DEATH ALONG THE SHORE

By
Michael Pritzkow

ISBN: 9798404458572 (paperback)

Dedication

To the memory of my friend and assistant of twenty-seven years, Jessie Downer.

Chapter One

Detective Tara Sullivan was halfway through her morning jog along Lake Michigan's Bradford Beach and Lincoln Memorial Drive. The beautiful lakefront was a favorite place for Milwaukee's Eastside joggers to run, play volleyball or just hang out. As she approached the McKinley Marina's boat launch, she spotted the Milwaukee Police coroner's blue Suburban turning into the parking lot.

What's that all about? she wondered, changing directions. Taking a shortcut across a portion of the beach, she arrived at the boat ramp and saw three parked police cruisers, and an unmarked white Crown Victoria, all with their lights flashing. She slowed her pace to a walk, recognizing Detective Tim O'Malley.

Notebook out, O'Malley was talking to two fishermen in their boat tied to one of the marina's four piers in the launch area.

She spotted a black body bag atop a chrome gurney. She watched Detective Frank Pinkowski zip the bag close and turn toward her.

When he saw, it was her, he smiled. "Hi Tara. Up kind of early, aren't you for a Saturday? Isn't today your off day?"

She wiped the sweat from her face with the corner of her gray Milwaukee Police Department tee shirt.

"Hi Pinkie. Yes, it's early. My first day off in two weeks. Just trying to stay in shape. What have we got here?"

He nodded toward the fishing boat tied up at the boat ramp. "On their way to do some salmon fishing this morning, these two guys found the body of a naked woman floating in the lake, about three miles out from the harbor's north entrance. A scarf was tied around her neck. There are bruises on her neck. My guess is she was strangled and dumped overboard last night or early this morning. We'll get more on that later from the coroner."

"Mind if I look? I still need more experience with this part of the business."

He nodded. "I guess it's OK, but don't touch anything."

"I might be a rookie," she said, "but I know enough not to touch anything."

"Yeah, OK. Just wanted to make sure."

Beads of water and bits of algae still clung to the body bag. Tara glanced at the nearby fishermen's boat with its fishing electronics, downriggers and four fishing poles, standing up like antennas, gently rocking at the nearby dock. She took a step to the chrome gurney.

It had only been two weeks since she had been promoted to the Homicide division, and she was still excited about the new assignment. She had worked hard over the past years, moving from dispatcher, to patrol officer, to burglary, and now to her ultimate goal, homicide detective. This was where she wanted to be, even as she knew she still had a lot to learn.

Tara braced herself as she reached for the zipper. It always was a shock to see death up close. She had seen way too many deaths when responding to motor vehicle accidents, but this was different. This probably would be a murder.

She reviewed the facts in her mind. A naked woman. Probably blue from being in the cold water. Tara steadied herself and pulled the zipper.

Her eyes grew wide as the victim's face registered in her mind. Tara's mind raced in disbelief for a horrific moment before the shock twisted her stomach. She turned and threw up. Acid from her stomach burnt her throat.

"Jesus Christ!" Pinkowski said. "What's wrong with you?"

Her eyes misted over. Taking the bottom of her tee shirt, she pulled it up to wipe the vomit from her lips and chin. Tears streamed down her cheeks, but she choked out, "It's Cate, my sister."

Tara slowly zipped the bag closed and then bent her upper torso over the bag, feeling the firm body inside. She broke into uncontrollable sobs at the contact, her body shaking the gurney with tiny movements.

She heard Pinkowski's shoes crunch on the gravel and asphalt, then she felt his hand on her back, trying to comfort her.

"Geez, Tara, I'm really sorry. I didn't know. We didn't know."

"I guess you and O'Malley never met Cate. She's my older sister, the lawyer."

"No, we never did."

She knew Pinkowski was never good with small talk, especially when he had to talk to the victim's family, but today he was trying his best because Tara was police family. She was one of the department's own.

"O'Malley!" he shouted.

O'Malley looked over at Pinkowski. "I'll be there in a second. I'm just finishing up here."

Pinkowski nodded, staying close to Tara.

"What gives?" O'Malley asked.

Hearing him, Tara slowly straightened her back, wiping away tears with the back of her hand.

"What's going on? Why are you crying?" a confused O'Malley asked as he looked at her, then to Pinkowski.

Pinkowski pointed to the body bag. "Tara's older sister."

"Jesus Christ," he said with a tight-lipped grimace. Tara watched his eyes move to the bag, then to her. He stepped in front of her, his big arms pulled her into a gentle hug.

"I'm so sorry," he whispered before stepping back. "Is there anything we can do for you? Do you need a ride home? Need to contact someone?"

"No, I'm close to home. I'll walk back. It's just up the hill."

Her eyes moved from Pinkowski to O'Malley. "I need to walk right now. It'll give me a chance to think, a chance to figure out what I need to do. Who I need to call."

Pinkowski put his notebook in his pocket. "We'll check in later. We need to ask you some questions about your sister. You know, procedure."

She nodded, rubbing the toe of her running shoe lightly across a yellow ramp line used to help fisherman align their boat trailers into the water.

Tara knew the procedure. She didn't know what she could tell them that might help. It had been a couple of weeks since she'd spoken to Cate. They only lived a few blocks apart, but they didn't get together often. Hadn't wanted to. They were too busy and involved with their careers, and then there was the jealousy. Now Cate was gone, and the two would never get a chance to patch up their differences.

Tara turned and started walking home, past Colectivo, the coffee roaster and popular coffee shop located in an old pump house across the street from the marina. Everything and everyone around her appeared so normal as she walked past the courtyard full of people having a Saturday morning cup of coffee, eating a sweet roll, or reading the paper. Some were laughing and talking about last night's events, or discussing today's events, not realizing tomorrow's headline was only 500 yards away now in the coroner's van. As Tara walked up Lafayette Hill, she wanted to scream at them, "Shut up! Don't you know my sister is dead—murdered?" She began sobbing again as she made her way home.

How was Tara going to tell her dad his favorite daughter was dead?

* * *

Drew Thompson got up early Saturday morning and started working on yesterday's fire damaged sailboat. First, he collected his clothing he had washed the evening before and placed them all in the marina's clothes dryers. Then he put the rest of the wet, soot-stained clothing and cushion covers into the washers. After that, he returned to his damaged boat. He had a lot of work to do if he was going to get back on schedule to start his sailing trip in early September. This journey had been meant to be therapeutic, but so far it was just more misery caused by his own poor judgment, once again.

The fire damage was mostly limited to a small forward area. Not hard work, he thought, but time-consuming. He got going, prepping the soot-darkened fiberglass and wood.

After hours of sanding *Courage*'s fire-damaged wood and fiberglass, it started to look better. His stomach growled. He glanced at his watch. Lunchtime. Why not Riptide Bar and Grill? Didn't Cate say last night they had good food? He'd grab a bowl of some chowder, a burger and a cold beer.

Ten minutes later, he sat down at the main bar. After ordering, Drew looked out at the Tiki area and reflected on Cate Sullivan and last night with her.

His thoughts were interrupted when he heard, "There's the son of a bitch I was telling you about. He almost ripped my shoulder out of my socket last night."

Drew turned toward the voice, and saw the "Jerk" from last night pointing at him. "Shit." He hoped this wasn't about pressing charges. Sure, he used a little muscle to move the guy away from Cate, but she asked him to.

"He was with her last night, Officer. I'd swear to it. I'll tell you one thing: he'd have no problem doing it. He's strong enough. I can attest to that. My wrist and shoulder still hurt from what he did to me."

Drew watched the Jerk move his shoulder in a circular motion. The plainclothes cop standing next to him nodded. "Thank you, Mr. Ream. We'll take it from here. We've got your address, and phone number if we need anything more."

"Any time, Officer. Always willing to help." He looked at Drew and gave him the finger.

OK, maybe he did use a little too much of his Marine Corps training on him but he deserved it. Besides, she wanted his help.

Out of the corner of his eye, Drew saw the approach of another policeman, or so he assumed, by his military looking brush haircut and clothing.

Drew lifted a draft beer to his lips as the first officer stood in front of him. The cop reached into his sport coat and produced a shiny gold detective badge.

"Mind if we ask you a few questions? I'm Detective Pinkowski and this is Detective O'Malley."

"Detectives? Don't you think this is a little overkill, two detectives for just helping a lady avoid being hassled by that jerk?"

Drew took another drag on his beer as the frost slide down the bottle and dripped on his soiled tee shirt and jeans.

"I don't know why you'd be talking to me." He pointed to the back of the jerk walking away. "He's the one that was bugging the lady last night. All I did was convince him he should leave her alone. He was bothering someone that didn't want anything to do with him. She asked me to help and I was only too happy to do just that."

"Can I see a driver's license or some form of identification?"

Drew reached into his back pocket, got out his wallet and handed over his driver's license.

"Michigan?" Pinkowski said.

"I'm from the Upper Peninsula of Michigan. My mother

still lives there. I was in the Marine Corps until recently, but that's my address of record."

"OK. Thank you for serving your country, Mr. Thompson." After writing down notes, Pinkowski handed back the license. "Were you an officer or a grunt?"

"I was an officer, a major." Drew watched Detective Pinkowski reach into his sport coat and produce a photo. "Do you recognize her?"

He grabbed the photo and looked at a dead Cate Sullivan. The photo was of her face and shoulders. Her face had a painful expression. Her complexion looked a bluish purple, and her eyes were bulging open. Around her neck was a silk scarf. Suddenly, Drew didn't feel like eating anymore. He placed the half empty beer on the bar.

"Yeah, Cate Sullivan. I met her here last night. Like I said before, she needed help with that guy. He was harassing her and she didn't like it. What happened to her?"

"Cate Sullivan ended up in the lake. We believe she was murdered. As you heard, Mr. Ream places you with her last night."

"I was with her last night. No crime in that."

O'Malley stepped closer to Drew's face. "You're right, unless she's found dead, murdered. We're checking out people of interest. So far, you seem to be one of those people."

Drew turned and just stared at O'Malley. "Is that so?" O'Malley looked like he could be a West Point graduate: strong, tall, with short cropped hair, a square jaw and dark eyes. He looked tough. Drew could tell already he had a short temper and liked to intimidate.

Drew reached for his beer, took a swallow, then placed it on the bar with a thud. That got the bartender's attention and Drew pointed for another beer. He wasn't thirsty enough for another beer yet, but taking a drink gave him more time to think.

"So where were you last night?" O'Malley asked.

Drew looked at the detective with unblinking eyes before a slight smile crossed his face.

"After I left Riptide, I went back to my boat. The security guy at the Milwaukee Yacht Club saw me come home alone. We chatted a while, I got a bag of ice out of the yacht club cooler, and then I headed back to my boat. I had a nightcap and a cigar." Drew brought the new bottle of beer to his lips, took a drink, and set it down.

"When was that?" asked Pinkowski.

"About 8:30 or nine o'clock."

"Oh, did I tell you, I had a fire on my boat yesterday."

Pinkowski looked up from his notepad. "A fire?"

Drew continued. "Last night my boat smelled like a fire pit at a campground—in other words, not the place I'd likely take someone I wanted to show a good time and have sex with. Because of that, I had lots to do last night. I worked late getting most of my wet, soot stained stuff into the washers. What was left, I decided could wait until this morning. Then I took a shower and went to bed. This morning I worked on my boat, as you can see by the sawdust on my jeans. Check it out. O'Malley. My boat's still a mess."

He handed the photo back to Pinkowski. "Too bad about Cate," said Drew. "She seemed like a nice person."

They held each other's stare for a while before Pinkowski looked down at the picture, and then put it in his sport coat.

"I wasn't on my boat with anyone."

O'Malley moved closer. "One thing we've got is a lot of time when it comes to murder, Mr. Thompson. We're going to check everything about your story, you can be sure of that. Where are you staying?"

"I'm at McKinley Marina on my boat. Dock B. Slip 22. It's next to the yacht club. The security guy is Travis—he'll vouch for me."

"OK, Thompson. Here are our cards. If you think of anything that might help us get Cate Sullivan's killer, we'd appreciate it."

He looked at the cards. "OK, Detectives. I've told you everything I know. I'd like to help." He looked at each detective. "I'll call you if I can think of anything else."

He watched them nod, turn, and walk away.

"Detectives?" He watched as they turned back to him. "There's a couple of things I just remembered."

"What?" Pinkowski asked.

"She told me she had three arguments at work with a jealous wife of a client, an old boyfriend, and most important a convicted child molester that threatened to kill her for suing him. Might want to check them out.

"Thanks for the information," Pinkowski said. "We will."

Drew watched them leave Riptide.

He sat there a moment. He'd seen a lot of dead people, including his best friend. Even though he had just met Cate and shared a few drinks and one long lingering kiss, this one stung too. Time to get back to *Courage*. He had a lot of work to do on his boat, and he also needed to talk to Travis before the detectives got to him.

* * *

Tara had never seen her father cry before that Saturday afternoon. They held hands, looking out at the cold, blue, Lake Michigan from a window in his high-rise condo on Prospect Avenue. After he composed himself from the initial shock, he broke the silence.

"How did it happen?" Peter Sullivan asked his daughter.

"I don't know, Dad. Some fishermen found her this morning. Cate was dumped in the lake late last night or early this morning." Tara wiped her eyes. "I just happened to be jogging past the boat ramp. I never guessed . . . "

He let go of her hand and tumbled into his favorite worn brown leather reading chair, dropping with a sound like a bag of cement hitting the floor. He let out a deep sigh.

"O'Malley and Pinkowski are working the case," said Tara. "They'll be calling you and me with questions about Cate's friends, work—anything that might give them a lead."

As her detective mode started to kick in, Tara felt she was gaining some control of her emotions. "They'll be looking for anyone with a motive. Maybe a disgruntled client, or someone on the losing side of a case she litigated."

"I understand," he said in a flat voice. Tara saw him looking out through the living room glass balcony doors at McKinley Marina, and then farther out in the lake, where Cate's body was found.

"You know she hated to go swimming in that lake, even in August. Said it was too cold. Ironic that they found her floating in it. Life doesn't make sense sometimes."

"Dad, was Cate dating anyone that was giving her concern or anxiety?"

"Not that I'm aware of. You know your sister. She attracts lots of men, and that's the way she liked it."

Tara watched a slight smile form, and then just as quickly disappear from his face.

"When I'd ask her if she was ready to settle down with one guy, she'd just smile. 'Oh Dad, you know the old saying, so many guys, so little time.' Then she'd laugh and kiss me on the cheek."

He turned and looked back out at the lake. A tear slid down his face, then another. Tara knew Cate was his favorite. She got the attention Tara had always craved but never seemed to get. Maybe because Cate was the oldest, the one that naturally was expected to follow in his footsteps. The one that battled her dad toe to toe on everything from the time she was a little girl to their work together at the firm. Now Cate was gone. Tara moved to his side, sitting on the armrest next to him. She moved her hand to his shoulder and then leaned against him, giving him a hug, then resting her cheek on the top of his head.

"I love you, Dad. I promise I won't stop investigating her case until I get this guy. I promise." *Then you'll see I'm just as good as Cate.*

Chapter Two

That night, Drew took his usual spot on his boat—a tradition he looked forward to each night. He poured himself a tumbler of Johnny Walker Black Scotch on ice, then lit up a cigar. He got a lot done to the boat since the fire Friday. The sanding and teak oiling was done. All his clothes were clean. He was tired, but satisfied to be almost back on schedule. He had gotten a lot accomplished on *Courage*. A couple more days like today and Drew still might meet his sailing deadline.

The marina basin was like glass. White lights of office buildings and high-rise condos cast an eerie reflection on the black water. From somewhere around his pier, he heard the *honk, honk* of geese in flight, and then the *whoosh* of them landing on still water. A family of six ducklings paddled around the stern of his boat. He broke up a handful of stale saltine crackers and tossed them to the baby ducks. After Afghanistan, he liked nature and all living things.

After finishing his Scotch, he continued puffing on his cigar. Then he got up and poured a second glass of Scotch trying to numb his mind before turning in for the night. Sunrise came early at 5:15 and he had a lot to do. He needed a good night's sleep and hoped he didn't have the dream.

* * *

Drew tossed and turned in a fitful sleep, and then he was dreaming he was back in Afghanistan in 2016. The Humvee convoy bounced along a potholed road, approaching the mountain valley area and a meeting with Afghan village elders. He and best friend Gunny Sergeant Tom Robb looked out at the all too familiar terrain through dusty, scratched windows. Private First Class Jacobs was driving the Humvee, a cigarette dangling from his mouth. He hummed most of Johnny Paycheck's country western song, but when he got to the chorus he'd shout, "Take this job and shove it!" and laugh his head off.

Another marine perched atop the roof behind a protective armor plate, manning a moderate caliber machine gun. They were the second vehicle in a convoy of three—the first being mine-resistant, followed by two lighter armored vehicles. They slowly moved toward the village, checking the way for IEDs.

"I can't believe they actually have a village out here," said Gunny. "It's nothing but rock, dirt and scrub trees." He was quiet for a moment. "I can't believe we're fighting for these people in this godforsaken country." He shook his head, "Let them grow their damn poppies, cut wood and tend their sheep. We've been here over twenty years and I don't think we've accomplished anything."

"It's where the Taliban was before 9/11, after 9/11 and still today," Drew countered. "They helped topple the Twin Towers and killed a lot of military in the Pentagon building—besides all the people in the airplanes. That's why we're here! These people are tough. Hell, the Russians couldn't beat them. Afghanistan turned out to be their Vietnam." Drew gathered his thoughts. "I don't know if we're making a difference here either. I sure hope so. No one wants to give their life for a senseless war." He looked around the inside of the Humvee. "Gunny, do we have the food, medicine and clothing for the village elders that we usually give them?"

"Yes, sir. It's in the last vehicle." He shook his head in disgust. "What was Command thinking, when they decided to send us to this village? We have to walk over a kilometer and a half in fucking broad daylight to get to the village because we can't get the Humvees up the narrow trail. It's bad enough at night, but during the day?"

Drew laughed. "Probably some intelligence planner that never set foot on one of these trails in an area like this and has never seen combat. He's probably a desk jockey. He asked to be stationed here so he can tell his buddies later that he had time in a combat zone, but he'll never tell them he didn't see any fighting."

"Why are you even here?" Gunny asked. "You don't need to be. They normally don't send a major for something like this. That's what lieutenants are for, someone of lower rank to gather and check out information. Someone expendable."

"Hey, I was a lieutenant once. Actually, I wanted to go—to get a better feel about what's happening in this area. We've had too many casualties in these valleys. Besides, I promised Connie I'd watch over you. Right out on the tarmac, before we got on the plane, she made me promise to keep you safe."

Gunny laughed. "Yeah, I remember. Like you're God or something."

Both men fell silent as they bumped along. Finally, Drew asked, "Any new pictures of my godson, Andrew?"

Gunny's face lit up. "Yes, sir. Actually, I got some pictures yesterday and I didn't get a chance to show you." He reached behind his body armor vest and pulled out a Ziploc bag with three pictures. One picture of Andrew, one picture of the twins and one of the whole family holding a birthday cake that had "Happy Birthday Dad" spelled out in red frosting. Drew saw a letter too, and assumed it was from Connie.

"Here's one with Andrew playing with the Monster Truck you gave him for Christmas."

Drew looked at the twins in matching outfits and then the family picture. "Nice. You're a lucky man to have a woman like Connie." Drew thought of Clair, then forced himself to block that memory. It was still too painful, even now. He handed the pictures back to Gunny.

"Don't I know that." Gunny kissed the family pictures, and carefully put them and the letter back in the Ziploc bag, placing it behind his body armor in his shirt pocket over his heart.

Drew smiled as he watched him pat the spot after he buttoned the shirt flap.

"Connie says Andrew plays with that truck all the time and tells her, 'Uncle Drew bought this for me.'"

Moments later, the Humvee rolled to a stop.

"I guess it's time to get going," Drew said as they piled out of the armored vehicle. "Nothing says we have to make the walk back in daylight. We'll get intelligence from the village Elders, then stay in the village until after dark. Then we'll walk back. Leave four here to guard the vehicles. Tell them if they hear anything to contact Command and call in support. I don't like this walk."

"Major?"

"Yes, Gunny."

"We've done this before."

"Yeah, I know but I still don't like it."

* * *

The Elders had requested the meeting. They said they had new, significant information about the Taliban. Drew knew they often used this type of request to get food, medicine and clothing for the village. He hoped they really did have new, significant, information.

The trail followed a winding creek bed one and a half kilometers up to the flat spot where the small village perched. As Drew looked up the winding trail, he said, "Let's hope the Taliban aren't in the rocks above us. We'd be sitting ducks. We've got no place to really take cover if they start shooting. Spread out as we move up the trail. Let's go."

Gunny and the others nodded their heads in the affirmative.

The air was clear and cool, easy for snipers to zero in on them. The men moved slowly, up the moderately steep trail, each carrying an extra fifty pounds of supplies and ammo. Drew was in the middle of the patrol, with Gunny number two in line. Jacobs, as usual, had the lead position. He had the best eyesight of the team, able to see things most marines missed. Back in South Carolina, Drew knew Jacobs was a good hunter and excellent shot.

They were about 300 meters from the village when a young man stood on a wall and yelled in broken English, "Welcome

Americans" and another unintelligible greeting. He was waving a small American flag.

Drew heard Gunny say "Shit" just as the first shot rang out. They hit the ground, rolled and started looking for muzzle flashes to return fire. Seconds seemed like minutes, and minutes like hours. The packs came off and were used for cover, but there was nothing between where they were now and the village. Rocks and trees were what they needed.

Jacobs got up and tried to run zigzag towards the safety of the village wall. He got thirty meters before he went down with a shot to the leg. Once he hit the ground, the area around him looked like it was boiling, dirty water, with dirt and dust popping up as the Taliban took aim at the downed marine. Jacob's body armor bounced as it took hits. He tried to get up, but his helmet flew off and he lay still.

"Gunny, we need to get to the village or they're going to pick us off right here," Drew yelled over the gunfire.

"Right. I'll get the rest moving towards the wall." They got up from the ground and started moving in erratic paths, like a bunch of ants moving towards a candy bar, but the village seemed a long way to safety. Drew got on the radios and called to the leader of the four marines he left back at the Humvees. "Call for a medical chopper and air support, ASAP."

"Major, we already did, when we heard the shooting start. They said it would be fifteen minutes before they got to you."

"That's going to be too late," Drew said. "We're making for the village now. Tell Command the whole thing was a set up. The enemy is in the hills. Tell them to light up the hills surrounding the village fast or we're all dead."

He got up and started moving with the others towards the village feeling the dirt and rocks spitting up around him as he did. Drew heard a scream from behind, then another. He knew the others would help their buddies get to cover if they could. He needed to get to that village wall and its cover. Keep moving.

About fifty meters away from the village and cover, Drew saw Gunny stop, turn and fire toward a low muzzle flash. It seemed nearer than the others from just across the nearby creek. Drew heard a scream, then he saw a Taliban fighter fall over.

Gunny dropped, rolled and came up shooting again. Drew looked around the valley. The valley looked like someone had strung red twinkling Christmas lights along the lower level. Very pretty, except the twinkling lights were tracer fire from Taliban guns, and they were pointing at him and his men.

Gunny was only twenty-five meters away, moving slowly towards the village, when Drew saw him twist at the waist and tip over on his face. When Gunny rolled over, Drew saw a grimace on his face, his hand moving just below his groin area on his left side.

Drew ran to him. He could see the hole in his camouflage pants surrounded by dark red spreading fast. "Hang on, buddy." Drew grabbed his arm, pulled him up and across his shoulders in a fireman's carry as he zig-zagged to the village, slower now with Gunny's added weight. He felt the thuds of rounds hitting Gunny's body armor. There was nothing he could do about that. They needed to get to the safety of the village wall. "We're almost there, buddy. Hang on!" It took

Drew another minute to reach the village, but it seemed like an hour. He finally sank behind the wall and rolled Gunny off his shoulder. He knew it was going to be bad.

"We made it, Gunny, we made it!" Drew just got behind a low stone wall as rounds were pinging off the rock. Drew's body shuddered, and he felt two searing pains go off through his body. "Fuck."

He was hit: one to his buttock, and another to his side, just above his waist where he knew his body armor must have rose up when he rolled Gunny to the ground. It hurt like hell, but his attention was focused on Gunny.

His best friend's face was ashen and he was bleeding badly. A major wound just below his groin on his left thigh was gushing blood. Drew got out a compression bandage from his belt, ripped Gunny's blood-soaked pants leg and applied direct pressure to the wound. In seconds, the bandage was saturated with blood. Oh God, Drew thought, Gunny's going to bleed out right here if I don't stop it now. He tried to get a tourniquet around the leg, just above the wound, but Drew couldn't put enough pressure above the artery to cut off the blood flow. "Hang in there, buddy, the choppers are coming. We'll get you home back to Connie and the kids. Just hang in there." Stone chips rained down on Drew and he instinctively leaned over Gunny to protect him.

Gunny whispered, "Drew, take care of Connie and . . . "

Drew sat up, and watched his best friend's eyes roll back in his head. "I know, Gunny, I know." He pressed two fingers against Gunny's neck and felt no pulse. He was gone. Drew grabbed him by his shoulders, pulled him tight against his chest and cried. Drew had failed his promise to Connie to keep Gunny safe.

Then Drew felt a sharp pain to his head followed by blackness.

Drew woke with a start, drenched in sweat and hugging his pillow aboard *Courage*, not in Afghanistan.

When would these nightmares end? He rolled out of his bunk, and climbed the three steps to the cockpit, waiting for Sunday's sunrise.

Tara got up early Sunday morning. She sat on the side of her bed, her fingers combing through her tangled red hair. Yesterday, her sister was found dead. Tara's mind had been restless all night, trying to reason out what had happened.

"God, I feel like shit," she said aloud, reaching for her robe. Slipping it on, she made her way to the kitchen. She started a pot of coffee and sat at the kitchen table. She knew she should go back to bed and try to get some needed rest, but all Tara wanted to do was get to work and start solving her sister's murder.

She'd have to talk to Captain Blake tomorrow and plead with him about getting assigned to the case with O'Malley and Pinkowski. She'd make him understand. She had to be involved in some way. It was her sister, for Christ sake. She had promised her father she would find the killer. She sighed. Deep down, she knew what Captain Blake's answer would be. She could hear him say, "Your judgment could be clouded and swayed by it being family. Let others handle it." She'd try anyhow. If Blake wouldn't let her work on it she'd go rogue, investigating it on her own, in secret.

The coffee was ready. She had a half cup, and then went to her room, slipped on her jogging outfit and was out the door.

After yesterday, her usual three-mile run along Bradford Beach felt anything but normal. Still for a few seconds here and there, she felt better.

Once back home, she picked the Sunday paper off the stoop and deposited it on the kitchen table. She sat down and poured herself a fresh cup of coffee. Her eyes moved to the paper sitting on the table and back to the view out her third story window. It seems so quiet, so normal, but it wasn't.

She stared at the still untouched Sunday paper. After ten minutes and another cup of coffee, she got the courage to see if there was an article about Cate.

Tara found it in the local section. Amazed at how short the article was, Tara stared at the closing sentences: "Ms. Sullivan was the oldest daughter of Peter Sullivan, Senior Partner of Sullivan, Sullivan, Peterson, Smith and Associates. She is survived by a younger sister, Ms. Tara Sullivan."

After reading it a couple more times, she carefully refolded the section, slid the paper neatly back into its original sequence and then screamed. She violently threw the paper against the kitchen wall, knocking a picture off its hook.

"For Christ sake, she was murdered!"

Leaving her unfinished cup of coffee, she got up and in a daze, went to her bathroom, stripped off her jogging outfit. Then she pulled back the shower curtain, turned the water to almost full hot, and stepped in. The water cascaded over her head, stinging, and as it did, she started to cry, slowly at first, and then the sobs gaining intensity until Tara was howling in agony as she wedged herself back into the corner of her white tiled shower stall and slowly slid down to a squat and let loose the pent-up emotions of her sister's death.

On Tuesday morning, Alex West stepped out on the front stoop and picked up the morning paper. Shading his eyes against the sun, he looked up and down the block but saw no one, not even the paperboy making deliveries. He looked at his watch, 5:08 a.m. Good kid, he thought, as he turned and stepped back inside, tossing the paper on the kitchen table before moving to the old familiar dented gray coffee pot. He loved the old fashion coffee pot his dad had purchased years ago in Chesapeake. His dad bought it for boating because it made perfect coffee on the boat's stove and was stable with its wide base. Alex used it now all the time because of the good memories. It brought back all the times sailing with his father. Not a day went by that Alex didn't think of his father, even though it had been almost twenty years since his death.

He watched the dented coffee pot start to perk, and smiled as the smell of the coffee was like sunshine to his senses. The *blurb, blurb, blurb* sound started and then the water began turning a light brown as he watched brown liquid hit the tiny glass on top of the pot. He went upstairs to change into his running shorts, shoes and an old ratty tee shirt he always wore when he jogged. When he came down to the kitchen again, he turned the burner to warm and headed out the side door to his driveway.

He loved his Tudor house on Lake Drive, a house in which he had spent many a happy summer as a child. Was it really fifteen years already since their mother's death? Alex and his brother George had inherited this house in Milwaukee, as well as a large Colonial style house in Annapolis, Maryland.

Alex smiled. Not many kids had an opulent summer house like this. Situated in a lovely area just off Lake Michigan, he stood on the driveway, looking across the street at scenic Lake Park before starting his daily run. The sunlight was peeking through tall mature trees and illuminated several of the park's flower gardens. Alex had always felt his roots were more in Milwaukee than the Chesapeake/Annapolis area, which was why as an adult he had chosen to live here year-round. And of course, it also made sense because Alex was CEO and president of the family business, West Industries, headquartered in Milwaukee.

He started with a slow easy jog, heading down a winding street through the park to Lincoln Memorial Drive. Moving along Bradford Beach and its lakefront path, he smiled as he broke out into the bright sunlight. The cleaning machines were moving on the sand, around the volleyball courts and the main beach, grooming and picking up refuse before everyone arrived. Alex's eyes turned down the beach: the sun's orange ball reflected off office and condo windows facing east.

He needed the workout today. He hated being out of shape and prided himself on not having "love handles" on his thirty-five-year-old body. He kept running, past the marina, around a large lakefront lagoon where he saw several paddle-boats tied up, then headed back, completing the three-mile circuit as he reached the canopy of trees and the hill. He looked at his watch: twenty-four minutes. Not bad, he thought, and slowly walked back to his house and his waiting coffee and paper.

That same afternoon, Alex drove from his office to the Milwaukee Yacht Club. He entered the boatyard to inspect *Passage Maker*, the beloved family sailboat. Looking at it on its wooden cradle, he was surprised how excited he was for the boating season to start. The boatyard was busy, but then it was always busy in early June. The "Woody's" were usually the last to go in the water because they took more care and feeding than the modern fiberglass boats. Alex loved the look and feel of his classic Hinckley Bermuda 40.

Standing there, he heard the usual sounds of owners and crew and the club's yard help working on several boats, yelling instructions back and forth. The high-pitched wine of orbital sanders and buffing machines filled the air. Several boaters were outfitted in white toxic preventive outfits and surgical masks as they finished painting the bottom of their boat. He walked toward his boat and saw Nathan, his varnish guy, already hard at work, lightly sanding the teak, putting on the finishing touches. It looked like the varnish work was all done. Alex loved the smell of paint, varnish and turpentine as it mixed with the fresh air of Lake Michigan, giving this area a special feel of late spring.

"How's it going, Nathan?" He shaded his eyes from the sun. "You've got *Passage Maker* looking just the way she's meant to. Thanks."

Nathan smiled as he patted the long wooden masts laying on several sawhorses. "She looks pretty good, Mr. West," he said. "I love working on boats like this. Fiberglass is nice, but wood—" He paused. "Wood is what boating is all about." He laughed. "Besides, it gives a poor college student like me a job."

Alex smiled. "Glad I could help pay for your education."

"I finished putting a second coat of varnish on the mast yesterday," Nathan said, sliding his callused hand along the smooth finish. "I also checked the hardware, fittings and stays to make sure everything was ready. The light bulbs on the running lights, including the anchor, spreader and masthead lights are OK. One more coat of varnish on a couple of the spots and she's ready to be launched. Dan and Travis said they could step the mast tomorrow."

"Great, I'm really antsy to get sailing." Alex moved around *Passage Maker's* smooth, freshly bottom-painted hull until he reached the wooden ladder. Bounding up like a teenager, he settled in the cockpit, sitting to the side of the traditional wooden spoke steering wheel. There was a light breeze blowing from the southwest, and for just a moment, Alex fantasized he was sailing. His left hand on the wooden spoke, he looked out across the freshly cleaned teak deck. In the distance were the waters of Lake Michigan, and the several smokestacks billowing white smoke towards the open sky. The marina basin had several boats already in their slips or bobbing on their moorings.

"Beautiful boat." He heard someone say.

Alex turned trying to locate the source of the voice. Leaning over the edge of the cockpit, he saw a sweat-stained baseball cap and the back of a crouched, muscular torso moving closer to the boat. He watched the man's left hand reach out to caress the hull as if it were the soft cheek of a new love. At his feet, Alex saw the worn canvas bag of assorted tools, sandpaper and scrapers.

"It's a Hinckley, isn't it?" the man asked. "Probably built in the 60s. I saw a few of them when I was at Annapolis." The guy moved around the hull, as Alex's eyes followed him. Alex got up and made his way to the stern, and down the wooden ladder.

Alex smiled. He recognized the military look. The curious man had to be either navy or a marine. It fit: the baseball cap, military sunglasses, erect posture and his reference to Annapolis. His eyes followed the stranger as the man inspected the boat. He circled the boat a second time, and finished in front of Alex.

"What a beauty. How long have you owned her?"

Alex smiled at the question. "My whole life. Actually, she was my father's. And you're right; he bought *Passage Make*r in the 60s before I was born. He loved sailing. He loved the look and feel of wood. At that time, they didn't produce many fiberglass boats. The only negative with a 'woody' is the amount of work and money it takes to keep the boat in perfect condition."

The man laughed. "I can only imagine. I remember at the

academy, the hours we spent varnishing, polishing and general maintenance of the sloops, keeping them up to the Navy's standards."

Alex snickered. "Now it's my turn to say, I can only imagine."

Alex stuck out his hand, "Alex West."

The man took off his cap. "Drew Thompson, Nice to meet you." He put his cap back on. "Actually, when I look back at my time at Annapolis and the Naval Academy, the time working on boats was my happiest. I grew to love boating and taking care of all the little things associated with the love of water. I can spend hours and hours fiddling with anything associated with a sailboat, like I'm doing now."

"I wish I had the time to do that," Alex said. "Unfortunately, I don't, so I write checks to Nathan, and keep college kids like him employed during the summer. Actually, I like it that way. I like to sail. Don't get me wrong, I like to tinker too, but I can only stand so much. When you have a limited amount of time to spend sailing, you must set priorities. My dad instilled that in me. He loved sailing, but business came first. He'd sneak away at Annapolis, and here, whenever he could get away. When I was old enough, he'd take me along."

"Annapolis and here?" asked Drew. "I don't understand."

Alex leaned against the wooden ladder, his deck shoes resting on the first rung. "Dad's business was involved with the government, primarily with the Navy. Even though most of his businesses were located in Milwaukee and the Midwest, he spent half his time in Washington lobbying for the company. It made sense for him to have a second residence in the

Washington/Annapolis area. My dad was a visionary, but he also liked to make money. So do I." Alex smiled at Drew as he finished. "What brings you here?"

"I retired from the Marines," he said, standing almost at attention, shoulders back, feet close together. His arms hung straight down at his side. His canvas tool bucket touched his worn deck shoes.

"You look pretty young to be retired."

"I hear that a lot. I like being where the action is but on my last tour of duty," he pointed to his head. "I got one wound that prevented me from being in combat. So I retired ..." Drew paused, momentarily lost in memories. "Anyway, I decided to see the world from the deck of a sailboat."

"Really. You look fit and happy, no worse for your injuries."

"I am, for the most part. The boat I bought was already located in Milwaukee, here at the yacht club. Milwaukee seemed like a good spot to get things ready. The people are friendly here, and I like beer."

Alex laughed. "Twenty years ago, Schlitz, Blatz, Pabst and Miller were all made here. Now only Miller is, although they are trying to resurrect the other brands. It would be nice to have them all brewed here again."

Drew nodded.

"Where's your boat?" asked Alex.

"It's in the water on B Dock. I got all the bottom preparations and painting done at the yacht club yard before launching it. Now I'm working on the outside teak and the interior wood. I had a little fire inside the cabin the other day, but that's a minor setback now. Then there are the electronic odds and ends that need to be upgraded or replaced. I need to get all this done before I go on my trip."

"When's that?"

"I'm shooting for just after Labor Day. I plan on doing my shakedown sailing on the Great Lakes before I hit the East Coast. By then, hurricane season will almost be over."

"Sounds like you've thought everything out. I'm putting my boat in the water this week so you're welcome to sail with me. It would be nice to have company. I can sail *Passage Maker* myself," Alex said, patting the hull, "but usually with reduced sail. That's no fun unless I line up a crew to help. That's the way I have to do it."

"I'll take you up on that," Drew said, sticking his hand out to shake. "Let's go to the Tiki Hut, and have a drink. I need a break from sanding."

"Good," Alex said.

"I'll drop this stuff on the boat and see you in ten minutes."

Alex watched Drew turn and head for his boat.

* * *

Tara reached for her Coke as she thought about the funeral the day before on Monday. As hard as it was for her, it was even harder on her dad. While he was tough as nails in court, yesterday Peter Sullivan's eyes were wet and his shoulders shook as the priest performed the graveside service. Tara's father had leaned heavily on her and could not even place a rose atop Cate's coffin. Tara still couldn't believe she was gone.

It was good to be working today at the department, even if

it was only busy work, filing last week's reports. All day long, fellow police officers and detectives had stopped by her cubicle to pay respects, and each time she talked about Cate, the image of her in the body bag flashed before Tara's eyes. They all showed her compassion, even the tough guys.

It saddened Tara that the sight of Cate's body inside the black body bag would be forever tattooed in her mind when thinking about her sister.

Tara got through the day. She craved a glass of white wine at home, after which she planned to collapse and sleep.

Ready to head home, she collected her things. As she walked past O'Malley's cubicle, Tara saw a manila file with her sister's name on it peeking out from the murder folder. Looking around and seeing no one paying attention, Tara grabbed the file and slipped out the paperwork. O'Malley's notes listed a suspect Drew Thompson, indicating his involvement with Cate Sullivan the night of her death.

Thompson's address was a boat located at McKinley Marina, B Dock, slip 22—not so far from where her sister's body was found. Interesting, she thought.

Tara headed to McKinley Marina.

Moving down B Dock, she passed family cruisers, several boats for salmon fishing, and a few for sailing. On slip 22, she saw a figure bent over the opening to the cabin, sliding the boat's wooden hatch boards into place. Was Drew Thompson going someplace?

She walked down a finger pier, and said in a firm voice, "Drew Thompson?"

He turned towards her, looking curious. "Yes?"

"Detective Sullivan. I'm with the Milwaukee Police Department." Tara showed her badge. "I'd like to ask a few questions." She looked into his piercing blue eyes. Time froze as she took in the rest of him: rugged face, strong jaw, short brown hair with just a scattering of gray in the sideburns and temple. Her eyes moved lower, to a strong upper body, well developed shoulders and forearms. He had a tapered waist that led to jeans worn in all the right places. Thighs that looked strong but allowed for flexibility and speed. She knew he had a great butt, which had been evident when Tara saw him bending over. He was handsome—yes, Cate would be attracted to him. That attraction may have killed her.

"I thought I already answered your department's questions on Saturday with Detectives O'Malley and Pinkowski."

Tara got down to business. "The report from Detectives O'Malley and Pinkowski stated that you were one of the last people to see Cate Sullivan alive. Can you tell me more about that?"

Drew frowned. "When I left her that night at Riptide, she was very much alive." He squinted at Tara. "You look like her."

Tara smiled. "Actually, she's my adopted sister. We did look like sisters. Funny. Dad used to say when questioned about the resemblance, he thought it was the Irish in both of us. My parents knew her nationality when they adopted her." Then she paused. "Why am I telling you all this?"

"Thought so. Cate was a very nice person, although I only met her briefly. I'm really sorry for your loss."

"Thank you. Well, I just wanted to verify information I saw on their report."

He nodded. "I understand. Go ahead with any questions you have."

"How did you two meet?"

"She and I were both at Riptide, having drinks. I helped her out with a guy who was harassing her. She bought me a couple of drinks after that, and even offered to buy me dinner. Unfortunately, I took a rain check. I had work to do on this boat after the fire I had on it that day.

She wanted me to come back after I cleaned up the mess. I said I would try my best. Now, I'm sorry I didn't take her up on her offer for dinner and stay, because if I had, she'd still be alive."

She stared, trying to decide if she believed him.

"You'll have to excuse me," he said, "but I'm late to meet someone at the yacht club for a drink. Why don't you join my friend and me? You can ask your questions there. It's just a few piers over." He pointed to a big tan building with several flags flying from a tall flagpole. "I don't have anything to hide. If you're as nice as her, I'll enjoy talking to you."

"I don't know . . . "

Before she could finish, Drew padlocked the boat and stepped off the sailboat onto the narrow finger pier. His quick movement off the boat and onto the floating pier caused a rocking motion. A surprised Tara took a quick step back and lost her balance.

Drew grabbed her and pulled her close, saving her from falling in the water. She let out a gasp of surprise at the sudden movement and resulting contact. She felt strong arms as she grabbed him for support.

"I can't," Tara said. "It's against department rules. I need to have another detective with me."

"Suit yourself. You don't have one here now, and you're talking to me. If you have more questions, you're going to have to follow me there because I'm late. I don't like being late."

He started walking down the pier towards the Milwaukee Yacht Club, leaving her open mouthed and staring.

"Wait! I'm not done with my questions. Son of a bitch." She hurriedly followed. She saw a playful grin on his face as he continued down the floating dock and that really pissed her off. "Asshole!"

Chapter Three

Alex West had just ordered a second Ketel One and tonic when he saw Drew Thompson rounding the corner of the Milwaukee Yacht Club building and walking towards the Tiki Hut. Alex was surprised to see Drew look over his shoulder and laugh. Then he saw an upset red-haired beauty right on his tail.

Drew plopped down on a stool, leaving an open stool between Alex and himself.

"Sorry I'm late, but I was delayed." He turned his head toward the pursuing redhead.

"Mr. Thompson, I wasn't done with our conversation," she said.

"I know you weren't done but I was late and it's rude to keep people waiting. Besides, I thought this was a good way to have a drink with you, and have you meet my new friend. Now, of course, I'll be happy to answer your questions. Alex, this is Detective Sullivan. Detective Sullivan, this is Alex West."

Drew nodded at the empty stool. "Please, have a seat. What would you like to drink?"

Alex almost laughed out loud when he heard her say, "Shit." She sighed and sat.

Glaring at Drew, Detective Sullivan turned to Alex and

gave him a curt smile. "I'll have a white wine, since I'm technically off duty."

"Good." Drew turned to the bartender and smiled. "Give Detective Sullivan a white wine, and I'll have a Corona and lime."

Alex extended his hand in greeting.

"Nice to meet you, Detective Sullivan. Is there a first name that goes with Detective?" God, she was gorgeous, he thought.

"Tara." She shook his hand, smiling at him before turning and glaring at Drew. "Sorry, Alex, I'm normally not this *rude*, but this is not a social call." She turned back to Drew. "You were the last person to see my sister alive, and you're a person of interest with the Homicide Department. While I'm not officially assigned to the case, I wanted to check you out myself."

Drew's face turned solemn. "I was not the last person to see her alive, Detective Sullivan. The killer was, and that's not me." Drew spoke in a calm, soft voice. "She's your sister, and I understand you want to find the killer, but like I said before, that's not me."

They held eye contact, and then she pulled her glance away. She took a sip of wine before saying, "Yes, I want to find the killer—or, I should say, Milwaukee Homicide wants to find the killer."

Drew softened his gaze. "I'm sorry again about Cate. I told the detectives Saturday, after I helped her get rid of a guy harassing her, she and I had a few drinks. Then I left. I didn't know about her death until I showed up at Riptide the next day, and met your colleagues."

"Their report said you left Riptide, and came right back to your boat? You don't live in an apartment or home?"

"I live on my boat. I got back around 8 that night. I talked to Travis here at the yacht club for a few minutes."

"What did you talk about?"

"Nothing important—the weather, boating, the latest Brewers game and a bag of ice. Then, like I said to the other detectives, I came back to my boat."

"Anyone else see you onboard?"

"Not that I'm aware of. There weren't many people around, even for a Friday night."

Tara hesitated. "You didn't have any companion with you on the boat to . . . to keep you company?"

"I didn't have your sister on the boat, if that's what you're asking. No just me and my Johnny Walker Black," he said. "Again, I told all this to Detective Pinkowski and O'Malley."

Tara turned toward Alex, quietly sipping a vodka tonic. "How long have you known Mr. Thompson?"

"I was wondering how long it was going to take for you to get to me," he said, briefly smiling. "Actually, we just met today. He was admiring my boat over there in the yard." He pointed towards the dock. "We decided to have a drink and talk more about sailing. Simple as that. I'm so sorry to hear about your sister. If there's anything I can do to help, please don't hesitate to ask." He touched her arm.

She pulled her arm back, "Thank you."

He smiled again. "I have a great idea. I'm putting my boat in the water tomorrow. It'll take all day to get everything shipshape. Why don't the three of us go out for a shakedown cruise tomorrow evening, say 5:00? I know you'll love to sail on my boat, Drew." Looking at Tara, he said, "And you, Detective, could use some fresh lake breezes to clear your mind, if only for a little while to relax and get your mind off your sister's death." Alex took a swallow of his drink. "We'll meet here at the Tiki Hut. I'll get some ice, wine, rum and beer and we'll be on our way for a nice relaxing cruise."

"Sounds like a great idea to me." Drew said.

When Tara didn't say anything, Alex asked, "What's wrong? You don't think you need to relax? This will help you think clearly. What do you say?"

"Getting my mind off my sister's murder, even for a short time would be good, I agree," said Tara, "but not with both of you. Only you, Alex."

She looked at Drew. "It's against procedure to go out with a suspect, especially alone, with no partner or backup. I really shouldn't even be here with you now."

"I understand." Drew said, obviously disappointed.

"But I'll go sailing with you, Alex," she said.

"Great. I'll buy another round."

***

The next day at the Yacht Club, Tara met Alex at the Tiki Hut, and they made their way down the pier to his boat. Once on board, Alex gave Tara a short tour of *Passage Maker* before they cast off. Once on the water, he took her on a slow motor tour around the marina basin, getting her used to being on a sailboat and a chance to see the other crafts and the sights of the city from the water.

"Look at that big yacht," she said, pointing. "The one

named *Condor.* It looks like it's made of wood like yours. It's huge."

Alex smiled. "You have a good eye for beauty. That's actually a classic motor yacht. It's sixty-five feet long and was built by Burger Motor Yacht Company."

"You seem to know a lot about that particular boat."

"I should. It belongs to my twin brother. Technically, it's mine too, but really it's my brother George's."

"You have a twin brother?"

"Identical. When my dad died, he had two boats, one power and the other sail. He loved the water. When he had the time—not often—he'd sail with me on *Passage Maker.* And when he didn't have as much time, he'd take that motor yacht, *Condor*. George usually went then. He doesn't have the patience for sailing like I do. He liked motors boats when we were kids and still does—anything that goes fast. I, on the other hand, like the quiet of no motor, and the navigation aspect of sailing just using the wind. If someone likes geometry, they usually like sailing, because of the angles required to sail off the wind. You just can't point and go where you want to. It requires visualizing the route you want to sail and that calculation the course."

"Sounds complicated."

"Anyhow, my dad was great to both of us. He tried to spend as much time as he could with each of us separately because George and I were very different. Water was the place to be together with Dad. I miss sailing with him."

"That's nice that you had that relationship with your dad that way, and sad that he's gone now."

"Actually, our company owns the boats. George uses the motor yacht and I use this one. We're twins, but he and I stopped being around each other at an early age. I don't know why except he would throw a fit when Mom mentioned me or compared us to one another, so they separated us as best they could. We might look the same but that's as far as it goes. George is a no-nonsense type of guy. Loves photography, taking pictures of things that go fast and those associated with it. Racing boat, sailboats, racecars, planes. He especially likes taking pictures of the women at those events. He somehow manages to talk them into posing for his pictures. He sells his photos to several organizations for their annual reports and advertisements. He even has a darkroom on the boat."

Tara turned and looked back at George's boat. "Well, it sure is big enough to have a darkroom."

"Yes, it is." Alex patted her hand. "I'm really the romantic. I love the arts, the symphony and fine paintings, all supported through a foundation I've set up. Matter of fact, when I went to Paris on business, I took off a couple of days after lobbying the French Naval Department for our Company and visited the Louvre. I still marvel at how realistic the paintings by Da Vinci were. One painting of a woman mesmerized me. When I looked at the veins in her hands, arms and breasts, it seemed as if I could actually see a beating pulse. It looked so real. It was hard to believe someone could paint that realistically back then. The painting actually looked like a photograph if you stepped back from it. To think that back then, artists even mixed their own paints. It must have taken days, weeks or months to paint some of the pictures I saw." Alex looked at Tara. "Da Vinci would have loved to paint you, Tara." His eyes moved over her body. "You're very beautiful."

She shrugged off the compliment. "I'm sure he could find others more beautiful." Tara stared at him.

Alex smiled. "That's why I like sailing and maintaining wooden boats." Alex caressed the varnished wood. "It's special and takes time to build and maintain. My brother George and I both got what we each wanted. Our boats match our lifestyles and philosophy."

Close to six o'clock, Detective Pinkowski was ready to call it a day. He was at his desk at the station house, again going over his notes on the Sullivan case, when O'Malley walked in the room. Pinkowski's partner threw down his notepad and sank into his chair.

"We need to bring Thompson in for questioning," said O'Malley.

Pinkowski looked up. "Why? What have you got?"

"Several employees at Riptide saw Thompson later that evening, around 11 p.m. They said he got into a dispute with some guy over a woman. I showed them a picture of Cate Sullivan I got from the Tara. They said the woman he left with looked a lot like her."

"Maybe Cate went home and changed, then came back to Riptide to meet him," Pinkowski said.

"Maybe," O'Malley said. "Anyhow, the waitress who was

servicing the area said the woman looking like Cate Sullivan had a lot to drink and was talking to Thompson soon after he arrived. The waitress was taking a drink order from some guy Cate seemed to be with most of the evening. She said the guy Cate was with was drunk and slurring his words. The waitress said the drunk thought he was God's gift to the world. Taking their drink orders, the waitress was facing Thompson and this guy's girlfriend. She said the woman ran her hands down Thompson's chest and then kissed him full on the lips. The waitress wasn't sure if the drunk saw that, but soon after the drunk turned around just in time to see Thompson putting his arm around the lady's waist, evidently to steady her from falling. The waitress said the drunk went ballistic and came at Thompson, swinging and swearing. Thompson pulled the woman aside, at the same time ducking the guy's roundhouse punch. When the guy tried hitting him again, Thompson cold cocked him with one punch to the jaw and dropped the guy. Then he and the woman whispered to each other, and they left Riptide in a hurry. The waitress said the woman was hanging all over Thompson as they took off.

"As they walked past her, another waitress heard the woman say 'I want some sex tonight, and after what I just saw, you're just the guy I'm looking for.' That waitress said Thompson did not look too happy as they left, but they did leave together."

"Anyone say anything else?" Pinkowski asked.

"The bartender witnessed the fight and saw the two leave together. Said he didn't hear any conversation, but he confirmed this woman with Thompson looked like Ms. Sullivan."

Pinkowski closed the notebook. “OK. Back to the marina to ask Thompson a few more questions about the lady who wanted sex.”

Pinkowski grabbed the car keys and his sport coat. “Let’s go.”

Chapter Four

Alex turned the *Passage Maker* into the wind when they motored out of the harbor. Then he turned the boat's autopilot on.

"Tara, help me raise the mainsail. You can't learn sailing sitting. You need to be doing something. For a cop, you look pretty fit, not like you sit around all day eating donuts." He playfully squeezed her right bicep. "Follow me up to the mast and I'll show you how to raise the mainsail."

"I thought I was just going out for a ride. I didn't think I'd actually have to do anything." She smiled. "OK. It can't be that hard. Should we sing sea shanties like when the sailors hoisted up the tall ships' sails?"

"I don't sing," Alex snapped.

"Oh, excuse me."

"Give me your hand." Alex helped her step up on the cabin top, and then they both moved forward towards the mast while the boat motored slowly into the wind.

Alex loosened the main halyard and attached it to the mainsail. Next, he grabbed the main halyard line that fed out of the base of the mast and put three wraps around the winch located on the side of the mast. He inserted the winch handle. "Ready to start working?"

"I really have to do this?"

Alex ignored her comment. "Crank the winch handle around and around. Now as you crank, the mainsail should go up the mast track and when we get it up to the top, we'll cleat it off here." He pointed to a cleat on the mast. "Nothing to it, really. I do it all the time by myself but it's nice to have help. Ready?"

Tara nodded yes.

"Start cranking." Soon the sail started unfolding off the boom. The sound of the *click*, *click*, and *click* of the winch could be heard above the labored breathing of Tara as she cranked.

"This is harder than I thought," she said between breaths.

"It will all be worth it when we turn off the motor and all you hear is the sound of the water lapping against the hull." Alex smiled as he looked at her, but his smile was really about the silhouette of Tara, her sweater pressed tight against her body in the evening breeze.

After a minute or two of hard cranking, Alex said, "Stop! That's high enough." Taking the end of the line, he cleated it off.

"Good job. Let's move back into the cockpit." He held her hand as they moved across the cabin top. In the cockpit, he moved to the side of the wheel and turned off the autopilot. He turned the wheel and the wind filled the mainsail. He turned off the diesel.

The sound of the motor was replaced by a soothing *pat, pat, pat* as waves struck against the wooden hull.

"*Whew.*" Tara plopped down on one of the many cockpit cushions. "That sail is heavy."

Alex laughed. "What about the jib?"

"The jib?" Tara looked at Alex perplexed. "I thought I was done."

"It's OK, I'll do that. Hold the wheel."

She slid over, holding the wooden wheel spoke with a death grip.

He grabbed the jib's roller furling line, loosened it a bit and then gave the jib line a tug, pulling the edge of the headsail out enough for the wind to grab it and unroll it. Then he put a few wraps around the self-tailing winch and started cranking. Soon the big headsail was drawing air. He continued tightening it, creating a curved sail shape. The boat slowly heeled over a bit more. "That looks about right." He took the wheel from Tara and guided the boat further out into Lake Michigan.

After a few more minutes of sailing, Tara sighed. "This is great. I feel the tension of the last few days ooze out of my body. Thank you for talking me into this."

"How about a ration of rum and coke for the captain and crew after a job well done?" Alex looked at Tara. "Would you mind going down below and making us a drink? Of course, if you prefer wine, I can hop down and make the drinks for us. I'll just put the autopilot on."

"Would you? That would be great. I'm enjoying just sitting here in the cockpit. I've never seen Milwaukee from the water like this. The skyline is so beautiful, especially with all the new buildings going up. And the art museum looks like a beautiful giant swan ready to spread it wings and take off. Milwaukee is so gorgeous from out here. A glass of wine would go great with this view."

"Aye, aye. I'll be back in a second with our drinks. Enjoy."

He flipped on the autopilot again and went below to get the drinks. Five minutes later, Alex came up with two drinks, wine for Tara and rum and Coke for him.

Tara took a sip of Sauvignon Blanc. "Perfect."

The wind tousled her red hair, giving her a vibrant, free spirited look. Alex raised his drink. "To the crew."

"What are you smirking at?" Tara said.

"Am I smirking? I'm admiring how you look. If my brother were here, he'd be going nuts wanting to take pictures of you. I have to admit, he's a talented photographer, and he likes beautiful women like you. You'll have to meet him someday, then you'll see what I mean."

"He's the one that owns the *Condor*?"

"Yep, that's George—my older brother, by twelve minutes." Alex took a drink. "He can do wonderful things with his camera, and with the right subject to photograph. You're a natural for him, although he'd make you get into something more" he paused, "to his taste in boating attire."

"I'm a cop, not a model. I think there was a female cop a few years ago that got into big time trouble when she showed up in *Playboy*. Besides. My sister was the pretty one. She used to help me put make up on, but I was always shy around boys. Cate was the outgoing one. Men threw themselves at her feet. They all wanted Cate's attention and she theirs. She would unbutton one more button on her blouse than necessary to get their attention. Me, I'd wear a sweater."

"Like tonight?" Alex said with a grin.

"Yes, like tonight."

But he noticed there was no humor in her reply.

"I loved her dearly." Tara drained her glass of wine. "She was my older sister, and I looked up to her. The only thing that hurt me about our relationship back then was that my dad gave her most of his attention. I guess I understand that, because Cate worked with him, went into the same field as he. I became a cop. They had more in common, more of a bond."

She stared at her empty wine glass.

"Cate was family, and I loved her. Lately, we hit some rough spots. We always celebrated Mother's Day, even though my mother died giving birth to me. This year, though, Cate and I got into an argument about something. It wasn't even important but my dad sided with her . . . again. It really upset me, and I said a few things I probably shouldn't have to both of them. Now I can't make things right between me and Cate, and never will."

She looked up at the Milwaukee skyline, and sniffled.

Alex broke the silence that followed. "I never get tired of this view, especially at this time of day." He gazed at the skyline below a dramatic sky. "The sun's setting rays do special things to the tall downtown buildings—especially to the winged silhouette of Milwaukee Art Museum."

She nodded.

"How about another glass of wine?" he asked.

"OK. I guess I did drink all of this one."

They sailed for another hour. "I think it's time we head back to the yacht club to meet Drew."

Tara took a deep breath. "I just hate to see this end. I am so relaxed and enjoying myself."

"That was the whole idea of you going sailing. That, and

the thrill for me of spending time with someone that probably carries a gun in her purse." He noticed a faint smile.

"I do," she said, patting the purse. "Regulations."

He turned the wooden spokes of the wheel, so *Passage Maker's* bow was pointing at the Milwaukee skyline and the harbor's entrance. He settled back as Tara gazed ahead. Alex hoped the evening didn't end with just a sail.

Alex skillfully eased the big boat into his slip. After folding the mainsail on the boom and putting on the canvas sail cover, he checked the last of the boat's dock lines and stepped off. Holding his hand out for Tara, he said, "All shipshape and ready for our next sail."

"Thanks, Alex, for the wonderful adventure. It was just what I needed." Leaning over, Tara gave him a kiss on the cheek. "And thanks for showing me how to raise the mainsail."

He grabbed her hand and looked into her eyes. "I'd like to see you again. How about dinner tonight?"

"I'd love..." but before Tara finished answering Alex, her eyes saw Pinkowski and O'Malley standing near the end of the Milwaukee Yacht Club pier. They were looking her way. She frowned. "Shit, what are they doing here?"

Tara and Alex watched as the two detectives made their way down the pier, the cops sticking out like sore thumbs in their non-boating attire of leather shoes, tie and shirts, and sport coats.

"Hi Tara, funny meeting you here with—?" Pinkowski paused, waiting for clarification.

"Alex West. I'm a friend of Detective Sullivan's."

Tara stepped towards Pinkowski. "As you can see, we were out sailing. I am allowed to have a personal life, right?"

"Of course you are. I was just surprised to see you here, that's all."

"Why are you here?" she asked.

"We're trying to find Drew Thompson. We need to ask him more questions, and then we saw you. That's all, nothing personal."

"Funny you'd be down here—that's all Pinkowski meant," said O'Malley. "You don't have to get defensive."

"I know all about Drew Thompson. I looked at your notes and saw he was a suspect."

Pinkowski motioned for her to move towards him, out of earshot of Alex and O'Malley.

"Tara, the captain doesn't want you anywhere near this case. He told you that the other day. It's off limits, you know that. You could compromise our investigation. The captain would be royally pissed if he knew you were nosing around here. You understand why, don't you?"

"She was my sister!"

"I get it," said Pinkowski. "I'd feel the same way, but rules are rules. Just try to stay out of our hair on this one, please? There's plenty of other cases in homicide for you to cut your teeth on. You've got a good experienced partner now with

Sabina. She'll teach you a lot about this business but stay away from your sister's case. Understand?"

"OK, but keep me informed. That's all I ask."

"We will. Now we got to find Thompson."

"You won't have to look too far. He just sat down at the Tiki Hut." Tara pointed.

Pinkowski and O'Malley turned, and the group of four started walking toward Drew.

"Hi, how was the sail?" Drew asked. "You didn't pick these two up and take them on the sail too, did you?"

O'Malley stepped in front of Drew. "We need to ask more questions, this time downtown. We have a nice comfortable room for just that purpose. Seems you forgot to mention a few things to us. I told you we'd check out your alibi, Mr. Thompson, and we did."

Pinkowski moved to the other side of Drew, so he and O'Malley were on either side. "Witnesses say you left with someone with a striking resemblance to Cate Sullivan." Pinkowski looked at Tara. "There are a few other things we we'd like to clarify, but we can get into them downtown."

Pinkowski moved towards Drew. "Oh, by the way, you can give us your keys now to your boat and your car, or we can get a court order. If we get a court order, we'll probably have to use force to get inside your boat without the keys—and you wouldn't like that—so we'd appreciate the keys. Make it easy for all of us and sign a consent form. If the search is clean, you'll get out earlier. If we have to go to court, it could be days."

Drew handed his keys to Pinkowski. "I'll sign the form. I don't have anything to hide."

"We'll see," O'Malley said.

"I'm coming along!" Tara said, her eyes searching Drew's face.

"No, you're not!" O'Malley said forcefully.

Pinkowski looked at Tara. "What'd I just tell you?"

"If it's Thompson, I want to know." Tara turned to Drew. "I believed you. Now I learn you lied and might have left with my sister that night, after all."

She squared off at O'Malley. "I'm going to see the captain about this and change his mind."

"Good luck with that." O'Malley said. "If you know what's good for your career, drop it, or you might get transferred back to Burglary."

Now Alex was glad Drew didn't go on the boat tonight. He might have gotten mixed up in the investigation by just being Drew's friend. Besides, he didn't want Drew to distract Tara. Alex could be possessive about his interests, and he decided that he was very interested in Detective Tara Sullivan.

Chapter Five

Drew sat at a gray steel table facing a beat-up light green wall. On the ceiling above the door were two black bubbles; he assumed they hid camera and audio equipment directed at the table and chairs, taping and recording his conversation with O'Malley and Pinkowski.

Drew was surprised how small the interrogation room was. Waiting for Pinkowski to come in, he counted the nine linoleum squares back to the door and six across. Not unlike a normal police cell, he thought. Next to his seat, he noticed a steel ring bolted to the concrete wall used to secure a person being interrogated if needed. He was glad they had taken off the cuffs before leading him into the room.

Was Tara Sullivan watching? He assumed she would see the tape later even if she weren't allowed to observe now.

He knew the procedure. Drew had been one of the best intelligence officers for the Marines in Afghanistan.

Pinkowski entered the integration room with an extra chair.

O'Malley followed. "Mr. Thompson, please go over the events of last Friday night one more time, just to refresh our memory of what went on with you and Ms. Sullivan."

"OK."

Give short answers, nothing more, Drew thought.

"You told us you had a couple of drinks Friday at Riptide with Ms. Sullivan. Were those drinks before or after you got rid of Mr. Ream?"

"After."

"And after you took care of Mr. Ream, what did you do?"

"She thanked me for saving her night from the jerk. She bought me a couple of drinks and I bought her a couple. We enjoyed each other's company. She asked if I wanted to have dinner—her treat, she said."

"She was a beautiful woman," said Pinkowski. "You two seemed to hit it off. Is that all that happened?"

"I told her I had to take a rain check on dinner because of the fire on my boat. She gave me her card with her cell number." He reached for his wallet and got out the business card with the number written on it. "We were going to get together in a few days if I didn't get back that night. I never got a chance to call her back for that dinner. She was a nice person."

"Really?" O'Malley said. "How touching."

"No way I'd take someone like her, the way she was dressed, to my boat with the way it was. It smelled like a campground after a rainstorm. I was a combat marine, I'm used to being wet and sleeping in those conditions, but not someone like her."

Pinkowski looked at his notes. "You went home, had a cigar, some scotch and called it a night. Is that right?"

Drew stared at him. So far, everything he had told them was accurate, but now he was in trouble. They knew he had gone back after a few hours of work on the boat. Drew had wanted to spend more time with Cate Sullivan. She had made it very clear to him, if he came back, they'd spend the night together. He definitely wanted to spend the night with her.

"Mr. Thompson, I'm waiting for your answer."

"You took someone to your boat that night," barked O'Malley. "We have a witness that saw you with a woman staggering down the pier and stepping onto your boat. Several witnesses from Riptide say you left late that evening with a woman resembling Cate Sullivan. You're lying."

"Yes, that's what I did."

"You went back to Riptide," O'Malley summarized, "you met up again with Cate Sullivan, and took her to your boat."

"No. When I returned, Cate was gone. The woman I left with might have looked like her, but it wasn't her. What I told you was true, but after I got back to my boat I decided that I did want to have dinner with her. She was smart, attractive and liked to have a good time. She made that apparent to me."

"What do you mean—apparent?" Pinkowski asked.

"She kissed me, touched my arm, and the final thing she said was, 'Don't wait too long to get back to me,' and I knew why."

"She was hot for you and you just walked away?" Pinkowski said.

O'Malley laughed. "And you expect us to believe this? Amazing."

Drew glared at him. "I said goodbye and walked the short distance to the door leading back inside. I thought about changing my mind, but when I turned around to head back, there was another guy already hitting on her, and she was laughing. That's the last I saw her alive."

Pinkowski looked up from his steno pad. "OK. Can you describe the guy?"

"Tall, brown hair, broad shoulders, black polo shirt, and jeans. I never saw his face. He kind of looked like O'Malley but he obviously was friendlier than O'Malley."

O'Malley started getting up, but Pinkowski grabbed his arm restraining him.

Drew smiled. He didn't like O'Malley at all.

"You sure you didn't call her cell phone later after you cleaned up?"

"No. She was too classy to sleep on my smelly boat, like I said."

"But later you thought you'd go back and see if she was still there. Did you call her phone then?"

"I did go back, but no, I didn't call her."

"You know we're going to check your cell phone record and hers," Pinkowski said.

O'Malley asked. "So how come we have witnesses that said they saw you later leaving with Ms. Sullivan?"

Drew took a deep breath. He could feel the pressure building. He was used to being the guy asking the questions, not answering them.

"I went back later. As I was walking around Riptide looking for Cate, another woman grabbed me and we started talking. I guess she did look somewhat like Cate. She was really drunk and almost fell over. I grabbed her to keep her from falling. Her boyfriend was the jealous type. When he saw my hand around her waist and her giving me a wet kiss, he jumped to conclusions and exploded. I don't know why she gave me the kiss, but she did. Her boyfriend came at me, swinging."

He paused. "Marines teach you how to handle yourself. Fights don't bother me. Besides, he telegraphed his punch. I moved my new best friend out of the way and ducked the roundhouse punch. Now he was really mad. I had made him look like a fool in front of his girl and his friends. He came at me a second time, but this time I decided to end it right then and there, so I decked him."

"Jessica wanted to leave with me after that. She said I was just her type, someone strong. Besides, she said she was horny." He smiled. "I mentioned having to get back to my boat. She said she wanted to see it. I tried to explain about the fire and what shape it was in. She didn't care. She thought boats were romantic, so I took her back to the boat to get a few things. She was still drunk and was loud, laughing and talking as we walked down the pier. I showed her the boat and the marina bathroom before we went to a hotel she liked."

"What was her name again?" O'Malley asked.

"Her first name was Jessica. I never heard her last name. We wanted to keep it simple."

"Simple?" Pinkowski said.

Drew nodded. "Yeah. Sex can be simple and straightforward if you leave out all the emotion."

Pinkowski and O'Malley looked at each other but didn't say anything.

"Anyhow, Jessica said she was a nurse at one of the hospitals close by and had come to this hotel once before with a different boyfriend. She told me she needed someone romantic that night. Someone to make her feel special because she was fed up with her current boyfriend. Besides, she said, he couldn't get it up anymore. She told me she was going to break up with him after tonight. She decided I was the guy that was going to make her feel special. She was hot and horny. What could I do?"

"What was the hotel name?" Pinkowski asked.

"I think it had an animal name or something."

"Iron Horse?" O'Malley said.

"That could be it. We both needed to freshen up. Jessica thought the Iron Horse Hotel was a romantic place to spend the night. Our room had a big shower with a glass wall separating the bathroom and bedroom. She was right, it was romantic."

O'Malley grunted. "Been there once, with my wife for our anniversary . . . before kids. God, it seems like ages ago we did that. It has a nice bar, and really good food. It had nice rooms too, for a special night, or for a hook-up like with you two."

Pinkowski looked from O'Malley to Drew. "Sure you don't remember her last name?"

"I didn't ask, remember? It's in the hotel registry and on her credit card. Check it out."

"Who paid for the room?"

"She did. I didn't bring much cash with me that night."

"How convenient," Pinkowski said. "In the meantime, we'll let you be our guest for twenty-four hours in one of the Milwaukee Police Department's finer suites. Let's go." Pinkowski grabbed Drew's arm. "We need to process you in after failing to tell us about this other person."

***

After processing his personal possessions, Drew was taken to get a mugshot and fingerprinted. O'Malley and Pinkowski walked him to the holding cell.

"Here we are," O'Malley said. "Enjoy Milwaukee's hospitality, Mr. Thompson. See you in about twenty-four hours."

The large, beat up holding cell reeked of body odor and puke. It had been a long while since Drew had been in a place like this.

Actually, it was like a hotel compared to the last time he'd been cooped up. That had been Paris, 2011. He was on leave when an army sergeant made unflattering comments about the woman Drew was with. Drew hadn't been sure if he was angry because the guy was making fun of him or if he was just an army asshole making fun of a marine. And even if she was a working girl, Drew took offense at the guy for calling her one. She was his whore, and she was nice and had made Drew feel good when he needed it. Maybe he had been just looking for a fight.

His dad told him a long time ago, "Never back away from a fight if you're right." He was right, of course and the first time Drew got in a fight in grade school, his mom was horrified, but his dad was proud. He had stuck up for a friend getting bullied. Drew felt he was right then and he felt he was right in Paris. After he beat the shit out of the army guy, she gave Drew a kiss on the lips, and said to look her up after he got out of jail.

He never got a chance because the Marines cancelled the rest of his leave and shipped him back to Afghanistan. He'd have to be more careful when deciding to help a damsel in distress.

The holding cell in Milwaukee was uncrowded, but it was early in the evening. There was one guy in the corner, sitting with his head against the wall, looking like he was trying to sleep. As Drew walked past him, he smelled the sour smell of stale beer. He was probably drunk and trying to sleep it off. Not a bad idea. He knew as the night wore on, it was going to fill up, and sleep might be elusive. In the opposite corner, Drew found a spot on the metal bench, stretched out, and tried to get some shut-eye.

Two hours later, Tara Sullivan was able to sneak a look at the disk of Drew Thompson's interrogation. She watched the whole thing, ending with him being led out of the interview room. Tara turned off the machine and placed the disk back in its envelope, putting it back in the investigation folder.

She sat in a slight daze at the desk in her cubicle. Until now, she hadn't heard about the other person Cate supposedly met after Drew walked away.

She'd check out Iron Horse after Pinkowski or O'Malley or one of the other homicide teams went to the hotel. Milwaukee's Homicide Department might have three teams working a case on eight-hour shifts, so any case was theoretically worked 24/7. Tara knew she and her partner Sabina Bennett would be prevented from working this case but Tara still could snoop into the file. Of course, if Cate wasn't on the hotel's CCTV camera with Thompson that night, it was unlikely he was her killer because she definitely was killed that night. He couldn't be in two places at once.

Drew Thompson had seemed genuinely sorry about her sister's death when she talked to him that first time at the Tiki bar, but did Tara believe him now? She had believed him once, and he had lied about going back to Rip Tide. She could see how her sister—or anyone, for that matter—might be attracted to him. No one really knew much about who this Drew Thompson guy was, but Tara was going to find out.

He didn't know how long he was dozing when he heard the cell door unlatch, then the slide of metal against metal as it screeched open. He watched as a new guest entered, looking unhappy. Drew watched him walk to the center of the room, slowly taking in his surroundings. Then he moved to the side where the drunk was blissfully sleeping and took a seat.

"Well at least there are no Blacks or Mexicans in here yet. This city is full of them," he said with agitation, looking at Drew.

Drew didn't comment. Drew guessed he was high on something, drugs or booze. Drew closed his eyes and hoped he would be quiet like the other cellmate. The quiet lasted about five minutes when the big guy said, "Wake up!" Drew heard a thud of a boot kicking something, followed by a yelp of pain from the drunken cellmate.

"I want to sit where you are and stretch out. Move!"

Confused, the drunk in the rumpled dark suit said, "I was sleeping. Why don't you go over to the other side? No one's there."

"I said I want to sleep in your spot. Move!"

Drew watched as he grabbed the guy's suit collar and yanked him off the bench, tossing him to the floor. Then he kicked him in the ribs and in the leg. "I'm the boss in here. My bitch girlfriend found that out when I roughed her up for talking back and arguing. Can you believe she called the cops? She'll find out who the boss is when I get out, restraining order or not. She'll pay for calling the cops."

The drunk rolled on the floor and moaned.

The bully turned and looked at Drew. "What are you looking at?"

Drew smiled at the big hulk. "Not much, if you ask me. You like picking on weak people who are intimidated by your size. It makes you feel strong, but I know your type. You're basically a weak, insecure asshole."

"Don't make me laugh, fuckhead. I could take you out with one hand tied behind my back, but I'm feeling generous and won't make a mess of you. Besides, I'm comfy now." He leaned back and clasped his hands behind his head.

"You're a coward." Drew said, smiling. "You better just sit there and be quiet and leave our friend alone or you'll deal with someone that can take care of himself and you."

"Oh, do I look scared?"

But Drew noticed the big man didn't move except to lean his head back and close his eyes.

It quieted down for about twenty minutes when the drunk said, "I don't feel so good. I think I'm going to get sick." And started moving towards the cell's stainless steel commode.

He didn't make it. Puke splattered the floor and the big guy's shoes and pants leg.

That's all it took for him to lose control.

"You fucking idiot, look what you did. Now I'm going to smell like puke." He grabbed the soused guy by the throat and was about to punch him when his arm was suddenly halted.

"I told you, don't touch him."

"He just fucking puked on my shoes and pants. He's going to feel a lot sicker when I get through with him."

"I don't think so," Drew said. "First, you're going to have to deal with me, and I don't think you're going to want to do that."

"You aren't so tough, and I'm going to prove it." He let go of the drunk. When he turned towards Drew, he smiled showing off a missing front tooth. Drew knew what this bully's first move was going to be. He saw him fist his right hand, lean back turning his shoulders telegraphing a big roundhouse right. Drew moved back as he was still winding up so when the guy delivered an intended blow, he missed Drew by six inches.

Drew ducked under the follow-through and delivered a solid punch to the stomach, then a quick jab to the jaw. He saw surprise in the dude's eyes as his head recoiled back. Drew had learned at Annapolis and Marine training that you end a fight as fast as you can and you don't pussyfoot around. You don't fight fair, you fight to win. While the big thug was reeling from the punch to the gut and jab to the jaw, Drew grabbed him and slammed his head into the wall. Then he bent him over near the metal toilet rim. Ten seconds tops Drew figured, and it was over. He was bleeding and out cold, but not dead.

He turned to the drunk. "He slipped on your puke, hit the wall and then fell on the toilet— right?"

The drunk looked dazed but knew enough that Drew saved him from being beaten up. "That's what I saw. Thanks."

"No problem, I hate cowards."

"Thanks again. I'm a CPA in Milwaukee. I know it doesn't look like it right now, but I have my own firm. If I can ever help you, let me know. My name is John Paul Jones."

"Like the father of the Navy. I can remember that. Thanks. Now let's get some rest. He's going to be out for a while."

"What the fuck happened here?" the guard said as he opened the cell door and saw the bloody mess, with the big hulk sprawled on the floor.

"He slipped and hit his head on the wall, or the toilet— I don't really know. I was trying to sleep but then Mr. Jones puked on the guy as he tried to get to the toilet. This guy got pissed off and came at him, but slipped on the puke and hit his head. That's all I know."

The guard turned to Jones for confirmation.

"I got sick. I don't drink very often. Sorry."

"He's breathing. It just knocked him out." Drew continued. "Guess someone that big is not too coordinated."

The guard turned to the new detainee, who also looked like he'd had too much to drink. "Sit down. I'll be back with someone to clean this mess up and check on the guy."

Drew shrugged his shoulders and closed his eyes.

After the guard closed the door with a *clank*, Jones turned to Drew. "You think he bought it?"

"For now," Drew said. "We'll find out if they have a camera

covering the cell or if our friend here complains. Get some rest. It's going to get busy in here as the night goes on. Things like this happen all the time, especially with big obnoxious, drunks like him. Besides, he swung at me first so it was self-defense. Right?"

Jones nodded.

Drew thought about what he'd just done. He didn't need to give the police more reasons to hold him, or to show them what he was capable of doing with his hands. Sometimes he acted before thinking, and that led to trouble. He'd already had enough of that kind of trouble.

He let out a cleansing breath and tried to relax. But his memories from past events felt too close tonight and he knew he wasn't going to get much sleep.

* * *

The next afternoon, O'Malley and Pinkowski pulled up to the Iron Horse Hotel. "I wonder what the building looked like before it was converted," said O'Malley.

Pinkowski answered. "It was a one hundred-year-old warehouse before the developer renovated it into trendy loft style rooms and a bar."

Six Harley bikes were parked near the entrance. "They're probably staying here," O'Malley said, "so they could visit the nearby the Harley-Davidson Museum. Look at all that chrome on those bikes. I wish I could afford one of these. That one costs just about what we pay a year to keep my wife a stay at home mom—at least for a couple more years until the kids are ready for school. I had an old beat up Harley when I was younger but it was a piece of shit. Not like Harleys today. Someday I'm going to get one so my wife and I can cruise."

Pinkowski smiled. "I never was that adventuresome. My old red Corvette convertible has four wheels and I get the feel of the wind blowing in my limited hair, plus I don't have to worry about someone not seeing me. It's safer."

Both smiled at the Hog machines as they walked into the lobby. Approaching the reception desk, it took a few moments for their eyes to adjust to the interior after coming in from the bright sunlight.

They heard laughter coming from the bar off to the side and noticed male and female leather-clad bikers at the bar, along with several other patrons at tables.

It looks like a nice place to stay, O'Malley thought. Contrary to what many people thought, he could be a fun and loving husband. Maybe he'd get a chance to visit with Helen, his wife, after all this was over.

Pinkowski said, "We'll have to see if there are any cameras covering the bar area, besides the front desk."

"I'll check that out."

At the front desk, they waited their turn in line.

"Can I help you?" Pinkowski's head turned to a young woman in her early twenties, dressed in a smart looking suit.

They showed their badges. "I'm Detective Pinkowski and he is Detective O'Malley. We're working on a murder investigation and need your help. We need to talk to the manager. Can you help us with that?"

She gave a stiff smile and nodded. "Let me get him." She

turned and walked to a near office disappearing inside. A minute later, she returned with the manager.

"How can I help you, Detectives? Is something wrong? I'm not aware of anything happening at our hotel."

They looked at the name on the hotel badge: Frank.

"I hope so. We're investigating a murder that occurred last Friday or early Saturday morning. We have reason to believe the suspect and victim might have stayed at your hotel that night. Do you have surveillance disks of the front desk and bar area from last Friday night?"

"Detective, we did not find any body here at the hotel or we would have contacted you so I doubt if anything like that happened here."

"The event may have happened later at some other location, but we have reason to believe they might have stayed here before the crime was committed. Right now, we need to look at your recordings of the front desk and bar area. Do you have them?"

"Friday night or early Saturday morning? If you'll wait, I'll get them."

"Do you have a disk of the front entrance too?" They hoped they might see Drew leaving with Cate Sullivan.

"No, just the check-in and bar area. That's where money changes hands," Frank said. "I'll get those disks for you. Please have a seat."

"Thank you." Pinkowski got out his cell phone and called Tara.

"Homicide, Detective Sullivan."

"Hi Tara. O'Malley and I are at the Iron Horse. The hotel

manager is getting the disk for Friday night and early Saturday morning. Can you come downtown and look at the CCTV disk, to see if it's Cate?"

"I'm with Sabina checking out a lead on a shooting, but I can come in right now."

"If it's Cate on the disk, we have her killer, Drew Thompson. If it not Cate on the disk, we have a lot of work to do." Pinkowski knew the odds of solving the case got slimmer after forty-eight hours passed, and right now it was close to six days since the murder.

Chapter Six

"Thanks for coming in, Tara," said Pinkowski. "Even though you can't work on this case, you'll be helping us get closer to the killer. This is the hotel's CCTV recording and let's see what we've got. O'Malley, fast forward it until we get to around 10 p.m."

The three huddled around the monitor on a large table in the police station's operations room, watching the time on the screen move toward the appointed hour. O'Malley slowed down the fast-forward and took closer looks at various male-female couples, focusing on the female guest as they checked in.

"There!" Tara said as O'Malley stopped the frame. "That looks like Thompson from the back."

"I guess you got a better look at his ass than we did, Tara." O'Malley said with a smile.

"Fuck you, O'Malley."

"All right, you two. Let's just watch the tape and try to identify the lady," Pinkowski said. "Sometimes O'Malley, you can be such an asshole," she said.

"Yeah, I know. My wife says the same thing. Sorry, Tara."

They watched the images as a female leaned against Thompson's shoulder while her right hand rubbed his ass. She moved her hand up his back.

"God she's all over him, right at the desk," Pinkowski said.

"Tara, can you tell if it's your sister?" asked O'Malley.

"It looks like Cate from the back, but I've never seen Cate wear a sweatshirt—not even a Green Bay Packers one." Tara continued looking at the monitor, moving the scene forward with the control, now in her hand.

"Come on," O'Malley pleaded to the sketchy figure on-screen. "Turn around so we can see your face."

"There!" Pinkowski said. "Freeze it there. Is that your sister?" His eyes focused on Tara's face, hoping that they already had their killer in the holding cell. Instead, he heard a soft moan, and "Shit" from Tara.

"What? Tell us: yes or no?"

Tara lowered her head to her forearms now resting on the table. "It's not her."

"We had to make sure," said Pinkowski. "Your sister wasn't registered at the hotel. This confirms what Thompson said. He was with someone else." They watched as the hotel clerk said something to Drew and the woman. She took out a credit card and placed it on the desk.

"Well, at least we'll have her last name, if we need to question her," said Pinkowski.

"Why?" Tara said.

"Good point," O'Malley said.

Tara got up from the large table in the operations room and looked at Pinkowski and O'Malley, teary eyed. "The killer is still out there." *And if you two can't find him, I will!*

***

Now that Drew Thompson was eliminated for all intents and purposes as the killer, Pinkowski and O'Malley drove to the law firm where Cate had worked to follow up on information about any arguments at work. The firm was located on the lakefront in one of Milwaukee's newer glass buildings.

"Nice building to work in. Great view of the harbor," O'Malley said. "I wonder what they charge an hour?"

"You don't even work in a building like this unless you charge at least $500.00 an hour, that's for sure," Pinkowski said. "Their office is on the sixth floor."

Five minutes later they entered the cherry paneled law office. The receptionist greeting them was a pert, mid-twenties woman with black rimmed glasses and long black hair. On her desk was a large box of tissues with a few crumpled next to the box. Pinkowski noticed her red eyes, and slightly smeared mascara and knew she had been crying.

"Good morning, gentlemen, May I help you?"

Pinkowski looked at the name on the desk. "Yes, Ms. Nicklaus. We're Detectives O'Malley and Pinkowski with the Milwaukee Homicide Department. We'd like to speak with Mr. Sullivan, please, if he's in?"

"He just called, and said he was going to be late, and would be here in ten minutes. Can I get you some coffee while you wait?"

O'Malley smiled. "That would be great. Black for me. Thank you."

"I'm fine but thank you," Pinkowski said. "As you might expect, we're here to investigate the death of Cate Sullivan. Do you happen to have a photo of her that we might use? We really don't want to use our photo, if you know what I mean."

"I can't believe she's gone. She was so nice, and everyone loved her. That is except Mrs. Reynolds."

"Oh?" Pinkowski lifted an eyebrow at her comment, and then watched as she opened a drawer from a cadenza behind her, and pulled from a legal-size file two glossy profiles with Cate Sullivan's picture on it.

"Would this work, or do you need just a corporate photo?"

"What did you mean by 'everyone but Mrs. Reynolds?' Did something happen to give you that impression?"

"Yes. Last week, I think it was Friday afternoon, Ms. Sullivan had a meeting with Mr. and Mrs. Reynolds. Cate represented them in a legal matter that did not work out as they had expected. I guess they were meeting to determine if they were going to appeal. Mrs. Reynolds and Ms. Sullivan got into an argument. Mrs. Reynolds was quite upset with the outcome of their lawsuit, but I think there could have been more to it than that. I think she thought Cate, I mean Ms. Sullivan was making a play for Mr. Reynolds. Anyhow, they went at it, even knocking over a chair and ripping Ms. Sullivan's blouse. Nasty scene that had the whole office talking. Cate had to go home and change her blouse. She came back later."

"Do you happen to have their address?" O'Malley asked. "We're going to need to talk to them."

"I probably shouldn't give you the address but you could Google it, so here it is." She wrote it down on a piece of paper and gave it to O'Malley.

"Thank you."

"Let me get you that coffee. Mr. Sullivan will be here shortly."

Ten minutes later, Peter Sullivan entered the office wearing a black suit, white shirt and black shined shoes carrying a thin briefcase.

"Good morning, Miss Nicklaus. Sorry I'm late but I'll only be in for a short time this morning. I don't know how I'm going to get through today. The funeral the other day did me in. Hold all calls, and tell them I'll call them back tomorrow."

"Mr. Sullivan, these two men are here to see you. They're police detectives."

Turning, he looked at O'Malley and Pinkowski. Both were getting up and pulling out their shields. "Tara said you would be stopping by to ask a few questions. Come into my office and we'll get this over with. I'm sorry but my mind is not very good this morning, but of course I want to help as much as I can."

"Thank you, Mr. Sullivan, you have our condolences on the loss of your daughter," Pinkowski said.

They took a seat in the large richly appointed corner office. The view was of Lake Michigan, Milwaukee Harbor and up the north shore towards Shorewood and Whitefish Bay. Pinkowski thought how difficult it would be to get any work done with a view like that, but then he noticed that Sullivan's desk was turned away from the view. The man didn't want to be distracted and that was a simple way to do it.

"How can I help you find the killer of my daughter?" he said, sitting upright in his leather swivel chair, his hands folded in front of him.

"Is there anyone that might want your daughter dead?" asked O'Malley. "Maybe a disgruntled client or employee?"

"Not that I'm aware of. I guess there could be. Cate was

successful at litigation and won big cases for our clients and the firm. That's why she was a partner. She was great at her job. It wasn't because she was my daughter. She earned the partnership. She got along with everyone here as far as I know. Sure, there were squabbles now and then, but nothing serious."

"Last Friday, Ms. Sullivan had a heated disagreement with the wife of one of her clients. Do you know what that was all about?"

"Not really. I heard about it later when I came back to the office from court. Seems it was mainly a disagreement with the wife of the client. I guess it was like an old fashion cat fight. Guess his wife got nasty and scratched Cate, even pulling some of her hair and ripping Cate's blouse. Cate sometimes dresses a little provocatively. I guess in this instance the client's wife took exception."

O'Malley made notes.

"Did your daughter have a boyfriend?" Pinkowski asked.

Mr. Sullivan pressed his fingers tips together like a steeple and thought. A smile came to his face. "Cate was very attractive and liked to have a good time. She attracted several friends and lovers. I can't say she ever mentioned being afraid of any of them. This last one did grab her arm and left a bruise. She told me they got into a fight. She said he grabbed her and escorted her out the door a little too forcefully, bruising her arm in the process. Guess she also did some damage to a few of his things. You might want to talk to him. He's the only one who ever hurt Cate that I'm aware of."

"Do you know his name? His address?" O'Malley asked.

"He's in real estate. His name is Steven Tizanglo. He sold

her the condo she lived in, and that's how they met. His office is on Prospect."

"Anything else you can think of that might help?" Pinkowski asked.

"No. I just can't believe someone would want to hurt my Cate. She was so beautiful and kind."

"Thank you, Mr. Sullivan. Again, our condolences on your loss. If you think of anything more, please call us." He said, giving him their card.

Later that afternoon, O'Malley stood next to Pinkowski's cubicle. "I called a few minutes ago to make sure Tizanglo was in. He's back in his office now. I thought we'd surprise him. Not give him a chance to think too much about what happened."

"Yes, that's good." Pinkowski said.

O'Malley and Pinkowski entered the small real estate office of Tizanglo and Associates and were ushered into his office.

Steven Tizanglo stood up from behind a large wood desk, and came around to shake their hands before returning to his seat. "I thought someone would be calling on me. I didn't realize it would be so soon. You guys don't waste time."

"Yes, you're right. We understand you were involved with Ms. Sullivan until last week—Wednesday, to be exact."

"Yeah, we had an argument that got nasty. Cate was a beautiful, exciting woman who liked to have fun, eat, drink and loved to have wild sex. I was more than willing to participate. After all, I'm Italian."

Pinkowski looked O'Malley, and silently mouthed "Italian?"

"We met about a year ago, when I showed her the condo she bought. Being a successful litigation attorney, she could get a little high-strung and domineering. I'm Italian and I know I can get moody and controlling too, so we'd have disagreements from time to time. What can I say?"

"Mr. Tizanglo, did you ever strike Ms. Sullivan in one of these arguments or last Wednesday specifically?"

"Well, maybe I slapped her once or twice but never more than that. She'd slap me and then I'd slap her. Sort of tit for tat. I could have easily nailed her good Wednesday. As I said, she could get pushy. I'm not proud of what I'm going to tell you, but I got fed up. We did a lot of things with her best friend and her boyfriend. One thing led to another and her friend and I started seeing each other on the sly. She surprised me Wednesday with a bottle of champagne and strawberries. It's too bad about the whole thing. Cate had every right to yell and scream, but then she grabbed two of my prized glass trophies and smashed them on the floor. I could have killed her when she did that. Oops, I didn't mean that, really it was a wrong choice of words. Hey, you can ask her best friend what happened."

O'Malley leaned forward. "We will, Mr. Tizanglo, we will. What's her name?"

"Ginger Nelson. She lives in 1503, the same condo complex as Cate."

"OK, Mr. Tizanglo. We're going to check out your story. We'd like to take a DNA sample from you. It's a simple mouth swab."

"Sure, go ahead. I have nothing to hide."

"Oh, by the way, where were you last Friday evening and early Saturday morning?"

"Ah, Friday night . . . I was with Ginger at my house. We went to dinner at Buckley's and then to my house for the rest of the night. You can check that out too."

"OK, Mr. Tizanglo. If you think of anything else, please call. One last thing: don't leave town unless you check with us until we clear you."

"Right."

Pinkowski and O'Malley drove back to the Homicide. "Why don't you interview Ms. Nelson and see if we can get any more information from her?" Pinkowski said. "I'll contact Mrs. Reynolds and try to set up an interview tomorrow morning with her and her husband."

"OK."

***

The next morning Pinkowski pulled in front of a large red brick home with black shutters, several white-trimmed windows, a circle drive, and a three car garage. The large two-acre lot had several large blue spruce pine trees scattered around and he could see a large flower garden in the backyard. "Wow, so this is how the affluent live in River Hills. Nice."

Pinkowski turned off the engine of his old red Corvette. He loved driving the car when he could. As he walked to the black front door with a large brass knocker, it swung open. The policeman was greeted by a tall, black haired man, dressed in light gray suit pants, shined shoes and a starched white shirt unbuttoned at the collar. No tie.

"Detective Pinkowski, please come in. My name is Dennis Reynolds. My wife Rose is in the kitchen with a fresh pot of coffee and a few pastries. Can we do the interview there?"

"That would be fine." He followed him into the kitchen and sat across from Rose Reynold as she pushed a cup of steaming coffee toward him.

"Cream or sugar, Detective Pinkowski?" she asked.

"Black is fine." She looked like she was ready to go to the country club and play cards with her lady friends. She did not look happy being interviewed. Pinkowski started in.

"As you know, your attorney Cate Sullivan was found floating in Lake Michigan Saturday morning. We have every reason to believe it was not an accidental death. The reason I'm here is to get more information on the altercation you had at her law firm Friday."

Mr. Reynolds cleared his throat. "Ahh, an unfortunate situation, a terrible misunderstanding. My wife Rose overreacted to a situation she believed was happening." Pinkowski saw him turn toward his wife for confirmation.

Instead, Mrs. Reynolds slapped her hand on the kitchen table. "My intuition is pretty good, Detective. I think Cate Sullivan was giving a little more of herself than just practicing law with my husband. My husband might be smart in business but when women are involved, he thinks and acts with his dick."

"Rose, that's not true and you know it."

"No, I don't. When I showed up with you and surprised her that day, she was very unprofessional." Rose looked at

Pinkowski. "Cate Sullivan was always smiling and would bend over showing my husband a good view of her breasts, even when I was there. I even saw her unbutton an extra button to give him a better view a couple of times. After we basically lost our lawsuit against a former partner, I couldn't take it any-more and we had an unfortunate disagreement. I have to say it felt good what I did to her last Friday, but I would never kill her. Unfortunately, my husband has done this sort of thing too many times before with others."

"Rose, shut up. The detective isn't interested in our dirty laundry, even if it is not true."

"Bullshit," she said under her breath.

Pinkowski wrote in his notebook, then looked up at the two. "I need to know where you were late Friday night and early Saturday morning from about 9 p.m. Friday until 3 a.m. Saturday."

Reynolds turned toward his wife, then back to Pinkowski. "We went to the country club for Friday fish dinner about 7:30 p.m., like we usually do, had a few drinks with dinner. We talked afterwards with our friends at the bar. After that, we came home. I went to my study and read a John Grisham novel, *A Time to Kill*, until midnight and then went to bed. Rose went to her bedroom and read for a while I assume, and went to sleep. The lights were off in her room when I went to bed so I assume she was sleeping late Friday, and Saturday morning."

"You sleep in separate rooms?"

Pinkowski turned and saw Mrs. Reynolds nodding yes. "Is there anyone that can vouch for you both being here late Friday and Saturday?"

Mr. Reynolds frowned. "No, we didn't have people over, if that's what you were wondering and we don't like to drive after we've had a few drinks. We came home, like I said."

"I will be contacting the country club. Do you have the names of the people at the bar you had drinks with?"

"They were the Howards and the Atwoods." He said.

Pinkowski closed his notebook and stood up. "I think I have enough information from you both for now. If you can remember anything else to verify your time between nine and three, please call me." He handed them a card. "I can let myself out. Thank you for the coffee. It was very good."

***

When Pinkowski got back to the station, he saw O'Malley slam the phone down.

"Shit."

"Why are you so mad?"

"I just got off the phone about that Child molester Thompson told us about. I got the name of the guy from the office. Then I did a check on him and found out the guy was in jail when Ms. Sullivan was killed. Seems he got beat up by an adult neighbor of a kid he was trying to entice in his car. A neighbor heard him try to get the kid to get in his car help him look for a lost puppy. Lucky for the kid, the neighbor ran over to the car before he got in his car and drove off. The neighbor pulled the guy out of the car, and then started beating the shit out of the guy. Neighbors pulled him off the guy before he almost killed him, and called the police. The guy is out of the hospital now but is in jail awaiting charges again for child molesting. Nobody likes a child molester. He's probably going to have a hard time in jail when the guys in there with him find out. No one like people like him that do nasty thing to kids"

"I guess we don't have to interview him. Thank god for the neighbor. Who knows what would have happen to the kid?" Pinkowski said.

"That's for sure. The neighbor is a hero as far as I'm concerned."

Chapter Seven

Ever since he had been old enough to wear one, Alex West liked putting on a tuxedo. He used to watch his dad get dressed for various functions in Washington D.C. and in Milwaukee.

Alex enjoyed community service. The annual Boys and Girls Club picnic his company sponsored was always fun. Alex thought it helped bring single parents and their children closer together. Then there was the Winter Carnival he sponsored at one of Milwaukee's ice ponds, with tubing and sledding. He still loved the feel of the old wooden toboggan he had in the garage. It was thrilling racing down the ice track with three or four others, yelling and screaming along the way.

Alex's favorite was the Make-A-Wish functions. Each year an event was held at the Milwaukee Yacht Club. Boaters—both power and sail—got together and provided rides for kids who were very sick or terminally ill, who wanted one wish to come true. It might be a simple boat ride or something more. It gave Alex a chance to use *Passage Maker* for a good cause.

He wrote big checks for the *Race for the Cure* and his company sponsored a refreshment stand on the route. He even sponsored a table for his brother at the Humane Society Gala because George loved dogs. It was nice that Alex had the money to help out, but he did it because he cared for the city he loved, Milwaukee.

Tonight's event was a black-tie affair for the Milwaukee Symphony. Alex was excited about it—not just because the music would be great, but the gala would be fun.

Ever since their sail last week, Alex could not get Tara out of his mind. Something about her felt familiar, but he hadn't put his finger on it until he was playing his baby grand piano in his living room. Looking at a family picture of his mother and father resting on the corner of the piano, he suddenly noticed that Tara bore a striking resemblance to his mother, Gloria. It was an old black and white photo taken of his parents when they were at some society function, before Alex was born. His mother's hair was brunette, and Tara's was red, but the face, eyebrows, and eyes were alike.

Not a day went by that Alex didn't think of his mother. Poor George couldn't seem to do anything right in her eyes. Alex had been her favorite. She had doted on him. She used to call him "Alexander the Great" with her soft Southern accent. Then she'd pat the top of his head or give him a kiss on the cheek.

Last week, when he had phoned Tara to ask if she'd like to go to the symphony fundraising gala, she had sounded excited to go.

"What type of dress should I wear?"

"You looked pretty good in a simple sailing outfit." Alex could only imagine how extraordinary she'd look dressed up. He felt his face break into a smile as he remembered when he explained it was a black-tie affair.

"I'll see if I could find one of my old prom dresses. Would that work?" She laughed so he knew she was kidding. "I was looking for an excuse to buy a fancy dress, so now I'll go shopping with a purpose. If Cate were still alive, I'd borrow one of hers. She went to a lot of these events. Is it real fancy?"

"It's more like an upscale wedding. I'll wear a tux. It isn't New York, but it is Milwaukee's finest."

"Milwaukee's finest? Are you sure you want to go with me, a lowly rookie homicide detective?"

Alex had sensed her uneasiness about being out of her social comfort zone. He tried to ease her anxiety. "I want to be with no one else but you."

After that conversation last week, he could hardly wait to see her. Alex grabbed his keys and went to the garage and his black Jaguar convertible. After sliding behind the leather covered steering wheel, he adjusted the mirror, looking to see if his tie was straight and his hair looked OK. Satisfied, he turned the Jag's key, and the big engine came to life with a low rumble. He liked the slow speed of his sailboat, but he loved the power and speed of this car. Like his boat, it was a classic. No top down tonight, he thought, at least going there. He didn't want to mess up her hair—or his own, for that matter. He looked in the mirror again, then chuckled at his vanity before backing out the long Jaguar.

He gazed at the rich black leather seat. He had it detailed for tonight's event, wanting everything to be perfect for Tara. He could still smell the leather conditioner the company used on the interior. His mother, Gloria, had owned this car, an XKE from 1962. It cost a fortune to maintain, but Alex loved it as she had, especially with the top down. She'd say, "With this big engine, it's as spirited as my favorite thoroughbred horse, *Midnight.*" The leather seats touching her skin, she said, reminded her of her black leather English jumping saddle.

The image of her tugging on black leather driving gloves when she drove flashed in his mind. Alex slipped on the gloves his mother had given him on his sixteenth birthday. He'd have to get a new pair, as these were almost worn through. Backing into the street, he made sure he didn't scrape the long tail pipe that gave the Jag its distinctive sound.

On Monday afternoon, O'Malley was on his third cup of acidic coffee causing the pain in his gut to make him grumpy. O'Malley ran his hand through his hair and grunted. "I'm brain dead." He dropped the reports on his desk. "I don't see anything new on this case. Riptide's CCTV of the tiki area doesn't cover the area where Cate Sullivan was."

"It's over two weeks since the crime was committed," Pinkowski said. "CSI said Thompson's boat came up empty. He's right about bringing a woman there for the night; it was still a mess from his fire and his work, even after he worked on it for a couple of days cleaning it up. No hair or anything that wasn't his. As much as I hate to, I almost believe him."

"Tara is going to keep bugging us on this case, in addition to the captain." O'Malley slid his notes into the accordion murder file. "Tara and her new partner can help us with that—what's her name again?"

"Sabina Bennett. Good idea, O'Malley. They can go through Cate's computer. Check out her personal items at home. Maybe two women will have a better insight for what's important than you or me. Teaming Tara and Bennett was a good idea. Sabina's been on the job a while, first in Los Angeles and now here. She'll train Tara on what it takes to be a good detective and follow procedure."

O'Malley rubbed his eyes. "Hopefully, Sabina can keep Tara out of trouble. At least doing this work will make her feel like she's helping."

"Right. Have we got everything from pathology?" Pinkowski asked.

O'Malley slid over a yellow file. "Cate Sullivan didn't drown. No water in the lungs. Surprising, there was no semen in her either. He must have used a condom, or he never ejaculated. She appeared to have had sexual intercourse recently with the marks on her breast and vaginal area. The thorax was crushed, and she had bruises on her neck that looked like finger marks so let's assume she was strangled. She might have been raped and then killed, or just had rough sex because of the bruising. Her being in the water didn't help."

"It might be just what Thompson said when he was leaving. He looked back, and she was already with another guy," Pinkowski said. "She got picked up at Riptide, taken someplace, and killed."

"What about that shlubby guy, Jasper Ream?" O'Malley said. "He waits for her to leave Riptide. He follows her to a car. Sees she's alone, overpowers and kills her? He's furious because she rejected him. He waits and gets his revenge." He narrowed his eyes in concentration. "She couldn't have drifted out that far in the lake, even with a good wind, so the killer had a boat. The fishermen found her almost three miles out. We should find out if Jasper Ream has a boat."

"Let's see what shakes out of that tree. He seemed pretty angry about the whole thing with Sullivan and Thompson. We don't have anything else to go on."

Drew sat on one of the high bar chairs under the canopy of the yacht club's Tiki Hut. He didn't need any more sun, that was for sure. His body was as brown as a nut from working on the boat. He was almost done with the repairs. His last project inside was replacing the cushions. There was no way he was ever going to get the soot smells out of them, and they were old anyway.

Boats are always damp. He could smell a hint of the fire, even without the cushions in the boat. Once he was sailing, the continual fresh air rushing through the open forward hatch would help give it a clean, fresh smell. At least he hoped so. The new cushions would be delivered in a couple of days. He could hardly wait to finally take *Courage* out on Lake Michigan.

His train of thought was broken when he saw a familiar figure walking towards the boatyard office in shorts and a wild Hawaiian shirt. He had not seen Alex that much to know if he usually wore something that colorful.

"Alex! Alex, wait up." But Alex kept walking. Drew watched him go into the yard office and heard the screen door slam. A minute later, Drew walked into the yard office and saw Alex talking to Dan, the yard manager. Drew waited for him to finish his business with Dan.

He was surprised when Alex again didn't acknowledge him. Was he angry with him? "Alex, I guess you didn't hear me. How are you doing?"

Alex turned toward him with a surprised look.

Drew persisted. "We didn't get a chance to talk when you and Tara came in from sailing last week. How are you?"

"You have me confused with my twin brother. Happens all the time. I'm Alex's older brother, George, the black sheep of the family. Alex gets all the publicity and awards, and that's fine with me." George laughed. "I get the girls."

"He never mentioned you to me, but then, we just met a short time ago," said Drew. "We were going to go sailing on his boat, *Passage Maker*, but I got delayed, and couldn't make it. When I saw you just now, I was hoping we could reschedule."

"I think Alex will be around later. I came over to fuel my boat. I'm going to motor down to Chicago for the start of the Mac Race. I'm a photographer, and part of the marketing department with our company."

"I see. He mentioned the business, but we really didn't talk about that as much as we talked about sailing."

"My parents knew I'd never take to business like Alex, so he got the business, and I got the freedom to do my art. He does pay me a small salary that just about covers my gas for the boat, but I really live on my trust fund money and work on photography."

"Wow, nice for you."

"Yes, I'm what many would call a Trust Fund Brat, and Alex will tell you that too. I have work to do now. I'm going down to Chicago early to capture the excitement of the race. And the beautiful people there."

"Nice work if you can get it," Drew said, smiling.

"Someone's got to do it and I'm the right guy. If you're going down to Chicago for the race, stop by." George reached into his pocket and handed Drew his card. "Call me. We'll have a good time. There are lots of women down there that like to party. And several will be on my boat. You won't have any trouble meeting someone."

"I just might do that. I don't think I've ever been to the start of a big race like that. I used to race at the Naval Academy, but that's about it."

"Well, come down. You sail, so you'll enjoy what's happening on the water and off." He laughed.

"OK, sounds like a good time. I'll call you on your cell if I decide to come down. Won't be until later in the week. probably Friday. Where will I find you and your boat in Chicago?"

"I'll be at one of the marinas near the Chicago Yacht Club. I think it's called Monroe Marina."

"Need any help handling the boat today and getting it to the gas dock?"

"No, I'm pretty good handling the boat by myself. Besides Dan and Travis are always around." He paused. "Don't forget to call if you get down to Chicago. Call and I'll let you in at the gate. There are lots of hotels around the area, but you might want to book something today. They do fill up. I'd normally say you can stay with me, but I'll be busy with the event, and I'll have a guest or two staying on the boat."

Chapter Eight

Tara decided to skip her morning jog and spend the extra time in bed. Her thoughts turned to last night's symphony gala. That had been the first night she had been able to forget about her sister's murder since the sail with Alex. It was like Cinderella getting away from her wicked stepmother and stepsisters, except it didn't end at the stroke of midnight. Far from it.

She could feel the big grin form on her face, as her eyes turned to the black lace dress tossed across her bedroom dressing chair. Last night, Alex was truly her Prince Charming.

What a spectacular night they'd had, dancing and drinking champagne. They'd ended the night at her place.

She had not wanted the night to end. Alex introduced her to everyone with, "This is my special friend, Tara Sullivan," and after a while she started to believe she *was* special to him. As they walked around and mingled, Alex put his arm around her waist and squeezed. He'd look deep into her eyes, and she saw a twinkle of excitement in his. And after a couple hours and a few dances he said, "We need to get out of here and be alone."

But then he'd meet more people, and they'd have more champagne and dance. Tara remembered his body pressed against her and she could feel his excitement. When he kissed her neck, a tingle raced from her spine to her toes. Pretty soon, it was one in the morning.

"Let's go to one more place I know that's still open and it's a lot of fun," he said.

At Speakeasy, most of the women were dressed as flappers. Because of the way Alex and Tara were dressed, some people thought they worked there and asked them to get drinks. Alex thought it was very funny. At least there he could kiss her on the lips.

Mmm, she felt herself getting warm right now as she remembered his tongue dancing in her mouth. Alex West was a wonderful kisser. When they closed the place at 4 a.m., it was time for him to take her home.

When he stopped his black Jag in front of her building, he kissed her again. His hand had moved to her thigh. Her hand went to her thigh stopping him from going any higher. That's when she decided she had to invite him up to her apartment for coffee. After all, she was an officer of the law, and she couldn't let him drive Milwaukee's streets unless he was absolutely sober. Besides, sometimes a girl wants to taste a little honey, and he was the drone.

As they walked up to her apartment, she said, "I bet you thought I was going to make some excuse and hurry up to my apartment? I'll make us coffee, OK?"

He just smiled and nodded. She unlocked the door.

"Allow me, madame," he said with a flourish and a slight slur. She stood back as Alex moved to the door and turned the knob. He pushed it inward and stepped into her small living room. She followed him in.

"It's nice," he said. "The teak and the modern Scandinavian design look reminds me of the woodwork on my boat."

"It's not big but it's the perfect size for me. I don't require much. Have a seat. It will only take a few minutes to make the coffee."

She watched as he unbuttoned his stiff white collar, and untied his bowtie, letting the ends hang loose. He took off his tuxedo jacket, tossing it over an easy chair in the living room. God, he's sexy, she thought.

Cate would have no qualms about jumping into bed with him, but Tara wasn't Cate. It had been a long, long time since Tara had slept with a man. As she made coffee, she watched him. He seemed at ease as he moved around her small apartment, looking at her photos and books in her small bookcase.

When the coffee was done, they sat on the sofa and made casual conversation until the talking got personal and eventually got around to kissing.

She sighed now as she lay in bed. Tara remembered how hard it was to stop his advances as his lips and hands roamed her body. She felt herself getting aroused even now as she lay in her bed thinking of him. When her hand rested on his pants and Tara felt his hardness, she squeezed it at the same time his hand caressed her breast and his tongue swirled against hers. Then he loosened the straps of her dress and eased the top down, exposing her breasts. He gently kissed her until she moaned with his attention to her nipples.

She had almost let things get too far but when she asked him to stop, he did. Now she hoped he didn't think she was a prude.

Lying in bed this morning, she thought, would he call her again? He didn't say he would, but he did say he had a good time and had given her a long lingering kiss at the door. Oh well, she thought, it was a nice time. He was a nice guy, and she never would have met all those people. She wasn't going to sit around all day, waiting for his call.

A few hours later, she was at work at her desk. Today was another day in homicide, and another day to sneak around her sister's case.

She and Tara's partner, Sabina Bennett were assigned with four other detectives to team up and work on a couple gang-related murders so common in Milwaukee.

Tara knew Sabina had come to Milwaukee to be closer to family in the Midwest after being a detective for a long time in L.A. The new job was a good fit for her and so far, the two women had gotten along well. Having a black partner also helped their policing in the community with its large African American population.

Unfortunately, there was always work in the homicide division, and not just gang related killings. Murders happen across all social groups, as Tara well knew.

Chicago.

Stella Carpenter was a beautiful loner. She had long legs

that seemed to go to the sky, a trim upper body, medium breasts, and had grown up an Air Force brat. As a child, she had moved from base to base and never developed close friends. Instead, Stella developed a protective attitude. She'd smile to herself after saying something designed to shock people. She knew who she was.

After she graduated from Luke AFB High School, she decided she was sick of the heat of Arizona and the dust of the desert area. She came to live with her Uncle Frank in Chicago. The wind and cold up north seemed better than Arizona's heat, dust and snakes. While she tried not to draw attention to herself, it was almost impossible not to because Uncle Frank, who managed a marina in Chicago, decided to have her work the gas dock, servicing the sail and power boats.

She remembered Uncle Frank telling her, "Be prepared for hearing all the pickup lines in the world from the guys with the big yachts or fast cigarette boats. They likely have big stomachs, big egos and lots of money—or their parent's money if they're your age—but they all want to get in your pants, so be careful."

She laughed when he told her that, but she soon found out he was right. Still, she often got twenty to a hundred-dollar tips for gassing up their boats. At the rate she was going, she was easily going to pay college tuition for the whole year.

Here comes a nice one, she thought, as the boat made its way towards the gas dock. It was an older design but looked in great shape. Don't see too many like that. She saw it had lots of varnished wood topside. "Nice."

She watched the captain skillfully maneuver the boat

towards the gas dock. As she positioned herself to grab his lines, she saw the name *Condor.*

This guy was good, she observed as he brought the boat sideways to the marina's long gas dock. He had his bumpers and lines all set so all she had to do was grab and cleat the lines off. She wondered how he did that since it seemed like he was all alone.

George West saw Stella as he rounded the last marker to the marina gas dock. When she bent over to cleat the bowline, giving him a good view, he saw what a beauty she was. He watched as she went to the stern and wrapped a couple turns around the cleat before tying it off. Nice ass, too. Finally, stepping out of the cabin, he threw her the spring lines.

"Nice job bringing it in," she said. "How did you get the lines and bumpers ready when you were the captain and crew?"

"I've done this a million times. I just studied your dock configuration on the way down from Milwaukee." While he spoke, his eyes never left hers. "You do a nice job yourself. I enjoyed watching you tie up my boat."

She laughed.

"I'm a photographer. I'm down here early for the Mac Race. I'm always looking for fresh faces. I'd love to take shots of you, perhaps on my boat? You'll get paid for modeling, and if I sell the photo, you'll get paid more. You don't need to tell me now. How about later, after you give me 300 gallons of diesel? My boat likes to drink lots of fuel. She's beautiful like you, but high maintenance. Come over later and I'll give you a tour. We can have a drink and talk about modeling."

"That's nice of you, and I'm flattered, but no thanks on the modeling," Stella said. "I might take you up on the tour of your boat and that drink, though. Since I've been working here, I enjoy a glimpse seeing how different boats are decorated and laid out. I'd love to see the inside of your boat."

"That's good enough. Now, if you can tell me my slip and have someone stand by and handle the lines for me. Maneuvering in a confined area is when I like a little help, just in case the wind comes up."

"Actually, we have you on the end of a pier so your slip is just like here, and you should be able to use the same setup you have now," said Stella. "I'll have Chet go over and help you. By the time I have you gassed up, he'll be over there."

"Thank you," George said. "I'm sorry. I don't know your name."

"It's Stella, Stella Carpenter. And yours?"

"George West. Nice to meet you Stella, I hope to see you later."

Stella went to the diesel pump, turned it on while George unscrewed the diesel cap. Walking over with the hose, she liked what she saw in George West too, and it just wasn't his boat.

The next morning, when O'Malley entered the homicide assembly area, he saw Pinkowski sitting at his desk, shaking his head.

"What a sick bastard. You won't believe what I discovered about our Jasper Ream."

O'Malley sat at his desk. "Here, I brought you better coffee from the shop next door."

"Thanks." Pinkowski nodded at the folder in front of him. "Ream lives in a condo on the river, just down from Riptide. Not only that, but he has a slip there and a boat with a cabin. It would be easy for him to come up behind Cate as she was leaving, attack and strangle her and then dump her body."

"What does he do for a living?" O'Malley asked.

"He's a funeral homeowner and director."

"Oh my. Let's pay a visit to Jasper Ream."

Twenty minutes later Pinkowski pulled their police vehicle into the parking lot of the Ream Funeral Home.

"No cars in the lot," he said. "I guess no one is getting buried today." The two detectives entered the funeral home and saw a tall young man, sandy brown hair, tortoise shell glass frames, and white shirt with a skinny black tie wearing a rumpled black suit, with both hands in his pants pocket. He stood in a side office, looking out the window, scowling.

"Excuse me, is Mr. Jasper Ream here? We're with the Milwaukee Police Department." O'Malley showed him his badge and ID. "We'd like to talk to him."

"It took you guys long enough. I was wondering when you were going to show up. We called in to complain about him a couple of weeks ago about his sick behavior. He's sick, real sick."

O'Malley and Pinkowski looked at each other and then back at the employee. "You called in a complaint?" asked Pinkowski.

"Yes. You know, we caught him having sex with a dead woman."

"We?"

"Yes, another employee and me. His name is Eric."

"And you and Eric are still working here after that?" Pinkowski asked.

"Yes, the police said they would keep it anonymous. I'm surprised we're still working here myself."

"Where is Jasper Ream now?" asked Pinkowski.

"He went to pick up a body at a nursing home. He should be back in about twenty minutes if you want to wait?"

"We'll wait," Pinkowski said. "You got any coffee?"

***

Stella knocked on the side of the hull. "Anyone onboard?"

"Just a second."

She heard a muffled response from somewhere in the yacht: "Who's knocking?"

"Stella, from the gas dock?"

"Don't leave." Thirty seconds later, George West's head appeared. "I was hoping you'd show up. Are you here to tell me you'll model for me, or are you here for a tour and drink? I hope all three." He reached out to help her up the three dock-side steps to the cabin entrance.

"Just the drink and the tour," Stella said. "I don't see myself as a model. I told you that before. I just had to see this boat. It's not glitzy fiberglass like the ones that normally berth at the marina. It intrigued me."

"It's a Burger. It was built in the mid 60s for my father and has been in our family since, though I added a darkroom for developing film."

"I bet that comes in handy."

"Not as much as it used to because now just about everything I do is digital, but I still like to use film once in a while. It brings out the artist in me. Before I give you the grand tour, how about a drink. What would you like?"

"How about a beer? Do you have a Stella? I know it's my name, but it's also good beer."

He laughed. "I should have known. No, I don't have any Stella, but I'll make sure I do in the future. I'm going to have a party Saturday night after the start of the race. It's for friends, models, and others I work with in Chicago. I'd like it if you'd come."

"Saturday night? I think I can do that." She smiled. "How about that beer? I'm really thirsty after work. Do you have a Heineken?"

"That I can do." George opened the boat's refrigerator and grabbed two beers. "Here you go. Now let's relax and tell me about you." She watched his eyes as he moved from her face to her breasts and then back to her eyes. Why did she suddenly feel like Little Red Riding Hood looking at a leering, hungry wolf?

Chapter Nine

Waiting for Jasper to arrive, Pinkowski called over his partner to look at his iPhone "Take a look at this. I just pulled this up from records. Says here, one of Jasper Ream's employees did file a complaint after catching him having sex with dead women's corpses—probably ones he would never have a chance with, if they were alive. Then I looked up his divorce file. Ream used to tie up his wife with scarves and have her lie still and not move when they had sex. He would tell her to play like she was dead. It freaked her out so much, it was one of the reasons cited for the divorce."

"Really sicko." O'Malley grabbed the file and read. "We need to get a search warrant and visit Ream's condo. He just moved to the top of our suspect list."

Pinkowski looked at the open folder in front of him, and across at Jasper Ream. "Thanks again for meeting us today to answer a few more questions about the night Cate Sullivan was killed."

"Sure, no problem. I hope this doesn't take too long."

Pinkowski looked at Ream. He was dressed like you might expect an undertaker to be dressed: black shoes, white shirt, black suit and navy tie. He sat at his desk, shifting his body, trying to get comfortable.

"Let's go over your story again," Pinkowski said. "Tell us exactly what you did that Friday night when Ms. Sullivan was killed."

"Like I told you before, I didn't do anything to her. I came up to her, put my arm around her, real friendly-like, and asked if I could buy her a drink. That's all. She turned and looked at me like I was dogshit on her fancy white high heels and told me to fuck off. Before I could do anything, this guy comes up, grabs my arm and almost twists it off and then leads me away. I say something to him and then go find my friends."

O'Malley leaned forward. "If it wasn't you, who was she with later?"

"I only looked a couple of times, but I know she was with the guy who twisted my arm. I saw them drinking and once she gave him a long kiss. Seems like they were real cozy."

"You didn't see her with anyone else?" asked O'Malley.

"I might have, but all I saw was the back of a head. After being told to fuck off, I didn't pay close attention."

"How long were you there?" asked Pinkowski.

"A couple of hours. I went to another place to have a few drinks and dinner. I was hungry by then."

"What other place?" Pinkowski asked.

"Crazy Waters. It's close to Riptide in a roundabout way. It's a neighborhood restaurant I like. Good food and drink if you haven't been there."

O'Malley nodded. "I've been there. You're right. It is good.

Nice garden dining area, but we aren't here to give a food review for the paper."

"Were you with anyone else? Pinkowski asked.

"No just me. I like to go alone in case I meet somebody."

O'Malley leaned forward. "Here is what I think happened that night. You went to Crazy Waters for dinner. Then you decided to stop back at Riptide because it's close to your condo. You see Ms. Sullivan is still there and you wait. She gets drunk and decides to leave. To your surprise, she leaves alone. This is your chance to get even. You come up behind her while she's walking to her car, and overpower her, knocking her out. Then you drag her to your boat on the dock. You decorate her with a silk scarf and have sex with her. She wakes up and struggles with you. You didn't mean to kill her, but when she started screaming, you had to shut her up. You choked her, killing her. Then you motored out into Lake Michigan and dumped her naked body. Is that how it went, Jasper?"

"What? What do you mean? You think I killed her? I told you the truth. I didn't kill her. Someone else did!"

"Look, Jasper, we know you get off having sex with dead women. Employees from your funeral home said if women were good looking and not too messed up, you got them ready. I guess you gave them special prep work."

"You guys are wrong. I had dinner after leaving Riptide at Crazy Waters, and then went home alone!"

"You might as well come clean, Jasper. We got a search warrant for your boat, your house, and your car so were going to find something. You'd save us all a lot of time. Tell us how it happened," said Pinkowski.

"I want a lawyer before I talk anymore."

Pinkowski looked at O'Malley. "Let him call his attorney."

Someone at the yacht club had told Drew to take the train from Milwaukee to Chicago so he wouldn't have to pay for tolls and parking. It was good advice. It was a nice ride, and not too crowded. He had a couple of beers as he watched the countryside flow past.

Drew stepped off the train in downtown Chicago, his backpack slung over his shoulder. While not New York City, Chicago had its own energy level, and Drew could feel it as he started walking from the train station. Now that he was here, it felt good to walk, especially now, since he was retired from the Marines, and he didn't have to carry a rifle or sidearm. He'd had to hike into the hills often enough over the years as a marine when he was scoping out a village, or meeting with troops to get information. He might, once in a while, have to carry a pack just in case he had to stay a while, but that happened less often as he rose through the ranks.

He thought of the time he'd visited a village and was walking down one of its narrow alleys. A young Taliban fighter leapt out of a doorway and attacked with a dagger. His Marine training kicked in. Drew glanced at the scar on his left forearm, the result of deflecting the attempt to stab him. His teenaged assailant had jumped out of a small doorway, arm raised with the dagger. Drew redirected the weapon with his hands and continued the knife's arc until turning it towards the attacker's own stomach. That the attacker was a little more than a kid made no difference. He was a killer. In Afghanistan, the young were more dangerous than the old. With blood seeping around the dagger and his hands, the look in his young attacker's eyes told the story of death.

Chicago wasn't Afghanistan, and while Drew didn't have a gun with him right now, he did always carry a folding knife. That would be enough if he got in a tight spot.

He smiled and shook his head. Why did he think of that knife and a weapon? He was down here looking for fun, meet women, spend time on boats and enjoy time away from sanding and varnish.

Also, he was looking forward to getting to know George West better. Drew thought George had it made, and he could tell already that George and Alex were very different. In what ways, he wasn't sure, but Drew would find out over the next few days.

Drew checked into the *House of Blues* on the Illinois River. He remembered the building and parking ramp from the old *Bob Newhart Show* reruns at home. The hotel was close enough to the Mac race area and near State Street and Rush Street, the action spots.

Walking along the river, Drew made his way toward the Mackinac Race staging area and George West's *Condor*. He was awed by Chicago's architecture. He could only imagine what it was going to look like tonight with all the lights. As he passed the Tribune Tower, in the distance he saw masts silhouetted like a forest of trees. Walking closer, he observed many boats displaying their previous Mackinac pennants, hoisted up on their halyards. Crossing the bridge, there was a hum and laugher as the crews were preparing for the race or tipping back a few drinks. What was sailing if not a good excuse for a drink? Drew surmised that once the race started there wouldn't be much drinking, for safety reasons, until their final destination, Mackinac Island.

Walking down the marina dock, Drew saw an attractive woman in a tight, white polo shirt and short khaki shorts. Walking over to her, he said, "You look like you work here."

"Yes, I do. Can I help you?"

"I'm trying to find George West. He told me he would have a slip here. He's got a big motor yacht named *Condor*. Do you know what pier he's on, by chance?"

"Are you another of his clients? He's got a bunch of people stopping by later for a big party. Are you going to it, or are you crew for another boat?"

"No, I'm just here to see the start of the race."

She looked him up and down. "Are you military?"

"I was. Marines. How did you know?"

"My dad's in the air force. The good ones stay in shape, and have a certain look, like you." She smiled. "Maybe we can have a drink later. George invited me to his party on his boat too. After I get off from work. You'll find him on Pier B, at the end of the dock. You can't miss him."

"Thanks, I didn't catch your name?"

"My name is Stella. I left my nametag at home this morning."

"Mine is Drew. I'll look forward to that drink with you Stella. See you later."

Drew stood at the end of the dock and looked at *Condor*. God, it's a beautiful boat, he thought. Then he saw George come out the side door of the yacht's main cabin, followed by three gorgeous women all in tiny bikinis.

"Sit over here, on the railing." George said to a redhead. "Turn your head slightly to the right and up, as if looking at the skyline."

Drew heard the camera's shutter snapping as George scurried around the bow area, getting different angles of his model.

"Now light me up with a sexy smile, as if I'm Brad Pitt and you want to get my attention."

Drew watched as the redhead leaned slightly forward and pressed her outstretched arms against her breasts to show more fullness.

"How's that, George?"

"Great, just what I wanted to see, now stand up so I can take some shots of those long legs."

She got up and put her arms on the mahogany railing and shook her butt at George while looking at Drew. She smiled at him.

George moved for a better angle and saw Drew. He took a few more pictures of Ashley, then said, "Hi, you made it down. Great." He turned to the models. "April and Ava, why don't you and Ashley take a break for five minutes while I talk to my friend here? Get a soda or water. You know where I keep them."

They nodded and as the trio walked past Drew and smiled at him, the fresh scents they wore lingered in the air.

"Did you see those legs?" asked George.

Drew smiled. "Yes, I did."

"Nursing students."

Drew shook his head. "Tough job you've got."

"All in a day's work. Look, I'm going to be finishing up here with Ashley in an hour and then I've got to get some candid shots with the other two around the dock. After that, maybe we can motor out and get shots of the boats practice sailing. I need someone to steer while I shoot. Could you help? I'd appreciate it."

"Sure. What time?"

"Say, 1:30?"

"See you then."

"By the way, I'm having a little party tonight. Hope you can make it. Should be lots of women like Ashley here, and support crews from other boats. I guarantee you'll have a good time."

"No doubt," said Drew. "I already heard about your party and am planning on coming. See you at 1330 hours."

Chapter Ten

Everyone was excited about the race. God, Drew wished he were sailing on one of those beautiful boats. He guessed he could have been a crew on one if he wanted. But he didn't want to take at least a week or more off from working on *Courage* just to sail the race.

Because George had made it sound like Chicago and the start of the race was the place to be, Drew was happy to get a break from all the issues back in Milwaukee. Walking back to his hotel room, along the docks, he saw the shapely behind of a woman bending over, securing the bowline to a dock cleat. When the woman stood up and turned, he recognized who it was. Stella. She smiled and waved, then walked over to him.

"Hi, did you find George West?"

"Yes, I did. He talked me into helping him later with his boat. He wants me to steer while he takes shots of the boats practicing. And then later, the onboard party. I hope you're going."

"What's not to like about free beer?"

"Good. I'll look forward to seeing you there."

"I'll be a little late. I want to go home, shower, and change into something more presentable than these shorts and shirt."

"Looks good to me. I don't think anyone is going to be dressed up except maybe some of his models. Most of the women will be casual from sailing or getting the boats provisioned."

"Well, George finally convinced me earlier today to take a couple of pictures of me, so I better try to do something with myself. I'm not too interested in modeling, but he seems to think I have a look that can sell so I said I might give it a try. I'm saving money for law school."

"Law school? I don't picture you as a lawyer."

"What, you think all I have are these," she said testy.

He watched her eyes burn into his.

"Spoken as a true military male. Most of you guys never think a woman could have anything up here." She knocked the side of her skull. "I saw plenty of your type at Luke AFB. I'm tired of being thought of as a piece of ass. You military guys think you're God's gift to the world."

He raised the palms of his hands in surrender. "At ease. I'm just saying, I never thought of you as an attorney type, that's all. That's great that you want to be an attorney. Make something of your life." He watched the stare soften.

"Sorry. I get kind of touchy about that subject. That's why I came to Chicago, to get away from all you military jocks and pilots. I'll see you later. Maybe we can start this conversation over."

"I'd like that. See you there."

Returning later that day, Drew spotted a couple of the boats from the Milwaukee Yacht Club. He went over to chat with a few of the skippers at the marina before making his way to

Condor. When he arrived, he saw George busy at work, giving instructions to a tall black-haired model, who was wearing a deep cut, one-piece swimsuit with a white flowing scarf draped over her shoulders.

Her bright blue eyes offered a stunning contrast to the black of the suit and hair. At the bow of the boat, Drew saw two other models, sitting on cushions and sunning themselves. He placed his windbreaker near the boat's controls and waited for George to finish his shoot.

Twenty minutes later, George entered the pilothouse of *Condor*. "Glad you're here to help. The sky is perfect, the wind is not too strong so the boat won't bounce around too much, and there are a lot of boats out practicing. I saw a few flying their spinnakers, which always makes for great calendar shots. Have you piloted a boat this size before?"

"Not really. Biggest one was a forty-footer at the academy and that was a sailboat."

"You're still used to a larger boat moving through the water. I just want you to steer the boat at about three knots. No fancy turns. Just motor a straight course and if a sailboat gets in your way, slow down and pass behind them. We don't want to hit anyone or get any skipper pissed. These two levers control the speed for each propeller while these levers control the direction of the propellers spin."

"I think I have it figured out," Drew said, nodding.

"Good. I'll take her out of the marina, but once we're out on the lake, she's all yours. Follow my hand directions and just steer the *Condor* back and forth where the boats are practicing, so I can get good action shots."

"No problem," Drew said. "I just hope I don't hit anyone."

"You won't, unless you get distracted by the women on board. There's three more, changing swimsuits down below." George winked. "I love going swimsuit shopping."

Drew laughed.

"I got to get my cameras ready. We'll get going in ten minutes, so have a soft drink or water. No beer or booze until later. Then I'll bring in the boat."

"Aye, aye, Captain." Drew gave a short salute as George went below to get a different camera. Ten minutes later, he watched George start the engines. "We'll let them warm up for a few minutes while I show you a few things."

George grabbed the wheel. "While I have a rudder to steer the boat while underway, at the pier I use the two props and bow thrusters to move the boat."

Drew nodded. "I have one throttle like yours on my boat, but no bow thruster so I'll be interested to watch how you use that."

"There's so much windage on a boat this size that you sometimes need it to move the bow off the pier. Today, I think we can just move off the pier by pushing one of the prop levers forward and the other in reverse. It will spin the bow away from the dock. Go and un-cleat the stern line but feed it around the cleat and then bring the loose end back on board. Tie it off on the stern cleat, then untie the other lines and we'll rotate off that stern line. Once we pivot, let go of the loose end and pull it on board. It should slip around the cleat on the dock. We'll be moving out by then."

"Got it," Drew said. "I do the same thing on my boat."

Thirty minutes later they were out motoring, Drew behind the wheel turning *Condor* into the wind. He steered a straight course through the many boats.

Several were raising the multicolored spinnakers for a downwind leg, which all photographers like to shoot. Others were just sailing, letting new crewmembers get a last-minute chance to become acquainted with a new boat, the placement of equipment, different sails.

Above the low rumble of *Condor's* engines, Drew heard the frantic yelling of the captain's instructions at a crewmember from passing boats. Once in a while, he'd hear a frantic scream of "Starboard," meaning an approaching boat had right of way.

Drew kept a steady course as sailboats moved around him. He laughed as he watched George run around the deck snapping pictures, getting a model in a certain position, visualizing the shot, then waiting for another sailboat to move into the background to get the perfect shot.

The crewmembers from other boats gawked, watching the models get into position. They'd stare, forgetting to haul in a line. Drew could hear the boats skipper yell, "What the hell is going on!" And then the crew jumped and tried to recover.

Drew observed George at work. It took a lot of skill to be a good photographer.

Getting what you wanted meant a lot of planning—just like in Afghanistan, except here no one got killed if the shot didn't turn out. Drew thought about his last operation with Gunny. Then he heard a scream and watched a large wave collide with *Condor's* bow, splashing two of George's lovelies. He hoped that George got the shot. The surprise on the models' faces was priceless.

It was enough to break the negative spell Afghanistan cast on him. He got back to enjoying the moment.

Two hours later, George declared he was done shooting for the day, and it was time to start partying. He moved *Condor* off to a quiet spot on the water, turned off the engines and drifted.

"I love how quiet it gets when the engines are off, and you can just enjoy the sights. I don't say this often, but I think my brother Alex has that part about boating right: just enjoying the quiet and what nature offers you."

George moved over to a refrigerator in the pilot area and grabbed two Heinekens, passing one to Drew. "You did a good job this afternoon. Let's do this again. It would be great to have someone reliable that can handle the boat while I shoot."

George's eyes focused on a brunette model in a small turquoise one-piece. "Bridget's the one for me tonight. She doesn't think she's pretty enough to be a model, but her mother thinks she is, so she keeps trying. Mothers can fuck things up for their kids." He took a swig of the Heinekens. I know that from first-hand experience." He took another long drink of his beer. "I told Bridget I'd make her better than she thinks she is . . . and I can. I'm good at what I do. There are benefits."

Drew laughed. "You got any extra cameras laying around here?"

George smiled. "I do, but I don't think you'll need a camera for help in that area. You've got that rugged military look. You'll have no problem hooking up."

"Actually, there is someone I hope to get to know better: the dock girl, Stella."

George laughed. "She is a beauty. I thought I could get her drunk and then she might like to try out the captain's quarters. That girl can drink. She almost put me out of commission when I had her over last night for a tour. Be careful. If you have to pay for all her drinks, you might exceed your credit card limit."

"Thanks for the warning," said Drew, "but it might be worth it. Besides, we have a few things in common. She's an Air Force brat and I'm a marine, so we're screwed up in a similar way." He smiled. "Anyhow, she said she'd stop by, so we'll drink your stuff first."

"Good," George said. "Let's go outside. It's too nice to be inside the cabin." George grabbed another beer for himself and one for Drew and they headed to the deck chairs in the aft part of the boat, where shapely Bridget sat. Drew followed, but headed to the bow where there were three other women to talk to.

Everyone was in a mellow mood, and they watched boats of many different sizes and classes start the race. It was quite the sight. Finally, when the racing fleet was on their way, George headed *Condor* back to the end of the dock, and the start of the party.

Life is good, Drew thought.

Chapter Eleven

The party was in full swing when Drew caught sight of Stella walking down the pier. She hadn't changed from her work outfit of tan shorts and marina polo white shirt, but that didn't matter to Drew. He liked the idea that she was comfortable. He felt the same way and had not gone back to the *House of Blues* to change after they got *Condor* tied up.

He stepped out to meet her as she came to the boarding stairs.

"Thanks," she said, grabbing his hand. "Looking at the number of people on the bow, it looks like George has a lot of new friends to take pictures of."

"I think he's got enough pictures for the day. How about a beer, or would you like something stronger?"

"No, a beer is okay. Did he get some Stella like he said he would?"

"Actually, he did. I put it in a hidden spot he showed me so it wouldn't disappear before you got here. He told me about how you wanted your namesake beer." He reached into the back of the refrigerator. "Here you go."

"Thanks."

She brought the bottle to her lips and drank a third of it.

"God, that tasted good. I guess I was thirsty after the day I had."

"Good for you." Drew turned to the Chicago skyline, and then turned back to Stella. "You have a great office view here."

"Yeah, it is kind of nice until winter, but then I'll head someplace warm or go back to Arizona. My uncle is good to me."

"Let's go sit in the back of the boat so we can talk." They moved toward the stern and a rattan sofa flanked by two deck chairs. They sat, facing each other.

"So what kind of law do you want to go into?" he asked.

"I want to be an advocate for women. Growing up in the military, I saw everything. Some things were kept a secret by the wife and girlfriends, but there is a lot of drinking, and with that there is often domestic and sexual abuse. Even kids get caught in it." She paused and took a drink.

"My dad is cool. That didn't happen in our family, but it did with lots of his friends. I'd hear Mom and Dad talk about this person or that person. How you could see the bruises on their face or arms. They'd say they fell, or the kids would say they fell off their bike or something, but you could tell they were lying. It happens across the ranks, from enlisted personnel to officers. There is no boundary to this. It's not just limited to military. It's in the private sector too. Then there is the sexual harassment thing. I think I'm going to be pretty busy."

"Good for you, Stella. That is a great area to focus on. You'll be making a difference in many people's lives."

"Tell me about you. Where are you from?"

He smiled. "I grew up about 500 miles north of here, in the Michigan's Upper Peninsula, in a town called Houghton-Hancock. I loved growing up there. It's a beautiful area. I hunted, fished and played sports. My dad worked at a copper mine, maintaining the mining equipment, but when the mine eventually closed down after the Vietnam War, he maintained the mining area until he retired. He was a marine in Vietnam. His best friend in basic and advanced training was from the UP. Dad was from Georgia originally. When they got leave together, they would go back to his home there and visit. That's how he met Mom, my uncle's sister.

"My Uncle Drew never made it home from Vietnam. When Dad's tour was over, he went to the Upper Peninsula, looking for closure while he visited my Uncle Drew's family to pay his respects. That's when Dad and Mom got to know each other, and eventually they fell in love. Obviously, I'm named for my uncle."

"That's a sad and happy story. Sad because your uncle died, but happy because your mom and dad met. Because of him, they made you."

"I wish I could have met my uncle, but that's life and war." Drew brought the bottle of beer to his lips, thinking about how life can repeat itself—Vietnam for his uncle and Afghanistan for him. His uncle didn't make it home, and his best friend didn't either. Hell, Drew almost met the same fate.

"I got an appointment to attend Annapolis Naval Academy and got a great education and I was guaranteed a job when I graduated." Drew smiled. "I played sports like I did at home. Football and basketball, but I got to crew on some of the Academy boats and fell in love with sailing. At the Academy, my junior year, you make a choice of whether you want to be in the navy or the marines. Family tradition made the decision an easy one for me, as you might expect: I became a marine.

"Funny, my whole time in Afghanistan, I thought about sailing. When I retired from the Marines, I found me a boat that needed a little fixing up so I could pursue my dream. When I get *Courage* just the way I want her, I'm going to live on the boat and see all the little towns you normally just pass by, but at a slow five knots an hour. I'll see the real America most people are too busy to take time to see and know."

"How romantic. Can I visit you along the way?"

"What about school? Think you can afford the time from saving women and kids?" He saw her hazel eyes twinkle with merriment.

"You might be worth the risk now and then." Stella leaned over and kissed Drew on the lips. Her fingers moved to the scar on his head and caressed it. "Afghanistan?"

"Yes, and one of the reasons for retirement."

"*One* of the reasons?"

She moved back from her kiss. Her eyes held on his and she smiled.

"If I'm going sailing with you, I need to get to know you better. Chicago tonight seems like a great place to start. What do you say about a tour?"

"How about another beer before we leave?"

"I'd like that."

An hour and a half passed when Drew said. "I thought you said we were going to have just one more beer. George warned me about you."

"I think we only had five each, if my count is right." She winked at him. "I don't know if I can trust you now that I've had all this beer."

"Trust me?" Drew looked at her, waiting for her to explain.

"I thought we should drink up all my namesake beer so no one else could have them."

"How greedy. In that case, you're all mine tonight—I mean the Stella beer and you." He leaned in and gave her a light kiss. He felt her hand slip into his back pocket, and when he pulled back, heard her giggle.

"I'm all yours tonight? Is that so?" she said. "Then really kiss me so I know if you're worth my time."

Moving in front of her, he wrapped his arms around her, cupping her ass and pulling her closer. He felt her firm breasts tight against his chest. His lips met hers, but unlike others he'd kissed, she attacked his mouth with her lips and tongue. The two fought for control and when he overwhelmed her with his, he felt her relax in his arms.

Then he heard a familiar voice yell, "Get a hotel room, will you two!" Drew pulled back and saw George smiling, camera in his hand.

"I should be able to sell this to the *Enquire*, at least to pay for the beer you two consumed. See you later, I hope."

Drew turned to Stella. "Come on, let's get away from this place and George's cameras. I have a hotel room close by. Should we go to a few more places first? I think there's some neat bars around here."

"Don't make me wait too long," she said with arched eyebrows.

"Just let me know when you're getting bored, and I'll change that."

"I'm expecting you'll do lots of things, at least I'm hoping so. Just in case you didn't notice, I'm not wearing anything under my shorts and shirt."

"I did tell you I was with military intelligence, with the Marines, didn't I? Nothing gets past me, especially in that area." He gave her a gentle push forward. "Let's go, times a wasting."

Four hours later, the two entered the empty elevator at the House of Blues. As the door closed, they turned toward each other and started a slow kiss, tongues intertwining, bodies pressing against each other, trying to pretend their clothes were not on. Finally, the slow elevator reached the sixth floor as Drew's hands slipped under Stella's white Polo shirt to her breasts. He heard her sigh.

She whispered, "No, Drew. I want it too, but not here. The room, please?"

"Yeah, sorry. It's just you got me so damn excited and hard."

She smiled. Her hand reached down and pressed his manhood. "How does it go with you Marines? The few, the proud, the Marines, you're all Marine, Major Thompson." And then she lowered herself and kissed the bulge of his jeans, stood up and said, "Your room, quick."

He woke up the next morning. The sun was peeking between the two drapes as he got up from the bed. Pulling back the drape to gaze out from the sixth-floor room, he saw not a ripple on the surface of Lake Michigan.

There is nothing worse than no wind in a long sailing race, he thought. Then he looked over at the bed, and realized Stella was gone. It dawned on him: she probably had to be at work this morning and had slipped out while he slept. Oh well, he thought, she's younger than me. She had to be to do the things she did last night. He pulled the drape all the way back, letting the full blast of the sun shower his naked body and the room. Then he went to the small Mr. Coffee in the room and made a cup.

After a breakfast at the *House of Blues*, Drew headed to the marina to see if Stella was working, and to meet up with George on *Condor*.

Saturday morning in any city is usually busy, and Chicago was no exception. As Drew walked the street to the marina, it reminded him of apocalyptic movies with the streets chaotic, lots of people moving with a purpose. It was only 8 a.m. He headed over to the gas dock to see Stella first.

His knuckles rapped the small building that housed the dock master, cash register and marina office. "Anyone home?"

"Yeah, come on in." Stella's face glowed with delight. She leaned into Drew and kissed him.

"I didn't even hear you leave this morning. What time was it?"

"Five a.m."

"Shit, you didn't get any sleep. It was close to four when we quit. You must be exhausted. I know I am."

"Luckily, I only work until noon. I'm going home and nap,

and then I'm supposed to go to George's boat for a photo session. I need to get the bags under my eyes covered up. Maybe I'll try putting on tea bags." She cocked her head. "Are you going over there?"

"I'm heading over to *Condor* too, then I need to get back to Milwaukee, back to work on my own boat. Why don't you come up and visit?"

"I'd like that. I'll see you later at George's, if you're still around." She got up and wrapped her arms around his neck, pulled him against her. Her kiss did its trick as he felt himself get aroused.

When she pulled back, she looked down. "Oh, he's a happy boy now. You are amazing." She said, touching his bulge. "I hope we can continue our romance tonight. You can delay your trip back to Milwaukee, can't you? Didn't you say you were retired?"

"Let's see, more varnishing and electrical work or . . . He smiled. "You won't have any arguments from me on that score." I'll see you at George's later, and we can continue where we left off last night—I mean, this morning. Tomorrow, I'll really need to get back. You'll just have to come see me in Milwaukee and spend a few days."

"Sounds like a deal to me. How about Thursday?" she said. "I'm off for two whole days."

"It's a date."

***

"Drew. Where did you two go last night? I thought you'd be on my boat later."

"Ah, Stella and I had some places to go check out. We got to know each other a little better. She's fun."

"Stella's coming over later today for a photo shoot. I'll have to think up something special for her. She's not like the others. She's fresh. I love fresh."

"Fresh. Now that's a new way to describe someone. You going out on the water today?"

"No. I need to clean up the boat. It's a mess."

Drew looked around the cabin, and afterdeck and had to agree. "I can help. What do you want me to do?"

"That's great. How about you clean the foredeck and hose it down? There are spills all over. I'll get the inside shipshape. Besides, I have a guest still sleeping down below that I need to get going. You didn't have all the fun last night."

Drew heard a plaintive voice call up from down below. "George, are you coming back to bed? I'm cold and I need you!"

Drew raised an eyebrow.

"Oops. Why don't you come back in say a couple of hours, and help clean up? Then we can have a bloody mary and wait for Stella."

"Sure. Is that enough time for you to warm her up?"

"Yeah, I'll have plenty of time for that."

"Sounds good. I need to go back to my hotel and extend my stay another night. Have fun. See you in a couple of hours."

Drew turned and stepped off the boat. He'd head back and maybe catch an hour of sleep. He'd need it, if last night was any indication of what might happen again tonight.

Chapter Twelve

Back at the hotel, lying in bed, Drew's thoughts returned to a former love, Clair. Stella was about the same age as Clair was when he first met her: twenty or twenty-two. Young, beautiful, but it was always a woman's eyes that captured his attention. Then, he'd check out the rest of her body like any American male would. God, they'd had fun.

Back then, Clair was Drew's best friend. They'd talk about anything. He had met her at the U. P.'s Copper Grid Saloon in Houghton-Hancock, Michigan. Entering the bar, Drew had seen her surrounded by a bunch of local Michigan Tech college hockey players. It was summer. She was wearing short gym shorts and a tee shirt that was too small—but just right to attract the attention of all the guys, including Drew. He walked to the end of the bar and got a frosty mug of beer. Drew had drained about half of it when he saw her eyes focus on him.

A smile crossed her face. Then he saw her mouth the words, "Excuse me, boys, but I need to say hello to someone I haven't seen in a long, long time."

She pushed through the group and walked straight up to him. "Hi, I'm Jasmine Hurley. You probably don't remember me because I was five years behind you in school, but I remember you. I lived down the street from your parent's house on Adams Street."

"You're right. I don't remember you." Drew leaned back against the bar and looked her up and down. "I don't know how I missed you."

"Well, I could see how you could back then. I had a flat chest and was gangly. These days, I get more attention."

"Well, you have my attention."

"Aren't you in the army or something?"

"I'm a marine. I went to the Naval Academy at Annapolis—that's what you probably remember. I had to decide if I wanted to be in the navy or be a marine like my dad. I'm a First Lieutenant now in the Marines."

"Oh, an officer," she said, saluting.

"I'm home on leave for a month after my first tour of duty."

"First? Are you going back?"

"Yes."

"Well, First Lieutenant, can a grateful citizen buy you another beer or are you going to be one of those guys that say I can buy my own?"

"I never turn down a free beer. I might be a marine but I'm not stupid." Then he told her he was so hot from working at his parent's place that afternoon, doing repairs, since his dad had his hunting accident. "Dad can't do the repairs himself anymore. A lot of things needed to be done so I'm doing them before I go back."

"Oh yeah," she said. "I seem to remember something about an accident." She waved to the bartender. "Can we get two more, please?" She turned back to Drew. "How's your dad doing since the accident?

"About as well as can be expected. A ricocheted bullet from

someone in our deer-hunting group hit him in the head. He has balance issues and vision problems. Nothing life-threatening, but he's not able to do much around the house—at least not like he used to. I send money home to help mom financially, but it's tough for her until I got leave and could get back to help her and dad."

The bartender brought the beers. Grabbing a frosty mug, she said, "Here's to a grateful American." She clinked her beer to his.

"So what have you been doing for the last six years or so?" Drew asked Clair, wiping his lips with the back of his hand.

"I went to college and got a teaching degree. I'm teaching first grade. I love the young ones. Not much more than that. Living with Mom and Dad still. Need to get a place of my own. I need to get away from here, really. I'm dying here. It's boring. Nothing's happening, not like with you. How about you? You married, got a girlfriend?"

"Not much time to find someone when you're in combat or moving around. That's basically what I've done since graduation. It's not fair to put someone else through that. Someday I'll settle down, but after this war is over."

"But you like to have fun, right? It's summer vacation and I'm up for a good time. Do you think you could help out?" She asked the question with a big smile on her face.

"When I was being shot at overseas I prayed a lot, and not just to save my life. I knew I was fighting for something over there. Now that I'm back, I just realized you are the reason."

When she laughed at that, Drew leaned over, wrapping his arms around her waist and holding her close. He kissed her. Pulling back, he said, "Thank you, God, for answering my prayers."

Clair was an answer to Drew's prayers, at least for a while. They were inseparable for the next 25 days. Then came their tearful goodbye.

He and Clair had been sitting on her parent's front porch swing when he finally got up to leave. Looking at Drew, tears streaming down her face, she said, "I'll stop by your parents' house and keep your mother company, now that I know your family better, and I'll write to you every day. I'll wait for you, Drew. I love you."

"I love you, too Clair." They kissed goodbye for long minutes, not wanting to let go.

For the first time in his life, Drew was in love. He got into his red Camaro convertible, adjusted the mirror and drove off, watching her stand there, crying, and waving goodbye. He had to go back to war.

Stella was not like Clair, or Drew didn't think so. It was hard to tell after just one night. Stella was confident, driven to get a law degree and to help society. She was independent, not needy or clinging to her man. Thinking back to Clair and that first goodbye, she did keep her promise and wrote every day. Drew wrote back as often as a guy in combat could. From the letters or their first 26 days together, he never saw what was coming. He wished he had.

Six months into Drew's second tour, his dad's injuries from

the hunting accident caught up with him and he died. Drew remembered how horrible he felt because of the possibility he might have caused his injury. The head wound might have been from his gun or from someone else in the hunting party as they made a drive through the woods.

A big buck had run parallel to the line of hunters. Several in the party took a shot at it, including Drew, as it moved down the firing line. Drew's dad was the last hunter in line and as the animal got closer to him, the shooting continued. His dad dropped just after the deer moved past him. The only thing shot was his dad.

When Drew got home for the funeral, Clair was waiting.

But she wasn't the same person she was when he left six months before. She looked the same, but something inside had changed. She seemed to have a black cloud hanging over her. She was needy, possessive, not wanting to share Drew with his own mourning mother. Clair also did not understand his guilt for possibly causing his father's death at the relatively young age of 56.

Later that night after the funeral, Drew and Clair made love. Lying in bed in each other's arms, she startled him with, "Drew, let's get married. We love each other. I want to be with you always. I want to have your babies."

He said nothing for a long while. She rolled off him and sat up straight, agitated. "Well, what do you think? I'm waiting."

"You know, Clair, usually it's the guy that proposes. Besides that, I'm a marine. All I can tell you is not now. I love you, Clair, but I'm in a war. I don't want this added worry about us. I definitely want a child but later, when I'm done fighting and back in the States. I want to make sure I'm around to raise my child. Let me get through all this. Let me get back from this tour of duty, then we'll talk about marriage and kids."

It sounded reasonable to him, but not to her. She started crying, then became angry, saying he just wanted her for the sex, which wasn't true. He had meant what he said, but for the next seven days, Clair hammered him with the same line, and he responded the only way he could. "Not yet, later."

When he left this time, it was not a loving goodbye. A month later, while waiting in Restrepo, he got an urgent message to call her.

When he phoned, she had a surprise. "Guess what, Drew? I'm pregnant. You need to come home. We need to get married right now, before I start showing. I'm a teacher . . . you know people will talk."

He was shocked. "You told me you were on the pill."

"I guess I missed one or two, I don't know. I do know that I love you. You need to come home, like on emergency leave, so we can get married."

He laughed. "You don't know the Marines. Getting pregnant or getting married is not an emergency." He waited for her comments but not hearing one, he continued, "I love you too, Clair and I want to get married and have children, but the Marines are not going to let me come home right now. I'm excited about being a dad and you'll be a great mom. I'll send you money to help with expenses. Don't worry. People don't think too much about unwed couples having a baby anymore, and you can tell them that as soon as I get back home, we'll get married. I love you, Clair. Why don't you go pick out a ring now? That will shut people up."

She started crying. "You don't want me or our baby, or you'd find a way to get home."

"Were you listening? I do want a baby, and I want to marry you, but the Marines will decide when I can get home and do that. That's just the way it is. I'm sorry."

"No, you're wrong, Drew. People won't understand, not up here. Just remember, Drew, I loved you. Goodbye." Clair hung up.

A week later, he got a letter. *Dear Drew, just thought you'd like to know I'll take care of everything. I hope you and your Marines have fun at your war. Love, Clair*

The day she wrote the letter, Clair hung herself. He couldn't make it back in time for the funeral before she and his unborn child were buried. Drew had lost two more people.

Chapter Thirteen

Since Drew was no longer a suspect in Cate Sullivan's murder, Alex had thought it was fine to invite Drew for an afternoon sail with Tara aboard *Passage Maker*. Now, walking down the long dock to Alex's boat, Drew turned at the slip's finger pier to see the off-duty cop onboard, red hair blowing in the wind. It reminded him of a horse's mane flowing back on a full gallop. She took his breath away.

"Detective Sullivan, nice to see you again."

"Oh hi." She waved. "Alex told me you were coming along. Just call me Tara."

"And call me Drew." He stepped on board. "You look very nautical with that blue and white striped top and blue shorts. Is that purse next to you for your gun?"

She looked down and laughed. "It's in the purse. I hope I don't needed the Glock today." Then she smiled. "Regulations are regulations." As she patted the purse.

Drew raised his right hand in the three-finger Boy Scout sign. "I promise to do my best, to do my duty, to God and my country. How's that?"

Alex came up from the boat's cabin.

"Let's go sailing. There's a nice wind out there and I want to get some of it. First, who wants a drink, and then we'll get going. A beer, Drew?"

"I'm OK for now." Drew moved to the bow. "I'll get the lines when you're ready and we can get going." Alex started the engine, letting it warm up, and then went below to get Tara white wine.

Fifteen minutes later, they were out past the north entrance to Milwaukee's harbor, sailing northeast with a full main and headsail.

With the trio sitting in the cockpit, Alex pointed out to Drew, "Did you notice that Tara winched in the headsail? She's become a fantastic crew member."

"Thanks, Alex, I try, now that I know a little of what to do."

Drew raised his eyebrows. "It seems you two have been sailing together quite a bit."

Alex grinned. "Tara and I have been doing a few social things besides sailing too. Thursday we had the Symphony gala, and this Saturday we have a fundraiser for the Milwaukee Boys and Girls Club. I'm involved with a lot of causes. Tara is making it more fun to attend the related social events."

In her seat, Tara stretched out her long legs, and looked up at Drew. "Yes, Alex and I have been an item since that evening when you were carted away by O'Malley and Pinkowski."

"Fond memories," said Drew. "As long as you brought those two up, may I ask how the investigation is going? Even though we just met briefly, I liked your sister. I'd still like to help. I was in Military Intelligence with the Marines, so I know a few things about studying the facts."

"I probably shouldn't tell you this but there is a prime suspect. I believe you have an arm's length knowledge of him, a man named Jasper Ream."

"Yeah, the bastard tried to pin your sister's murder on me."

"Yes, he is a disturbed man. But you'll have to take some of the blame for getting tossed in jail. You lied about where you were that whole night. You're lucky I could tell from the hotel CCTV that the woman with you wasn't Cate. You can thank *me* for getting you out."

"I thank you. I didn't know you were my savior. I just wanted to let you know I want to help."

Tara's voice was firm but not unfriendly. "I think we can handle it from here Mr. Thompson—I mean, Drew."

"Can we move on to something else?" Alex said. "Drew, could you handle the boat while I fetch some drinks?"

"I thought you'd never ask." When Drew slid behind the wooden wheel, his eyes met Tara's. Was there something there? He remembered how she had looked at him the first time on the dock.

"Here we go," said Alex. "A Greenie for Drew, another white wine for you, Tara, and a Rum and Coke for me."

Ten minutes later, as *Passage Ma*ker slid through Lake Michigan's light chop, Drew watched Alex and Tara make their way to the bow of the boat. They chatted and kissed while holding on to the front stay. Drew felt like hired help as the captain had his way with the crew. He wished Stella was along to enjoy the sail with him.

The sail back to the harbor was uneventful, and they arrived back at the slip just after sunset. The Wednesday night race crowd was at the Tiki Hut, and they decided to join the racers for the traditional buffet dinner. Tonight, it was boiled shrimp.

After a few more beers, Drew said goodbye to Alex and Tara. Being around Tara, he realized he missed the company of a woman. Slightly weaving as he walked back to *Courage*, he thought of Stella's arrival tomorrow. He had better clean the boat up tomorrow morning. Women like things clean and neat. Being an Annapolis Naval Academy graduate, Drew knew what shipshape meant. He had work to do.

Thursday came and went. Friday came and went. Where the hell was Stella? She had promised to meet Drew in Milwaukee at McKinley Marina. She had his cell number and she said she would call.

He thought he was pretty good at judging people, but then he had misjudged Clair's intentions. And with Stella, it really had only been a couple of nights . . . but what a couple of nights.

He got his Great Lakes Boating Guild out and looked up the marina's number where she worked. If she had second thoughts, he could handle that, although he hoped that wasn't the reason.

The marina's phone rang and rang. She was probably gassing up a big yacht. Those babies took hundreds of gallons of fuel if they traveled any significant distance. It was expensive to travel. A lot of the big boats were just glorified condos on the waterfront. One more ring and he was hanging up.

"Monroe Marina. Can I help you?"

"Yes. This is Drew Thompson. I'd like to talk to Stella Carpenter. She was going to drive up here to Milwaukee and go sailing and have dinner with me. She didn't show up on Thursday. I'm trying to find her and make sure she's OK. Can you help me?"

Silence.

"Hello, are you still there?"

"Yes. Let me get your phone or cell number and I'll have her get back to you. If you don't get a call back, she's not interested."

"Is everything okay?"

"Yes. Give me your number. She'll get back to you soon. I have my instructions."

"Instructions? Fine, here it is." That was strange. He just wanted to talk to her.

"Drew, it's Stella. Oh, I'm so glad you called. I lost your cell phone number. I didn't think I'd really need it because I was going to meet you Thursday, but then I had to work unexpectedly and had no way of finding you, except driving up and it's a long way. I hope you aren't mad at me. I'm so sorry."

"Oh, I was for a while. I was bummed out. Who was that guy on the phone? He didn't sound friendly."

She laughed. "That's my Uncle Frank. He's protective of me. We had a problem last night with a guy with a big boat and a little dick." She laughed again. "He gave me a big tip after filling his tank with diesel, and thought the tip entitled him to sample my goods. He was drunk and tried to force himself on me. Uncle Frank walked in as the guy had his pants down around his ankles and was pressing me against the counter. Uncle Frank just about killed the guy with a kick between his legs and a right to the jaw before we called the cops."

"He sounds like a good man but I'm not sure I want to meet him. With your permission, I did sample the goods. Remember?"

"How could I forget? I had made it a rule: never go out with boaters from here, but then you were just visiting, so technically I didn't break my rule. I miss you. Can I still come up and visit?"

"When can you get away?"

"I can leave today at noon. I can grab a few things from home and be up there, say around three. How's that?"

"Great. It's Irish Fest this weekend at the nearby Summerfest grounds, and Saturday is always a good time. A few hours' time will give me a chance to tidy up the boat."

"Oh that's nice but you really don't have to. If you saw my room at Uncle Frank's, you'd see I'm probably just as messy as you. Got to go. Bye until three."

* * *

That afternoon, precisely at three o'clock, Drew spotted her standing at the gate. Another boater opened the locked gate as he was leaving, and Stella slipped past him and halfway-ran down the dock to him. He couldn't believe that he was so excited to see her after just a couple of nights, but he was.

When she reached him, she dropped her backpack and jumped into his arms, wrapping her legs around him, like a catcher does after winning the World Series. Their kiss brought hoots and hollers from Robert and Lou, two charter fishing boat owners on the dock, but Drew and Stella didn't care. After a few more kisses, Stella pulled back from Drew's embrace, and picked up her backpack.

"I guess I really missed you." She smiled. "Which boat is yours?"

He pointed. "*Courage* is her name. She's a Pacific Seacraft 34. She even has ice-cold Stella beer in her cooler. Then again, I'm not sure we have enough, if I remember Chicago."

"How thoughtful of you to get my favorite brand. I'm thirsty after the drive up. What a great view you have of the Milwaukee skyline. Driving down to the marina, I noticed the nice waterfront and park. Is that a kite park I see across the marina basin?"

"Yep."

She pointed. "I like the flying pink flamingo."

They moved down the finger pier of his slip and he stepped onto the boat's stern. Drew reached for Stella's hand. When she stepped on, he pulled her against him and kissed her again.

"Welcome aboard *Courage*. Let me show you the boat." They stepped down into the cabin. "Pretty standard layout, sink, refrigerator, stove, settee, head. And here is the master's V-berth."

"Looks roomy. Is there room for two?" Stella dropped her backpack, sat on the edge of the berth, bouncing up and down a couple of times. "Pretty firm, but it seems comfy." She pulled her tee-shirt and sports bra over her head, looked up at him. "Shall we try it out and see? I sure missed you."

"Beer can wait until later," he said as he shucked his shorts and his tee shirt. "Here, let me help you with your shorts."

She slid back on the berth, raised her hips as Drew slid off her shorts and thong. He moved into her outstretched open arms.

Later, her head was on his chest, but they said nothing, enjoying the gentle rocking of the boat and the sound of the *pat, pat, pat* as the wavelets struck the hull.

Stella broke the silence. "There is something so sensuous about sleeping or making love on a boat. It must be the idea of freedom a boat represents, what do you think?"

"Freedom is more sensuous when you have someone to share it with," he said, kissing the top of her head.

She looked up at him. "Now that we got our hellos out of the way, how about that cold beer? I'm thirsty."

He retrieved two Stellas from the refrigerator. She slipped on her shorts and tee shirt, then moved to the main cabin.

"You forgot your thong," he said.

She grinned. "You look good drinking beer naked."

"You got dressed so soon. I hoped we both could drink beer naked."

"I want a shower after this. You said you were going to show me a good time, remember? Irish Fest sounds like fun. I even brought a green tee shirt."

"Nice, let's finish these beers. Here's an extra key to the shower and bathroom building you'll need to get in, and then to get back through the gate at the end of the pier."

"Too bad we can't take a shower together," she said.

"I have a shower on board this boat, but I think it might be a little crowded in the head with two of us . . . but if we plan to do it later, I have a solar shower we can hang outdoors."

"Won't the neighbors talk?"

"Not if we do it at night."

"Right now I want to hear some music, drink beer and eat."

After dark, George West fingered one of the new silk scarves while sitting on a white rattan lounge chair on the stern of *Condor*. After docking the boat at the Milwaukee Yacht Club, he'd had a busy day shopping on Wisconsin Avenue. It was hot—even for a late July afternoon—but he'd enjoyed himself. He went to several stores to get just the style, color and right number of scarves for his models. He liked the long, colorful ones. Buying one or two at time shouldn't raise suspicion, he thought. The salespeople would assume he was just another thoughtful husband or boyfriend, buying a scarf for his wife or girlfriend. George figured fifteen should be enough for a while.

The women in his life were mostly models: young, vibrant, with so much life. Sometimes these beautiful women displeased him, did something naughty, and then they had to pay for his displeasure. Hard not to think of his mother when his mind wandered that way.

His preferred method was to tie their wrists and ankles with silk scarves, pretending he liked it that way or needed a photo shot to be set up that way. Those that displeased him felt the strength and power of silk. He'd tighten the fifth scarf around their neck until they passed out. George had a short fuse, especially if someone brought up his childhood.

He thought of himself as a compassionate guy in general, but if a woman really pissed him off, he toyed with them like cats did with mice, and slowly killed them. He liked seeing terror in their eyes. They struggled as he tightened the scarf and when they passed out, he gave them just enough air to revive them. Towards the end, he'd look for a sign of resignation to their fate. They knew they were going to die, and their terrified look was replaced with regret and sorrow. This was the payback George sought. Unfortunately, it wasn't against them personally but his dead mother. Too bad. He knew he was sick but . . .

He folded the last scarf after examining it, poured himself a glass of Glenlivet Scotch, and sat down. He tried to enjoy the warm July evening and the Milwaukee skyline, but for some reason his sudden deep anger from his past—from Mommy—came flooding back. He felt his mood swing to rage. He slammed the Scotch back in one swallow. It burned going down. Then he threw the crystal W-engraved tumbler at a buoy bobbing on the black water off the boat. He stuffed a black silk scarf, along with others, into a silver shopping bag, and slowly walked below to the master cabin.

Feeling his rage subside, he carefully placed them neatly in his nightstand drawer.

He returned topside to the boat's bar, got a newly engraved tumbler and poured himself another drink. Then he raised another crystal tumbler to the black night.

"To beautiful women." George West settled into one of

Condor's embroidered deck chairs to enjoy the Irish music blaring from the Summerfest grounds and the rest of the night, numbing himself and the memory of Gloria, his mother.

Irish Fest was still going strong when Drew and Stella started back. With green, white and orange beads draped around her neck, and two shamrocks pasted in two prominent places on her tee shirt, Stella and Drew ambled along in Milwaukee's Veteran Park towards the yacht club's Tiki Hut for one last drink before calling it quits for the night.

Music could be heard in the distance. When fireworks started from the Summerfest grounds at 10:30 p.m., all they could do was stop and marvel at the marvelous sights and sounds.

Drew kissed her neck, then her lips. "I'm looking forward to fireworks of our own."

She pulled away, licking her lips. "I sure hope so. I have to work for the next seven days without a break, so if you want any more of what I have, you'll have to come and visit me in Chicago."

"Sounds fair. How about a Guinness and shot of Jamison whiskey to salute Irish Fest at the Club?"

"Aye, aye, Captain. Let's hurry. Morning comes soon enough, and I have to get back to Chicago around three tomorrow afternoon for a family dinner. It's a tradition at Uncle Frank's and I can't miss it. Sorry, Drew."

"Really? I'm disappointed. I'd hoped we could spend a

couple of days together. There are so many great spots to see in Milwaukee."

"It is what it is, and we still have lots of time to be together tonight."

"Right," he mumbled.

Thirty minutes later, they were climbing down into *Courage's* cabin.

***

As the sun spread its rays through the front hatch and the cabin's portholes, Drew got up and closed the V-berth door, trying not to wake Stella while he made a pot of strong coffee. He slipped on his shorts and boat shoes and made his way down the pier to the marina's toilets and shower. He knew the smell of the perking coffee would wake Stella. When he got back from his morning constitution and stepped on board, Stella was sitting just outside the cabin, in the shade of the dodger, sipping the fresh coffee in one of his clean tee shirts.

"Hungry?" he asked.

"Starved."

"I'll fry up eggs and bacon."

"That's great. Usually I just have what I have in my hand, but right now, bacon and eggs sounds great."

As he cooked, he felt her come up behind him and press herself against his back, wrap her arms around his waist, and kiss his neck. "You were wonderful last night. I wish I could stay longer but I have to get back for dinner at Uncle Frank's."

"I know. Let's not think about you leaving just yet. We have breakfast and one last time to say goodbye."

"Yes, to both."

Later, Drew and Stella walked hand and hand to her car, saying goodbye to several of the boaters as they made their way down the dock and to the parking lot.

She pulled away. "I'll call next week when I get my schedule set. I'll drive up for the night, and you can show me Milwaukee's *other* night life—besides the Tiki Hut, OK?"

"Sounds good. It's only an hour's drive here or you can take the train. I'll pick you up if you come by train."

"I'll probably drive. See you at the end of next week."

Drew kissed her, turned, and missed her already when walking back to *Courage*.

George had just finished breakfast at the yacht club when he saw Drew and a woman walking across the marina parking lot. Soon after, Drew returned and went through the gate leading to the boat slips, disappearing from sight.

George's gaze shifted to the woman, and he saw it was Stella.

She was getting into an older gray Grand Am. Hearing the car's engine start energized George, and he jogged over, knocking on the driver's window as Stella was adjusting the car's mirror.

She jumped at the surprising knock, but then a big smile

appeared on her face as she recognized him. Stella lowered the window.

"Hi, George, what a pleasant surprise."

"Same here. I guess you were up here visiting Drew?" he asked.

"Yeah, we hit it off at your boat party."

"That's fantastic. If you have a few moments, I have some extra money for you."

"Money? But you paid me before for modeling."

"I know, but I sold a couple of your shots so I owe you a little more. If you have a few minutes, I can pay you and show you the finished work. Your pics really turned out well."

Stella looked at her watch. "If we can get it done in a half an hour, I can just make it home in time."

"Park your car at the lot near my dock. My boat's at the end of H Dock." He pointed. "Just over there. I'll wait for you at the gate."

It was just a few minutes later that Stella and George walked down the long pier to its end, where *Condor* was tied up.

"Gee, it's really empty around here for a pretty Sunday afternoon," she said. "So quiet. Creepy like. It's not like I remember it, when you were in Chicago."

"Yes, it gets quiet that way sometimes."

"You had women sleeping in every cabin. You don't have any models down below in the bedrooms sleeping now do you?"

"No. Today it's just you and me, Stella. Sit here in the cabin area. If you want something to drink, you know where the refrigerator is. Help yourself, I'll be right back with the pictures, your money, and my camera."

"I'm not really thirsty, but thanks. I'll just wait."

George went to his darkroom and got the pictures and his digital camera. In his bedroom, he went to the special drawer where he kept his collection of silk scarves and a few bikini bottoms. He grabbed a few, holding them up to the light streaming in through a porthole. He grabbed some money and returned to the cabin.

"Not too long of a wait. Here is your money for the three pictures I sold and here's the rest of the photos I took of you." George watched her as she studied the nine photos.

"Wow, George. I didn't realize I could look that good." Stella looked up and smiled at him. "Thanks for the extra money. It'll help with school costs."

"That's right, school. You told me about that. I was hoping I could take a few more pictures. I have this idea about using scarves to show off your body and my boat. Would you mind? Here's what I was thinking. I'd like to take a couple scarves and make a swimsuit out of them: two on top and a third one a bikini bottom or cover-up. Just make the top loose enough to show some skin. Get the idea?"

"Yeah, I think I got it."

"I love working with scarves. I guess I got that from my mother. She used to dress with scarves all the time. Here let me show you what I mean."

"I think I get it."

"Here, it will only take a second. If you like the idea, you can go down below and change into the bikini and scarves. Then we can go out on the bow, and I can take a few shots with the skyline in the background." He got up and quickly moved towards her. "Here's what I had in mind." He draped two scarves over her. "There. What do you think? Of course, it will look better without your tee shirt and shorts on."

"I like it, George, but this can't take too long. I have to get back to Chicago."

"I promise, thirty minutes more, tops. Now go down below and change. Here is a pair of turquoise scarves. If this works, we can try a different color too. I'll be out on the bow waiting."

She grabbed the black bikini bottom he brought up and the scarves and headed below.

When she stepped out of the cabin door and walked towards the bow, he got excited. "You look just as I pictured you would. Totally fantastic. Sit on the big circular bow cushion with your knee crossed slightly over your leg and lean on your elbows."

"Like this?"

"Yes. That's it. Good. Now tilt your body like you might roll over, so your breast sags like it might slip out of the scarf. Wait, the scarf is too tight, I need to see more breast." He leaned over and loosened the scarf so that her breast slipped out.

"George, what are you doing?"

He saw anger in her eyes. "Nice, but that's too loose. Sorry. Here, let's try this." And he moved the loose scarf so it just covered her nipple. "Yes, that's the look I want. God, you look seductive. That's just what I wanted to capture."

George moved around the bow, snapping shots.

"Now sit up, lean forward and with your arms pressed against the sides of your breasts, make more cleavage. That right. Perfect. Now place your hands so they're resting on your bikini bottom like you are covering your pubic area. Now slowly, wet your lips with just a little bit of your tongue." *Click, click*, and *click*. He went on, moving faster. *Click, click* and *click*. "Great, I'm getting the sun and the shadows just right. Yes, you are good. So hot! No wonder Drew fucked you all night in Chicago and up here."

"What! What did you say?" Stella jumped up. She grabbed the other scarves and started back to the cabin. "I'm done with this shoot. How dare you say that?"

Knowing she was going down to his cabin, George quickly followed. When he got to his cabin, she was slipping out of the bikini bottom, showing a small patch of hair.

"What are you doing in here?" Stella was unashamed of her nudity but furious, nonetheless. "Get out of here while I dress. You are bad. Here you talk about your mother loving scarves. I bet she never taught you to act like you just did. You're an asshole, George, bad through and through! I never want to see you again."

She turned her back to him. Stella was wrong; George's mother did call him "bad" all the time. His brother Alex was always the good one.

George lost it anytime he heard those words directed at him. No one talked to him like that anymore and got away with it!

"My mother did teach me to act this way, Stella, and you're right, you won't be seeing me again." George clenched and unclenched his fingers as he watched her try to get into her shorts. She had one leg in the air and one leg in her shorts when he grabbed her neck, pushing her off balance, pushing her facedown to the cabin floor. His right knee moved to the middle of her back, pinning her down. Then George grabbed the scarves' loose ends and wrapped them around her neck. Stella struggled trying to push him off. He grabbed the two scarf ends and pulled, tightening the scarf, bending her back.

"You fucking bitch! You're just like my mother, and this is what I did to her."

He heard a throaty, "No!"

He pulled with all his might. He couldn't see her face, but imagined her eyes bulging, fear, and then panic. Yes, just like Mom did. George enjoyed Stella's struggle. She tried to twist and throw him off, but he was too big, and strong. He rode her like she was a bucking horse, keeping the pressure tight on her neck.

"I liked you, Stella," he said to the back of her head, "but no one lives after calling me names like Mom used to." George felt her losing the fight, and moved his fingers to her silk covered neck, finishing the job.

Stella lay still. He held the end of the knotted scarf and sat on her a few more minutes, letting his anger subside. Then he unwrapped the scarf and rolled her over, looking at her semi-naked body.

"Just like Mom, you got what you deserved. Wasn't I good to you in Chicago? I'm not so bad when you want something, am I? All I wanted was a little love, Stella, just a little love."

He gently slipped her shirt over her head, then put on her shorts.

Going topside, he thought he better get rid of her car

quick, before someone noticed it there. He would make it look like Stella got a flat, letting the air out the tire near the off ramp by the big freighter pier. George could dump her body later, maybe on his way back from Barnacle Bud's after dark.

He knew just the place to dump her car. His folding boat bike would fit in her trunk, and he could ride it back. Anyone seeing him would think George West was just out for a pleasant Sunday afternoon bike ride.

Chapter Fourteen

Two days later, Tuesday morning, Drew heard a knock on his hull. Standing in the cabin, he looked out and saw Detectives O'Malley and Pinkowski on the pier.

"Now what?" He climbed the three cabin steps out into the cockpit of *Courage*.

Pinkowski took the lead. "Hi, Thompson. Surprised? We thought you might be. We have a few questions we'd like to ask you down at the station. Seems we found a woman's body floating in the Kinnickinnic River, and she was last seen with you. Stella Carpenter's uncle said she was supposed to be home for a family dinner Sunday afternoon. When she didn't show up, he called the police. Of course, we had already found her body by then."

"Stella! You found Stella dead?" Drew staggered back and sat down in the cockpit. "That can't be. She was just with me a couple of days ago, Sunday. She was fine when I walked her to her car. How can she be dead?"

"That's what we'd like to talk to you about," Pinkowski said.

"Yeah," O'Malley said. "Seems like beautiful women you meet get murdered and end up in the water. Let's go."

***

Later that morning, Tara and her partner Sabina were sitting in front of a monitor in the department meeting room, as Drew was brought into the green interrogation room he was in before. They each had a copy of the initial murder report in front of them looking over the facts. The size of the small interrogation room prevented them from being in the same room as Pinkowski and O'Malley. This time, they were going to be part of the investigation team working with Pinkowski and O'Malley, there being no conflict of interest with Drew since he was suspected of killing someone Tara didn't know.

Pinkowski said, "We need to read you your rights."

"I don't need an attorney because I didn't do anything."

"Great. We're glad you feel that way." Pinkowski opened a folder, taking out a paper and sliding it across the table toward Thompson. "Then you won't mind signing this form. It says you are giving up your right to an attorney, and we have read you your rights."

"Fine." Drew signed it, sliding it back to Pinkowski.

"Let's start from the beginning: how did you meet Stella Carpenter?" Pinkowski asked.

Drew felt sick to his stomach. He was in shock, like when he'd seen his fellow marines killed in Afghanistan. Even though he wasn't wounded or hurt, his mind was disorientated.

"What? What did you ask me?"

"Aw, come off it, Thompson," O'Malley jumped in. "You knew we were coming after you. People saw you with her. Is this like the Sullivan case? A little sex and then you killed her and dumped her in the river like garbage?"

Drew lunged at him, but Pinkowski stopped him, pushing him back in his chair.

"Fuck you, O'Malley! I really liked her. We were going to get together later this week when she had a few days off. I was going to tell you that, but you didn't let me."

Pinkowski looked at his partner. "O'Malley shut up and give him a chance to explain will you."

Good cop, bad cop? Fuck them, Drew thought. He didn't do anything, and he was the one who had lost someone he really cared about. Again! He sat still for a few moments, staring at his hands, and then recounted meeting and romancing Stella, ending with, "I kissed her in the parking lot. I turned and walked back to my boat and that's the last I saw her. She was alive and smiling."

"So you met her Saturday here, went to Irish Fest and had sex. Is that it?" O'Malley asked.

"Yeah, O'Malley, that's it. We had lots of sex, if you want to know. Is that what you were getting at, O'Malley. Go fuck yourself!"

"Simmer down, Thompson." Pinkowski said. "We're just trying to figure out what happened from the time you said you saw her alive, and when Stella Carpenter was found in the river."

"Lots of people saw us," said Drew. "There was Lou, across from me, and Robert and his wife Carrie Ann from the boat *Relaxation*, next to me. Aaron and Dorf, two fishermen, talked to her too. They talked to Stella just before she left. People saw her walking with me down the pier. Then they talked to me again when I came back alone. I stayed on my boat until around five in the afternoon and then went to the Tiki Hut, had a few beers, talking to some people there until around seven. Then I headed back to my boat."

"What kind of car did she have?"

"I think it was a Pontiac Grand Am, older model. Gray. Why?"

"Did you ever ride in it?" Pinkowski asked.

"No, I never got in it. We walked everywhere in Chicago, and the same here. She wasn't in Milwaukee that long. Maybe I put my hand on the driver's side roof when I walked her to the car Sunday, but I don't think I even did that."

Pinkowski opened the folder in front of him and then looked at Drew. "We need to know. We found her car parked off I-794, on a side street near one of the cement freighter piers. We're checking for prints. You ever have a reason to go there?"

"No."

What kinds of car do you drive, Thompson?"

"I have a black BMW convertible, older model. Why?"

"Just in case a witness saw a black BMW in the area. Thank you," Pinkowski said. "Did you go out for a drive Sunday afternoon after she left?"

"No. I was on my boat or the pier all afternoon. I told you that already."

"Right. We found her ripped shirt and purse thrown on the front passenger's floor mat with its contents spilled out on the front seat like it was dumped—quick, like it might have been a robbery gone bad. Her front left tire was flat, but we found no puncture in the tire when we examined it."

O'Malley cut in. "Or it could have been set up that way, to

make it look like it was a robbery, sexual assault? There were marks around her neck. Looked like finger marks. Let's see your hands, Thompson. They look like they're big enough and you sure are strong enough to kill her. Weren't you a marine?"

"You know that."

"Your training in the military would make it easy for you to kill, I bet," said O'Malley. "Hand to hand combat training. Were you Special Forces or a Seal?"

"I was in intelligence, on the ground. My last station was Afghanistan."

"You kill anyone over there?" O'Malley asked.

"Only when I had to protect myself or my men. Protecting my men is how I got wounded and because of that, I took early retirement. That's why I'm here in Milwaukee, remember, my boat? I'm fixing *Courage* up for a long sailing trip."

"A trip? Where are you going?" Pinkowski asked, smiling.

"Away from Milwaukee and you guys. I want to see the perimeter of the United States. I want to get to know America at a slow pace. I want to visit the little towns, big cities. Enjoy life and meet people." He looked at O'Malley, "Not kill them."

"Very touching, Thompson," O'Malley said. "Let's go over again: where were you after you say Stella Carpenter left?"

"Like I said, I went back to my boat, did some work. Then later, I went over to the Tiki Hut and had a burger, a few beers. There I talked to Brian and Vickie, Rick and Madonna about sailing over to Michigan. We talked about planning a trip later in August. By that time, it was nine at night and I headed back to my boat. I have lots of witnesses to verify all this, like I said. I am not your killer."

"Well, Thompson, we'll check your story out with these people. You told us a story before, and then we found out that you left a lot out. Until we check your alibi with your boating friends, don't leave Milwaukee. We are waiting to hear from forensics on Ms. Carpenter. We need to take a DNA swab from you."

"Guess what, O'Malley? You're going to find my sperm inside her because we made love in the morning, and just before she headed home."

O'Malley and Pinkowski looked at each other and smiled. O'Malley got a swab and took a sample from Drew's mouth.

The next day, Pinkowski joined his colleagues in the large detective briefing room and sat down at the large table. "Here's the report from Forensics." He held it up.

That got the attention of O'Malley, Tara, and her partner Sabina.

"What does it say?" asked Tara.

He put on his reading glasses. "I hate wearing these things but if I don't wear them everything is fuzzy. Here's what we have. I'll highlight, minus all the technical stuff we'd use in court."

O'Malley nodded. "Yeah, go ahead."

"Carpet traces found under Stella's fingernails. It also verifies what Thompson said: his sperm was in her vagina. They're no identifiable fingerprints on her neck. There was a wide ligature type mark on her neck and the burst blood vessels in her eyes. They found no water in her lungs."

"Just like my sister," Tara said.

"Yes, like your sister," Pinkowski said.

"Stella Carpenter did not drown," Tara said.

"No trauma to her body, indicating she was beat up, except to her neck," Pinkowski continued. "But she did have a bruise on the small of her back. Usual pooling of blood, but not consistent with someone dumped in the water." Pinkowski looked at Sabina, sliding the report over.

Sabina looked the report over. "Says here that the body was dumped in the water hours after death occurred."

O'Malley cut in. "Maybe Thompson stashed her body someplace, and dumped it later, making it look like a robbery?"

"Maybe," Pinkowski said. "We'll need to verify with Thompson's boating friends how long it was before he returned to his boat after saying goodbye to the victim."

Tara said, "I'll check with the marina and get the phone numbers and addresses of the people Drew Thompson said he talked to. Sabina and I can check his alibi with those people."

"Good, I don't want too much time to pass on this. The recollection of time gets fuzzy after a while," Pinkowski said, looking at the report. "It looks like the carjacking was a set up. No fingerprints inside of the car. We checked her credit cards to see if they were used but there were no charges except for a gas charge on Saturday afternoon in Chicago. Probably before she drove up here."

He scanned the report. "Bruising angle indicates she was attacked from behind as the bruises were angling upward and back. She might have been surprised by another she didn't see, like two gang members looking for an easy hit if it was robbery.

That's about it. Let's get going on the boating people at the yacht club and McKinley."

Sabina said, "I'll ask Eric, the marina manager, for a list of the people on the three docks around Thompson's and set up interviews." She looked at Tara, "You go to the yacht club and get the names there: the bartender at the Tiki Hut, and other folks Thompson said he was talking to."

O'Malley said, "I don't like him. I know he did it."

Pinkowski was less sure. "Don't get clouded by your emotions O'Malley. Let's gather the facts. They'll prove him guilty or innocent."

"Yeah, yeah. I know. I'm no rookie, Pinkie."

Sabina had stayed behind at the station, but Tara headed to the yacht club. In the parking lot, she spotted a familiar face.

"Alex! Alex!" Tara yelled, but the person kept walking toward a black Corvette convertible with its top down. After he got into the convertible, she swung her car in front of it at an angle, stopped, and got out.

"Didn't you hear me?" she said, a little irked. She looked at his car. "Did you get a new car? What happen to the Jag?"

Sitting in the open sports car, George looked at Tara and smiled. "I am almost tempted to play a joke on you, but you have me mixed up with my brother. Alex and I are identical twins so this confusion happens all the time. It's hard to tell us apart, but I can tell you I'm much more fun to be with then Alex." He laughed. "My name's George." He held out his hand.

Tara studied him more closely, moving around to the driver's side to get a better look at him. She shook George's hand, even leaning down closer to get a better look. "You really aren't Alex?"

"No, he's my younger brother by twelve minutes."

"Amazing. I would have sworn—"

"Happens all the time. How do you know Alex?"

"We've been going out. Your brother is a great guy, like I assume you are. I love sailing with him. After I saw your boat *Condor* in the harbor the first night we went sailing, Alex told me about it. It really is nice."

"Oh yes, it is nice, but I boat on the dark side if you listen to him and other sailors." George pointed south of the yacht club. "*Condor* is at the end of H Dock. I'm just going over there now. Would you like to join me for a drink and I can show you how the other half of the Wests live? Then you'll realize I'm more fun. I'm sure, you can already tell I'm better looking than Alex."

She looked at her watch. "I can't right now but I'd take you up on your offer after I'm done with my shift. I have to question people about a case, but I should be finished by four o'clock. After that is good."

"Sounds great. Here's my card with my cell number on it. Call when you're done working and I'll come open the gate. Remember, H Dock.

"Got it. See you around four, or earlier if I can manage it."

***

Five minutes before four o'clock, Tara called George.

"Welcome to Dock H, home to beautiful *Condor*." George said soon after, as he opened the heavy steel gate. They walked down the sloping ramp to the main pier before turning onto H Dock.

"There are lots of larger power boats and sailboats on these docks," Tara said as they walked. "Wow, your boat takes up the whole end of the pier."

"I like it that way—just enough room for an inflatable run-about off the stern, if I want."

They walked up the three steps and boarded *Condor*.

"Would you like a drink? I probably have whatever you like."

He pointed to two large refrigerators built into the bulk-head below a granite bar. "I also have a nice selection of white wines. I only allow guests to drink white, just in case you spill on my white rug. We can sit inside in the salon area or outside on the afterdeck."

"A vodka tonic would be great, if you don't mind."

"Coming right up."

A minute later, he handed Tara her drink. Then he poured himself a Glenlivet Scotch on the rocks. "Shall we go out on the afterdeck? For once, there isn't a cold wind coming off the lake."

She nodded. "That would be great." They moved to the afterdeck with the large sliding doors open so it felt like it was outside and sat on a white rattan sofa facing each other.

"Tell me again how you met my boring younger brother?"

She smiled. "I was questioning a suspect we thought was involved in a homicide. The suspect was meeting Alex for a drink."

"So, you like my brother?"

"Yes. Alex is such a nice guy, but I admit he not as good looking as you. Don't tell him I said that." They laughed as they touched glasses.

"You don't look like any cop I've ever seen or met, but then I've only got speeding tickets for driving too fast in the Corvette."

"Actually, I'm a detective in Homicide. It sounds classier, doesn't it?" she said. "I moved up through the ranks for six years. I just started working Homicide just before my sister Cate was killed. Ironic and sad timing, isn't it? I can't even work on my sister's case but am working on a new case with my new partner. It's similar to my sister's case. That's why I was on B and C Dock: verifying a suspect's information. Same guy from my sister's case is a suspect in this murder too. Creepy. His alibi checks out again too, but he sure ends up being around a lot of dead women." She slapped her forehead with her open palm. "Shit. I shouldn't be telling you this. I could get into lots of trouble. I guess I shouldn't drink on an empty stomach."

He moved two fingers across his lips. "My lips are sealed. Besides, who am I going to tell? I'm not a reporter or the killer, so it doesn't matter."

"Yeah, you're right. Let's talk about you. I know something about your family from your brother but tell me something I don't know."

"We'll, I'm a photographer. I started at an early age. My dad got me a Polaroid camera for my sixth birthday. Remember Polaroid cameras and film? Like most six-year-olds, I didn't have a lot of patience. That Polaroid took pictures that were almost instant, not like today's digital, but still fast enough. It was ahead of its time. For a six-year-old, that was fantastic. My mom loved me to take pictures of her. She especially liked it when she and Dad got dressed up. It was about the only thing that I did that she really liked. Alex got all the praise from her. 'Alexander the Great,' she'd say. Alex could do no wrong, but not me, not George. I could never do anything right in her eyes."

"That sounds familiar," Tara said. "That's kind of the way it was with my dad and sister."

George drained the rest of his Scotch and got up to make another one. "Can I freshen your drink?"

"Sure, why not? I'm off duty now."

"Here you go." After giving her the glass, he stood there looking at her, thinking of his mother.

"Thank you. Why are you frowning? You asked if I wanted another drink?"

George sat down again. "Just talking about my mother, the way she treated me, makes me upset." *And you look like her.*

He sat closer to her. "I was named after George Washington, our first president, maybe because I was born first. But I never seemed to measure up to Alex in my mom's eyes."

"Oh, George, that's sad, but like I said, I know how you feel." Tara sipped her fresh drink. "With my dad, I could never measure up to my sister. In his eyes, she was always the special one. Cate went into law like him. She was a top attorney, like Dad. I became a cop, starting at the bottom, and working my way up. I understand my dad's feeling about me," Tara said, the words tumbling out. "My mother died giving birth to me.

Actually, my sister was adopted. They didn't think mom could get pregnant and have kids. Cate being their first, she got all the attention. It didn't matter that she was adopted. My mom kept trying to get pregnant and prove to Dad that she could conceive a child like any other woman. She did, and three years later I was born, but that killed her. I think Dad felt one child was enough. His ego was strong enough that he didn't need biological offspring. These days, everytime I look into his eyes I feel like it pains him to look at me. He sees her in me. Dad still deeply loves Cate and misses her. I see the regret."

A tear slid down her face.

George said, "My mom wanted to prove she was still beautiful and wanted by men. I think she'd be called a trophy wife today," he said with a chuckle. "Mom was twenty years younger than Dad, and a real looker." He took another drink. "She fooled around a lot to feed her need. I walked in on her once. Caught her in the act with a big strapping deliveryman.

"I remember the day like it was yesterday. I was forbidden to go into their bedroom, even when Dad was home. I had a golden retriever named Buddy. He was my best pal. I loved him more than anyone except maybe Dad. Anyhow, that day I taught Buddy how to shake his paw and wanted to show Mother the trick. I burst into her bedroom, all excited. That's when I caught her fucking this guy. She screamed at me and slapped me. Then she took me into my room and tied me to the bed and gagged me until she was done with her sex.

"From then on, if someone was coming over, she'd grab my arm, drag me into my room and tie me up, spread-eagle to my bedposts, or worst of all, lock me in my bedroom closet. I hated those days. I'd plead 'Please Mommy, don't tie me up. I won't come in I promise. I'll just go play with Buddy.' But she'd say, 'No, I don't trust you and you aren't going to wreck my fun.'

"She knew how much I loved Buddy, and said, "You tell your father about these other men and I'll kill Buddy." Buddy was the only one that unquestionably loved me, so I stayed quiet for years, taking her abuse. By the time Buddy died of natural causes, Dad was dead, I was older and there was no one to tell."

"How horrible for you," she said. "What about Alex? Couldn't you tell him when it happened?"

"I was afraid if I told him about her, he'd tell her. Alex was her favorite, and he'd do anything to stay in her good graces. He usually squealed on me, so I kept the secret so I couldn't take that chance. Yeah. I hated her for a long time, but I loved her too. I just wanted her to love me. Kind of like a Greek tragedy." He stared at Tara.

"Why are you looking at me like that?"

"Actually, Tara, you look more and more like her the longer I look at you." George got up and went into the main cabin, returning with a framed picture. "Look at this."

Tara studied the picture. "I guess I do, sort of, but I think you're saying that because of the hairstyle in this picture."

"It's more than your hair. It's your face, eyes, legs, and hips. Even your breasts are about the same size as Mom's."

"George, your analysis is embarrassing me."

He saw her face get red. "I'm sorry. I didn't mean it to come out that way, but I'm a photographer. That's how I see things. Actually, just looking at you gives me comfort because I miss my mother. I just wish she had loved me as much as she loved Alex. That's maybe why he and I don't get along."

"Alex told me you aren't close. Your mother is dead, isn't she?"

"Yes. She hung herself after she shot our chauffeur in a jealous rage. He was her lover, and she found out he was going to leave her for someone younger."

His face looked deeply troubled. "I lost the two things I love the most in the world—Mom and my dog Buddy. She's been dead," he looked to the sky as if the answer was written in the clouds, "a little over fifteen years. I still have the house in Annapolis where Alex and I grew up. I usually go there in the winter and stay here for the summer on *Condor*. It works out well."

"Wow. I'm sorry about your mom. It's tough when they take their own life and even tougher when they take another person with them. It's selfish to kill yourself. The guilt stays with the survivors."

"Thanks for your thoughts. It was tough for both Alex and me. I was the one that found her so it's hard to erase that final image of her." *He loved that image. It excited him. And he would do the same to Tara if she wasn't nice.*

"Can you show me around? This boat looks amazing."

"Sure. Follow me," he said, and gave her the grand tour. "Here's the galley, fairly modern. Here is the engine room, no secrets here, just two big diesel engines. Here's one of the guest bedrooms. Here are the crew's quarters, or kids' room, if I had any. Next is my pride and joy of the boat, the darkroom."

"Do you still develop pictures? I thought everything is done digitally."

"Sometimes I like to be more creative. Film is special. The art is in the developing."

"I guess. Can you show me some of your work?

"Sure, look at this." He got out some disks, loaded one into a big Apple computer and screen and started scanning through pictures.

"They're great," she said. "All these women look fabulous."

"It's my job to make them look good. I bet you would look fantastic in front of my lens."

She laughed. "Your brother said the same thing when we passed your boat the first time he took me out."

George smiled. "I guess we both recognize beauty." He leaned down and kissed her gently, putting his arms around her. He felt her tense up.

"You're good, George, really good, like your brother, but I'm happy dating him. I have to ask, are all you West's good kissers?" She laughed. "I think one West is enough."

"So once again Alex is Alex the Great?"

"Since you put it that way, yes. He is Alex the Great. Sorry, George."

"Can't help a guy for trying." He gave her a peck on the forehead. "Let's finish the tour with my room, no sex, and then we can go topside."

"I'd like that, but George, you and I have a connection—in a way that Alex can't compete against."

"We do?"

She looked into his eyes. "We both have a parent that held back their love to us."

Tara stepped towards George, stood on her tiptoes and kissed him lightly on his lips.

"Remember that," she said.

"Tara, if friendship is the most I can expect from you, I can live with that. I feel like you're the first person in a very long time that likes me for me. Let's have another drink on deck. It should be a nice sunset and I'd like to share it with you."

Chapter Fifteen

The next day as he pulled into the parking lot at the yacht club, Alex saw Drew walking to the nearby McKinley Marina roundhouse. He powered down his car window.

"Drew, wait up, let me park the car, and I'll walk over and have a cup of coffee with you." Drew nodded.

Alex said, "How's it going? Ready to do some sailing? I need someone to crew with me for a few days. I want to sail over to Michigan. Spend a day or two over there and then sail back. How about it?"

"Sounds good but I have another situation going on with Milwaukee's Finest that might prevent me from going. When were you thinking of?"

"Not for a week or ten days at the most. Why? What happened?"

"You don't know?"

"No. I've been out of town on business."

They entered the Pitch's Express at the roundhouse. Drew said. "Hi John, how about two hot dogs and a couple of coffees?"

"You bet. I'll bring it outside."

"I love the hot dogs here. They're so good," Drew said to Alex.

Getting their coffee, they sat outside at one of the picnic

tables, enjoying the bright Saturday morning, watching joggers, bikers and all the people with their assorted dogs. It was a great spot to boat and people watch.

"Tell me what's going on," Alex said.

"When I was down in Chicago for the start of the Mac Race, I met this smart, attractive, fun woman. Anyhow, after she came up to see me in Milwaukee, she disappeared. The police found her body floating in the river, and guess who the last known person was to see her alive?"

"You again?" Alex set his coffee down, looking hard at Drew as he digested this latest unsettling news.

"Yes, me, but this time I have several witnesses to vouch for me."

"Well, then you should be in the clear, right?"

"I should be except we made love that morning, and my sperm was inside her. We made love the last time, just before she started for home."

"Shit. That's not good. You're having a run of bad luck in Milwaukee, Drew."

"Don't I know it. Tara and her partner Sabina are working this case, along with my buddies Pinkowski and O'Malley. They told me not to leave town. Until I get the OK from them, I have to stay here."

"Well I hope you're cleared by the time I take my trip. I'll make a few calls to the higher ups and see what I can do."

"Thanks. I'd appreciate that."

"We'll have a great time. I just got a new jib and mainsail so I'm excited to use them."

"I'd love to help you. I hope Tara and her partner can find

Stella's killer. Not to change the subject, but how is Tara doing? You guys going out?"

"Not as much as I'd like to but enough. I've had her to a few social events and we've gone out to dinner."

"I'm jealous, but you also have a lot to offer Tara. You travel in all the right circles."

Alex nodded. "It doesn't hurt our relationship if I can spend time with her at fancy events. We've argued a few times about her work schedule and mine. She spends lots of her free time trying to find her sister's killer, tracking down leads. I understand that. Hell, I'm gone a lot too, with company travel. Thank God I have great division managers who basically run the day-to-day operations of the companies or I couldn't go anywhere . . . like this trip coming up."

"I bet. Tara's focused on finding her sister's killer, but she still likes all the perks of being with a pillar of the community, and all the social events and things you do," Drew said.

"That she does. How about we go sailing this afternoon, 1 p.m. I've been working and traveling, and I need time on my boat. How's that?"

"Great. See you then."

That afternoon, O'Malley, Pinkowski, Sabina and Tara were sitting around the big table in the conference room going over the Stella Carpenter Murder Book, looking once again at the evidence.

Pinkowski stood next to a big greaseboard on the wall. On

it was a drawing showing Carpenter's car in relation to the river and where the body was found. There were several photos of the front and back seat of her vehicle. On the table was a yellow folder holding pictures of her semi-nude body and pictures of her bruised neck.

Pinkowski banged the board with his pen. "I told you, O'Malley. We don't have anything outside of his sperm inside her to make him a bona fide suspect." He looked over at Tara and Sabina. "Tell him. You talked to all the witnesses he gave us, right?"

"Right," said Sabina. "They all check out."

"Thompson could have killed her in the car, in the parking lot, driven it someplace and then came back later, and dumped her," O'Malley said.

"Come on, O'Malley, you're a professional," Pinkowski said. "You know it didn't happen that way. His prints were not inside or outside of the car. They dusted the whole thing. It was clean."

O'Malley stood up and began pacing.

Pinkowski said, "I know you don't like this guy, but his story checks out. Forensics says it didn't happen that way. Thompson's clean."

Tara looked at O'Malley. "Tim, as much you hate this guy, I don't think he's the

killer. Stella Carpenter was in the wrong place at the wrong time. Pinky said he really looked surprised and broken up when you told him Stella Carpenter was dead."

"That's right," said Pinkowski. "I agree with Tara. My gut says he's not our man."

"Alright, I get it. But who then?" O'Malley took a seat again.

"There are enough guys looking for ways to get cash by any means," Sabina said. "You know that, O'Malley. When they are hurting, the crackheads, meth-heads or heroin druggies will look for any way to score. And if they're desperate, they'll kill if they have too. They hit and move fast. They even break into homes when the people are there, killing anyone in their way. If Carpenter was pulled off the road with mechanical problems, she was an easy mark. It happened all the time when I was working in LA. Milwaukee is no different."

Tara looked at the report. "There was no cash or credit cards found, and most of her stuff was scattered in the car so it looks like she struggled and they killed her. Looks like a robbery gone bad."

O'Malley said. "When she tried to call for help, they shut her up by strangling her."

Pinkowski nodded. "Probably two guys, one in front and the second comes around the rear of the car. She doesn't see him come around behind her. He grabs her from behind. The report says she was killed from behind. They put her in the car, then one drove the car near the river and dumped her. Messy killing."

"Maybe when they put her in the car, they were pushing her face down and that's when she got the carpet burn to her face and carpet fibers attached to her earring?" Tara said.

"Could be," Pinkowski said. "I don't see anything in the report that says it matches the car fibers. We'll have to check that out. We'll need to make sure if they don't match the fibers from the car, then she was killed some other place."

"Tara and I will check on the car fibers found with the earrings," Sabina said.

Tara got out her smart phone and typed it down on her to-do list. "I'll call forensics and coordinate with the garage to check the car for matching fibers."

"This all sounds plausible," O'Malley said, "but there were no prints found in the car except the victim's. These types of people wouldn't take the time to wipe down a car or wear gloves. I don't like that. That just doesn't fit. I still think Thompson did it or someone else that had the time."

"Let's go with what we know," said Pinkowski.

***

A week later, Drew stood on the pier in front of *Passage Maker* at 8 a.m. duffle bag in hand.

"I wasn't sure you could make the trip," Alex said, shaking Drew's hand. "You can put that duffle down below later but tell me how you got permission to leave Milwaukee. It sounded like the cops were going to keep you here for a while."

Drew smiled. "It seemed like it to me too, but I called Tara at her work and told her that I had a chance to go sailing with you across the lake for a few days to Ludington, Muskegon, Holland and then back. She said my alibi checked out. She said they were pursuing other leads, but she trusted you and as long as I checked in daily, telling her where I am. If you verified it, they'd let me leave. Seems like you're my babysitter, Alex. Tara trusts you."

"Oh, great. You better not get into trouble over in Michigan. I'm already *persona non grata* with Tara. We had a fight last night—once again, about her work and her sister's case. She was tracking down a lead about a former client's wife. Tara was supposed to have dinner with me and say goodbye, but the case came first. I'm not too happy with her right now. The romantic dinner and sendoff didn't happen."

"Sorry about that. Well, it's all in your hands now. I promised Tara not to get into trouble, unless you lead me astray."

"Great. I was looking forward to having fun over there, especially after last night," Alex said.

"Let's get going. Stow your gear in the stern quarter berth. I have the boat provisioned, but I was planning on mostly eating out over there, so it's snacks and sandwiches until our first stop—probably Holland or Muskegon. We'll see which is most favorable, based on the wind." Alex moved to the engine panel and started the diesel engine. "Sounds good, doesn't it? I just had the maintenance done on her so the engine should run perfectly. Hope we don't have to use it much. I like the sound of the wind in the rigging and water against the hull, not the drone of a diesel."

"I couldn't agree with you more. I'll be ready to get us going and untie the lines in five minutes after I stow my gear."

"The captain gets the spacious V-berth." He laughed. "You get the smaller bunk in the stern quarter."

After motoring out the harbor's north entrance, they raised *Passage Maker's* sails and set out for Muskegon, heading due east. The prevailing wind was from the southwest so they had a nice reach directly across the lake from Milwaukee to Muskegon.

"Seven knots are good. At this rate, we should make it in

twelve hours' time for a late dinner and a nightcap. I'll call one of the marinas now and get a slip assigned. We could anchor, but usually I like to get a slip the first night, just to get a good night sleep and plug into the marina's power hook ups and charge the batteries. It's nice to start the day with a shower and top off the diesel if need be. We should arrive around seven or eight tonight."

"I hear the Michigan shoreline is great for boating," Drew said.

"Yes it is." Alex said. "The towns and harbors go all the way around Lake Michigan to Lake Huron about every twenty miles or so. Wherever a river flowed into Lake Michigan or Lake Huron, the lumber industry in the late 1900s dredged out the rivers and created lakes to hold logs before they rafted them up or shipped them to the big cities around the Great Lakes like Chicago. Most of Chicago was built on log pilings."

"Really? I didn't know that," Drew said.

"It really is a beautiful and historic area," Alex said. "People are friendly and there are a lot of great restaurants and townie bars."

"I can hardly wait."

***

After crossing Lake Michigan, they tied up *Passage Maker* at the marina in Muskegon's lake entrance, then headed off in the inflatable in search of food.

Five minutes later, Drew looked at the peeling paint on the

wood-sided building displaying a sign that said it all: "BAR." It was a place one would associate with a working, industrial area, not a picturesque resort like Muskegon, but it turned out to be perfect for two hungry guys trying to get away from their yacht club routine. It was some ways down the shoreline, near where the high-speed ferry docked.

"If the yacht club members could see us now in this dive, what would they think?" Alex said with a smile.

"Speak for yourself. I'm just a retired military officer with a patched-up hole in my head. I like bars like this. We marines hung around bars like this all over the world."

"Did I ever thank you for serving our county? I'll buy dinner tonight and all the drinks. A unique place like this, shouldn't cost me more than 50 bucks for the two of us."

"I accept your kind offer. Let's eat, I'm starved."

Later, as they motored back to the marina in the inflatable dingy, and turned off the small outboard, they heard music. Alex said, "I'm up for a little action after dinner. Look at that place up the hill with the lights and music. We could even stumble back to the boat if we got really loaded. Lead the way, Major."

The restaurant and bar was called Dockers.

"Hey, the place is jumping and it's a Thursday night," Alex said. "Great band and looks like lots of women."

"Give me a vodka tonic with two limes since you're buying," Drew said. "In the meantime, I'll try to cozy up to the bar while you find a waitress and get us a drink just in case you're delayed. I see a couple of women to chat with while you get the drinks." Drew smiled at Alex.

Alex nodded. "I'll be back soon with the drinks."

The bar was several deep and the bartenders were swamped trying to fill orders. A man of his word, Drew spotted a small opening between two attractive women.

"Good evening, ladies, mind if I slip between you two to get a drink order for me and my buddy? We're mighty thirsty and he seems to be having trouble getting an order filled with one of the roving waitresses."

Drew watched the shapely brunette give him the onceover. She glanced over to her blond friend. "Sure. Slip right in here between my friend and me. Where's your friend?"

Drew smiled. "He's right over there, near the table with the three big guys wearing green Michigan State tee shirts. He thought he could get a drink faster from a waitress out there than at this crowded bar."

"Oh, he's even better looking than you, honey. Why don't you wave him over here? We'll keep you company if you buy us a drink. My name is Roberta and this is Amber—like the color of whiskey."

"Roberta!" said Amber. "What's gotten into you? You never were like that before when you were married."

"When I was married, I never had a chance to act like I do now, because of you know who. Now, there's these two, and I got me some new boobs. I've been working out and toned up the rest of me too. Time to show it all off."

"Too much information," Drew said with a laugh. He

waved to Alex who nodded and then pointed to Amber and Roberta. Drew saw Roberta lick her lips as she watched Alex walk over.

"No offense . . . what did you say your name was?" Roberta said.

"Drew, Drew Thompson."

"Well, Drew, no offense to you, but he's mine. Amber, you get Drew here."

Amber smiled. "Fine with me."

Alex was his usual suave self, bowing to the ladies. "Good evening. How nice of you to make room for us."

"It's the least we could do since you're buying us a drink," Roberta said.

"Actually, Marine Major Drew Thompson, retired, is buying your drinks."

"I am not. You are. Remember?"

"Oh yeah. I forgot." Alex pulled out a hundred-dollar bill.

"Marine? Retired?" Amber said. "You look too young to be retired."

"Long story we can talk about later. First let me get our drinks." Drew grabbed the hundred-dollar bill from Alex and waved to the bartender.

"Are you two from around here?" asked Amber. "I don't think I've seen you at any of the restaurants or bars around Muskegon, especially Dockers. We come here a lot on Thursday night and the weekends, don't we, Roberta?"

"Yes, we do. I know I wouldn't forget seeing either one of you."

Drew turned his attention back to Amber. She was more to

his liking, with green eyes, shoulder length strawberry blond hair, a pretty roundish face, and a petite body. Maybe a jogger? "So Amber, tell me about yourself. You must live nearby if you two come here often."

"I live about a mile away in an apartment close to where I work. Roberta lives in a house a few miles from here. She works at a beauty salon and I work at a day spa located in the same mall. That's how we met. I'm a masseuse." She smiled at Drew. "Seems you've kept your Marine body in retirement."

"A massage sounds like a good idea to me, but I don't think we'll be here long enough for me to get one. Alex and I sailed over today from Milwaukee. We're going up the coast for a few days sailing on Alex's boat, and then we're going to head back."

"How exciting. I used to sail when I was a kid," Roberta said. "Could Amber and I be your crew? We're both off tomorrow, so we have a long three-day weekend. We were just going to go to the beach and hang out. It's supposed to be nice weather. You could teach us the finer points of sailing." She turned her attention back to Alex, now that she knew whom the owner of the boat was. "I could even give you guys a haircut. You both look like you could use a trim." She ran her fingers through Alex's hair.

"Interesting proposition," Alex said. "Let's finish these drinks and the four of us can head over to my boat at the marina next door." He pointed to *Passage Maker*. "Looks like I have the fixing for all our drinks on the boat. It's quieter there. We can even talk about being part of the crew, if you really want to do what you said. I enjoy Drew's company, but it would be more fun with you two along."

Roberta pressed herself tight against Alex, and then kissed him as Amber and Drew looked on.

"I've never done it on a boat before," she said.

"Roberta!" Amber said, her eyes wide in amazement.

"What? Okay, I guess I had a few drinks and," she paused, "I want to go sailing with these guys and have some fun for a change. I know you do too. When do we get a chance to go sailing with two good-looking guys, with no strings attached? Am I right?"

Alex smiled and nodded. "I bet we can hear the band's music from my boat. Let's go."

"My car?" Amber said. "What do I do with my car?"

"You can leave it in the parking lot for the time being," said Roberta. "No one will care. Besides, we have to go home and get some clothes if we go."

They headed for *Passage Maker.*

Drew wasn't sure about all this. He was still upset about Stella's murder and while company might be good, he wasn't sure about anything more than that. He could be cordial.

He guessed the argument Alex had with Tara must have been a little more heated than he had let on earlier.

Chapter Sixteen

The morning was sunny and clear. A wind was blowing about 12 knots from the southwest. It was a perfect day for a journey up the shore. But before that, Drew and Alex sat on the *Passage Maker*, finishing their coffee, enjoying the warm morning sun and waiting for Roberta and Amber to return with their clothing.

"Where do you want to head next?" Drew asked.

"Let's try Ludington. I checked the chart this morning. It's 56 miles up the coast. With this wind, and the waves helping push the boat a bit forward, it should be a nice easy sail for our new crew. I'll call and get us a slip later when I know we're far enough to make it. They have floating docks, and it says a pool and hot tub. If we can't get in, we can always anchor out."

Twenty minutes later, Drew saw an SUV pull into the marina's parking lot.

"Looks like they brought snacks besides their duffle bags," Drew said. "Must have bought enough food for a whole navy."

Alex laughed. "I think we lucked out when you spotted them last night. Keep a man full with food and you've got a happy man. Throw in sex, and he'll think of a woman as an angel and worship the ground they fly over."

"Really?" Drew said.

With Amber in her wake, Roberta bounced down the pier.

"Hi boys, missed us? We're ready to go once we get these supplies put away and our clothes stowed. Hope it's warm enough to wear my new bikini."

"Anything you wear, Roberta, is fine with me," Alex said.

"I'm not as wild as she is but I think you'll find my attire to your liking, Drew." Amber climbed on the boat and lightly kissed Drew on the lips. Moving to his ear, she whispered. "Thank you for being kind and considerate last night. I'm looking forward to being with you today and tonight." She slipped down below to stow her gear.

"What are you smiling at, Drew?" asked Alex.

"Oh nothing. Just a compliment on my manners, you know I'm an officer and a gentleman."

"Bullshit!" Alex said. "Let's get going. They can put their things away while we motor out the channel. I'll start the engine, and you loosen the lines."

Drew unwrapped the lines from the cleat, and they moved out.

Drew watched as Roberta and Amber behaved like two college students on spring break even though they were years past that. They tried their hand at steering. The vodka tonics and beers worked their magic, and around two in the afternoon, he noticed them both napping. Drew smiled. He wanted them to be rested for the evening of dinner and bar hopping. He watched Amber curl into the fetal position. He went down below and got a blanket. Placing it over her body, she made a soft cooing sound, then said in a soft voice, "Thank you."

He moved back to the port corner of the cockpit. "Want me to take over for a while?" he asked Alex.

"That's all right. I don't get a chance to steer on a reach like this very often without a care in the world. You can take over when Roberta wakes up."

"Got it."

Everything was right with the world, Drew thought, as he watched Little Sable Point pass by from two miles out. The homes on the shore were made of weathered gray wood, as if all the paint had been sand blasted off by the beach sand and the prevailing wind. He thought that someday he'd drive over to this side of the lake, and check the towns out, maybe with Amber, if life started getting better.

Late that afternoon, *Passage Maker* pulled into Harbor View Marina. Alex checked in with the marina's dockmaster, getting a slip on the end of a pier. It was still warm and they decided to go for a swim in the marina's pool. After that, they moved to the hot tub, enjoying glasses of wine as the sun went down.

Feeling pangs of hunger, the group set off to Jamesport Brewing Company just across the parking lot from the marina.

"We can start with a few appetizers, see how the food is," Amber said. "It looks good and they have a band setting up."

The four eventually got a table out on the back porch. It was warm for a late July evening and they all ordered the Friday night fish special, a tradition in the Midwest.

The view overlooked the marina and the sunset was replaced by the twinkle of stars.

After dinner, they moved down James Street and found

Gasoline Alley, another bar with a smoking hot band. The two couples danced to classic rock songs that they all knew the lyrics to, changing partners occasionally. Two hours later, slightly drunk and sweaty, they made it back to the boat. It was a long first day together and they decided to sleep longer in the morning before taking off for the next stop.

Lying in their berth, Amber snuggled close to Drew. Even though the hour was late, it was still warm in the cabin. The boat's fans made a humming noise, almost blocking the moans coming from the forward part of the boat.

"Stuff a rag in my mouth if I start making noise like Roberta is."

Drew laughed. "It's OK, she's having a good time. I know Alex is."

"I'd be too embarrassed if I made all that racket." Amber listened for a while and then the moaning quieted down. "Alex must be really good or it's just the act of making love on a boat that lets her go."

"Can't say I know much about Alex's lovemaking skills. This is our first trip together." His hand stroked her hair as she lay on his chest. "We only met maybe a month ago but we hit it off. We both have a love of sailing. Sometimes he needs help sailing this boat because of its size. I have my own boat, but it's nice to have a companion to sail with."

"You guys seem to get along like you've known each other for a long time. Thanks again for taking us along. I'm enjoying it and I know Roberta is too. She had to do some promising this morning just getting her ex-husband to take their son for three days so she could come. She was pleading and crying with Joe, that's her ex. She said a once in a lifetime trip had dropped in her lap. I even had to get on the phone with Joe and say I was going along. When he heard that, he softened and said yes. Little did he know that she and I were going sailing with two handsome, sexy men." Drew felt her give him a squeeze, then her lips kissed his naked chest.

"She loves that little boy of hers, but hardly ever gets a break. Joe is a drinker and she doesn't like to leave Billy with him very much. I usually take him if she needs to go someplace, but obviously that wouldn't work this time so Joe's got him. I hope he makes the most of his time with his son and doesn't get drunk. Now that Billy is twelve years old, I'm sure he notices things like that."

"That explains why she might like someone like Alex. He truly is a nice guy." He felt her fingers exploring his chest, stopping when they hit two scars to the side of his ribcage, and then she continued to explore the rest of him with her sensitive fingers.

"Are those scars from bullets?"

"Yes, Afghanistan." He took her hand and moved it to his scalp, hidden by his hair. "This one got me out of the Marines. I can't hear in this ear, just in case you talk to me and I don't answer."

She propped herself up on an elbow. Moonlight from the open cabin hatch cast light upon her nakedness, as she moved on top of him and kissed him. Resting her head against his, she said, "I guess you're a hero?"

He suddenly rolled on his side, and she toppled off. "No, Amber, the guys that died that day are the heroes. I'm the one that probably made an error in judgment about the mission, and I got them killed and the rest of us wounded."

"I'm sorry. I didn't mean . . . "

He put his fingers on her lips. "We have better things to talk about."

"I think you're still a hero, Drew." Amber moved to him and started kissing him, down his chest, kissing scars as she went.

***

"What a gorgeous morning," Amber said, stretching and reaching for the sky as she stood in the cockpit, wearing only a sleeping tee shirt. "I'm starving! Do you think we could get some bacon and eggs? I'd love bacon this morning."

"That does sound good," Drew said with a smile. "Let's sneak off the boat before Roberta and Alex wake up. I think there's a café open a couple blocks over on Main Street." He looked at his watch. "It's 6:30. I know they won't be getting up early, so let's go."

"I can't listen anymore to their primal sounds." Amber stood on her toes and kissed him. "We're much quieter." She smiled. "Let's go. I'll get my shoes and slip into a clean shirt and shorts and be ready."

Minutes later they were walking to the café, hand in hand. They were waiting by the door when it opened at seven.

"Take your pick," said a man with a nametag reading Jerry. "You're our first customers. Want coffee?"

"Yes, please," Amber said. She watched Jerry do an about face, and head for the coffee pot dripping rich, brown liquid, the first pot of the day. He was rail thin, with a spotless white apron tied in front, to protect starched blue jeans. He wore a plain white tee shirt, and a red farmer's bandana tied into a do rag.

They watched him come back with their coffee. "Here you go, hot and black," he said, placing two steamy cups of coffee in front of them. "Now, what did you want?"

"Bacon, eggs over easy, and toast," said Drew. "We're sailors. We need to get an early start. Could you make two egg and bacon sandwiches to go in about a half an hour for the sleeping couple still back at the boat?"

"No problem. You look military. Early riser, right?"

"Yes, sir. Marine."

Jerry slapped his hand on his thigh and smiled. "I knew it! Me, too. Vietnam. Got me a Purple Heart, but nobody cared in that war," he said, shaking his head, side to side.

"Drew got the Purple Heart too in Afghanistan," Amber said excitedly.

"Quiet, Amber. We don't need to talk about that now. It's history."

"I'm sorry, Drew, I just thought . . . you two had something in common."

"We do, young lady," Jerry said. "It's called war. Until you've been in one, you realize you don't want to talk about it. Talking makes you remember friends that never made it home. I do, especially when I see our flag and what it cost to keep it flying."

Drew patted her back. "Don't worry about it. You meant

well. Let's drink this coffee and eat our grub when Jerry brings it, and then get back to the boat and wake the other two up. Times a'wasting."

* * *

"Hey, get out of bed, you two. We brought breakfast," Drew yelled as he pounded on the cabin roof, and then they stepped down into the main cabin.

"Alex? Roberta? Get up." No answer.

"Where are they?" Amber said.

"I bet they went and took a shower in the marina's clubhouse. Let's go take one, too."

After getting back, they found Alex and Roberta waiting in the cockpit, drinking coffee and talking.

"Thanks for the breakfast sandwiches," Alex said. "We saw you were gone someplace, so we went and got coffee." He smiled. "Let's get going. The wind is right for a trip up the shore to Frankfort. We can have a late lunch there, and then head back here or anchor in Lake Pentwater. Then it's a short sail back to Muskegon Sunday, drop off our crew, and head back to Milwaukee sailing through the night."

"Maybe we'll keep you for Sunday night, and you can leave in the morning?" Amber said, looking at Drew.

"That might work," Alex said. "We'll see what the weather looks like."

"Let's not think about that yet," Roberta said. "We have today and part of tomorrow, and I'm ready to play and sail. Let's get going."

The weather continued to be perfect, with *Passage Maker* making fast time on another broad reach. The prevailing wind made the sail comfortable, with minimal rocking. Both Amber and Roberta found places to lay out, Amber stretching out in the cockpit. Roberta, being more adventuresome, decided to lie out on the long section of the bow.

Alex was at the wheel, drinking coffee. Nothing like the slow pulsing of the bow on a reach. The boat rises and falls with the swells. "Not too big today with this wind. What do you think Drew, a foot and a half?"

Drew nodded, taking a drink of his bottle of water. "That seems about right. At this rate, we'll get to Frankfort about 11. Let's have a quick lunch, walk the harbor area for a while and head back. Whitehall or Pentwater would be a nice place to spend the night, but it's going to take us longer going back. No easy sail like now. We're going to have to tack out into the lake, and then tack back for a while."

"I was thinking about anchoring out tonight," Alex said.

"That would be great.

"Do you have any poles and fishing stuff? I think the girls would like to fish when we anchor."

"We can do that," Alex said. "Take over. I'll check the locker you're sitting on, and if the fishing stuff isn't there I'll go below and see where it is."

Drew slid next to the wheel and took control.

Alex lifted the wooden lid. Moved a few cushions and boat bumpers. "Ah, there they are, and a bunch of lures. We're in business." Looking forward, he saw Roberta lying on her back, the curve of the forward cabin top providing a nice backrest.

Looking closer, he noticed she had her top off, tanning. He went down below and got tanning lotion.

"Roberta looks like she might need help applying this lotion. I'll be back in a while."

Drew saw the smile on Alex's face, and then he looked closer at Roberta. Indeed, she was topless. He noticed the bikini tied to the fore stay. As Alex walked up, she turned slightly, revealing her full breasts.

This was what sailing was all about: wind, water, and a bare breasted crew. Now if only Drew could get Amber to do the same, that would be great but he wasn't about to push it. Besides, he had seen her body in the light of the full moon. He knew all her special places. At that moment, Amber turned her head toward him, opened her eyes and smiled.

"I love sailing. It's so relaxing after a long night." She rolled over onto her stomach, closed her eyes and went back to sleep.

Could she read his mind? He flipped on the autopilot, got up and went down below to get a cup of coffee from the thermos. Soon he was behind the wheel again, steering a course north.

Drew's mind went back to this morning's meeting in the café with the Vietnam vet. Jerry was right, he thought. Not a day goes by without thinking about the guys Drew lost on that last mission. Was he trying to escape that day by sailing? It was supposed to be a simple village meeting that day, but things went terribly wrong, and it changed his life forever.

Chapter Seventeen

Drew needed this sail to try and help him forget Afghanistan, but some things he'd never forget. The look Connie, his best friend's wife, gave him when he went to visit her after getting out of the hospital. That look said it all, but didn't stop her from saying, "How could you let this happen to my husband, my boy's father and your best friend? I thought you were going to protect him and now he's dead. Now I'm alone, and I have to raise them all by myself." When Connie slapped Drew, it felt like someone had put a hot branding iron to his cheek. Then she slammed the door in his face.

He thought about the teary-eyed look she gave him every day, and the nightmares he'd had just about every night, trying to change the outcome. He'd wake up and eventually fall back to sleep, and then the whole thing would start over again, with the shooting and dying. The same results every night. Insanity, he thought.

"Drew, what are you thinking about so hard?" Amber asked, looking up at Drew steering the boat.

"Nothing. Just something that happened in the past. Did you have a nice sleep?"

"Yes, this being crew is hard work." She smiled. "Can I sail?"

"Sure, sit where I am and I'll show you the finer points of sailing, and how to steer."

"Oh. I'm excited."

Ten minutes later, Amber was steering a straight course. "You're a natural, Amber. I'll be right back."

He went down below and got them two Heinekens. Handing one to Amber, Drew said, "So tell me about yourself. I don't know too much about you except I like being with you."

"I'm glad." Amber opened the cold beer. "I don't let too many people get close to me."

He took a sip of his Heineken. "Why? Maybe I can help. Is it something you want to tell me?"

She let out a deep sigh, saying nothing for a while. She drank several swallows of beer, then looked at the shore off the starboard side. Her eyes moistened.

"The night of my high school graduation, a bunch of us got some beer and went to a beach to party on the dunes. I drank too much I guess. I must have passed out, or nearly passed out because sometime late that night, I was gang raped—fucked, whatever you want to call it—by my so-called friends behind a dune. One of my girlfriends found me curled up, my jeans in a crumpled heap, bra off, shirt ripped and laying on an old ratty blanket someone brought."

Drew let her talk.

She looked at him with tears on her cheeks. "My friends had disappeared. I don't know if it was guys from our group, or a bunch of guys from another party that took advantage of me when I must have gone behind the dune to take a pee or a walk on a warm graduation night."

"Did you file charges?"

"No. I was too embarrassed. Besides, I didn't know who

did it. I was so drunk that night. It's haunted me ever since. I don't let too many people get close to me unless I really trust them. For some reason, I trust you Drew." She leaned over and squeezed his leg. "I hope I'm right."

"Thank you, Amber, but I'm not perfect." He tilted his beer back and took several swallows. "I have issues myself that I'm trying to work out. I guess I need to tell you this before you find out from someone else. Let me start by saying I did not do anything."

"You didn't do anything? Anything what?" She said, now looking confused, and a bit scared.

"A person I met at a bar in June in Milwaukee was found dead, floating in Lake Michigan, and at first the police thought I did it. I was thought to be one the last person to be seen with her, and I became a suspect. I was later cleared.

"Then about ten days ago, a woman I met in Chicago, came up to Milwaukee to visit me for the night. The day after she left, she was found dead, murdered. I have witnesses proving I had nothing to do with her murder. The police think maybe it was a robbery, or drug related. I liked her. I did not kill her."

Amber's eyes got big. She moved a short distance away from the wheel and him. Her eyes remained focused on his.

She took a deep breath and then exhaled. "That's not what I expected to hear when you said you had something to tell me. I appreciate you telling me face to face. I'd hate to find out from the paper or the Internet." She tilted back the beer and drank it all. Then she just gave him a questioning look.

"I needed this trip," he said, "and another big trip this fall on my own boat to try and forget about all this and the other things that have happened in my life."

He laughed without humor, but Amber didn't even crack a smile. She just kept staring. Then after a few seconds, she moved closer to the boat's wheel and him.

"Let me think about all this new stuff," she said. "I appreciate you being honest and telling me. That says something about your character. I can see Alex is comfortable with you. I just need time to process this. I'm not a trusting person after what happened to me. I can't make another mistake like that. It's taken me years to get to where I am now and an almost normal life."

"I get it. I'll give you space, Amber." Drew shook his beer can. "Would you like another?"

"Under the circumstances, yes, I think I could use another." And then she finally laughed. "Maybe two, now that I think about it. Can you get arrested for being drunk and driving a boat out here?"

"Sure can, but we're far enough out and no one is around so I think you're safe. I'll get the beers."

Amber sighed. It had been a couple hours and a total of three beers later. Now slightly tipsy, Amber leaned against Drew, his arm around her holding her close.

"I believe you didn't kill those women. But if you didn't, who did?"

"No one knows. It makes me sad, and I want to be happy so let's not go there."

"Oh, I can make you happy." Amber's hand slid inside his swimsuit, and she giggled.

"Amber, not right now?"

"Oh, I understand. Can I take another nap? The beer made me tired."

"Sure." Seems like everyone is napping or taking a break, he thought, as he looked forward and saw bare breasted Roberta resting on Alex's chest. Drew leaned back, flipped on the autopilot. Feeling the warm July sun and breeze engulf him, he closed his eyes.

He opened his eyes when he heard the steady drone of a powerboat off his port side. He looked forward and saw Alex was handing Roberta her top. He only hoped Alex put tanning lotion on Roberta or the moans tonight would not be about pleasure.

Amber opened her eyes and smiled at him. "Do you have any water?"

"No, try the cooler down below. I think there are bottles there. Bring me one too if you would."

Soon she was back with four bottles. "I figured Alex and Roberta might be thirsty too. Is that the lighthouse for Frankfort?"

"I sure hope so or we sailed by when we were all dozing." He grabbed the binoculars out of their case and looked. "Yeah, it's Frankfort."

Drew flipped off the autopilot and angled toward the canal opening as Alex stepped into the cockpit, and then reached over to loosen the jib sheet and started rolling in the headsail. "Do you want to start the diesel? I'll drop the main and tie it down. Roberta, come up here and help. I'll show you what an actual crew member does."

"Good, I want to be useful so you'll take me along again."

"Don't worry about that."

***

After tying up, they consulted the Internet for places to eat and decided on trying Dinghy's Restaurant and Bar. They just wanted bar food, and that's what Dinghy's advertised. After their meal, they walked the streets for an hour before heading back to the boat.

"My bacon mac and cheese was the best," Amber said.

"The BLT was great too," said Roberta.

"Drew's and my cheeseburgers were good too," said Alex. "Simple, but good. I'd come back again. Let's get going."

"We might want to get more beer. Amber and I had a few while you were tanning and napping," Drew said to Alex.

"Fine, there's a place to get beer next to the marina. You get the beer and ice with the girls while I top off the diesel. You never know if we'll need to motor. I don't like the tank to get too low. Besides, we tied up at their dock for a few hours and they were nice to us."

"Let's go and get that ice and beer, girls."

Ten minutes later, they were back.

"We got more wine too," Roberta said.

Alex was sitting on a cushion having a bottle of water. "I think we'll sail out into the lake, and then tack down farther south. We'll see how things go."

They sailed out about ten miles before tacking south, close hauled, bringing the sails in tight, about 40 degrees off the wind and heading for White Lake, and its small town, arriving around sunset.

The boat heeled over, occasionally taking spray over the bow as the waves collided against its wooden hull. It was a faster point of sailing, and exhilarating. The women let out screams of delight as the lake's cold spray arched back occasionally drenching them. Everyone was excited by the change in speed and the boat's angle of heel.

Amber and Roberta decided sitting on the high side of the cockpit made sense and while Drew preferred the comfort of the lower side. He relaxed and stretched out as the warm July wind funneled back from the sails.

They saw the Ludington lighthouse pass astern. White Lake lay a few hours in the distance. Projected arrival time, according to Captain Alex, was just after sunset.

As 9:30 came, *Passage Maker* lined up with the entrance lights. They turned on the motor, after dropping sails, and motored into White Lake. Finding twelve feet of depth, Drew handled the anchor and pulled out eighty feet of anchor line. In the back of the boat, Alex turned off the engine, and heard the women down below getting *hors d'ouevres* and drinks ready.

"I'm starved!" Roberta said, munching a celery stick with cheese spread.

"Me too," Amber chimed in. "How about white wine for White Lake drinks tonight? I see there are a few bottles of white here but no red wine."

"I don't keep red wine on my boat," said Alex. "Red wine

stains the teak if it spills, and if you sail enough sooner or later you'll spill it. White wine doesn't show. In case you haven't noticed, I have lots of teak and wood on this boat besides white sails and light-colored cushions above and below deck."

Both women said "Oh" at the same time.

"We cut some cheese, sausage and veggies with some dip," said Roberta. "Do we still have time to fish?"

"I think it might be late if you want to eat soon. I'll get the grill ready and we can cook some ribeyes I have in the cooler and make a garden salad. I think I have corn in a can somewhere down there."

"That sounds good. The fish can wait until next time." Roberta said, then added, "I hope there is a next time."

"There will be when I come back," Alex said. He looked at Drew.

"Amber's the one that has to decide if there's a next time for her," he said.

All heads turned toward Amber.

"I'm thinking about it," she said with a forced smile. Looking at Drew, she added, "We'll talk more about it tonight.

"That's fine," he said. "I'll have wine if you don't mind."

Alex and Roberta looked at each other with questioning glances, unclear about the turn in the conversation. Then Alex said, "We'll have some white wine too, in honor of White Lake."

Dinner turned out just fine. With three bottles of wine consumed, the mood lightened.

The four called it a night around 1 a.m.

"See you guys tomorrow morning," said Alex.

"Yeah, morning." Roberta said and giggled.

Alex and Roberta headed for their cabin. Drew stretched his arms and made a groan. "I guess we can head below too, if you want?"

Amber turned away from him, toward the many lights gracing the lakeshore.

"It's beautiful here. Yesterday and today on the boat were really special for me. Being with you, Drew, made them more special." She looked over at him. "I know you have demons in you you're trying to get rid of from your past."

He moved closer. "You're right. I do have demons. Demons about Dad, about a girl named Clair from a long time ago, and Afghanistan. That's the reasons I bought and fixed up *Courage*. I'm hoping to come to grips with them and put them astern. The hardest one that I can't seem to shake is the loss of my best friend, and some other team members that relied on me to get them home. I still have nightmares, seeing my best friend getting shot, dying in my arms, me holding him and knowing there was nothing I could do to save him. I let them all down. I let their families down. Somehow I made it back home alive, and the guilt of that is killing me. Meeting people like you and Alex help. Meeting Jerry today makes me realize I'm not alone." Drew's arm made a sweeping gesture towards the sky. "I just hope I can find peace in all this."

"You will." Amber leaned over and kissed him gently on the lips, wrapping her arms around Drew and holding him close. "I know you will. I want to help. I want to see you again, Drew. I don't want this to be the only time, but if it is . . ." She stood up and pulled her shirt over her head, untied her bikini top, dropping it to the deck. She slipped out of her shorts and bottoms. "I want you to make love to me Drew, tonight, out here, with the stars and lights. I want this night to be special."

He got up and kissed her, pulling her close, as he continued to kiss her body. He slowly moved on top of her, his manhood poised over her hips.

Later, lying entwined, he kissed her, tasting salty tears on her cheek, feeling her hands caressing his back. He rolled on his side, looked at the sky and smiled. "Thank you, Amber. Maybe tonight is the start of getting back to normal. I hope so. I guess I needed to talk about Afghanistan and my demons. You helped."

"You helped me this morning, talking about my graduation night. It felt good to get it out there."

They held each other. Later that night they moved down below to their bunk and made love again before falling asleep.

Chapter Eighteen

Morning arrived with humidity and a light haze. Alex and Drew were up early, letting Roberta and Amber sleep in. Alex made coffee while Drew stowed loose items from last evening.

As the coffee perked, Drew asked, "What did you decide about going back to Milwaukee? Are we going to stay the night in Muskegon or leave and start sailing across tonight?"

"As much as I hate to leave our crew, I think we need to get back. I have meetings on Wednesday, and I need time to prepare. We should get back to Muskegon no later than noon. We can have lunch, then take off. It will be ten or twelve hours to get back, so we'd be back around midnight or two in the morning. Enough time for me to get some sleep and prepare for the Wednesday meetings."

Drew poured the coffee in a thermos and two cups for him and Alex.

"I understand. I just want to be prepared for Amber's disappointment. I think she was hoping to have another night together. I guess I'll just have to sail over another time on my own now that *Courage* is almost ready."

Alex said, "Let's hoist up the anchor and get going. I'll start the engine and you man the windless and raise the anchor."

Ten minutes later, *Passage Maker* was motoring out the

channel from White Lake to Lake Michigan, where they would turn south for a short morning sail to Muskegon.

There was a light breeze from the west. Alex set *Passage Maker* on a beam reach, with a full main and headsail up. Even with everything up, it was going to be late afternoon, Drew realized, before they reached Muskegon, not that he was in much of a hurry.

Soon Amber was up in the cockpit, coffee in hand just like a veteran sailor.

"Good morning," she said, sleepy eyed. "I'm going to miss the beautiful view when I get up tomorrow, but not the kink in my back. That bunk is not the most comfortable." She rubbed her back, then smiled at Drew. "And I will miss the special person that sleeps next to me and keeps me warm."

"You took the words out of my mouth," Drew said, leaning over, kissing her.

"Did you hear Roberta rustling up forward yet?" Alex asked.

"Not a sound," said Amber. "That's unusual. You must have really tired her out last night."

Alex smiled. "No comment. Maybe I should go down and see what she's doing. Can you take over, Drew?"

"Sure. See you in an hour?" Drew answered with a grin.

"No, I really am going to see if she's awake. Back in five minutes."

Amber was watching the shore slowly pass and sighed. "I suppose you guys are going to drop us off and head back."

"Something like that. I think we are planning on having lunch with you at Dockers and then head home. Alex has to get back for a meeting." When she didn't say anything, he continued. "This was an impromptu sailing trip. I'd say it worked out well, don't you?"

He watched her slowly turn and smile. "Yes, it worked out great. Will I ever see you again?"

"Yes. I can promise you that. I'll come over on my boat next time. You gave me your cell number and I'll call. Maybe I can come over next week. Would that be soon enough?"

She jumped up and sat in his lap, wrapped her arms around him, and kissed him.

"Yes. That would be great, just the two of us. It will give me something to think about all week and give my back a chance to recover too." She kissed him again.

Just then, Alex came on deck. "Hey, I don't mean to disturb you two. I can go down below if you need more time alone. Don't forget to put the autopilot on if you do anything where you have to take your hands off the wheel."

"No, I just told Amber I was going to come back soon on my boat, and she was just showing me her appreciation. How's Roberta?"

"She's on her way up. She had 'to get her face on to meet the new day,' she said. Glad I'm a man and can get by with the bad boy whisker look." He rubbed his hand over his cheek and chin.

"Right," Amber said. "Bad boys." She smiled as she reached over and rubbed Drew's chin.

***

Alex was stretched out with the autopilot sailing the boat. He took a drink of his rum and Coke. He was thinking about the past few days with Drew and Roberta. It was late Sunday afternoon and *Passage Maker*, twenty miles out from Muskegon, was heeled over, close hauled sailing at seven knots towards Milwaukee. He looked over at Drew, lying on his side, arm over his head, catching a few winks on the low side of the cockpit.

He wished he were retired too. He usually called his managers each day, to keep in touch with them when he traveled or did an occasional sail, like he had been doing these past days. He also connected with his office and his secretary, Jessie, to make sure he was on top of everything but this trip he'd considered a mini vacation and he hadn't done anything but enjoy sailing and the company. His dad first, and then he himself, had assembled a management team to run the many businesses and divisions of West Industries, but he was still responsible for keeping everything going smoothly.

If he just sold the company, he could sail whenever he wanted to, and not worry about anything but where the wind was going to take him and maybe the next woman in port. Then he thought of Tara. He had not been his usual self, cavorting with Roberta. He felt guilty about his actions this weekend now as he headed back, but he had really been pissed at Tara when leaving. Roberta was so much fun. He'd screwed up. He shouldn't have done what he did. He just should have gone sailing with Drew as originally planned. The open water, sailing back to Milwaukee, brought everything back into perspective.

He really enjoyed Roberta's company, but he realized she was not the type of person he pictured himself ending up with.

Tara reminded him of his mom in so many ways, and he missed his mom. He had always known he was her favorite. Her untimely death by suicide and the messy shooting of the chauffeur still upset him. He and his brother had known she cheated on their dad, but he was gone so much, and she liked attention, so when he was gone . . . Alex got why she did it, not that he liked when she did it.

Tara wouldn't do that to him if they ended up together. He was surprised at how comfortable she was at the social events they had attended. That was important to him. He liked being involved in Milwaukee's fundraising and social events. Being a former Milwaukee Man of the Year had its perks and obligations. Tara fit right in, charming those she met, not only with her good looks, but also taking an interest in others. She asked people she met a lot of questions about themselves, and then actually listened to their answers. It must be the detective in her, he thought. She knew people loved talking about themselves.

Besides all of that, she was honest, smart, beautiful and very sexy. He was looking forward to running his hands over her body. Maybe tomorrow evening after he rested from the sailing trip and was done preparing for his meeting the next day.

Yeah, Tuesday night, tomorrow. He could invite her to his home for a grilled dinner and wine. There would be no distractions, just them, a meal, and then to bed. He'd have to call his cleaning lady this afternoon to come over today or tomorrow morning to tidy up the house. Make sure there were none of those dust bunnies that seem to show up in plain view. It never bothered him, but they put off some women. He didn't want that to mess up her impression when she stayed over for the first time at his house.

Yes, Tara, I'm coming home for you, I hope you're ready for me.

Late Thursday afternoon, George was walking along Bradford Beach when he saw a golden retriever playing in the lake. He watched as it jumped in and out of the waves, biting at the curling waves. Then the golden retriever saw a piece of driftwood floating in the surf. The dog leaped and clamped his mouth down on it with strong jaws, slowly dragging it to shore, shaking his head the whole time until he dropped the branch on the beach.

That's when George noticed something red around the dog's neck. He walked closer, and saw a short red leash attached to his collar. He didn't see anyone nearby. Is the dog by itself? Maybe it's lost, or just ran away from its owner. George had loved his golden, Buddy, his one and only true friend growing up.

After a while, he walked over and approached the dog. He knew how much his dog, Buddy, liked to retrieve sticks, and how much he missed throwing a stick to a dog. He didn't see anyone around or whistling for the dog. Was it a runaway?

"Here boy, bring me the stick." The dog lowered its stance and shook the stick in his clenched jaws. His eyes said, "Play with me."

He bent over and grabbed the end of the stick and at the

same time grabbed the red leash. "Drop!" he commanded, and he did. "Good boy." He checked for a name on the collar but there was none. Then he unsnapped the leash. The dog sat down and waited. "You've done this before, haven't you?"

He grabbed the stick, leaned back and flung it as far as he could. The dog's eyes never left the stick, and when it splashed, the dog took off after it. He leaped and surged towards the stick. He could tell the dog was a powerful swimmer by the waves streaming back as he surged through the water. He came back and dropped the stick on the beach, waited.

"Good boy. You want me to do it again?" So he did.

Five minutes later, he heard a voice behind him. "There you are!" an angry female voice said. She walked up next to George.

"I've been looking for over an hour for this damn dog, and now I'm late getting home. I should have known he'd be here at the beach. He saw another dog and broke away from me, then he was gone."

"Nice dog. I had a golden once. I miss him more than anything."

"Well, this one is a pain in the ass. I'm sick of the wet fur and dog smell. It belonged to a friend of mine, but he turned out to be allergic to it and asked if I would take care of it. It's too much work. I'm going to give it to the Humane Society today. I don't have time for a dog."

"Well, I'd take him if you're going to do that. I'd love to have a golden retriever again."

"Deal." She reached into her purse and wrote down her address. "Why don't you stop by this afternoon? You can pick up the dog and all his stuff. I'll be glad to get rid of him." She reached for the leash. "Now if you'll help me get him, I can get home."

Moments later, he watched her walk away with the dog and smiled. *I'm getting a golden.*

George watched as the woman whipped the dog with the end of the leash on the top of his head, between the ears. Then, for good measure, she gave him a kick.

George felt the rage build in him, a rage to hurt. He looked at the card with her address. "I'll see you this afternoon," he whispered, "and we'll see how you like to be kicked and hurt."

Chapter Nineteen

Drew was just about to leave the Tiki Hut when George plopped down on the barstool next to him. At his feet was a golden retriever.

"Nice dog. Is he yours?" Drew asked as the dog looked up at him with its soft brown eyes and tail wagging. Drew reached over and scratched the dog's soft fur behind his ears.

"Yeah, I got him from someone that didn't want to take care of a dog anymore. I got there just in time. Seems after I picked up Buddy, his owner fell down her basement steps, broke her neck and died. I was shocked when I read it on the internet."

George scratched Buddy's neck. "Lucky for me I got him before all that happened, or I might never have this dog. I named him after the dog I had as a kid."

Drew watched as Buddy looked up at George like he knew he was talking about him and licked his dangling finger as if to say he understood.

"Drew, I hear you and my brother had a good time sailing last week. He said you met a couple of nice women."

Drew smiled. "That's right, Roberta and Amber. They definitely made the trip more fun. They got to be good sailors too. Roberta and Alex had a nice time together. I guess she doesn't get away too much because of her little boy."

"She has a son? Is she married?"

"Divorced. Her friend Amber says she's a good mom. Doesn't leave her son with just anyone, but family or Amber. It was a real treat for her to be with your brother on his boat for a couple of days. She even cried when we left on Sunday. I bet she'd love *Condor*."

"Alex said Roberta hangs out at a restaurant just across from the Marina in Muskegon. I'm thinking of taking *Condor* over there. Want to come along?"

"I'd love to, but I think I'm going to take *Courage* over for a shakedown cruise. It's August 1 and I only have a month to get everything ready for my big trip out through the Great Lakes and down the eastern part of the United States. I promised Amber I'd hook up with her if I were coming over and I'd like to do some more sailing with her. I'm sure we could hang out together on your boat in port for a while, or you can easily meet up with us wherever we are. *Condor* is so fast. You just have to point and move the throttles. Easy."

"Yeah, that's why I like motors," George said. "Just let me know when you leave and I'll call and reserve a slip, but let's try Muskegon first. I want to meet Roberta."

Drew watched George and Buddy head back to *Condor*, and decided he needed to do the same thing to get ready for his trip. He needed to get supplies, do the laundry and get *Courage* ready for the trip. He also needed to call Amber to see if she still wanted to see him and go sailing. He hoped so.

***

George was down in the engine compartment checking everything for the trip to Michigan, when he saw the black trash bag hiding behind his port engine. He looked at the pile of clothing jammed inside the bag—Cate Sullivan's clothes? *Shit*, he forgot to get rid of them. How stupid was that? Lucky for him Tara didn't see it on the boat tour he gave her.

His image of her sister was fuzzy with all the drinks they had that night, plus being up until the wee hours of the morning. Then he'd had to motor out in the lake and dump her body.

He was surprised at how easily she was lured to his boat and bed. Too bad it had ended the way it had.

What was it she'd said? He looked at her clothes in the trash bag. He picked out her silk blouse and brought it to his face. It smelled like diesel oil. Not the nice scent he smelled on her and in the morning.

He'd kept her jewelry, placing it in a separate purple *Crown Royal* cloth bag like a pirate might have used to hold his booty.

* * *

"Amber, it's Drew Thompson. Are you busy?"

"I'm free now. I'm in between massages. I was wondering if you were going to call."

"I'm going to bring my boat over, and hoped you'd be free. We talked about sailing on my boat, remember?"

"Yes, I remember. I'm glad we're not one and done. When are you coming?"

"I'll leave around 3 a.m. Thursday morning, and should

arrive late Thursday evening or Friday morning, depending on weather. Can you make time for me and sailing this weekend?"

"Of course, I can. I can hardly wait. Is Alex coming?"

"No, but his twin brother, George is coming with his big motor yacht. Wait till you see his boat. It's huge. I think he's going to call Roberta. Alex talked to him about her, and he wants to meet her."

"I know what else he wants. I'll call and warn her. It might be hard for her to get away after last weekend. Remember she has a little boy."

"Yes, I remember, and I also told him about her having a son. Just letting you know so you can tell her."

"Sounds good."

Drew turned his cell phone off. Amber made him feel comfortable, and she enjoyed sailing, which was an added bonus. It was fun to watch people embrace the wind, and water, and feel life slow down.

Enough daydreaming, he thought. He had things to do if he was going to take off in a couple of days, like pumping out the holding tank and topping off the diesel. Not that he would use the engine much unless the wind died, but it did happen, even in August. He could do that stuff tomorrow, but he needed to tweak the boat's rigging and add new lines. He decided to really clean the inside of the boat. Then he'd make a list for essential food items he needed like coffee, and a new bottle of Mount Gay Rum, and some more Johnny Walker Black Scotch. A few cigars to keep the bugs away would be good. Did Amber mind cigar smoke? Maybe she'd even like to smoke one with him. Right now, he should clean while he was in the mood.

***

The next day he motored over to MYC and saw Alex walking to *Passage Maker*. Drew called out his name.

Alex looked up, then motioned for him to come over.

Drew nodded. "I'm almost done getting diesel and pumping out the waste holding tank. I'll stop over when I'm done."

Walking down the dock, Drew spotted Tara Sullivan sitting in the stern on the boat's white cushions next to the boat's steering wheel.

"Hi, Tara. Are you going sailing?"

Behind him, he heard Alex's voice. "She's getting to be a good crew member. Not as good as you, but she's prettier, especially in a swimming suit."

Drew saw her smile, and blush at Alex's comment.

"No contest about looks," he said. "Tara, may I ask you a police question?"

He watched as her smile disappeared. "It all depends. I can't divulge confidential info, you know."

"I was just wondering how the two cases are coming, your sister's, and my friend's, Stella Carpenter?"

"The information I'm going to tell you was in the paper and Internet so it's nothing you couldn't read," said Tara. "We have one pretty serious suspect, a real sicko according to O'Malley. Cate pissed him off pretty good that night, so we think he might have been getting revenge."

"Is that Jasper Ream?"

"I can't say, but we think the suspect could have waited for Cate and killed her."

As creepy as Ream was, Drew wasn't convinced. "Like I told O'Malley and Pinkowski, he wasn't the man I saw her with when I left her that night. But I guess he could have waited until she left Riptide, if she left alone."

"Enough police stuff," Alex said. "I want to go sailing. Drew, would you like to join us?"

"Sounds like fun," said Drew. "I'll meet you in about ten minutes. Just need to put some stuff away. Are you all right with that, Tara?"

"I don't think it breaks any rules."

Drew could tell by the look she gave Alex that she wasn't happy with the invitation. He thought she just wanted to spend time with him, but Drew wanted to change the hard feelings she had for him.

It was warm on the water, even with the wind, but then it was August. Having spent days on *Passage Maker*, Drew knew the procedure on raising the main and getting the head sail set. As he moved up to the mast, he turned toward her.

"Tara, would you like to help me raise the sail?"

It would be nice to break the tension between them. He wanted to get her to no longer think of him as a suspect in her sister's murder. He wanted to be her friend.

She wasn't interested. "No, that's alright. I'm in charge of getting drinks and keeping Captain Alex company." She smiled and looked at Alex.

She was still unsure of Drew, and he guessed she was more entwined with Alex since the last time he saw them. He wasn't about to tell her about Roberta.

He shook his head as he looked at Alex. After several days sailing with him, Drew surmised Alex had a knack of going with the flow, and that included finding beautiful women who looked the other way, maybe knowing they're not the only one but still wanting his company and all the things he represented. Was that the case with Tara right now?

Drew was kind of surprised she was so taken by material things. And she must guess that he and Alex had not been monks on the sailing jaunt. She's a detective, after all.

"Tara, I think Alex has some Scotch down there. I think I'm in the mood for something a little stronger. Would you give me a couple of fingers full, on the rocks if you could? Thanks."

Alex looked at him surprised. "Are you all right?"

"Yeah, I just thought I'd try something stronger. Is that all right?"

"Sure, Tara, the Glenlivet is behind the brandy bottle next to the wine rack. Let me know if you can't find it, and I'll get it."

Drew heard the cupboard open and then close. "I got it." She stepped up into the cockpit and handed Drew his Scotch.

"Thanks." A minute later, she stepped up with two more drinks, and sat down on the cushion.

"Here." She passed a drink to Alex. "I made your usual vodka and tonic. I'm having a large glass of white to celebrate you gentlemen having a good time last week." She took a large gulp, then glanced first at Alex, then Drew.

"So, Drew, tell me about your trip last week. I didn't get much out of Alex. Where did you guys go again?"

Before he could answer, Alex cut in. "I told you when I got back. I guess you were so happy to see me you forgot."

"I guess I was happy to see you but that's past now. Now that I have more time, and we're out here sailing, I'd like to hear more about the trip. Did you go to any fancy restaurants, or meet any interesting people?"

Drew looked at Alex, then at Tara. Oh boy, here we go.

"We went to Muskegon, Ludington, Frankfort, White Lake and then back to Muskegon. We fueled up, and then took off, back to Milwaukee." Alex said.

Drew tried to run interference. "Actually, I met a really nice woman named Amber while we were sailing. We got along well, and I made a date to go back to Muskegon and take her sailing this coming weekend." He turned toward Alex. "Your brother George was so interested in the area and the sights I described that he's also going over on *Condor*. He plans on taking lots of pictures of the harbors and people there. We're going to meet up someplace."

Alex looked at Drew and smiled, but Tara didn't buy the lopsided story.

"It sounds like Drew met a woman over there, and enough happened that he's going to get together."

Drew saw her eyes zero in on Alex like she was looking down the barrel of her Glock.

"And Alex, you didn't have any company?"

Alex smiled. "Well, Amber did have a girlfriend, and she wanted to go along sailing with us, so we let her. There are a lot of places to sleep on this boat. It does sleep six."

"And where did Amber's friend sleep?

"We made a bed up where the cabin table is. It turns into a double bed when we lower the table and move the cushions on top. Very comfy."

"Oh, that seems like a shame when you have that big V-berth up front and you being all alone. It gets cold and lonely." Tara took a big cleansing breath and drank down her whole glass of wine in four large gulps.

"Drew, could you get me another glass of wine?"

"I'll get it," said Alex. "Drew, could you take over the helm?"

"Sure." He took the wheel. Alex got Tara's glass, went down below and returned with a wine glass filled to the brim.

"Here you go." Alex sat next to Tara, hesitating before draping his arm around her back and shoulders and giving her a squeeze. He leaned over and kissed her on the cheek.

She didn't acknowledge the kiss, but just sat there, back stiff, eyes straight ahead as if searching the horizon for a ship. Then she turned to him. "You're an asshole, Alex, to do what you did. It better not happen again, or you can find yourself another crew member."

"It won't," he said.

Drew watched Tara's eyes search Alex's face. She relented and kissed him.

He's a lucky asshole is what he is, Drew thought. Taking a sip of his scotch, he looked at the compass. He resisted watching Alex and Tara smooth over the indiscretion of last week, and continued to be a faithful, silent crewmember.

The next day, George took his newly renamed golden retriever Buddy for a long walk along Bradford Beach.

"Are you going to be a good boy while I'm gone?" He watched as the dog cocked his head. George thought of Bobby, the son of another boat owner on the dock, who was going to dogsit Buddy while George was cruising. "I'm going to miss you."

The dog's tail wagged, his soft brown eyes stared up at him with love as George reached into his jacket and gave him a treat. The golden took it softly from his hand. Then he bent down and gave Buddy a hug, patting the top of his head. "You love me, don't you, Buddy? I'm glad I got you away from that mean woman. She deserved what I gave her for being so rotten to you. She was like my mother, you know, and got what she deserved."

George walked back to the marina, stopping in front of Bobby's parents' boat. "Bobby, are you ready to take care of Buddy?"

"Yep. All set. My parents are waiting for me to call, and then they'll come and pick us up."

He handed Bobby the leash. "Here he is. I really appreciate this. He'll have a good time with your dog, I'm sure. Here's the money for taking care of him, and the address for the vet in case he gets sick. I'll be back in a couple of weeks. You have my cell phone, right?"

"Yes, Mr. West. Have a good time on your trip, and thanks for the money."

"Don't spend it all at once. Take good care of Buddy."

Ten minutes later, George was walking down the dock to *Condor*. Onboard, he checked the needles on the control panel. He waited to let the blower clear any vapor that might have accumulated, even though it was a diesel engine. Starting the two big diesels, he let the engines warm up as he prepared to shove off for Muskegon. His dad always did that procedure on *Condor* and George always followed what his dad did, even now. He missed his dad every day.

He stepped out, quickly pulling the last holding line onboard. Pressing the one shift lever forward and the other back, he moved the throttle levers slightly forward. The two engines rumbled, and George felt the vibration as the big boat moved off the dock. He wouldn't even need the bow thrusters, and he never touched the steering wheel.

He smiled. He loved the sound of power.

He turned *Condor* out toward the marina basin and Lake Michigan.

He liked doing everything himself. No crew was needed for this trip unless they were female, and he'd see about that later.

The Coast Guard's weather summary earlier that morning indicated the waves would be less than a foot and a half and the wind would help him going across. He figured it would take no more than seven hours to make the trip across, so he should arrive around five in the afternoon. Plenty of time to get situated in his slip and meet Drew, his friend Amber, and Roberta.

He laughed as he remembered his conversation with her. Roberta was so predictable. When he had phoned her earlier in the week, she seemed put off. Who was this guy calling her out of the blue, asking her to meet him Friday night? But after he explained that he was Alex's twin brother, and that Alex had mentioned to George that he should get in touch with her, Roberta seemed more receptive. She said she wasn't sure if she could get away for a whole weekend, like she did with Alex. She said she usually spent the weekend with her son Billy.

The clincher that sealed the deal was when George said, "Bring Billy along Saturday. He'll love the boat and I'll teach him photography." That's when George told her he was motoring over to take pictures of the Michigan shoreline and the locals.

"Really? You'd do that? Oh, Billy will be so excited, and so will I." There was a pause on the phone. "I'll get a babysitter for Friday night, so I can meet you first. And then the next day we'll go boating. Is that good with you?"

"Great. We can go from there."

George remembered loving it when his dad took him on sailing excursions on Chesapeake Bay. It will be fun having a kid around, maybe even more fun than sex. George could be nice if he wanted to.

Chapter Twenty

Drew was about four hours from Muskegon. He figured George was going to get there first. So far it had been a good sail. *Courage* had performed like the blue water sailboat it was reputed to be, and his new systems worked fine. His new GPS system told him his location within three feet and gave a speed and heading all in one glance. The autopilot system kept the boat on a straight course. Drew made heading corrections when the wind shifted.

He had placed most of the harbor's coordinates into the GPS so all he had to do was hit FIND on the autopilot screen for the intended harbor. It told him how far away he was and the heading he needed to take. He still used a paper chart, and made pencil markings of his location, in case the GPS conked out. Also, it gave him something to do on a long journey. It was peaceful sailing for the last few hours. The only thing he saw was water and a horizon line. Lake Michigan is one of the biggest freshwater lakes in the world.

When he was at the academy, Drew never got to be on a Navy ship. In the Marines, the closest he had gotten to a real ship was when they practiced amphibious landing. If he had signed up for the Navy, he might not have been shot, and would still be in the service. Maybe a Captain of his own ship by now. Most important, he wouldn't feel guilty about losing his buddies.

Pouring himself a cup of coffee from his thermos, Drew looked out at the blue water.

He smiled to himself, and then patted the teak cockpit railing. On second thought, I am the captain of my ship now. I guess I could have lost sailors on a ship I commanded through fighting or accident. Who knows?

He thought of his best friend, Tom Robb or as he called him, Gunny dying in his arms. Drew got angry at himself all over again, as he usually did, for not checking things out better than he did. He had relied on other people for the intelligence, but that was not the problem. The problem was Drew didn't verify the operation plan until it was too late. He would never have agreed to a daylight march to the village. That march had led to his injury and the other deaths.

He still was amazed he didn't get court marshalled for beating the shit out of the First Lieutenant who had given him the bad info and designed the operation. The guy had never been in combat. The fight happened later, after Drew had recovered, and he saw the guy in the Officer's Club. Drew probably would have killed him with his bare hands if others had not pulled him off the guy.

He hoped he could get over his mistake in judgment. Wasn't that why he was out here, sailing, trying to forget?

Amber might help, even though she had her own demons. She cried after they made love that first time. He was glad he had been gentle with her, not pushy, not worrying about his one-eyed monster, and getting his rocks off. He was amazed she had confided to him her dark secrets, but he knew how good it could feel to talk, to get the burden of guilt off one's chest. They were good for each other, even if this was a long way to go for a date.

***

George stood at the end of Muskegon Marina pier and watched as Drew turned *Courage* down the runway between pier C and B, and then turned again, finding his slip: number 13.

"Grab the bow line will you, and tie it off?" Drew called.

George leaned over and grabbed the line looped on the bow pulpit, as it slowly moved forward. He tied it off as he heard Drew reverse the engine, stopping its forward momentum.

The stern snuggled against the pier, Drew shifted the engine into neutral and then killed it. He stepped off the boat onto the floating dock and tied *Courage's* stern line to the dock. "Thanks for the help."

"I couldn't have done better myself," George said, smiling.

"Nice to know I'm in your league."

"You'd make a good crewmember on *Condor*. I guess you did graduate from the Academy after all," George said. "Stop over after you get settled, and we'll plan our strategy for tonight."

"Sounds good." Drew said.

***

Sitting on *Condor*, having his drink, Drew said, "After the cell service showed up on my phone, I talked to Amber. She said she was going to meet us at the restaurant with Roberta. Turns out Roberta's a little nervous about meeting you, sight unseen."

"What's to be nervous about? She met Alex, and I'm better looking and older."

"She told Amber she feels like a woman who gets calls and a bad reputation because someone put her name and phone number in the men's room with the message, 'For a good time call Roberta.' Anyhow, she said she would feel better if the four of us met at the same place we met when Alex was there."

"Well, my little brother did mention having sex with her, but he didn't go into great detail."

"I'm not sure you should play the sex thing with her," Drew said. "According to Amber, it was a fling with a handsome guy on a special boat. Roberta probably thought it was romantic, like in the movies. She felt safe too because Amber was along. She's an attractive woman, and a mom who had a chance to live out a fantasy weekend with your brother."

"I'll be a gentleman, I promise," George said. "How's that? Besides, I had a card up my sleeve. I invited her son to join us tomorrow. That was the deal closer." He sipped his drink. "I like kids. My dad took me boating, when he had a chance, and I loved it so why not give a little back? I could take pictures of her and her kid. I'll be nice. I promise."

"That's good because in the short time I've known Roberta, I care about her, and don't want to see her hurt and taken advantage of." Drew also knew Amber would never forgive him if that happened.

Earlier that day, Tara and Sabina sat in the police station

conference room across the table from O'Malley and Pinkowski. A file with the name CATE SULLIVAN was on the table in front of Tara. "What do you mean you *had* to turn Jasper Ream loose?" she asked.

"Without more evidence, the DA didn't think he could make a case. It was all circumstantial. Nothing to prove Cate was in his car, boat, or business. I'm sorry, Tara, but we had no choice. The spurned boyfriend, and angry wife of a client didn't turn out to be anything either. I did check on the child molester. He was in jail the night your sister was killed, so were out of suspects. We're back to square one."

"Someone who killed my sister is still out there. We're supposed to wait until he kills again and hope we can tie the two together?"

"We need a break," Pinkowski said. "Some hard evidence or a witness—something more than we have now, which is shit."

Tara glared at her fellow cops but said nothing. She promised her dad she was going to find the killer. She sure as hell wasn't going to let him down on this if it took her the rest of her life.

Tara would have to develop a better profile to narrow the search. Sabina could help. There were a lot of sick killers in Los Angeles, after all. Hopefully, the bad guy wasn't just passing through Milwaukee, and had stopped at Riptide on his way someplace else. Tara knew she'd have to do this work on her own time because she couldn't interfere in the official investigation. The captain would be all over her, and so would Sabina.

What she was going to do was a big no-no. But fuck them. Tara was going to find Cate's killer.

"Tara, hello. Earth to Tara, are you there?" Sabina asked.

"Yeah. Just thinking."

"We'll get him, Tara, don't you worry," O'Malley said. "I still think it's Thompson. He was associated with both dead women. That's too much of a coincidence, if you ask me."

Tara decided to go back to Riptide and question the people working the night Cate was killed. If it cost Tara her job, so be it. She'd tell the captain Sabina was not involved. She closed the file. Maybe she'd come back later and make copies of everything. She had been repeatedly told that cases were solved in the details: a missed clue, a description of someone that at first didn't seem important. She'd need to start at the beginning.

Chapter Twenty-One

After eating boiled shrimp and fries with cold beer, the four sat at an outside table at Dockers Bar. The sun was setting in an explosion of colors, but the group was oblivious to the sunset. The women were having a good time getting to know George.

Drew smiled as he watched George turn his charm on Roberta. Even Amber was impressed with him.

"I'm looking forward to having Billy on the boat tomorrow."

"He's so excited," said Roberta. "He's never been on a big boat. We're both looking forward to seeing it. When Billy did go on a boat, it was a small fishing boat, with one of his dad's buddies, usually on one of the small lakes around here. Never Lake Michigan."

"Good to know," George said. "We'll want to make sure he wears motion sickness wrist bands, so he doesn't get sick. I have some onboard. He just needs to wear them for a half an hour before we go out."

"OK." Roberta turned towards Drew. "Where are you and Amber going tomorrow? You aren't going to hang around here with us, are you? You said you were going sailing."

"That's right," Drew said. "I think we'll head up north again, or just see where the wind takes us." Drew looked at Amber, who smiled.

She leaned closer to Roberta. "Wherever we go is fine with me. Drew said he was going to teach me to sail and let me do real crew things so I can go with him on different parts of his journey later in the year. I'm excited."

"Sounds like fun," George said. "Drew, you have my cell phone number so if you find a nice place and anchor, call me and we'll cruise up if you aren't too far away." He looked at his watch. "Would you ladies like a tour of my boat? I have booze on board."

"Sure, let's go," said Roberta.

The group made the easy walk down the grassy dune to the marina.

"Just so you know, George, I can't stay too long," Roberta said. "Maybe long enough for one drink. Billy is with a friend, and I don't want to impose on her too much."

"No problem." George said. "Whenever you want to leave is fine. We have tomorrow."

They entered *Condor's* large cabin. Drew knew they would both be impressed. He was still impressed, though he had seen it before.

"My God," Roberta said. "I can't believe the room. It's much, much, bigger than Alex's boat."

"Thank you."

"It sure is," said Amber. "The salon is as big as my living room. I can hardly wait for the rest of the tour."

Drew saw George smile. "While you give them a tour, George, I'll be the bartender, and get out the drinks and chips for when you're done. Don't forget the darkroom. I think that's really neat for a boat."

"That's what I'm going to show them first, because I'm going to take lots of pictures tomorrow, and show Billy how to take pictures and develop them. I really don't use film too much anymore but once in a while I might take pictures with it for the fun of it. Black and white, usually."

Roberta beamed. "Maybe you can teach me too?"

"Why not? If you promise I can take pictures of you."

"Oh, sure."

"I have a bunch of suits you can try on that will make you even more special to the camera."

"Ooh," Amber said. "I can hardly wait to see those pictures. He'll make me look great like a fashion model?"

"That's what I do," said George. "Come on. Let's start the tour so we can have that drink before you leave."

He's got all the lines down pat, Drew thought. How can a woman resist getting her picture taken by a professional? When he's done with her, she'll never look so good again before a camera.

***

Drew sat and waited for the other three. He could hear them walking around down below, with the occasional "Wow" and "Look at the room." He'd heard it all before. He even said the same things when George gave him a tour the first time he was on *Condor*. Finally, he heard them come up from below.

"Pretty impressive, isn't it?" said Drew. "Amber, don't expect that much room on *Courage*, but it doesn't use as much fuel." They all laughed.

"That's for sure," George said. "There are drawbacks to a boat this size, but then I can live the way I want, and this is the way I want to live. Not in an old house, like my brother."

Drew was the first to bring up the idea of leaving. He reminded Amber they'd need to get back to *Courage* and pack if they were going to get an early start in the morning. He and Amber said their goodbyes to George and Roberta. Then Roberta gave George a quick kiss. "I'll be at the boat at 9 a.m. with Billy. I wish I could stay longer tonight, but I need to get back to him. See you tomorrow, George." She gave him a long kiss.

The three left George smiling as they walked to the cars at the restaurant parking lot. After saying goodbye to Roberta, Drew got in Amber's car, and they drove to the marina's lot to unload supplies. Drew carried Amber's overnight bag onto *Courage*.

After getting everything put away and giving Amber a much shorter tour of *Courage*, they sat in the cockpit and had another drink.

"I missed you this week," she said. "I thought I might be just a weekend fling, so your call surprised me. I'm glad."

"I wanted to spend more time with you. Besides, I needed a good excuse to get this boat ready for my big trip, which is coming up soon, just after Labor Day. I spend too much time alone on this boat so it's nice to have company."

He leaned over and kissed her. Amber moved close to him nestling her body next to his, resting her head on his chest. Talking of nothing in particular for the next hour, they finished their drinks and retired for the night to the boat's large V-birth. They made love, falling asleep in each other's arms.

***

At sunrise, Drew made coffee, putting much of it in a large thermos. After pouring himself a cup, he heard a cheerful "Good morning, Captain Drew. Your crew is ready for duty."

Amber made her way to the galley area and got herself a cup of java. "It's awfully hard to sleep when you smell coffee bubbling on the boat. What a great alarm clock. What time is it anyway?"

Drew looked at his watch. "6:31 a.m. We need to get going. If you're going to learn to do things a crew does, it's time to learn how to cast off and get sailing, so get your tennis shoes on and something warmer to wear."

"Yes, sir." She saluted and turned to get dressed. He laughed as she performed a sexy sashay back to the bunk and her duffle-bag. Amber slipped into a pair of jeans and a fleece pullover. When she returned, Drew pulled her close and kissed her.

"The captain approves of the crew's uniform for the day," he said, his hands lingering on the back of the tight jeans. They took a final sip of coffee and went topside, where he explained about the lines and how he wanted her to release the bow and spring lines. They went to the dock, untied it there, looped it around the cleat and then refastened it over the cleat so all Amber had to do was untie the line on the boat and pull the loose end on board. "If someone was on the dock helping," he said, "we wouldn't have to do that because they'd throw the line to you, but that isn't the case now."

He took care of the stern line. He showed her how to start the diesel, how the shift lever and throttle worked.

"Good, now let's back out of the slip. You go forward and release the lines on the bow, and spring lines and pull in the loose ends on board, like I showed you. Then place them in the lazaret. I'll do the same on the stern line. Let me know when you're done and I'll back out."

"Got it."

When she gave the signal, he untied his lines and backed *Courage* out of the slip, turned the wheel over hard, throttled up, and moved the sailboat towards the harbor and Lake Michigan.

"Nice job, Amber. Why don't you get the thermos, and add some coffee to our cups? Then we'll motor down the channel, past the lighthouse, and see where the wind is coming from. Once we get out into the lake, we'll motor into the wind, and I'll show you how to raise the main sail."

"Sounds like a plan. I really did fine on casting off?"

"You did great."

After Drew showed her how to raise the mainsail, he set the larger jib and headed north on a reach along the Michigan shore.

"We'll see how far the wind takes us. Do you want to steer?"

"In a little while. I just want to enjoy the morning before I do that. How about more coffee?"

They settled in. Drew sailing for a while, gradually moving farther offshore and then turning on the autopilot. "There, the boat's all yours to steer when you want. We'll just head up the coast for the next few hours."

***

George saw the SUV pull into the parking lot. A sandy-haired boy, wearing tennis shoes, a polo shirt, shorts and a Detroit Tigers baseball cap bounded out of the front seat and looked around. He could see him mouth the word "Wow!" and then turn to his mother.

Standing in the walkway of the boat, George waved. Roberta said something to her son, pointing at George. The boy reached into the backseat of the car and pulled out a small duffle bag before slamming the door shut and running around to take his mother's hand. The two made their way to his boat.

George stepped down the three steps to meet them.

"Is this your boat?" the boy asked.

"George, this is my son Billy. Billy, this is Mr. West."

"Nice to meet you, Billy. Yes, this is my boat. Do you like it?"

"It's as big as a house and it floats. Mom was telling me about it. She says it even has a darkroom because you take pictures, and you're going to teach me how to be a photographer. Is that right—you're going to teach me to take pictures?"

"Do you want to learn? Because if you'd rather do something else, we could do that instead."

"Yes, yes. I want to learn to be a photographer, but can I steer this boat too?"

George laughed. "Sure. You can do both. Now let's get

going because we have a lot to see and do. Give me your hand and I'll help you up this first step to the boat and then I'll show you the boat, and the darkroom. How's that?"

"That's great." Billy turned to Roberta. "I get to steer the boat too."

An hour later, George started the engines, but this time he was in luck: a couple of the nearby boaters at the marina helped untie the lines, and *Condor* slowly motored out from the dock and made its way out into Lake Michigan.

Once past the channel lighthouse, George turned the boat south towards Holland, Michigan. Once they'd get to Holland area, he'd motor down a channel from Lake Michigan into a large lake. The city of Holland was at the eastern most end. There were several spots to anchor or tie up in the lake. He was planning on anchoring for the afternoon. He looked over at Roberta and smiled. She was on her cell phone talking to her ex-husband, Joe, arranging Billy's pickup later tonight.

He heard her say, "What a wonderful opportunity this is for Billy. It's a once in a lifetime trip." She agreed he would pick up Billy at 6:30 p.m. "Wait until you see this boat," Roberta said. "You'll understand why it's a special treat for him to be doing this. You can have him an extra day another time, if you like. He's excited. Right now, he's steering the boat. George is taking a picture. Did I tell you George is a professional photographer? I'll make sure you get a copy of the pictures."

She gave George a thumb up sign.

George stood behind Billy, giving him encouragement. "You're doing a great job. The trick to steering is not to make quick movements with the wheel but to just make small adjustments and turns. The waves are trying to push the boat towards shore, so you turn the wheel just slightly to adjust for the wave action."

Grinning, George watched Billy. "Billy, you caught on quick. I couldn't have done it better myself."

"Really! Mom, did you hear that?"

"That's wonderful, honey."

George watched as Roberta smiled at him, beaming appreciation.

Turning back to Billy, George said, "When you get tired of steering, just let me know and we'll put on the autopilot. It will steer the boat all by itself. These wristbands are neat, aren't they?"

Billy nodded.

"You aren't sick to your stomach, are you?"

Billy shook his head no.

"Great. We have an hour and half before we get to Holland, and then I'll take over, but until then, you are doing a great job. When we get to Holland, I'll teach you how to take pictures."

Billy nodded but kept his eyes on the compass. George watched the wheel move in little back and forth movement. He turned to Roberta.

"You have a great kid. I don't know who's having more fun, him or me."

She leaned over and gave George a kiss on the cheek. "Thank you so much for doing this. I don't know how to thank you."

"Oh, I'm sure we'll figure something out. Maybe you can be a model for me later, after he's gone with his dad?"

She smiled. "I'd love to. I'll see exactly how good you are."

"As a photographer or as a something else?"

"Both, I hope. That bed I saw last night looked pretty big. I can hardly wait to take a nap . . . . . .with you."

Later that afternoon, Tara pulled up in front of Riptide in her car. It was her day off. She felt good about doing this on her own time. The employees at Riptide needed to be talked to again. Drew was over in Michigan with George, and who knows what women they would be involved with over there. She couldn't fault Drew because he was not going with anyone she knew about and she surmised the same with George. He probably had a woman in every port. Photography. What a perfect way to pick up women. He tried it even with me, she thought.

Just thinking about what had happened when Alex was in Michigan with Drew upset her. She was still pissed at Alex for cheating on her. Tara had thought he was a better man than that, but maybe all men were like that. In that regard, she lacked experience.

She grabbed the list of employees that worked that night—lifted from O'Malley's file—and headed into the bar. It was over a month since her sister's death, and Tara was worried that memories fade. Still, she'd search for any tiny detail that had been missed or overlooked.

Sitting at a small out of the way, table for two, in the dining room overlooking the Milwaukee River, Tara managed to interview numerous members of the staff who'd been working that Friday night, digging for anything to move her closer to finding her sister's killer.

Tara interviewed one of the waitresses at Riptide, assigned to the Tiki area the night of her sister's murder. She did not hear anything different than what O'Malley and Pinkowski had learned when they had questioned the same employees.

Colleen was the fifth person Tara spoke to that afternoon. The waitress was smaller than the others, slim like a runner, bleached blond hair with black roots starting to show. She had hazel eyes and a small mole near her mouth like Cindy Crawford. She wore dark blue Marquette running shorts and a white tee shirt with Miller Time stenciled across the front.

"The manager said you wanted to talk to me about some woman and some guy that were in here a month ago. I'm not sure I can help you. That's a while ago. Unless they're regulars, I'm not sure I remember them."

"I understand but I'd like you to look at this photo anyway." Tara pulled out a picture of her sister. Remembering Drew Thompson's description that Cate had looked like an attorney that night, Tara had brought the picture from her dad's desk at home. She handed it to Colleen.

"Who was in the bar that Friday night?" Tara asked. "It's very likely that someone Cate Sullivan met here murdered her. I'm trying to find who she might have left with that night. Do you recognize her?"

"It's been a long time, but yeah I do. She came in here often enough, sometimes dressed like this. She always tipped well, and I remember she had a fancy watch. I asked her what kind it was. She said some French or foreign name. It wasn't a Rolex; I see those all the time. It was real classy. Yeah, I remember her."

"We already know a couple of people who spoke with her that night." Tara first showed Colleen the picture of Drew. "This guy was with her earlier in the evening." Then she showed her the picture of Jasper Ream. "He was bugging her earlier too, and maybe later. Did any of these two men leave the bar with her?"

"I really don't keep a track of who hooks up and leaves with who. I just want to serve the food and drinks and get my tips. I'm working my way through Marquette. This is my last year, and then I can quit doing this shit."

"Good for you." Tara wiggled in her chair, moving closer to Colleen. "Now that you're remembering bits and pieces of that night, was another guy with her later? Good looking, tallish, broad shoulders. They probably talked for a long time and maybe had a lot to drink. Maybe sitting in the same spot."

"She was getting tipsy, I know that, because when she got up and went to the ladies' room, she banged into me and I dropped a whole tray of empty beer bottles. Luckily, we have enough sand like a real beach in that area, and none broke. It's a bitch to get broken glass out of the sand. We have to close down the area and sift the sand to get the pieces of glass out so no one cuts their feet. People like to walk around barefoot out there, you know. Anyway, when she came back, the guy said it was time to go. He gave me a big tip in cash for my troubles."

"Yes?"

Tara's heart raced with that answer. "You saw his face?"

"Not really that I remember. She was pretty drunk, hanging on him. One thing I remember about him. He had a funny gold earring in one ear, some type of big dog."

"A dog earring?"

"Yes, usually guys have a diamond or something like that, but I've never seen a dog earring. I don't know what kind of dog because I'm not into dogs. Cats, yes."

Tara got excited. "Really? Can you give me a description of the guy?"

"Well, he was good looking, like you said. Tall, brownish hair, blue eyes I think. Good build too. I can't remember what he wore. At the end, she was really drunk and hanging on him." She pointed to Drew's picture. "This guy came back later, looking for her. He came and asked me about her, but I said she was gone. Then before he could leave, he got into a fight with a guy after his girlfriend started hanging on him." She pointed to Drew's picture. "It didn't take him long to get rid of the boyfriend. The boyfriend came at him swearing and swinging. This guy punched him once and the dude was out. Then he left real fast with that guy's girl. Funny, don't you think?"

"Yeah, funny. If you remember anything else about them, the guy with this woman I showed you, give me a call." Tara handed Colleen her card. "Let me get your cell phone number just in case I need you to verify the earring. I'd like to get one of our police artists to sketch the man that left with her. It won't take too much time, but it would really help the investigation."

"Sure. I'm glad to help."

"Don't say anything else to any other detectives if you call.

Just ask for me. They get kind of testy if a woman shows them up, if you know what I mean."

"Do I ever. My boyfriend gets that way when I beat him in darts and bowling—testosterone or something, I guess."

Chapter Twenty-Two

When Tara got back to her car, she pumped her fist in the air. She had three solid new leads that the others had not come up with. First, there was the watch Colleen had spotted. Tara thought it was her mother's that Dad had probably given her. It would have been like her dad to give Cate something like that. Tara supposed it made more sense for Cate, an attorney, to wear the Piaget, rather than her, a cop. She'd have to ask her dad about it.

Then there was that distinctive dog earring. She'd have to track down jewelers who sold or made some custom ones for people who liked dogs.

She thought about the description of the new suspect. It was still too general.

She thought of Drew. Because of this new suspect, her attitude toward him changed.

George had given Billy a goodbye hug and patted the top of his head. He'd given Roberta's ex-husband Joe a copy of a photo of Billy at the wheel of *Condor.* Now George was waiting for Roberta to return from the marina's parking lot. It had been a lot more fun with Billy and Roberta then he had expected. He had taken several digital pictures of mother and son. He had even given Billy a small old Canon Power Shot digital camera that he never used anymore.

He made sure he put a new chip in the camera because he could not remember what he had on the old camera. It was safer, he thought, to put a new one in for Billy. George knew he had taken sexy pictures with that small camera that no youngster should see, and maybe if he really thought about it, most adults too. Anyway, he was safe giving Billy that camera with a clean chip. When the kid had realized it was for him, he had hopped up and down, holding it up close to his mother's face.

"Look, Mom! Look what George gave me," Billy said. "George, thank you again for all this stuff and teaching me to be a photographer. I love you, George." Then he turned to his mother and said, "Nobody but you ever given me anything so neat."

George had to bite his lip so he wouldn't get misty-eyed in front of them. No one had said "I love you" to George since his dad had died. Those three words meant everything to George.

Still waiting for Roberta to return, George went to the bar and poured himself a Scotch on the rocks, and then poured her a white wine. He was done with his drink and was just pouring a second when she came back, crying.

"Why are you crying?"

"My asshole ex-husband accused me of bringing Billy out here to you and your boat, to turn him against him, to make him insignificant in Billy's eyes versus you. Joe said, there is no way I can top him and his boat. He said: 'Now all I'm going to hear about is George did this and George did that. I hate you for making me small in my son's eyes. I'll get back at you, you wait and see the next time you want me to do something for you.'"

George gave her a tissue to wipe her tears. She continued, "Billy heard all that, and started crying because he knew his dad was angry at him and me. He also knew Joe had been drinking and that's when he makes things difficult for Billy. He's always drinking—that's why we got divorced."

George hugged her. "Don't worry, he'll settle down after a while. This boat and I are pretty impressive," he said. Roberta pulled back and looked at him, blinked twice, then realized he was joking.

He handed her the wine. "Drink this one and you'll relax. The sun's going to set soon, and we don't want to miss that. If you want, we can walk over to the dunes, and watch it from there. I've got blankets around here and a cooler and . . ."

"No. I just want to sit here in your arms and feel good. Today was so special for me. I want to enjoy the memories with you, and remember the fun Billy and I had today. You made us feel special, like letting me wear this watch and these gold earrings." She reached into her big purse and pulled out the pictures from today, taken by George and Billy.

She smiled through her tears as she looked at the photos of her and her son. She turned to George. "I really did look good in this bikini you had me wear today."

"Which one? You tried on about five."

"I like the turquoise one that hardly covered me up. But you're such a good photographer, the camera angle you took the picture at made my breasts look bigger and my bottom smaller. What more could a woman ask? And that gold watch and pearl earrings you let me wear really went perfectly with the turquoise suit. I don't think I ever felt so alive." Roberta took off the watch and earrings and handed them back to George. "This watch looks expensive, and I know the pearl earrings aren't cheap either."

"They're my mother's. I got them when she died. My father had given her the watch for a Christmas present, and the earrings probably for her birthday."

"These pictures of Billy and me are great," said Roberta. "Look, the little guy even took a nice picture of you and me. You're right; he might be a good photographer. This one is great just of him. I'm going to frame it." Roberta put it on the cocktail table with the others, smiled at George. and moved towards him. Her kiss was deep and full. His hand caressed her breasts, while his other hand pulled her closer.

Later, Roberta decided she didn't want to leave the boat even for dinner, so George ordered a pizza. After eating, they decided to stay on the boat with the shades drawn. It wasn't long after dinner, and a couple more glasses of wine, that Roberta suggested she wanted to try out the bed she talked about earlier. George led her to the master bedroom, and they slowly undressed each other.

George laid her down on the bed, kissing her deep, their tongues making love before he moved his lips to her throat, and then down to her breasts and her love triangle, where he kissed her until she was moaning and thrashing her hips.

When he entered her, she let out a loud gasp, her fingernails digging into his back. Roberta started moaning and talking dirty. They were both so primed with pent-up sexual energy from the afternoon and this evening that it only took a few minutes more for them to come.

He was still inside her when she said the words that changed everything.

"George, you are such a bad boy for taking advantage of me. You know I couldn't help myself."

In an instant, it was as if his mother was in the room. He had heard his mother say that phrase to her many lovers over and over again: "You know I can't help myself."

George hated it.

She's no better than her, he thought. He'd show her how bad he could be, but not now . . . Controlling his rage, he slowly rolled off her.

She kissed him gently. "That was wonderful." A few minutes later, she moved her hands to his manhood and started stroking him, but nothing happened. "Oh." She turned and looked at him quizzically. "Is everything OK?"

"Sure. I had a couple of drinks before, waiting for you to come back to the boat. Then we had a couple more when you got on the boat, and we just made love. I'm not Superman, Roberta; just give me a chance to recover. Men aren't like a woman in that respect, we need a little time, plus I'm not a twenty-something anymore. Don't worry. I'll be ready for you."

She giggled.

He smiled and nodded.

"This next time, I have a new way to make love to you that I've been dying to try out. It will make our lovemaking more intense, and your orgasm even stronger. Wait until you see what I do to you and you'll like the surprise at the end. I promise."

"I can hardly wait. Can I get more wine? My glass is empty."

"Sure. While you're getting it, I'll get my surprise ready. Don't be long. I can feel myself getting excited just thinking about it."

She leaned over and touched him. "Oh, you're right, it's getting frisky again." She sat up. "I'll be right back. I want to go and get the nice picture of Billy you took and put it on the nightstand. I won't miss him so much if I can see his picture beside me tonight."

He watched her hips sway as she moved naked across the room, and up the steps. Yes, he'd get frisky in a little while. At his dresser, George got out five scarves, inspecting each before placing them folded on the nightstand.

Earlier that same day as *Courage* moved north, up the coast of Michigan, Drew explained the finer points of sailing while he let Amber take the helm. He explained how dangerous it was when the wind gets behind the mainsail and whips across the deck. "If you're standing up and that happens, you can get seriously hurt or worse."

He did a normal tack. This time the boom moved across the boat, sweeping above the cockpit area and rattling the whole boat. "Even a normal tack causes the sail and boom to move with a lot of force. That's why I hate to sail straight downwind.

It's easy to jibe if you don't pay attention. I'll do anything not to be on a course like that. Now let's go back to our normal course."

After an hour, Amber said she had enough steering. "It's too nerve wracking. You take over."

"I'll just put on the autopilot." As he did, Amber got a glass of wine while Drew drank the last of the coffee. For the next few hours, the two watched sand dunes slowly pass on shore.

"Look at the families playing in the water and soaking up sun on the beach," Drew said. "It's a great day to be on the lake."

Soon after, Amber was leaning against Drew sleeping, and he decided that wasn't a bad idea. He closed his eyes, but not before scanning the horizon and checking to make sure the course was not edging them towards shore. He loved cat naps on his boat.

Ten minutes later, he woke when the wind shifted and the sails started flapping. "Sorry Amber, I have to get up and adjust the sails."

"Oh . . . do I need to do anything?"

"No, you're fine, but you might want to put on more sunblock. You're getting red."

"It's fine, I want to get a tan. I'm so white."

They pulled into Ludington around 4:30 and got a slip at the same marina they'd had with *Passage Maker*. After checking in, they got into swimsuits, grabbed drinks, and hit the whirlpool to watch the sunset. They had dinner on the boat, making a simple meal of spaghetti and Italian sausage. With it, they had a nice bottle of Chianti from a liquor store near the Marina.

When it was time for bed in the large V-berth, they made love, falling asleep with Amber nestled on Drew's chest. He loved the feel of her against his chest and the fresh smell of her hair.

They fell asleep to the soft sound of water lapping against the hull.

He got up early the next day and listened to the Great Lakes marine weather report for Ludington, and the eastern shore of Lake Michigan. There was a good chance of thunderstorms moving across the lake. After hearing that, he asked Amber if she had to get back home that day or could she wait until Monday to go back, explaining about the possible storms they might encounter on the return trip.

"I need to get back. We have two people on vacation tomorrow, and I'm the only one left. I'm sorry."

"We better get started." The sky was already getting a light gray-blue, but it was still just before sunrise when *Courage* motored past the Ludington lighthouse and turned south, back towards Muskegon. "There clear skies now, but on the horizon, see the tops of cumulus clouds? Those clouds are not good."

Drew decided to motor sail back. He wanted to keep his speed up to at least at six knots. With the sails set, the motor running, *Courage* was hauling south, as they moved just off the wind. This was Drew's favorite sailing direction because it was the fastest, even with the motor running.

He hoped to get back before the storms hit. It would be a

race to get there in eight hours. He knew the boat could handle anything thrown at it, but he wasn't sure if Amber could. She was new to sailing and a good sport, but she had never been in a storm before on Lake Michigan with high winds, waves and lightning.

Drew hadn't either, but he had endured similar hardships on Chesapeake Bay, when he was sailing on Academy boats. He didn't mind the first two things, but lightning scared him. It reminded him of being shelled in Afghanistan.

Chapter Twenty-Three

Drew listened as Amber talked about her childhood.

"I came from a dysfunctional family. Heck, my dad named me Amber because he liked the color of his favorite whiskey. That should tell you something about my family. If I had a brother, he probably would have named him Jack because all he drank was Jack Daniels.

"Anyhow, my dad came back from Vietnam, met my mom and had me in a few years later. He tried to work for the auto industry but the demons of the war, and an ungrateful nation caused him to use booze to medicate himself. In other words, he was a drunk. Most of the time, he couldn't hold a job. My mom did her best. She was a teacher. She stayed with him until I was a teenager, but then he got abusive. He started abusing me physically. One night, in a drunken rage, while my mom was at work, he attacked me, ripping my shirt off. I screamed, 'No Daddy, No!' I ran into the bathroom and locked the door. Luckily, my mom came home just then, with him pounding on the locked bathroom. I'm sure he would have raped me, or even worse if he got his hands on me. Mom and I moved out the next day."

She wiped her eyes with the sleeve of her fleece. "Of course, I was screwed up after that. In a twisted way, I felt I had somehow caused everything that happened, by the way I dressed at the time and of course drinking—just like my two role models.

"So, graduation night, down on the beach, after drinking way too much, I got raped, gang raped actually, like I told you before. Later that same summer, when I decided I wasn't going to put out with this certain guy, I got confirmation of the rape. He spilled the beans about everyone taking a turn with me after I had passed out. I was a slut, the easy one, all through my senior year of high school. After he told me that, I got help. I quit having sex and controlled my drinking. That was a long time ago. You're the first one I've had sex with since."

Drew said, "You're a special person, Amber. I knew that after I spent time with you that first evening."

She wiped her nose. "Tell me about you. Where did you grow up? I bet your parents were nice. You are. I know about the war and your injuries, but tell me again about why you're taking this trip again? It seems so lonely. Why does it mean so much to you?"

"That's a lot of things to know, but we have time. We're on a slow boat with hours until we get home so I'll try.

"I'm from Houghton-Hancock. My dad was originally from Charleston, South Carolina but became best buddies with my mother's brother, Andrew, in basic training. My uncle invited him up to visit when they got leave, and after meeting his sister, he kept coming up. Dad told me he never got along with his parents so he spent every chance he could up north. He says it was fresh and clean up there, and he loved Hemingway's Nick Adams stories that took place in that area. But it was really because of mom that drew him there. He and my uncle were best friends, and then they got sent to Vietnam together. My uncle Drew got killed over there in some rice patty, and when dad got out of the Marines, he came up to visit his family and my mom. They got married soon, and I came along about a year later, and then my sister. That was it. They always said two was enough. He loved my mom more than anything in the world. People say you can't love anyone more than your kids after you have some, but in Mom and Dad's case, I think they loved each other more than me and my sister. They loved us a lot, no question about that, but she was his life, and she loved him that much too. It was a special, deep lasting love, like the love between the characters Noah and Allie in the novel *The Notebook*, except Dad was the needy one. After a hunting accident, she took care of him.

"I was named after my Uncle Andrew—Drew for short. Dad did maintenance work at one of the copper mines but when it closed down after the war. He was kept on, working only part-time until his accident. He was always good with his hands and so he made a decent living doing odd jobs. It never was easy, but we never went hungry.

"I got nominated for West Point and the Naval Academy after high school. I was good in football, and All-State in basketball so that helped, although hockey was the only winter sport that counted up north. It was a no-brainer for me to pick where I was going to go, with Dad and my uncle being a marine. I went to the Naval Academy.

"I would have stayed in the Marines forever. I loved the service, but then I never planned on getting shot. So now I'm a sailor."

"Didn't you have a woman in every port?" she asked, smiling.

"There was one back home, Clair. Actually, she lived just down the block from us and was younger. We fell in love. She wanted to get married, have babies, all that stuff, but I was in Afghanistan and said we should wait. When she told me she was pregnant, I said we'd get married as soon as I got back home. About a week later, I got a letter from Mom, saying Clair had hung herself."

"Oh my god! I'm so sorry for you."

He looked at Amber. "Thanks." He took his cup and shook the last drops of cold coffee over the side and then looked at Amber. "Everyone around me dies: Amber, my dad, Clair and the guys in my unit I was responsible for. Even the women I told you about in Milwaukee and Chicago. They were brief encounters—like Stella, one I really cared about—but they died. I'm not sure I'm the guy you want to hang around with, Amber. Bad things happen to people who do."

She smiled, but he noticed she didn't move closer to him, even a few inches to reassure him. He had hoped she would.

"Nothing is going to happen to me, Drew," she said. "I like you. I like being with you. I want to see more of you, especially after this trip. Got it?"

"Thanks," he said, and then she did move closer, kissing him lightly on the lips.

"How about a sandwich?" said Amber. "I'll go down and make us a ham and cheese."

"Great, we might not get a chance to eat later." He pointed to the sky. "It looks like we're going to run into some storms. After you make the sandwiches, get the rain gear and life preservers out of the hanging locker next to the head. I'm going to reef the mainsail while the weather is still reasonably good. Reefing reduces the mainsail's area. When it starts to blow, we'll be able to control the boat easier, and go faster than if we had the full mainsail up."

He flipped the autopilot on, lowered the mainsail enough to start reefing the sail, and then raised the sail taut, and climbed back into the cockpit. By the time Amber had made the sandwiches and gotten the gear out of the hanging locker, Drew was done double reefing the mainsail. "I'd rather over reef than not reef enough. I don't want to go up in the middle of the storm and have to do it," he said to Amber as she put a plate of sandwiches down. They started eating.

The storm moved in fast. Drew felt the temperature drop. Then the wind picked up, and he saw whitecaps forming. Strong southwesterly winds pushed the waves across the long open water, causing them to build higher and steeper. Soon they were four feet to seven feet high and cresting, the spray blowing into their faces. The waves crashing into the side of the bow sounded like a flat hand slapping the top of a desk with a bang. The temperature dropped more, and the sky became dark and menacing.

"Amber, you better put on that life preserver. Bring mine after you get yours on, would you?"

He slipped his on, just as the squall hit. The boat heeled over thirty-five degrees. Lightning cracked to the starboard side. Drew instinctively counted . . . six before he heard the boom.

"Hang on. Don't be afraid. She'll right herself in a moment," he said, turning the boat slightly into the wind to relieve the pressure on the sails. After a short time, *Courage* settled into a steady angle of eighteen degree of heel. Then he moved to the port side winch and cranked in a little more of the headsail as he motored closer to the wind. After that, the autopilot kept *Courage* on a steady course.

Drew turned to Amber, smiling. "Isn't this fun? This is what sailing is all about, dealing with what nature throws at you."

Amber looked at him with disbelief. "If you say so."

Large drops of moisture hung from her long eyelashes, her yellow rain slicker's drawstrings tight around her face. He laughed. "You look like a crossing guard with the matching bibs and yellow life preserver."

"You're really sick, you know that, Drew? I think that bullet did more damage to your head than just your hearing." She laughed.

The storm's intensity increased, forcing Drew to adjust *Courage's* course closer to the Michigan shore to minimize the heeling effect of the wind and waves.

"We're going to have to make a tack soon I'm afraid, and away from the approaching near shore and move more out into the lake," he said. "Nothing to worry about. We've done tacking before, yesterday. This time it's windier, but the procedure is still the same."

At that moment, a gust hit. The wind shook the mast like a child shaking a ragdoll. The boat's rigging continued its high-pitched wail like a group of mourners lamenting the loss of a loved one. He moved to the free winch they would use when they tacked to the other side, preparing it for the tack.

He wrapped the loose jib line—currently not carrying a load—three times around the winch. He pulled it back near the wheel.

"Let me go over the procedure one more time," he shouted. "I'm going to turn *Courage* into the wind, and when I tell you, I want you to loosen the jib line from the wince where it is now, and let it run free. Remember: not until I tell you. You'll be on the low side of the boat when you do this, close to the water, but when we come about, you'll be on the high side and safe. So get down on the low side now, and let me know when you're ready."

"This is exciting," she said, moving to the low side. "Let's do it, I'm ready." She stood with the end of the jib line in her hand.

Just at that moment, a huge rogue wave came from an unexpected crossing direction, slamming full blast into the stern quarter, jerking the boat down and violently pushing it towards the unsuspecting Amber.

Drew watched in horror as Amber lost her balance and flew out of the small cockpit still holding on to the line. She looked like a gymnast doing a cartwheel. She let loose of the jib line, grabbing instead for the boat lifeline, but missing.

"Help!" he heard her cry, and then she was gone.

"Shit!" He hit the man overboard button on the GPS marking the current location, let loose all the sail lines for the reefed main and jib, causing the boom to swing madly, all the while keeping his eyes on the yellow spec moving steadily behind the boat in the seven and eight-foot waves.

He throttled up the boat's motor. He needed the added power to come about quickly. Drew wasn't worried about the sails, now flapping furiously. They could always be replaced. The wind was blowing on both sides, causing the sail to snap, making sounds like someone shooting a shotgun. The sail's jib lines tangled around the stays and the boat's lifelines, looking like a cobweb and sounding like a cowboy snapping a long bullwhip.

Drew didn't care. All that mattered was keeping his eyes on the yellow spot at the top of a wave, and then watching it disappearing into the bottom of a trough before it came to the top of the wave again.

He slowly got closer to Amber, then slowly motored to windward and circled above her. He shifted the boat into neutral, letting the boat drift towards her. He got the life ring out and threw it above her position and watched as she laboriously moved towards it. Amber wrapped her arms around it.

He grabbed the line, pulling her hand over hand towards the boat until she was near the stern and the ladder. He kicked the stainless-steel swim ladder down into the roiling water behind the rising and falling stern.

He yelled, "Let the boat's stern plunge down, and then grab for the ladder's rungs and it will pull you out of the water. Don't worry about drifting away. I've got you."

She tried to grab the ladder a few times, but her timing was off. Finally, she caught it and, as she came up with the rise of the stern, he grabbed the collar of the rain suit up and yanked her into the cockpit.

Laying prostrate in the cockpit, she started spitting water and crying.

"Are you all right?" he asked, the sound of the sails still snapping.

"Yes, nothing is broken." She coughed, and then threw up. "I'm not sure I like sailing as much as before."

She wasn't joking he knew. He watched as she got up, her face red like someone with a winter cold.

"I'm going below to change into dry clothes."

He put the autopilot on, and then Drew spent the next ten minutes getting the lines untangled, the jib rolled up, but he left the reefed main up. He set the autopilot on a course away from the shore. Soon after the accident, the wind and waves began to lose their intensity. The storm was passing and he saw clear sky on the horizon, to the southwest.

Too bad, Drew thought, his life couldn't be clear sailing ahead like he was seeing on the horizon. He couldn't help think he'd just almost lost another person he cared about.

Chapter Twenty-Four

The next morning, Sunday, Roberta and George leisurely lay in bed.

She said, "Sorry I fell asleep last night before you gave me your surprise. The events of the day, and then the fantastic lovemaking and that last glass of wine made me fall asleep as soon as my head hit the pillow. Maybe I had too much to drink." Roberta giggled.

"You know how to wreck my huge ego," George said. "I was going to use my scarves and make love to you in a special way." He brought his lips close to her ear and whispered, "In a way, you'll never forget." He kissed her gently.

"Oh, George. I'm sorry I spoiled your fun, but now I'm wide awake, clear headed and ready." Her eyes saw the scarves neatly piled on the nightstand. "Were you going to use those pretty scarves on me for your surprise, tying me up and then having your way with me? Was that your surprising way to make love to me?"

"In a way. If I tell you now, it won't be a surprise, will it?"

"I guess not. What time is it?"

George looked at his watch. "It's 9:45—really late, but you were really drunk when you came to bed the second time. You only stirred when I started kissing you."

"George, I'm sorry. Let me make it up to you."

George felt her hand move to his thigh and slid up. He felt his excitement grow as he pulled back the covers, exposing Roberta's nakedness.

"Your wish is my command," he said.

"Oh good. I was afraid I'd never get that surprise. Are you going to take pictures of me wearing the scarves?"

"I could, but not this time. I like to use scarves in my love-making to make your body come alive to the feel of silk. You'll see."

"If you say so."

"My surprise makes lovemaking, and your orgasm more intense. I read about this technique on some naughty website, and thought you'd be the perfect person to try it on."

Roberta reached over and looked at the picture of her and her son Billy and gave it a kiss.

"Let's do it now. I have to be home when Billy's father drops him off at my house. Please, can we do it now?"

She kissed the picture again, and then laid the picture face up on the nightstand.

"I'm sorry, it's just the picture you took of him. It's so nice. I just have to keep it close to me."

He nodded. "I understand. Ready?"

"Yes."

He grabbed her right wrist and with a scarf, tied her to a bedpost. Then he did the same with her left wrist.

"No one has ever tied me up and had sex with me before. You're a bad boy, George West." She laughed just like she had done last night.

"My mother used to say the same thing, and she loved

scarves when she had sex with many different lovers. She used to tie me up, too, so I wouldn't interrupt her and her lovers. I associate silk with sex. It gets me excited. My mother wasn't very nice to me. Did I tell you that?"

"No, you didn't, but if silk and tying me up gets you excited, go ahead. I'm getting excited myself, thinking about it."

He took her ankles and tied them to the frame. "There. Are you comfortable?"

"Yes. I can move a little but not much. See?"

"Yes, I want you to move, to enjoy the sexual journey you are about to take to darkness, and ecstasy."

"Darkness?"

A small amount of fear replaced excitement in her eyes.

"Relax, Roberta. Erotic asphyxiation is the intentional restriction of oxygen to the brain for the purpose of sexual arousal. This type of surprise has been going on since the seventeenth century."

She struggled with her arms and legs, even bucking on the bed. "Geez, George, I'm not sure I want this kind of surprise."

"Relax, you'll like it. I promise." He leaned over and started kissing her lips, her neck. She relaxed. He kissed her breasts, swirling his tongue on her nipples, his hands massaging.

"Oh, George."

Her chest started moving rapidly. He moved lower to her center and kissed her, his tongue probing, flicking until her hips started moving up and down, tugging the restraints.

"Yes, that's it, there, there. Yes, don't stop."

But he did. He got up from the bed and reached for the last

long silk scarf. He took the scarf, spreading his hands, snapping the silk taut.

"Kiss me. Taste your love on my tongue," he said before straddling her. He wrapped the long red scarf twice around her neck. "Are you ready for the surprise?"

She nodded, but her eyes told him she was afraid. He liked that.

He entered her, moving like a snake, undulating, heat building in him as Roberta moaned with his long strokes. George held himself above her, his elbows outside her slim shoulders as he tightened the scarf around her neck. Her eyes dilated as her breath became constricted, then he moved his fingers around her neck.

"This is the good part for you, bitch," he said, pressing tighter on her windpipe. He moved inside her, faster and faster, watching as her eyes rolled back into her head.

Roberta stiffened and then went limp.

His eyes just then caught the up turned picture of Billy. "Oh my God, what am I doing to her? She's a good mother, a great mother to Billy and I'm trying to kill her."

He quickly untied the scarf around her neck and placed his mouth on hers and tried to blow life back into her.

"Come on, come back. Come back for Billy." George blew more of his air into her, Roberta's chest rising and falling until finally, her eyes fluttered open and she looked at him, trying to remember what happened. He untied her wrists and pulled her to his chest.

"It was too close; it was too close."

"That was unbelievable. I've never had an orgasm like that.

It was so powerful and then so peaceful. I came so hard, I must have passed out or something."

"Or something," he repeated, holding her close to his chest, like he always wanted to be held by his mother. Alex was always the one that got held close, not him, but then he had killed his mother.

"We aren't going to do that again," he said. "It's too dangerous for you . . . and Billy."

***

Amber was quiet as she sat in the cockpit, a wool blanket wrapped around her, drinking the hot tea Drew had made. She had said nothing to him except "Thank You" when he handed her the mug of tea.

After twenty minutes of watching Lake Michigan's waters turn from gun metal gray to a bright blue, she asked, "Do you have any more tea?"

"Do you want to talk about it?"

"Why would I want to talk about the tea?" she said.

"No, not the tea," he said with a faint smile. "You falling in the water."

She shook her head no.

"It was an accident. A wave from a different direction hit the stern of the boat just as we were going to come about and you lost your balance."

Amber continued to stare at the blue horizon to the west.

He got up. "I'll be back with more tea."

Five minutes later, he had a steaming kettle of Earl Gray.

"Give me your cup. If the boat hits another wave, I don't want to burn your hand when I pour the hot water into the cup."

"But you'd let me go to a place on your boat where I got tossed off in an actual storm."

"You think I did it on purpose? Is that what you're saying?"

"All I remember is the boat lurching as if you turned the wheel, and I lost my balance and got tossed into the water. I don't know what I'm saying, but I'm uncomfortable being around you now, Drew."

"I hadn't turned the wheel yet. I didn't want you to fall overboard. If I wanted you dead, why did I have you wear a life preserver, and then come back and get you? I could have just left you there."

"Maybe you didn't want me dead, but like you said before, people around you seem to die. I think you're unlucky. I care about you, Drew. I really do, but I fear for my safety. I don't think we should see each other anymore after this."

"Just like that, it's over?" When he watched her nod yes to his question, he felt his stomach clench. He knew she was right.

Bad things did happen to good people around him. He had hoped his trip would change his karma from bad to good, but so far it only confirmed it.

* * *

At 5 p.m., he dropped Amber off at the marina dock. She did give him a kiss, but nothing more was said about getting together. When she disengaged herself from him, he saw sadness in her eyes.

He watched as she walked down the pier, a slow sway of the hips, and the hunched shoulders shaking. He knew she was crying.

He went down below in the cabin and put back items that had moved from their normal places in the storm. Then he made a peanut butter and jelly sandwich, a thermos of coffee and climbed the three steps back into the cockpit and started the diesel.

He guided *Courage* out into Lake Michigan, turning the wheel north again. This time he was sailing towards Beaver Island, a longer trip. He would sail through the night, alone with his thoughts, and his demons.

***

Monday. At her desk at the police stationhouse, Tara hung up the phone. She had finished checking out information on a drive-by shooting case.

"Time for lunch," Sabina said. But instead of eating her usual vending machine sandwich, Tara's partner wanted to go out for lunch at nearby Major Goolsby's. "I have a craving for a bacon cheeseburger with all the fixings. You want me to bring something back for you?"

"No, that's fine. I have something to do here. See you later."

Tara was following up on the dog earring lead. From her desk drawer, she pulled out the secret Marquette University steno pad she used to track her rogue investigation. Scanning the list of jewelers, she'd already phoned a number of them to see if they sold custom dog-related jewelry. Most of the names had already been crossed out.

Over the past few days, Tara had learned dog earrings were not a hot commodity. But today, on her twenty-third phone call, she got a hit. A jeweler in Whitefish Bay remembered a purchase similar to the earring Tara described.

Fifteen minutes later, Tara pulled in front the store, not wanting to do an interview on the phone. Already in her investigative career, she had found that it was important to be able to observe body language, facial expressions, not just voice inflections.

Entering the shop, she asked for Judy, the woman she'd spoken to on the phone.

"I'm Judy. How can I help you?" She was about fifty-five, medium height, short bleached blond hair with dark roots. She looked tanned and fit, with weathered skin on the face and arms, like a golfer or sailor might acquire after being out in the sun too long over the years without enough protection. She wore a simple lime green sleeveless cotton dress with lots of bracelets on her wrists and a single thick, flat, gold necklace. Tara confirmed she was the wife of the owner, and often handled purchases of small items, while her husband handled the diamond purchases.

Tara repeated the Riptide waitress' description of the unusual jewelry.

Judy nodded. "I remember a woman that bought that dog earring. She brought her dog into the store with her."

"The earring this woman bought was of a big dog?" asked Tara.

"No. It was a little dog. Her dog looked like a gray and brown little dustmop." Judy paused. "Can you believe she'd carry the tiny dog around in her purse? What happens if the pooch makes a mess?" Judy laughed.

Tara was less amused. "Oh, not a big dog earring? Do you think the earrings were for her? Were there two earrings or one?"

"She bought one pair of dog earrings, not just one earring. Sometimes a customer puts one in their ear, and the other in the dog's ear. Soulmates, I guess. It could be for a husband or boyfriend. This woman looked like she could have both, if you know what I mean." Judy raised her eyebrows. "Well, she was very attractive, all dressed up like she was going to a country club lunch or meeting someone. We get a lot of ladies like that in here. They're bored and like to shop. Find a little something, and either buy it or come back and bring the boyfriend or hubby if it's really expensive. This wasn't. It was only $350."

"Have you sold anymore?"

"No. They're so unusual, we special order them from a custom jewelry shop on the northeast side." Judy pointed toward the corner of the bright case they stood in front of. "See—we have a cat pair here."

"May I have the shop's name?"

"Sure, I'll get it for you. What's this all about?"

"I really can't go into what it is we're investigating, but this earring is important to a serious criminal matter."

"Hang on. It'll take me a moment to find it on the computer."

Soon after, Judy came out of the office. "Here it is. *Custom Gold and Silver* on Brady Street."

Tara drove down Prospect Avenue and turned left to Brady Street. She liked this area: a combination of unique restaurants and shops. She located the shop and found a parking spot on a nearby side street.

It was a hot August afternoon. She would have liked to take off her jacket but then everyone would see her Glock on her hip, so she kept it on. She walked quickly to the store and out of the heat.

Entering the door, she heard a little bell jingle as she entered. Then the cold blast of air hit her. "Ahh," she sighed, thankful for the cool air.

The place reminded Tara of an art studio where they made metal sculptures. There was a workbench, a couple of blowtorches, small vices, bright spotlights and a large magnifying glass with a circular light around its edge.

Wiping his mouth with a napkin, a short, white, balding man, wearing black slacks and a short-sleeved white dress shirt, emerged from behind a black curtain at the rear of the small store. Must be his office and storage back there.

"Sorry, you caught me having a late lunch. Can I help you find something?"

Tara pulled out her credentials. "I'm Detective Sullivan, checking out a lead on a case, and I hope you can help."

"Sure. I always try to cooperate with the police."

"I'm looking for a special earring shaped like a dog."

"Yeah, we make those—usually special orders because

clients want jewelry looking just like their own mutt. We'll do something with the dog's ears, body or tail."

"Do you get any men who buy those earrings? I'm looking for a guy wearing a dog earring, but I don't know the size of the dog, except it was probably a big one."

"Well, it's true that men can be pretty attached to dogs too, but I can't recall making any earrings for men this year."

Tara felt disappointment creep into her stomach. "How about last year? He could have had it for a while."

"We sell about five a year, but like I said, they usually want it customized to their dog, so I'd remember the client. They'll come in with pictures, or even with the dog. No, not any men lately."

"Is there anyone else that makes dog earrings that you know of?" She watched his eyes look to the ceiling as he thought about it.

"Milwaukee's a pretty big city with lots of people dealing in custom jewelry items like this. Sorry I can't help you more."

"Thank you for your time. If you think of anything, I'd appreciate a call." She handed him her card, with her phone numbers on it.

"I will, Detective."

As Tara was leaving, he said. "I just thought of something that might help. The Milwaukee Humane Society has a gala each year, and a silent auction. Last year I think I sent them a pair of cat earrings, and a pair of earrings of a bigger dog, maybe a hunting dog. A guy had ordered the dog and then cancelled the order after we'd already made it. His dog had died, and he said he was too sad to wear them. At least we got a tax deduction for donating the pair to the Humane Society for one of their galas. Maybe you want to check with them."

"Great idea, I will. Thank you again," she said with satisfaction. Funny how one lead led to another.

Outside, the heat engulfed her once again, but Tara didn't care. She had another lead. Each one brought her closer to Cate's killer. She got to her car, turned the AC to max, and headed to her office downtown to meet Sabina. She'd call the Humane Society later.

She had the next day off and started it off with a run. For weeks, Tara had changed her jogging path, avoiding running past the McKinley boat launch where she'd seen her sister's body wrapped in the black body bag, but today she managed to run past the area, focusing on the group of jogging women in pink.

She could easily have run past the slow-moving group, but found comfort overhearing the normal conversation of family, new loves, and cheating gossip.

She thought of Alex. He seemed to be gone a lot, probably fooling around. Drew had all but said he had done just that on his trip with him. Alex had called her only once this past week, telling her he was traveling.

Tara had called his office. His assistant said he was out all week, "but he usually checks his emails and calls. Why don't you email him?"

Tara didn't want him to know she was checking up on him,

like she didn't trust him. When he called her later, he said, "I should be home in a week. We need to spend more time together. I miss you, Tara. I'll make dinner for you at my place. Maybe we can invite friends over. I'm tired of eating out and we need to get reacquainted."

"That would be nice. I miss being with you too, but I have been busy with work like you. We've had a rash of drive-by shootings and Sabina and I are working one. I also developed a new lead on my sister's case."

"Really, what?"

"I can't tell you anything yet—confidential, you know." She had sounded so official when she said it, it almost made her laugh. She definitely didn't want to say anything to anyone until she had spoken with the Humane Society.

It was just after noon when she pulled up to the Humane Society's building. Even outside on the sidewalk, she could hear several dogs barking. She expected the place would be packed. A family walked out of the building with an ecstatic French bulldog, likely saved from the death sentence befalling dogs and cats not cuddly or too old.

She followed two other families into the building. The kids were jumping up and down, excited about getting their first family pet, making promises to their parents that they'd take care of the animals, duties Tara expected would eventually fall to Mom or Dad, and not to the kids who would soon be too busy playing video games to take the dog for a walk.

Tara had made those same promises to her dad when they got their one and only dog, a black poodle Tara named Zorro. Zorro lived to be fourteen. He had been Tara's dog, her pal.

Cate never had anything to do with him. She hated when Zorro would lick her or try to sit on her lap.

She hoped the Humane Society would still have the silent auction slip from a past gala, with a record of who bought the dog earrings. Tara might be able to trace the killer through a credit card.

When she finally talked to the manager, Tara was disappointed with the answer she got.

"We'll try our best," said Sandy, who looked weary and overworked. "I'm not sure if we have that stuff anymore. We usually destroy everything once we get the money, but I'll check. We're right in the middle of preparing for an upcoming event. We'll work on it, but first we have to do our fundraising event: *TAKE YOUR DOG FOR A RUN*. It will be a couple of weeks, I'm afraid. I'm not sure where we keep all that stuff, or even if we kept it."

"I understand, but this is very important. It could help solve a murder investigation, so we'd appreciate you working on it sooner rather than later."

"Oh, a murder investigation?" Sandy's eyes widened and eyebrows arched up. "I'll try to get to it ASAP, but I have so much to do for this event."

"Great, I really appreciate your time and your help, Sandy."

Chapter Twenty-Five

That same day after he almost killed her, and still feeling guilty about this one, George had brunch with Roberta. Thank goodness for the picture of Billy. George promised he'd be back to see Billy and her, and they'd go picture-taking and boating again.

"Tell Billy I want to see lots of his pictures when I come back to Michigan. You have a great kid and you're a wonderful mother, Roberta."

He kissed her and walked her back to her car. Ten minutes later, George was headed in *Condor* to Ludington for the night. After putting the autopilot on, he sat in the captain's chair, poured himself a cup of hot coffee, and thought about the weekend.

It was the first time he had pulled back from killing someone who had made fun of him being a bad boy. George was glad he had.

He wished he'd had a mother like Roberta when he was growing up. If he did, he wouldn't be who he was. He'd be more like Alex, although he hated to think that way. He'd like to meet more people like Roberta. George didn't think he could actually love anyone except dogs, because they returned unquestionable love, but maybe someone loving and exciting like Roberta might work out down the road.

He knew he was fucked up, but Roberta? Yeah, he could get used to someone like her and her son, Billy. He was such a good kid, and with George's photo instruction, Billy might even become a good photographer. George would see how things went the next time he visited Muskegon.

Condor moved easily through the swells from the afternoon storm, getting a push forward as it glided over and down two-foot swells. As it made slight adjustments to the boat's course, the autopilot sounded like a violin playing a tune by Vivaldi.

George planned on spending the night in Ludington, and then, depending on the weather, he'd motor to Beaver Island where he and Drew planned on meeting. Then they'd head towards Sturgeon Bay, and the Door County peninsula in Wisconsin. Motoring up the Green Bay side of the peninsula, he'd stop, and visit some of the resort towns like Egg Harbor, Fish Creek and Sister Bay. Then George would probably turn around and head home.

***

He reached Ludington around 5:30 p.m., hoping to locate Drew and *Courage*. But maybe Drew had already gone to Beaver Island. There was no answer on his cell phone when he tried calling, but then, there are lots of dead spots on the big lake. No big deal, George thought. He'd have dinner at the Jamesport Brewing Company, an easy walk from the marina. Where there was good food and drink, there were usually women. George would bring along his camera. It helped his socializing.

George got a table on the restaurant's raised covered deck. A soft rain was falling, but it was warm outside, and he liked the sound of the raindrops hitting the corrugated metal roof.

When it rained, however, it was more difficult for him to find subjects to photograph. He wanted to take pictures on the risqué side, the type he could sell to men's magazines, or calendar and poster companies. He sometimes told himself he did it to keep *Condor* in diesel money, but it was really for the thrill of working with beautiful women. And George could do so much with the hungry ones, the insecure ones. Praise went a long way, lies even further.

He desired a woman with a knockout body but an average face—maybe crooked teeth or a scar on their face, a flaw that left them weak and wanting. He'd take lots of shots of her in sexy poses, he'd fill her head with fancy ideas, ply her with drinks, and she was his.

He'd hide their flaws in his photos, either by the angle of his shot, or later he'd airbrush it out. But George would reel them in with his skill and their insecurities.

The luxurious boat helped a lot too, of course. He'd show them the darkroom, and so on, until they finally got to his bedroom. It didn't take long.

But it was Sunday night, and the steady drizzle on the deck's metal roof sounded harder. He might actually have to eat alone, and then head back to the boat.

He raised his drink to his lips and that's when he saw her walk in. Alone. She sat at the long bar inside. The bartender took her drink order. George waited a few minutes to make sure a companion of hers wasn't parking the car or coming to meet her. When the bartender placed a cosmo in front of her, George watched as she took a little sip, then started scanning her iPhone. Occasionally, she looked around to see if anyone noticed her, or maybe she was hoping for an interesting offer from one of her bar friends.

Her off-the-shoulder, gray sweater slid down to one side of a strong shoulder, revealing honey-colored skin made darker by her platinum blond hair. The presentation invited you to look at the rest of her body, and look George did. He knew her natural hair color was not the white blond she wore because her eyebrows were deep brown. She had bright blue eyes, so the blond coloring was good. He loved the full, puffy lips. They looked like Angelina Jolie's.

She laughed—an intoxicating laugh, like his mother's cackle when she was drinking, flirting, or ready to tie him up.

He walked over with his camera front and center. "Hi, my name is George. I'm a photographer. May I buy you a drink and take a few pictures of you? What's your name?"

Her eyes widened. "You want a take a picture of me? That's a new one. Sure, go ahead. My name's Betsy." Betsy smiled with those big lips.

"It sounds like you have a cold," said George. "I don't doubt it with this rainy weather." He liked her sexy throaty voice but not her laugh. Oh well, he thought, if she's the only girl at the dance, go with her. He circled her sitting at the bar, snapping pictures.

* * *

When the rain, winds and lightning hit, Drew was anchored at Saint James Harbor on Beaver Island. In the northeast corner of Lake Michigan, the island was like a sentinel guarding the straits of Mackinaw and the path of those leaving Lake Michigan to Lake Huron.

It was a sleepless night because of the weather, but also because of what had happened with Amber. Sleepless nights were nothing new to Drew. He had several recurring nightmares transporting him back to Afghanistan.

Why had fate dealt Drew such a shitty hand again and again since his father's accident? He had so many doubts about himself now, and his abilities. Especially this last fuck up with Amber.

He didn't have to put Amber in that position on the boat, but he hadn't figured on that rogue wave. The unexpected had led to his father being shot by a ricocheting bullet, a bullet Drew might have shot. The unexpected had led to Clair taking her life and the loss of his child. The *fucking* unexpected had led to the deaths of three of his team members, including his best friend.

And finally, in Milwaukee, the unexpected had led to Cate Sullivan and Stella Carpenter being murdered, and Drew becoming a suspect.

Buying and fixing up *Courage* was supposed to help him forget. To prove to him he could do something if he put his mind to it and not screw it up—but then he did. Amber didn't drown, but it had been too close.

And the earlier fire onboard in Milwaukee had almost cost Drew *Courage* and this trip. This trip was supposed to make him a better man, to heal his demons. Instead, it added to them.

A bolt of lightning hit a lighthouse nearby.

Was Drew a lightning rod for death to those around him? Amber thought so.

Late that night, after riding out another storm at anchor for hours, Drew felt that his anchorage was safe for the night. His stomach growled, reminding him he hadn't had anything to eat since daybreak. He went down below and heated up two cans of Dinty Moore beef stew. Many people scoffed at the idea of eating this way, but not him. From long experience eating C-Rations, this food was very good, and the gravy went great with French bread he'd brought along. To top off the meal, he'd even found an open bottle of wine left over from his time with Amber.

He tucked himself in the corner of the cockpit, behind the canvas dodger, out of the wind, and light rain. He began eating his steaming plate of stew. He sipped the wine and tried to enjoy the beauty of St. James Harbor and Beaver Island. He felt his anxiety ebb away.

He wondered where George was. When first pulling into the bay, Drew had been surprised when he did not see *Condor* anchored. Something or someone must have delayed him. Knowing his fondness for women, Drew was betting on the second.

The storm raged outside but George had checked the boat's bow, spring and stern lines before he entered his cabin. Knowing Betsy was coming, he did not want to be disturbed once he started taking pictures.

"George, I'm here. How do I get onboard this big boat?"

"I'll be right out and help."

George looked at her and started planning the pictures he wanted to take. Betsy's appearance was unique. She had well developed shoulders as he had noticed in the bar. She clearly worked out a lot. She also had nicely shaped breasts though George could tell they were fake. Still, they looked good in her black, lacy, push up bra. She didn't have a tapered waist like most of his models but was appealing for his photographic needs, and maybe his other needs tonight. He focused on her eyes. He loved her piercing blue eyes against the platinum blond hair.

Her enthusiasm and attention were good. George gave her instructions on positioning, her head, up, down, or turning her face, and Betsy hung on his every word, knowing this was a special moment for her. He climbed all over her at different angles, snapping away, working to accentuate her breasts, face and eyes. Yes, she was a willing subject.

"Do you want to slip out of your clothes and try some of my bikinis? I can take more pictures than this if you change. I'll set up lights so it will seem like daytime. You'll look really fabulous if you're out of the skirt and bra."

"No, George, I'm fine with my outfit. I'm dying to see the pictures you've taken so far. They're digital, aren't they?"

"Yes, they are."

"Can I see them now? It's getting kind of late. I've had lots to drink, and I need to be getting home."

He watched as she pushed away the glass of wine he'd just poured for her. She looked at the short jacket she'd been wearing and a small umbrella leaning against the rattan chair.

"Really? It's storming out. I have lots of room on my boat. We can look at the pictures, have a few more drinks, and see what happens tonight. Let me get my Mac Book, it shows my pictures better."

The lights flickered as a bolt of lightning followed a second later by a loud boom.

"Wow, that was close." Betsy got up, stepped close to the boat's windshield and looked out at the raging storm. "Wow, look at the spray from the waves hitting the lighthouse! When the light from the lighthouse sweeps across the breakwater pier, I can see giant waves crashing on the breakwater. Nasty night. Maybe you're right about tonight."

"Here we are." George popped the chip out of his camera and put it into the laptop. "Sit here on the sofa and we can look at the shots together. Want anything else to drink?"

"Sure, what are you drinking? I don't think I want another wine."

"I'm having a scotch—more of a man's drink," he said, chuckling.

"Sure, I'll have that. I have that sometimes."

He got up and poured her one, and another for himself. Now that he was done taking pictures, he could focus on her.

"O-M-G. I'm really great-looking in these photographs. You can't even see this." She pointed to the rose spot at her hairline. "You are awesome. I'm so happy. No one's ever made me feel so beautiful as you have tonight, George. I want to do something special for you."

She pushed him back on the sofa and started unzipping his khaki shorts.

"Betsy, let's go down to my bedroom. It's more comfortable there."

There was another loud boom and flash.

"That was even closer!" said Betsy. "The boat's rocking. I think I like being up here. I might get seasick downstairs."

"I say, down below."

"Well, I want to give you your surprise up here." And with that, she reached into George's shorts and pulled out his penis.

"Betsy, what do you think you're doing?"

"I love sucking cock. I can't get enough of it, and I'm also very good at it." She started stroking and sucking his cock.

George leaned back. Eight minutes later, he exploded in her throat.

She had not lied about her skills.

"Oh baby, that was fantastic. Now let me do the same to you." He grabbed her skirt and panties and pulled them down in one motion.

Betsy let out a panicked scream. "No, George, not yet. I need to explain."

He never expected to see male genitalia.

"How could I be so stupid?" George raged. He became incensed, stomping around the cabin. He had never done anything like this with a man. Never!

Betsy started crying.

e put his head in his hands. "I can't believe this is happening."

"George, I have other ways to please you, if you give me a chance. I could be good for you. You made me feel so special tonight. I want to repay you."

"You want to feel special?" His face twisted and his eyes

spotted the thick glass ashtray on the cocktail table in the salon. "I'll show you how special you are to me." He went ballistic, grabbing the ashtray from the cocktail table and slamming it with all his might against Betsy's head.

She collapsed in a heap on the floor. He had to get rid of her. With the storm raging, he picked her up in a fireman's carry and took her outside. She was probably still alive, but she wouldn't last long after he dumped her in the churning water. She'd pay for her deception.

He staggered down the pier in the blinding storm carrying the body. Heading to its very end, his mind raced with the night's events. George liked oral sex, but was furious Betsy was a male transsexual. No wonder she didn't want to take off her skirt and panties.

It was past midnight when he hauled the body off the boat, carrying Betsy to the pier's end. While it was a massive structure, the power of the waves crashing into the pier made it shake, and water swirled around his feet, making it tough for George to keep his balance. Finally, he got to the end, dropping the body in the swirling water close to the lighthouse. He watched as a giant wave grabbed Betsy, slamming her into the large rocks protecting the lighthouse. The undertow sucked her under.

As he walked back to his boat, George heard a hissing sound. The light from the lighthouse went dark and water slammed him into the concrete.

When George woke up, his body was wedged against a metal park bench bolted to the pier. That bench had saved him, but not without cuts and scratches to his arms and face. He could taste blood in his mouth. Getting to his feet, another wave caught him, moving him to the edge of the swirling mess. He saved himself again by holding onto the same bench. With his face close to the swirling water and jagged rocks, he saw Betsy's lifeless body emerge briefly from the surf before it was sucked underneath again as another wave smashed her again against the rocks. If Betsy hadn't been dead when George threw her in, water might even be found in the lungs later. George hoped that would mislead any authorities from thinking foul play when looking into her death.

Seeing George hanging onto the bench, some locals came to his rescue. He gave then an excuse for being out there, saying he saw someone get swept off the pier and came out to see if he could help like they had. In the process, he almost got swept off the same way, he told them. By then, his body had started shaking from the cold and shock. He thanked them and slowly headed back to his boat, thankful for his luck.

After cleaning up and resting, he decided to leave at sunrise. Just before sunrise, the high winds sounded like the screams Betsy never had a chance to make. As the two boat's powerful diesel engines warmed up, George stood in the pilothouse. The powerful beam of light from the lighthouse rotated in the predawn darkness. He saw ferocious waves crash into the breakwater, creating curtains of water almost as tall as the lighthouse. It was stormy but he congratulated himself on the perfect way to dispose of a body—even though it almost got him killed.

Fierce waves created strong undertows around the rocks and steel cement piers like Ludington's and carved out small caves underneath the pier structure. If George was lucky, it would be days before Betsy's body was found, probably when the water calmed and her bloated, battered corpse floated out. Betsy's once laughing eyes, George knew, would be picked clean by small fish. The local cops would probably conclude Betsy was swept off the breakwater and drowned.

By that time, he'd be long gone.

Four hours later, *Condor* was rolling violently as George steered the boat towards Beaver Island. The sky lightened to a menacing gray. The stormy sunrises was blocked by low racing clouds. He heard a mixture of sounds from below as his boat was tossed about in the ferocious waters. Earlier, he had pulled back on the throttles to slow the big vessel down from its normal cruising speed. Stuff continued to crash against the floor or furniture, displaced by the violent rocking. He had most things secured, so the shaking and rocking must have loosened books and kitchen stuff during the hours he'd been at sea. Just when he thought it was quieting down below, he heard glass break and he knew some plate or wine glass must have been jarred loose in the galley.

He grabbed a chart of the northern half of Lake Michigan, spreading it out over the instrument panel. He needed to change course away from Beaver Island. He decided to adjust his course towards Sturgeon Bay, Wisconsin, about forty-five miles from his current position. With this new heading, he would motor into the waves at a better angle. It would be a longer trip because of the storm, the waves, and his slower speed, but the boat wouldn't take the beating it was now taking. Besides, George had planned on going to Sturgeon Bay after Beaver Island. He'd just be early.

Spinning the wheel, he made his move when the boat approached the top of a wave. Pivoting like a ballerina on a pointed shoe, *Condor* moved down and into the bottom of a trough, between the huge waves in a new direction.

The trick was to get most of the boat's direction changed before the next wave swept toward the hull. *Condor* was a big pleasure yacht, but it was a weakling against the force and might of Lake Michigan's steep waves. If George's timing was off, a giant wave could roll the boat or at the least, cause great damage. As he moved the wheel, *Condor* rattled and shook. He heard more items falling down below. Cushions slid from the sofa and chairs onto the deck.

His eyes stayed focused on the waves. He hit the throttle more to help move the yacht in the right direction. The boat seemed to sigh in relief when he completed the maneuver. Once the change was done, he had a smoother ride.

Chapter Twenty-Six

Drew was up early the next day. He had gotten the call from George saying he had switched plans because of the storm and was now headed to Sturgeon Bay.

Drew had stayed an extra day anchored at Beaver Island because of the blustery weather and had no problem cruising over to Door County to meet George.

The sky was a bright blue, free of all clouds with a fifteen-knot wind—perfect for a brisk sail across the lake. After filling the thermos with coffee and making instant oatmeal for breakfast, Drew hauled up the anchor and headed into deeper water, towards Door County, Wisconsin.

Even with the favorable wind, it was going to require at least ten to twelve hours to get there. He loved sailing close hauled, pinching the angle of wind at about fifty degrees off the bow. Sailing *Courage* was like riding a loping horse, moving up and down at an easy pace. The boat was heeled over about twelve degrees, and he was comfortable just wearing a tee shirt, cargo shorts, and his ever-present aviator sunglasses.

An hour later, Beaver Island disappeared over his stern, and after three hours, all land was gone and Drew felt like he was out to sea, totally alone. It was a good feeling, giving him a chance to relax, and daydream about his future trip. He planned to leave Milwaukee a week after Labor Day. He'd retrace the route to

Beaver Island, then stop at Mackinac Island for a couple of days. Maybe he'd load up the boat with pounds of their famous fudge, then continue down Lake Huron, across Lake Erie to Buffalo, New York. He'd have to take down the mast, so he could motor through the seventeen locks and 376 miles of the Erie Canal to Albany, New York. Once through the canal, he'd raise the mast again and travel down the Hudson River to New York City. He'd probably stay a week there, and then head out into the Atlantic, sailing south to Chesapeake Bay and Annapolis. Drew planned on staying a month in the Chesapeake area.

It was one of the best places in the world to sail, and its seafood was like nowhere else. Was there anything better then crab cakes and oysters on the half shell?

After that, it would be a slow motor down the Intercostal Waterway until he found a place to stay. He might even head to Cuba . . . or the Bahamas and Virgin Islands.

Drew was planning on spending at least four months on the initial journey, but he had to get through the Erie Canal before it closed in mid-October. And he needed to avoid hurricane areas. The hurricane season officially ended December first.

Then his mind slipped again to why he was embarking on this journey, and in an instant his mood changed. He thought of his buddies who were gone. His dad. And Clair . . . the death of his unborn child. The only child Drew might ever father, unless he could find someone special.

Nothing in his life had worked out like he thought it would. Drew slammed his fist on the fiberglass cockpit. Then he said out loud, "Quit feeling sorry for yourself!"

He looked at the blue water, the horizon, and then the sun overhead. Noon: time for lunch. He wasn't hungry but needed to keep his mind from morbid thoughts. He looked at his handheld GPS and moved the curser from his current position to southern part of Washington Island and Death's Door. He decided to sail through the Death's Door passage, and then down the Green Bay shore to Sister Bay, where they had agreed to meet. Drew expected to arrive at around 6 p.m.

But first Drew sailed through Death's Door.

Last night George was exhausted when he finally docked at CenterPointe Marina. He didn't realize the tension he was under guiding the *Condor* through the large waves to Sturgeon Bay. When he finally turned off the two big diesel engines, he could feel a large knot in the center of his shoulder blades. It took him twenty minutes to get the big boat tied up and the lines set with the grateful help of the dock people. In the cabin, he made himself a double scotch, took a couple of large hits, then slumped on the couch, closing his eyes for a few minutes.

When he finally opened them again, those few minutes had turned into two hours. It was just past sunset.

He idly wondered if Betsey's body had been found. George wasn't worried because no one knew they had left the bar together. George had left before Betsy, to ready his boat for the shoot. Betsy had followed later.

It would be assumed that she had went on the breakwater pier late that night or early morning and had been swept off by a big wave. When she was found, Betsy would be so beat up, they'd probably think she hit her temple on the large rocks.

He wasn't going to worry about Betsy. Best to forget all about that sordid incident. In the meantime, he wanted to get things shipshape, and have a light supper. He remembered a place called Gray Stone or Gray Castle, something like that. He'd walk across the newer Oregon bridge and find food there. Then he'd head back and turn in. It was a long day and he wanted to get up early and start toward Sister Bay, where he was supposed to meet Drew.

***

"Detective Sullivan? This is Sandy from the Humane Society."

Tara sat up straight. "Yes, Sandy?"

"I wanted to get back to you about your request about purchase of the dog earrings at the gala. I'm sorry to tell you that we destroyed all the information once it was determined that everyone had paid for the merchandise. I was really hoping we could help you."

Tara's heart sank at the news.

"Thank you for getting back to me so fast. I really appreciate that. If you have a chance, maybe you could go back another year and see if you could find it back then."

"I'll try but we really try to destroy everything once we know we got our money for the item. I'm sure there is nothing there to help you. If I find something, I'll give you a call."

Tara closed her cell phone and put her head on her desk. She was right back to where she was before: nowhere!

"Out late last night partying, Tara?"

Tara looked up at Sabina. "I wish I had been, but I thought I had a lead on my sister's case."

Sabina lifted an eyebrow. "Tarrrra . . . you know you are not supposed to work on your sister's case."

Tara nodded. She knew. "The investigation was stalled so I went over to Riptide to see if anyone remembered something O'Malley or Pinkowski missed. They did."

"Someone remembered something new? What'd you find?"

"You're not mad?"

Sabina pulled up a chair next to Tara, she put her hand on her shoulder and squeezed lightly and left it there. When Tara turned to look at Sabina, she had tears in her eyes.

Sabina said, "Yes. We're partners. Partners don't withhold information from one another. We want to solve the case. If something important was missed, I don't care who finds it. We work as a team. That's the way it's done in L.A., and here in Milwaukee—you know that. Now what did you find?"

Tara summarized what she knew. "It turns out the Humane Society has no record of the person who purchased the earring. I'm so disappointed."

Sabina patted her shoulder. "We'll get the creep that killed Cate. We'll just keep looking until we do. Maybe we need to check other restaurants and bars around the Third Ward. Maybe he's a boater from out of town and just in Milwaukee for his twisted needs. We can check out Port Washington, Racine, and Kenosha. You have a good lead. Let's see where it takes us."

Tara smiled at her. "Thanks, Sabina."

"But you need to give this information to the other detectives. It could help the case."

"I will," Tara said.

"That's what we do, Tara. We share information so everyone knows what's going on. We might find something that helps a different team on another case. If we don't get this guy, maybe they will. I'm going to grab coffee down the street. Want any?"

As Sabina walked away, Tara looked out the dirty windows across the room, but really wasn't focusing on anything.

She would make a list of bars and restaurants around the water and see if anyone remembered a guy with a dog earring. But first, she had other things to work on. She and Sabina were trying to locate a suspect in the shooting of an Eastside gang member. Drive-by shootings of gang members happened all too frequently in highly-segregated Milwaukee.

When Sabina got back from getting her coffee, Tara handed Sabina a DMV picture of a young black female.

"One of the victim's gang members got a description of the car, a gray Malibu sedan, and three letters of the plate. We did a search based on the model and these three letters. The Malibu is registered to Etta Jones. She works at Mayfair Mall in one of the kiosks. I don't think she did the shooting, but you never know. Maybe Etta let somebody else use her car, but we definitely need to find out who it was driving that car that afternoon."

Sabina smiled. "Now this is one of those times I like this job. While we're at the mall, I can pick up a few things. I just love those kiosks that have makeup and hair stuff."

Tara laughed. "I didn't know you could be so much fun while working."

"Shit. Do you know how much time I have to do stuff like this? I work so many hours on this job, I think we can squeeze it in. I'll count the time we shop as a coffee break. How's that?"

"No. I think it makes us look normal. Not like cops looking for someone." Tara smiled. "We can get up close to her. Ask her non-threatening questions, and then, *Boom!* Zero in on her car, and where she was that night in question. We'll have her."

"Let's go. I need this stuff for a date I have next weekend. I'm excited about this one. He's not a cop for a change."

The Mayfair Mall was relatively quiet as they walked the center corridor, looking for Etta Jones. Sabina wasted little time buying hair beads and cosmetics. They stopped at several kiosks before they spotted Etta talking to a customer at a nail and perfume kiosk. The two cops walked up and waited. Five minutes later, Etta turned to Tara and Sabina.

"May I help you?"

"Yes." Sabina smiled. "I have this hot date with this CPA next week and I thought I should get new nails and perfume to get him to lust after me. Most CPAs are boring, if you know what I mean, but this guy is cute. I want to get him excited. I want to get accessories like the nails and French perfume. What do you think?"

"These long red nails are popular. The only French

perfume we have is this one. Give me your wrist and I'll spray a bit on you."

Sabina extended her wrist as Etta sprayed on the perfume.

"Oh, that is nice. How much is it?"

"Well, it's French. See, it's right here on the box, and it's $150 for the bottle."

"$150! It's just a first date—no man is worth $150 on a detective's salary." Sabina smiled at the clerk. "Are you Etta Jones?"

Her eyes got big, and she stepped back two steps before bumping into the side of the kiosk cart.

"What? Why do you want to know?"

"We'd like to ask you a few questions." They took out their badges. "We can do it here, or we can take you downtown to headquarters. I'm Detective Bennett, and this is my partner Detective Sullivan. We are with Milwaukee Homicide."

"Homicide! I didn't do anything. What do you want with me?"

Tara saw panic in her eyes as they darted left and right, looking for a place to run. Sabina saw it too and stepped in front of her, blocking any escape.

"A gray Malibu sedan was involved in a shooting two days ago."

Tara watched as Etta mouthed the word "My—" and then stopped. There were tears in the girl's eyes, and her body trembled.

"Look, Ms. Jones," said Sabina, "if you don't answer our questions right now, we'll have no choice but to take you downtown. Why not make it easy on everyone? Who was driving your car two days ago in the afternoon?" When she didn't answer, Sabina asked, "Were you at work here?"

"Yes, I was working."

"Then who was driving your car?" Sabina asked. "Right now you're an accessory to a murder."

Etta dropped onto the kiosk stool, looking down at her hands.

"I guess were going to have to do this the hard way, Ms. Jones. You need to close up here now. We're taking a ride downtown. Let's start moving." For effect, Sabina took out her handcuffs, tossing them from one hand to the next as Etta closed up shop. When she was done, Sabina grabbed her wrist and clamped the cuff on one wrist, then the other. "You can grab your purse now."

As they walked down the mall toward their car, Tara said. "A male was identified as the driver of the car that did the shooting. We want to know if you know who that driver is, and where he might be."

Sabina said, "Listen Etta, we won't book you like we were going to if you tell us who was driving your vehicle. Our second question is: do you know where this person is right now?"

Etta looked up, then to the side. She started crying.

"Come on," said Sabina, "let's go downtown. You can cry there." Sabina grabbed Etta's arm a little firmer and led her outside to the parking lot.

Etta abruptly stopped. She turned toward Sabina. "I don't want to go. I didn't do anything. My stupid brother used my car, without my permission I might add. I didn't know he even used it 'til later. I take the bus to work because my car is a beater and I never know if it's going to start. I might have a shitty job, but at least it's honest work. My brother Waldo, he's always looking for easy money. He's in a gang. They hang out at the park near the basketball courts a few blocks from my family's house. I live at home with my mother and help her pay for things. Waldo doesn't do anything to help.

"The gang used to come to our house and hang around, but my mom got sick of those losers and called the cops on them for trespassing. After a few tickets, they finally got the hint and moved to a new hangout. The basketball courts are in the neighborhood park. You can find them there."

Sabina unlocked the cuffs. "That's good, Etta, that's real good. You're still not off the hook as a possible accessory. That's up to the DA, but we'll tell him you cooperated with us. We know where you work, and live. Here's my card if you have any information that might help us more. Don't leave town, and don't do anything stupid. Got it?"

"Yes, ma'am."

Trying to determine Waldo Jones' whereabouts proved more difficult than expected. Tara and Sabina never thought they'd have trouble finding the park where the gang members hung out, but then they didn't realize there were three Milwaukee County parks near the Jones' house. Murphy's Law proved to be in effect: the third park was the right one.

They were sitting in the Crown Victoria with the air conditioner going full blast even though they were sitting in the shade of a massive oak tree. They had no problem spotting the gang at this park. They were in a group: black men, and a few black women all wearing Oakland Raiders shirts and hats sitting in a corner of one of the courts, rap music blaring, and no one was dressed for basketball. The half of the basketball court the group was hanging out near was empty, while at the other half, a game was in progress with non-gang members. That group and their game never went near the other half of the court to play.

The two cops watched the area for about twenty minutes, planning their strategy.

"Looks like the gang's half of the court is off limits to other players, and they aren't even playing," Tara said.

"Their turf?" Sabina said. "Small gang if they can't find any place better than a playground." Sabina laughed.

Tara grabbed the case folder. "I got the DMV picture of Waldo. Take a look."

"Nice looking kid. Probably still in high school. Too bad he got mixed up in this."

They watched a few more minutes.

"There he is." Tara pointed. "He's coming out of the shelter's restroom."

"Tara, why don't you let me do the talking? I know you can do the questioning, but I think I might be better at getting information from the brothers here, rather than a white cop. Understand?"

"Yeah, I understand."

"Just be ready to back me up. It might get dicey when we try to take Waldo in. You got back-up on speed dial? Use it if you think we'll need it. Don't wait for me to give you the OK. Just call. Ready?

"Just let me call the dispatcher and give the address to her now so they know where to come if we need them."

"Good idea."

A minute later, Tara hung up. "Let's go." They got out of the car and walked towards the gang.

Drew had been sailing for several hours when he reached the wide channel between the tip of the Door County peninsula and the islands creating Death's Door.

Odd name, he thought while looking at the channel between the tip of the Door County Peninsula, Washington Island and a smaller Detroit Island. Having time on his hands and a signal on his phone, he Googled the story. He read it got its peculiar name when a band of Indians were raiding another band of Indians. Canoeing across the open water, a storm came up, tipping their canoes, and they all died.

An hour later, Drew had made it through Death's Door and was making good time. He thought he'd arrive sometime around seven that evening. He had called Sister Bay Municipal Marina and reserved one of the last slips for the night.

When he arrived at the marina, he didn't see *Condor*. He took a shower, then called George.

"Come on down. I'm at the other marina, Yacht Works, at the end of town, out near the gas dock. Can't miss me."

It was about a mile away, and the walk gave Drew needed

exercise. Plus, he enjoyed checking out the houses along the way.

George's sixty-five foot boat was at the far end of the marina. Of course, once again Drew was impressed with *Condor*; its gleaming white hull and rich brown varnish made it hard to believe the boat was over fifty years old.

Drew saw George on the bow, adjusting deck chairs, tightening the bow and spring lines.

"Hey, Captain, can a guy get a drink around here?"

George's head snapped up and he smiled.

"I usually don't let sailors on my boat. Bad image but, in your case, come aboard. Make yourself a drink and bring me a Glenlivet on the rocks while I wipe down the cushions."

Drew noticed he had three deck chairs arranged around a small table on the bow. Before he could ask it, George answered his next question: why three chairs?

"I stopped at a really unusual bar called Fred and Fuzzy's, located at Little Sister Bay on the way up from Sturgeon Bay this morning. The place is right on the shore, with tables set out on a hill with trees, and grass sloping down to a pebble beach. It had a huge pier just big enough for *Condor*.

"Fred and Fuzzy's had great food, and lots of people looking at the water view with its high bluffs. It looked like Maine, except it's here in the Midwest on Lake Michigan. A waitress named Rhonda was a real looker, and friendly too. Naturally, they're all friendly when they see *Condor*. But Rhonda was especially nice, and photogenic. I talked her into stopping by for a drink after she gets done with work."

"Don't you ever stop? We're boating. Male bonding."

"You don't seem to have a problem finding women," George said. "Hell, you don't even go out of your way looking for them, like I do."

"It's not that, George. The problem is, there is only Rhonda stopping by. I'd hate to take her away from you once she sees me."

"That'll be the day," George shot back. "Besides, I have a bigger toy boat than you." He raised his tumbler of Scotch to Drew. "To women and the sea."

Drew nodded. "How was your trip? I assume you got caught in the storm."

"Did I ever! Waves were at least ten feet and steep. I had to change course, or I would have had a lot of damage. I lost about six wine glasses, one lamp, but that was about it. Pretty lucky, actually."

Drew nodded in agreement. "I hate being out on the water with lightning flashing and my boat's mast being the only thing sticking up for miles around. I know I have lightning protection but still, it's intimidating."

"Well, we both made it safe and sound. That's all that counts. Did you have a good sail over?"

"It was great. Going south from the tip of Door County was right out of *Sailing* magazine, with the high limestone bluffs, and deep green trees. When you spend time in Afghanistan, with its lunar landscape, you appreciate all the color." Drew drained his drink. "Mind if I have another? It's been a while since I've had rum on the rocks. Tasty."

"Sure, help yourself. I always have lots of rum."

"How was your time with Roberta and her son? It seemed like you were excited to take her boy out the next day."

"I was. We took a lot of pictures. Billy took some, and I took more of him and his mom, and of course later I took pictures of Roberta alone. Here, take a look."

George shoved a box with pictures in it.

Drew grabbed the box and was looking at the photos when he noticed the watch and earrings Roberta wore. "That's a pretty nice watch she's got on—looks like a Piaget or a good knock-off, if I'm not mistaken. That type of watch and the pearl earrings are pretty expensive. Unless I misjudged what Roberta earns, she doesn't make that much."

"Good eyes, Major Thompson. They were my mother's. I sometimes let a few of my models wear Mom's jewelry on shoots. I thought Roberta would enjoy something fancy. It made her feel special and set the right mood."

"She sure looks good and happy, all right. I'm glad you had a nice time with her and Billy. Sometimes George, you amaze me." Drew laughed, and so did George.

"Yes, I'm really just a big lovable teddy bear."

The two went back to talking about how difficult the conditions can get on Lake Michigan.

George sipped his drink. "I was surprised how steep and high the waves got. It was difficult and very dangerous."

"I can only imagine. It looks like you got a few cuts or bruises on your face. Something hit you?"

"A couple of the glass tumblers came flying across the cabin when I didn't secure them. Nothing major, they'll heal."

"A big boat like yours is pushed through the water, not like mine that slips through the water. The storm might have been easier on *Courage* than *Condor*."

"You might be right. Anyhow, we got here, and storms are all part of boating and the Great Lakes lore."

Drew said, "I heard on the radio two people were washed off the pier in Ludington, and one of them was saved but the other hasn't been found yet. The Coast Guard is still looking."

"Only two?" said George. "I'm surprised there weren't more. People do crazy things in conditions like that, walking out on the jetty and sightseeing. I saw spray reaching over the top of the lighthouse there, when I left that morning. That storm raged a long time, I can tell you that. People don't know the power of water, and how deadly it can be." George rubbed his scraped elbow.

Chapter Twenty-Seven

Waldo Jones sat on a green-painted courtside bench halfway from the baseline to the mid court line. Along with several of his gang members, he was calling out remarks and making fun of three young men actually playing a basketball game called Horse.

Tara and Sabina watched as a tall, lanky gang member sank a big "Sky Hook" **à** la Kareem Abdul Jabbar, which brought hoots and hollers from the group.

"You aren't that good a shooter, Skinny," Waldo yelled from the sidelines.

"Love the nicknames these guys have for each other," said Sabina.

When she and Tara, each wearing a short blazer hiding their weapons, walked across the basketball court, the games and conversation stopped. The gang members' eyes were all glued on the women as they stopped to stand in front of Waldo.

"Waldo Jones." Sabina pulled out the photo, looked at it, then back at him. She wanted them to know that they had done their homework. "I'm Detective Bennett and this is Detective Sullivan. We'd like to ask you a few questions." They both showed their badges.

"Why you want to ask me questions? I didn't do nothing." He looked nervous. His eyes darted to the other gang members, then back to the detectives. Tara watched as he started pulling his left earlobe. Yes, he is nervous, she thought.

"We'd like to ask you about driving your sister's car two afternoons ago. Do you remember driving her car? Let me help you a bit: it's a gray Malibu sedan."

"I don't remember nothing from two afternoons ago."

"Several witnesses saw you driving the gray Malibu."

"That wasn't me." Waldo smiled and pointed at several of the gang members. "They can tell you. I was here playing basketball and hanging out. I have my own witnesses. Right?"

Several heads nodded in the affirmative. Others voiced, "Yeah, Waldo was right here, right fucking here."

One in the group got up from a bench and slowly walked towards the two policewomen. He was big, at least six feet three inches, with wide shoulders, mirrored sunglasses, and weighed about 220 pounds. Tara could also tell he didn't work out much because she saw a protruding belly under his sleeveless Raiders shirt. Unlike the others, he wore no hat. When he was no more than arm's length away, he said to Sabina, "Waldo's our star basketball player. He was here playing, like he said. Besides, it's our word against theirs. Reasonable doubt, I think they call it. Why you two here anyway?"

He pointed at Tara. "Especially you, white lady cop? Don't you know it's dangerous for you to be in our area? We rule here, and you're not welcome."

"Well I'm black, Mister Big Shot," Sabina fired back. "What's your name?"

"I'm Reggie." He stepped closer to Sabina, his eyes moving up and down her body. "Now you, I can't believe you're a cop. You are real fine. Let's talk about something really important, like working for me. Give up this cop shit. You work for peanuts, I bet. Maybe you even get shot at. Work for my gang and me. With your body, and me handling you, you'll make lots of money. We'll dress you in fancy clothes like a movie star, and I'll personally take really good care of you."

Sabina laughed in his face. "That sounds incredibly tempting. Are you propositioning me, Reggie? I think you're more like a rooster, making lots of noise, acting like a big wheel, but not ever really doing anything big. Your office here is half a basketball court—not even the full court. Impressive." She stepped closer to him. "Look, Reggie, we're taking your star basketball player downtown and we don't want any trouble from you or your gang, so back off." She pulled out her cuffs.

"I don't think you are going to do that," Reggie said, grabbing her arm. "I told you Waldo was with us. He wasn't involved in any shooting or driving a car. He's not going anyplace downtown. We already answered your questions. He was here!"

"That's funny," said Sabina. "Did I say we were questioning him about a shooting? We asked him if he was driving a gray Malibu. Since you brought it up, maybe we'll question him about that." She smiled at Reggie. "If I were you, I'd take your fucking hand off my arm now or I'll break it."

He laughed. "I don't—"

Before he could finish, Sabina bent her leg and jammed it into his knee. Reggie lost his balance while she grabbed his wrist and twisted his arm, slamming him down towards the ground. In a fluid motion, she snapped a cuff to his right wrist, then grabbed the other and cuffed that.

"Reggie, the idea of *you* protecting *me* is funny. Now we'll take you both downtown for questioning. You, Reggie, for assaulting an officer, and Waldo here for his possible role in the shooting. Yes, Reggie, I think we might even find you were involved in the shooting, too." She glanced at Tara. "Time to call for back up, partner."

***

George's gaze moved from Drew toward the shore and long dock. "Ah, here comes my waitress friend. Rhonda—I think that's her name. Drew, introduce yourself so I don't look like a fool if I'm wrong with her name, will you?"

"I can do that," Drew said. "I'll go help her come aboard. That way she'll think I'm part of your crew."

"She knows you're not. You weren't with me today, remember?"

"Oh yeah. Well then, I'll tell her I'm captain of my own boat so we'll be on equal footing. Two captains. Duty calls."

He watched her walk towards him. Even from a distance, Drew could tell she was beautiful, as George had said. He noticed too, she favored her right leg. She had a slight limp. Her auburn hair glistened in the fading sunlight.

"Welcome aboard. I'm Drew Thompson, a friend of George's." He extended his hand.

"Hi, I'm Rhonda. I guess George told you about me."

"Not too much. He was trying to keep you a secret, and I can see why." He watched her smile, then led her to the bow of the boat.

"Rhonda, thanks for coming," George said. "Now what can I get you to drink? I have cheese and sausage, just in case you're hungry.

Drew sat back and watched George try his photographer pitch on Rhonda about modeling, and how he could hide the scar on her leg. However, instead of impressing her with his photographic skills, George's pressure was having a negative effect, and putting her off.

As the evening wore on, George was getting more frustrated with Rhonda. Applying his charm on her like he had with Roberta was having less success. As a result, Drew observed, George was getting drunker and slurring his words. Other women may get excited to have a moment of photographic fame as a model, but Rhonda didn't seem to care.

After a couple drinks, she looked at her watch. "I really need to go. Thank you for the hospitality, George, but I have to get up early tomorrow. It's been a long day on my feet, so I'm going home to take a long bath. Maybe another day, George?"

"Oh, sure, I understand," he said in a drunken voice, "but you can stay here. I have plenty of room as you can . . . "

She cut him off. "That's all right. I want to go home and rest. Maybe I'll see you again tomorrow, or another day. Drew, it was nice meeting you."

Drew chuckled to himself when he saw Rhonda wink at him. He said, "You know, George, I've had a long day too. I think I'll leave too. I'll see you tomorrow, and we can plan our trip, or see the sights of Sister Bay."

George scowled. "I can't believe you're both leaving me."

They walked together towards Yacht Works' parking lot.

"Can I give you a ride to your boat?" Rhonda said. "It's right on my way home."

"Sure. Where do you live?"

"Just down Highway 57, a couple of miles from Sister Bay. It's away from town and the water, so it's a lot cheaper. Not many people want to live in the middle of the peninsula, but it's fine with me. I see the water all the time at Fred and Fuzzy's, so it's no big deal. Where I live, I see lots of prairie grass and juniper bushes. Actually, I like it that way. I get lots of birds and small animals that come to my birdfeeder."

It only took a few minutes to get to the Drew's marina.

"Would you like to see how the other side lives, and have a drink?" asked Drew. "I only have wine or scotch."

"I guess I could do that." Rhonda parked in the lot next to the marina office. "I don't really have to work until one in the afternoon tomorrow, so I can stay out a little later than usual. I just wanted to get away from him."

He smiled. "Right this way," and they walked to his boat. After he helped her on *Courage*, he said. "You didn't like George, did you?'

"For some reason, he gave me the creeps. He was fine this afternoon, a gentleman, but tonight I saw something different. I didn't like it." She sat on one of the cockpit cushions.

"What do you want: rum and Coke, beer, or white wine?"

"I'll have wine. You know the view here is nice too. The town's lights along the shore, and the condo lights across the bay, really make it scenic."

"Yes, it's a nice little harbor," Drew said, admiring the view. A few minutes later, he sat next to her.

"Here you go. I've got cheese if you'd like something."

"No, I've had enough cheese. This wine is fine. Maybe later. I am getting hungry, but I can stop at Husby's for a burger on my way home."

"I detect a slight European accent. Where are you from? We didn't talk about that on the boat."

"Sarajevo. I came here twelve years ago. I got a green card, and then got my citizenship five years later. There was just too much fighting back home to stay there. The siege of our capital started in 1992 and lasted until 1996. Thousands of people were killed. Some of them were my family. I lost two brothers and an uncle.

"I was seven when it started. I remember back then: you got up in the morning, and never knew if it was going to be your last day. Bombed out buildings, deserted neighborhoods were all around where we lived. So much destruction, like we see in the Middle East now. My country was so beautiful, but now, with what's going on there, I'm not sure it can ever recover. They've tried to fix it up, but some things will never be fixed. I'm not sure I ever want to go back again. I feel safe here in Door County. Back home, the fighting has stopped but the anger and revenge is still hanging in the air, or maybe just under the surface, waiting for another spark to start it all over again. This is my home now. It's nice and quiet here. When winter comes, it even gets a little boring, but I like that too."

She took a sip of wine. "Fred and Fuzzy's closes later in the fall. In the winter, I waitress at Alexander's, between Fish Creek and Ephraim, so I have a place to work, and some years

I've gone to Florida in the winter. It's warmer, and I can easily find a job doing the same thing down there."

"Well, I'm glad you're here. Let's forget about war and killing and talk about something happier. Do you have any kids?"

"No, but I'd like to someday. This is a great place to raise kids, and Wisconsin is so pretty, even in the winter. You know Sarajevo had the Winter Olympics in 1984, before I was born, so we like the winter, and winter sports. About all I can do up here is cross country ski in Peninsula and Newport State Park. They have beautiful trails in both, and in the summer, I bike ride and get asked to go boating a lot. I can't imagine why." She laughed.

"I can. You are beautiful, Rhonda."

"Thank you. I guess I could be a model except for my limp and scar on my right leg. They don't give out medals to civilians for wartime wounds." She rubbed her leg. "Sometimes it hurts towards the end of a long shift, but I was luckier than most."

Drew nodded. "War is horrible. I lost my best friend in Afghanistan and took a few wounds myself.

"You did? Where?"

"Here, above my ear. I can't hear out of this ear. That's what got me early retirement, and here." He lifted up his shirt and pointed to the spots on his side. "Can't really show you the scar on my butt unless you really want to see it. That wound only hurts when I sit down, and only for a couple of weeks back then."

"So now you're doing what?"

"I'm getting ready to take a long trip along the eastern

part of the Great Loop Route, eventually sailing down to Chesapeake, where I'll spend a month. I went to the Naval Academy in Maryland so it will be fun seeing old friends and reliving good times there where they made me one of the few and proud. I decided to be a Marine like my dad. After that, I'm not sure. That should keep me busy. I have a lot to try to forget."

"We both do," Rhonda said. "Can I have another glass of wine?"

"Sure." He got up and poured her the last of the bottle, giving it a vigorous shake before resting it on the cockpit deck. "Sorry. I can only give you that. I usually drink beer or scotch."

"That's fine. I'm getting hungry, and I bet you are too. Let's finish these drinks and go to Husby's and get a burger. The pizza's good there too. If I'm not mistaken, they have a band playing tonight. Maybe we can even dance."

"Dance?"

"Marines know how to dance, don't they?"

"We'll see." He looked at her flip-flops and smiled. "I hope I don't hurt your toes too much."

Chapter Twenty-Eight

Husby's Bar was busy, but Drew and Rhonda managed to find a table far enough away from the booming band speakers. The singer was doing a good job of sounding like Johnny Cash, and the band played familiar tunes that kept everyone in a good mood.

They ordered the standard sixteen-inch pizza with the works and a pitcher of beer. As Drew finished the last piece and was wiping his mouth, Rhonda grabbed his hand. "C'mon, even a Marine can dance a slow dance."

He smiled. "Why not? Marines aren't stupid." The dance area was small, but was packed with tourists and locals, all having a good time. They found a spot, and when Drew wrapped his arms around Rhonda, she did likewise.

"It's been a while since I danced with someone like you," she said.

He looked at her. "And?"

"Nothing. I just like dancing. No strings attached, just a nice dance with someone who seems to care about me, not just my body. At least I think so," she said with a big smile. "You are an interesting person, Drew Thompson."

She rested her head against his chest, feeling good in his arms. And her words were so satisfying to hear, especially after what Amber had said a few days ago.

The song ended, and they walked back to their table. As they did, a guy with wild eyes, a dirty tee shirt, and hair that looked greasy and wild, blocked Rhonda's path, getting right in her face.

"Well, look who's here. You aren't at Fred and Fuzzy's now, so you can talk to me about going out, having some fun." He smiled, revealing a missing tooth. The rest of his teeth were nicotine stained. "You know what I mean, or am I not good enough for you?"

Rhonda jumped back, bumping into Drew and then moving behind him so Drew was acting like a shield.

"I told you earlier. I'm not interested in going out with you today, or any day. Just leave me alone!"

"Why? I can clean up real nice for you. I can be good. I get a little funny once in a while in the head because of Afghanistan, but I can be real nice to someone special like you. We'll have a good time. I'd take you to a fancy restaurant, and we can get to know each other. Come on." He tried to reach around Drew and touch her arm.

She jerked it back. "I told you this afternoon, *No*, and I mean No."

Drew had enough of this guy. He'd seen a few like him that couldn't handle life after the horrors of war. He sympathized. Hell, he was having a hard time himself.

He stepped in closer to him, shielding Rhonda more so he was right in his face. The dude's body odor was strong.

"The lady is not interested in you, so leave her alone, and back off."

"Oh, are you her husband?"

"No, I'm her friend. If you touch her again, you'll be sorry."

He stepped back, looked at Drew, appraising him. Drew saw him reach for something in his front pocket. A knife?

"If that hand comes out with anything in it, I'll break it," Drew said.

The packed crowd started to move back.

Drew watched as the hand slowly came out empty.

"That's the first smart thing you've done. Now leave us alone."

Drew grabbed Rhonda's hand while still staring at the guy and started walking her to their table. When they sat down, Rhonda let out a big sigh.

"Thank you. That guy has been coming to Fred and Fuzzy's for three days and keeps bugging me. I thought he'd get tired and leave me alone by now, but he seems to be stalking me. He freaks me out."

"He looks like he's on something," Drew said. "Don't worry about it. Let's have another drink and wait for another slow dance."

"I thought you said you didn't like to dance?"

"I like the slow ones. With you."

She reached over and touched his hand.

They ordered another drink and talked, not really hearing the music, but enjoying each other's company. After an hour, the tables started to empty around them. Drew looked at his watch.

"It's almost midnight. I should go back to my boat."

She looked around the area, and then at him. "Would you mind coming home with me? I mean, I'm afraid to go home alone because of that guy. He freaked me out tonight. He comes to my work, and just sits and watches me. You saw how he acted. I just don't feel safe."

"Do you want to go to my boat? He won't go there."

"No, I'd rather sleep in my own bed. Is that all right? The bed is big enough for two." She smiled.

"Sure, I can do that," said Drew. "I really don't need anything for the night. I can finger brush my teeth."

He paid for the pizza and drinks, and they headed to her car.

They walked across the main street of Sister Bay, past the bowling alley to a dark area where her car was parked. It was a big Chevy four door, with a little rust, but still a nice older model.

He opened the door for her. She slid behind the wheel, putting the key in the ignition. As he started walking around the back of the car to the passenger's side he noticed she didn't unlock the door.

A trusting soul, he thought to leave it unlocked? Then he saw quick movement in the back seat as two arms moved over her head, with some kind of thin rope. Rhonda tried to scream, but all that came out was a muffled sound as her head was pulled back, causing her body to straighten out as she was being pulled tight against the headrest.

Drew raced around, back to the driver's side and flung open the back door, surprising the guy, driving his fist into his face. The attacker's right hand let go of the rope, and Rhonda slid back down into the driver's seat, her hands around her neck, pulling away the loose ends.

Drew pulled the guy out of the car by his shirt where he pounded his face with a couple of punches. That's when he saw the guy reach into his pocket for a knife. Drew grabbed his wrist as his hand came out with a switchblade. Drew brought his knee up to the dude's arm and heard a crack, then a scream. The knife dropped to the pavement.

"You broke my fucking arm!" he screamed. "You broke my arm."

Drew silenced him with a strong right to the chin, and watched as he crumpled to the ground, out cold.

He rushed to Rhonda's side. "Are you okay?"

She was rubbing her throat and crying. "He would have killed me."

"You're OK now, it's all over." Drew wrapped his arms around her. "We need to call the police."

The next morning Drew woke on his back, with Rhonda snuggled tight against him, her arm across his chest, her face pressed against him, her long brunette hair splayed on his chest. While she wore a nightgown, it had ridden up, exposing her scarred leg and shapely bottom. She wasn't naked, they hadn't made love, but that didn't matter.

Drew had finally done something right: he had saved someone. For once, no one had died, and he felt good about himself. His hand moved to her exposed buttock, rubbing in gentle small circles. She made small sounds before opening her eyes and gazing at him.

"Good morning" she said. "My throat hurts." She touched her neck. "Is there a scar?"

"No, but its red."

"You saved me last night from that horrible man."

"'Probably. That's what knights are supposed to do, right?"

"I didn't know I had a knight, but I'm grateful."

"After saving the damsel in distress, doesn't the knight usually get the girl?"

"Something like that."

Drew felt a huge grin spread across his face, and Rhonda was smiling too. He felt her hand slide down his body.

She said, "I think it's my turn to say thank you."

* * *

Rhonda dropped Drew off at the marina parking lot a little after noon. When he walked down the pier, much to his surprise he saw George sitting in the cockpit of *Courage*.

"Where have you been?" he asked.

"I went for a walk and had breakfast."

George wasn't convinced. "I must have just missed you because I've been sitting here for an over an hour. What was her name?"

"I forgot," Drew said with a smile.

"Bullshit. It was Rhonda, I bet."

Drew didn't say anything and went below.

"It's all right if it was," George said. "I don't think she was going to let me take any pictures. I don't think she liked me. I was surprised she agreed to come to the boat for drinks in the first place. She must have been bored or something."

"Not to change the subject," Drew said, "but I think I'm

going to head back to Milwaukee. I'm going to take my time sailing back, but I need to make some final plans for my trip. I'm going to be traveling a long time, so I need to rest up and save my pennies. Slip fees are biting into my bank account."

"Yeah, you're right. I'll see you back there. I guess I can leave today too. We'll talk on the way back. Sorry I got so plastered last night. The scotch tasted especially good."

"No problem." Drew shook George's hand, and watched him walk down the pier and head to Yacht Works and his boat.

Drew went down below and went to sleep. He really didn't get any rest last night or this morning. He was still keyed up from Rhonda's assault and the fight.

When he woke up, he was surprised it was dusk. He called Rhonda.

***

Drew left before dawn the next day. It would take a couple of days to get back, and while he had enjoyed Door County and his time with Rhonda, he wanted to be in Milwaukee.

Later the next day he got a call from Alex, inviting him to a cookout at his house on Saturday. Today was Wednesday, so he had time to get stuff done.

For the first time in a long time, Drew felt good about himself.

***

It had been a couple of weeks since Alex last saw Tara. He

picked up his cell and called her. "We still on for tonight? No murders pulling you away from tonight's dinner?"

The plan was to have a nice, quiet dinner at the yacht club, and then perhaps watch a movie at his house. He had picked up Robert Redford's *All is Lost*, though Alex hoped they would not watch much of the movie.

"Hi to you too," said Tara, a smile in her voice. "Yes, so far so good. What time should I meet you at the yacht club?"

"Five thirty, or sixish."

"I'll see you then." She paused. "Alex, it's been a while. I thought you forgot about me."

"I'm sorry, darling. You know business consumes me when I travel away from home. I'll try and make it up to you tonight."

"That sounds promising. I can hardly wait, but you still could have called me a couple times to let me know you were alive."

"I'll try to be better about calling. See you tonight." And he clicked off.

With Tara, he realized, he needed to stay closer to her, if he wanted to keep her. He'd better get her flowers or jewelry. And then he thought of his mom's jewelry.

Dad always got Mom the best, and after what she's been through Tara deserves the best. Alex smiled as the image of Tara, and then the image of his loving mother flashed in his mind.

Alex was sitting at the Club's bar overlooking the marina basin when Tara walked in.

"Hi, I'm sorry I'm late, but I had to follow up on a drive-by shooting with some of the lucky people that didn't get shot. The person killed was an innocent bystander: a guy who just happened to be in the wrong place, standing next to his gang member nephew. Sad. Even a little girl six years old was wounded. It's so senseless." She shook her head, gathered her thoughts, and then leaned over and gave Alex a kiss. "Enough business. How are you?"

"I'm good, but one kiss is not enough. Come closer." He wrapped his arms around her, pulling her close and kissing her more. Hearing footsteps and voices, they broke their embrace, and Tara sat on a nearby barstool.

"I'll have a Pinot Grigio, please," she said to the bartender.

"And you, Mr. West, another Ketel One and tonic?" He asked.

"Just give it to me on the rocks. I'll sip this one while Tara and I catch up before dinner. We'll have dinner in about a half an hour. Window table, please."

"I'll get your table set up, and you can go over to it whenever you're ready, Mr. West."

"Thank you."

"So how was your trip?" Tara asked when she had his attention again.

"Usual stuff. Just visiting people in Washington, the navy, Department of Defense, congressmen and senators, answering questions on projects. Then I spent time in Annapolis, at my parent's house, which is now George's. I have the Tudor here, but we technically share both houses." Alex changed the subject. "And what about Homicide, downtown? Anything new with your sister's case, or can't you say anything?"

"I'm working with Sabina on a couple of gang type shootings. Actually, there are new developments in my sister's case, but let's not talk about that. Let's talk about us!"

Alex grinned. "What do you want to know about us? Do you want me to describe what I'm going to do to you tonight because I missed you so much?" He watched her cheeks flush a light pink. He smiled like the Cheshire Cat in *Alice in Wonderland*. Alex reached for her hand and squeezed it. "I really did miss you."

"You are so bad but . . . " Tara looked at him. "I can't figure out why you are interested in me." Cate would have been such a better match for him. She wondered why she always put herself down.

"You're the one I'm interested in," Alex reassured her. "You're more beautiful than anyone else I know, and you carry a Glock in your purse, so I feel safe." That made her laugh.

"Come on, let's have fun tonight. After dinner, we can go to my house and watch a movie. It's all about sailing and disaster at sea. If you don't like it, we can go upstairs and make love. Is that proof enough of my devotion?"

"You're impossible. I like the part about after dinner—I mean the movie. Maybe the movie will help me get better at sailing stuff." She laughed when she saw Alex's smile turn to a frown. "Only kidding. Let's eat, I'm hungry."

"Before I forget. I'm planning a backyard barbeque at my house this Saturday afternoon that should last into the evening, if I know my friends from the yacht club. Brats, hamburgers, chicken wings, simple stuff, so I hope you can make it. Just so you know, I invited Drew Thompson."

"That's fine. Drew didn't kill Cate. Besides, he's almost as handsome as you. And even more than that, he could protect me in case someone tried to rob or mug me. I'm not so sure about you."

"You really know how to hurt a guy's ego. Maybe I need to take up martial arts or something."

"Serves you right. I'll talk to my boss about getting off. You know, I'm a rookie so I'm at the bottom of the totem pole for nights off, especially a Saturday night."

"Tell him I'll invite him too, if it makes a difference. I could always invite the Chief. You met him at a couple functions so . . ."

"Just let me ask. I don't need you to ruffle feathers in the department. Besides, Labor Day weekend is just around the corner, so maybe I can trade some time then. If I get off this Saturday, it will cost you big time."

"No worries. I already have that all figured out." *The earrings from mother should do the trick.*

It was a short drive to Alex's stately Tudor from the yacht club.

"Why don't you sit on the couch and I'll get us an after-dinner drink? What would you like?"

"I'll have a sip of whatever your drinking. I have to get up early tomorrow, so I don't want to be hung over. I've already had a couple wines too many," she said. "You aren't trying to take advantage of a poor defenseless girl, are you?"

"I'd hardly call you defenseless. How about a little Cognac? The French call it *the water of life*."

"Oh, I'm impressed."

He handed her a snifter. "Smell it, swirl it and then sip it."

"Bossy, aren't you?" But Tara did as instructed. "Wow, it's warm going down. That's enough for me."

He took the glass, and did the same. "The perfect way to end a dinner. Let me find the movie."

"I was only kidding about the sailing movie." she said. "Forget it. Get your ass over here and kiss me!" She patted the sofa.

"Yes, mademoiselle, but first I have to get you something. You mentioned it would cost me big time. I want to give you something." He got up and went to a picture on the wall.

Alex grabbed the edge of the painting, a Van Gogh copy of sunflowers. The frame was hinged. When he swung it back, it revealed a built-in safe.

"Just like in the movies," he said. "I have something to give you." Pulling out a velvet box, Alex excitedly walked over to her.

"Open it. It's for all the trouble you have to go through to get Saturday off, and also all my traveling."

She looked at the box, and then at him. "Alex, what are you doing?"

"Shut up and open it. It's just a little present."

She opened the box. Inside were two huge, sparkling diamond earrings. "You can't be serious?"

He got up and went to the grand piano in the living room, removing the framed black and white picture of his mother, and brought it back to Tara.

"Put them on, please."

Her hands shook as she put on the earrings.

"Come with me." Alex grabbed her hand and walked her to a full-length mirror in the entranceway. "Look at this picture of my mother, and then look in the mirror. Do you see the resemblance?"

In the photo, his mother wore these same diamond earrings. Tara stared in the mirror, saying nothing. Her stomach got queasy, like something horrible was going to happen.

Alex grabbed Tara's hand, turning her toward him, and gently kissing her.

"Every time I see you, I think of my mother. She was everything to me, and I miss her so much. I thought you should have her earrings."

She stared at him, taken aback by this revelation. He'd mentioned the resemblance before, but she hadn't paid much attention—but now, the earrings?

As if he knew what she was thinking, Alex said, "Don't worry. It's not what you think. I don't want to make love to my mother."

They walked back to the living room sofa.

"They look beautiful on you," he said.

She touched one of her ears, then reached for the Cognac and drained it.

"Whoa," he said. "That's powerful stuff."

"I think I need it," she said. "Can we go to bed now?"

"That's my girl."

***

When Drew pulled up to Alex's house for the Saturday night cookout. He was impressed, but then he never really ever owned a home. While the big Tudor house didn't overlook the lake, it had a great view of the park, and its golf course. Lucky guy.

Grabbing the twelve pack of Heinekens he had brought to help the beer supply, Drew could already hear music, and laughter coming from the backyard. Rounding the rear corner of the house, he saw several of his friends from the yacht club: Brian and Vicky, Tom and Robyn, Bill and his wife Barbara, and Rick and Madonna. Matthew, and Pam from the club were helping set everything up. Walking over to them, Drew said. "So where's the host?"

Pam pointed to the house. "In there, with his girlfriend, I think. Oh, here comes the girlfriend now."

Tara was carrying a big bowl of boiled shrimp. Right behind her was Alex.

"Hi, Tara, need any help?" Drew asked.

"No," Alex answered for her. "We've already cooked the brats and hamburger so I think we're all set."

"Is that beer for us?" Tara asked. "I could use a cold one now."

"Yes, it is," Drew said.

"Just dump it in the big washtub full of ice over there," said Alex. "Thanks for bringing it."

Drew was focused on Tara. "Are we still friends?" he asked.

She smiled. "Yes. Stop asking that. We're friends. Where have you been? I stopped down at the marina to see if Alex was around the last couple of weeks, but he was out of town too, on business. You were gone, and so was George."

"Well, I can only speak for George and myself. We were on a boating trip. George took *Condor*, and I sailed *Courage*. It was a long and interesting trip."

He bent down and grabbed a beer from the tub. "Do you want this cold beer or wine?"

"I'll have a beer."

Drew pulled out another Budweiser and handed it to Tara. "The Heinekens should be cold in another ten minutes."

Alex looked at Drew and Tara. "You guys talk. I'm going to mingle with my guests."

Tara locked eyes with Drew. "Let's sit down, Drew. I want to bounce some things off you."

"Sure."

They walked to a couple of lawn chairs under a big oak tree, away from everyone else.

Drew was curious. "What do you want to ask me?"

"I've been going over everything involved with Cate's case."

"I'm listening. How can I help?"

"I've been working this on the Q.T. and can't talk about it to anyone at the stationhouse. You said you worked Intelligence, if I remember correctly. I need fresh eyes and ears on this. Sometimes you look so hard at things, you miss the obvious. I went back to Riptide on my own, and one of the waitresses remembered something about a guy that was with Cate that night. She couldn't remember much, except that my sister had on a fancy watch, and the guy had an earring in one ear that was some type of large dog."

"That's interesting about the earring, but I could have told you about the watch. Your sister had on nice jewelry that night. Even I noticed it, and I couldn't remember the last time I bought any jewelry except this Seiko dive watch I'm wearing," Drew held up his wrist. "In New York, I've seen watches like Cate had on that night, and I know they go for a lot of money. Some drugged-up guy or crook might kill for something like that, if they needed money for drugs."

They sat for a while, not saying anything but drinking their beer. Drew had been looking at Tara, thinking how nice she looked. "Nice earrings, Tara. Did you get a raise, or are they zirconium diamonds? It's hard to tell nowadays."

"Alex gave them to me the other night. He said his mother had lots of jewelry, and I reminded him of his mother."

"It must be true because George said almost the same thing. You know their mother committed suicide? Alex told me she hung herself."

Tara's eyes got wide.

"He said she did it with silk scarves."

Tara looked down at the ground.

"Cate was found with a silk scarf around her neck."

Tara looked up and made a funny face, and then she got white, paled. "Oh, Drew."

"Don't go jumping to conclusions, Tara. Maybe you should ask Alex if his mother had a watch like your sister's. "Do you think Cate bought the watch, or was it a gift?"

"It was my mom's. Dad gave it to her when they adopted Cate. That's why Cate got it. I got a tennis bracelet, and some gold earrings."

Drew thought about what should be her next step. "Find out the brand of Cate's watch if you can."

"It was a Piaget. I asked Dad once. I'll find it on the Internet, and print it out. It might be useful."

"When you find the right one, show me the picture. In a photo George showed me, I saw a woman on his boat—Roberta—wearing a similar watch. It could be just a coincidence. George didn't seem too concerned about me seeing the picture, even when I asked about the watch. He said it was his mom's. Ask Alex if his mom had a watch like that, and who got it."

"I will. He had all this stuff in a wall safe in the living room, behind a picture. Let's go in the house, and I'll show you the picture of his mother wearing the earrings, and the wall safe."

"OK, I guess."

Alex intercepted them before they entered his house. "There you are. I saw you two sitting back there talking intently. Drew, you aren't trying to steal Tara from me?"

Tara jumped in with a quick answer. "I was just going to show Drew the picture of your mother. He commented on how nice the diamond earrings you gave me were. I just wanted to show him how they looked on your mother, and to see if he thought I looked like her."

"Oh, sure, go ahead," Alex said. "I'd be interested in your opinion." He walked towards his guests.

* * *

They stood in front of the piano in the large living room. "Here. Look." Tara held up the framed photo.

"You do look like her! Now that I've seen his mother, let's grab a plate of food, and head back outside and eat. I'm hungry."

Tara had expected a stronger reaction. "That's all you're going to say? Men!"

As they came out of the house, Alex joined them. Looking around the backyard, he said, "Everyone seems to be doing just fine out here. Drew, did you look at the picture of my mom? Tell me if you think Tara looks like her."

"She does look like your mother."

"Let's finish eating inside," Alex said to Drew and Tara. They picked up their plates of food and headed back into the house, and its large formal dining room. Drew was surprised that no one was inside, but then it was ideal weather outside.

Drew looked at the room's fancy chandelier. "You're really lucky to have a house like this, Alex. They don't make homes like this anymore. It would cost a fortune in today's market."

"You're right, and it's no small feat keeping it in good shape and paying the property taxes. It's fine, though. I love this house. I have fond memories. It's like *Passage Maker*: It costs a fortune to maintain her, but she's worth it. I guess I'm not afraid to get things that are expensive if they're worth it."

Alex reached out to squeeze Tara's hand. "Don't those diamond earrings look great on her?"

Drew's eyes turned to Tara, and saw her force a smile.

When they finished dinner, they cleared the table into a big trash bin and went into the living room. There, on the piano, was the picture of Alex's mom.

Just to make conversation, Drew picked it up again. "I think you're right, Alex. Tara does look a lot like your mom."

"Really?" Tara said. "I just don't see it."

"Thank you, Drew, I knew you were my friend," said Alex. Then he leaned over and gave Tara a kiss on the cheek. "I better go out, and mingle more, or I'll hear about it from my friends at the yacht club. Tara, I didn't see your captain here tonight. Didn't you invite him?"

"No!" she said suddenly.

Drew laughed.

"Oh. Well. We'll talk later." Alex left the room, heading to the kitchen and back door.

"Now that he's gone, let me show you the safe." Tara swung back the faux Van Gogh. "See!"

"Yes, I see a safe. If I had valuable jewelry, I'd keep it in a safe too. So what?"

"I guess you're right." Tara looked around the room. "All I meant was, it's a nice cozy living room with a nice fireplace. I can imagine a fire going, stockings hanging on the mantel, with a big Christmas tree in front of the window decorated with a big star on top."

"Yes, that's the way my parents had our house decorated," Drew said.

"I wish it had been that way at our house. With Mom gone, Dad tried his best, and our housekeeper tried too, but it wasn't the same. Dad would look at us on Christmas morning, and he really tried to be happy and excited, but there was always sadness in his eyes, especially when he looked at me."

Tara started crying, and Drew put his arms around her.

After a couple of minutes, she stopped, pulled herself together and wiped her face with the back of her hand.

"Thank you. You're nice. I don't know why I started crying." She reached into a pocket, got a hanky, and blew her nose. "I guess I do know. I've never really gotten over the idea that my birth caused my mother's death and neither has my dad. I see it in his eyes. So, seeing all these pictures of Alex and George's family make me sad and maybe a little envious."

She started walking around the living room, looking at each picture, smiling, laughing.

"Oh, look, here is a picture of George or Alex with a golden retriever. I think it might be George's. Alex never talked about a dog, but George did."

"Yes, he recently got a golden," said Drew. "George keeps the dog on the boat when he's in Milwaukee, and when he's gone, he has some kid take care of it. I've seen him with that dog, and he loves it. He's a real dog person, that's for sure."

"I forgot about the new dog," Tara said.

They continued to walk around the house, looking at family pictures. After they finished, they went outside.

Tara walked across the lawn towards Alex, with Drew following. They joined a lively discussion about the yacht club races on Wednesday nights and Saturday mornings. Drew liked to crew occasionally, but he was a cruiser at heart. Everyone was laughing and telling tall tales.

Around midnight, Drew had enough. He shook everyone's hand, kissed all the women he knew and said goodnight. As he was walking to his car, Tara yelled to him. "Drew, wait." He watched her try to walk a straight line, but she was wobbling like someone learning how to wear high heels.

Standing in front of him, swaying, she slurred, "I know I've had too much to drink tonight, but we need to talk some more about all of this. I'll call you tomorrow."

"Fine. You aren't driving Detective Sullivan, are you?"

"No, I'm staying here." She giggled. "I won't forget. I'll call you tomorrow. I thought of something strange."

"Tomorrow. Yep."

Chapter Twenty-Nine

Two days later, Drew got a call from Tara. "Can we meet somewhere?" she asked.

"I thought you were going to call me yesterday."

"I had a pounding headache and couldn't think straight. Today's different. Are you free?

"Sure. Why don't you come down to my boat? I'm doing some last-minute varnish touch up. It's quiet there, and no one will disturb us."

"I'll be there in about an hour. I'll call so you can unlock the gate and let me in. See you then."

An hour later, Tara was sitting across from Drew in the cockpit, sipping a Coke.

Drew saw no reason to beat around the bush. "What do you need to talk to me about?"

"Several things have been gnawing at me, and maybe the two of us can figure out what I'm missing."

"OK. What stands out?"

"You said you saw George's friend in Michigan wearing a fancy watch?"

"Yes. A Piaget, I'm sure of it. Just a second." He got up and went down below into the cabin. A few minutes later, he came up with a picture of a watch from an old Piaget ad.

"I printed this off the Internet. It's an old one, 34 years old, to be exact."

Tara inhaled sharply. "Look at this." She showed Drew an old photograph of her mother wearing a posh watch. "Dad said when they adopted Cate, he bought this watch for my mother. After she died, he gave it to Cate. They're the same watches—same year, same style, same everything."

"I don't know what to conclude from that," said Drew. "It just seems like a coincidence. It doesn't prove George murdered your sister, if that's what you're driving at."

"True." Tara took a deep breath. "Here's another one: earlier this summer George and I had a heart-to-heart talk on his boat about our families. He said his mother had killed herself by hanging herself with scarves—Cate died with a scarf around her neck. Anyway, I checked with the Annapolis Police Department. No one was ever charged in Gloria West's death. It was ruled a suicide."

"Suicide is not a rational act, Tara. Unfortunately, people do it every day. The scarves were probably just handy."

"It just seems like a lot of strange coincidences: the watch, then the scarves. George said his mother did mean things to him and tied him up with scarves. She threatened to kill his dog if he told his father she was screwing around—a golden retriever, like he has now. I already told you about the dog earring—a golden is a big dog."

"All this sounds very circumstantial," Drew said, "but you're onto something. Find out who bought that earring. If it's George, he's our man. Or if you think Cate's watch is aboard his boat, get a search warrant. Are there any identifying marks on the watch?"

"My mom's initials are on the back."

"Next week I'm going to Virginia, and then Washington, to finish some Marine business. After that, I'm going to Annapolis. I could go to the police department and try to check things out if you like but I'll need your help. Do you think you could call the detective on Gloria West's suicide case and set up an appointment for me to go over the file?"

"Sure."

* * *

The following week, Drew pulled up in front of the house he knew all so well, the home of his best friend Gunnery Sergeant Tom Robb. When Drew walked to the front door, he heard the boys playing inside. He also heard Connie talking on the phone.

He stood there, stomach churning, but had to do it; he had to see her. He rang the bell.

"Just a second, someone's at the door," Connie Robb said on the phone. He heard footsteps, and the door opened.

"Hi, Connie."

She looked thinner, her hair disheveled, and she wore no makeup. She was barefoot and wore jeans. A food-stained kitchen apron covered a wrinkled, white tee shirt. He saw the look when she opened the door. She quietly said, "I'll call you back. Drew Thompson is here. Yes, that Drew." Her eyes had a fury like a drill sergeant.

"What do you want? Didn't I tell you, I didn't want to see you ever again?"

Just then, Andrew, Drew's godson, the oldest of their three boys, ran and hugged Drew's leg. "Uncle Drew, Uncle Drew . . . I missed you, Uncle Drew. Where have you been? Mommy's crying all the time. I'm so glad you're here to fix it. I don't like to hear Mommy cry."

Connie turned away, her hand to her face, eyes misty.

"Andrew, that's just why I came. I wanted to talk to your mom and see you guys too."

James and Mike, the twins, ran up now, jumping up and down around Drew, chanting "Uncle Drew, Uncle Drew" like a mantra. He bent down and pulled the two in his arms, giving them a hug.

"How are you guys—OK? Are you listening to your mom?" They shook their heads yes, and then started squirming. He set them down. "Why don't you guys go play, and when I'm done talking to your mom, we'll all go and get some ice cream? How's that?"

All he heard was "Yeah" and they took off.

"Connie, we need to talk. May I come in?"

She turned and resignedly moved to the living room, dropping into a chair. "I don't have any coffee. I need to go shopping today. The kids keep me so busy, I can't seem to even do the simplest things. I'm a big mess." Tears rolled down her cheeks.

"I miss him so," Connie said, wiping her face. "I mean, Tom was gone a lot—you know the Corps—but I always knew he was coming back to the kids and me. We'd talk on the phone when we could, and I'd send him pictures and letters so he'd keep up with the kids." She stopped and took a big, gasping breath. "Now I know he's not coming back."

A minute passed with no one saying anything. Connie looked up and wiped her eyes. "I miss him so much, and the kids do too. They're too young to understand he's never coming back." She got up and grabbed a tissue.

When she sat again, he said, "I know how you feel. I have a hole in my heart because I miss him too. Gunny was my best friend. We made a promise to watch each other's back, and to make sure we both came home. We got bad intelligence that day. I should have known. Our contact in the village who was going to facilitate the meeting with the village elder never showed up. He just disappeared or was shot, just before the shooting started. It was an ambush. I should have figured it out, but I didn't. He died in my arms, Connie. His last words were to tell you he loved you and the boys. He said, 'Take care of them, Drew.'"

As he said the words, he broke down and started sobbing uncontrollably. Through the tears, he felt Connie's arms around him, holding him. He kept on crying hard sobs. After a few long minutes, Drew finally managed to stop.

"I'm sorry. I've kept it in for so long."

Red-faced too, Connie managed a smile. "That's all right. It's tough to be a marine—keeping up the image."

"Yeah, the image. But I can tell you, there's a lot of crying that goes on when you lose a buddy." He did his best to collect himself. "Connie, I've come to tell you I'm here for you and the boys—anytime, anywhere, just call. I'm going to try to make up in some way for Tom not being here. I've set up a 529 plan for the boy's education, just in case they don't get to go to the Academy." He laughed. "I can just hear Gunny say, 'I don't want them to be no stinking officer!'"

Connie laughed, a twinkle in her wet eyes. "Yeah. That would be Tom. He loved being a Gunny."

"Can we be friends again?"

"We can be family, Drew, like before. We all need that." Connie leaned over, giving Drew a hug and a kiss on the cheek.

"Thanks. I'd like that. Now let's get that ice cream I promised the boys. Then we'll go shopping."

Late that day, almost at sunset, Drew drove along a gray asphalt street in Arlington Cemetery. He looked down the seemingly endless rows of white stone markers turning a light shade of pink-orange as the sun's rays defused the light. With the right section and row number written on a piece of paper, he finally found it. Parking his car, he made his way to the headstone.

Drew stood looking at it, tears again streaming down his face. How much could one man cry?

"Hi Gunny," he said out loud, not caring if anyone was listening. "I miss you so much, buddy. I saw Connie and the kids. They look just like you, poor kids, except for Andrew. He's the best looking because he's named after me. I just wanted you to know that I'll raise them just like you would want them to be raised. Connie's a strong woman, like most military women.

She's been getting support from the widows' group. She'll be OK."

He went down on one knee, grabbing grass from around the stone marker and pulling it free. "Sorry I let you down. I let you all down. Can you forgive me, all of you?" He kneeled there a few minutes, as if waiting for a voice to say, "You are forgiven, go on and lead a normal life." He heard nothing. Did he really expect to hear something? That happens only in the movies.

He got up, dusted his knee off, and walked back to his car. Then he heard it, the clear notes of a bugle playing "Taps." He turned, looking to the flag waving in the falling light. Standing at attention, Drew saluted.

He held the salute until the last note echoed through the hills of Arlington. Then he heard Tom's voice in his head say, "It's OK, Drew. We forgive you."

The following morning Drew parked in front of the police station, a multi-level, red brick structure, with the customary flags fluttering. At the front desk, he asked the desk sergeant for Detective Woods.

"And you are who?"

"I'm Major Drew Thompson, Marine Intelligence, Retired. Detective Tara Sullivan of the Milwaukee Police Department set up a meeting for me with Detective Woods. He has information we requested."

"Have a seat. He'll be out in a few minutes."

He hoped his hunch would pay off. Minutes later, a tall, crew cut military type came down the hall.

"Mr. Thompson, I'm Detective John Woods." The two men shook hands. "I have what you and Detective Sullivan requested, but it seems kind of odd after so many years to ask for this case file on a suicide-murder case. It was pretty straightforward. I looked over the case again, just to refresh my memory. I don't see anything new."

"I'm not doubting your investigation. I just wanted to look over a few things, and ask you a couple questions, if I could, after I look over the file. I'm a retired Marine major and did investigation as a normal part of my intelligence work for the military, so I'm familiar with investigation procedures. But Detective Sullivan and I just wanted to check a few facts for a couple of cases in Milwaukee."

"OK, you can use that room over there, but the info needs to stay here."

"Fine and when I'm done, I'll have a few questions for you, and I'll be out of your hair."

"Fine."

***

Alex looked at his watch: 8:00 a.m. He knew it was Tara's day off, but she must be awake by now. He listened to Tara's phone ringing.

"Tara Sullivan."

"Good morning, Tara. How are you this bright sunny day?"

"Well, if you really want to know, I'm totally sweaty from

my morning jog. I'm a little late today because I overslept, but it's my weekday off so no big deal. What's up? You don't usually call this early in the day."

"I know but I was pretty sure this was your day off, and I hoped to take you out sailing today. It's supposed to be perfect weather. We could go for a short sail up to Whitefish Bay, anchor there, and then have a picnic on the boat, maybe even go swimming. The water is warm this time of the year. We might even fool around. It's really important to me. What do you say?

"Well, since it's that important to you, I guess I can postpone cleaning the apartment today and spend time with you. Sure."

"Great. I'll pick you up at 9:30. How's that? It even gives you time to do a little cleaning."

"I was only kidding about the cleaning, Alex."

"Tara, I'm really looking forward to our sail today. I'll pick you up out front of your apartment. See you at 9:30."

"See you then." Tara looked at her phone and pressed End. She wasn't sure what that was all about. Alex had sounded funny, actually giddy.

Drew went into the precinct's conference room to go over the Gloria West file. He read about the West's chauffeur, Peter Owen, being shot in her bed, then she hung herself from the ceiling fan with two silk scarves. George West found his mother's body and summoned the police. The deaths were determined to be a murder-suicide.

Drew appeared next to Detective Woods' desk. "Here you go, Detective. May I ask you a couple of things?"

When the policeman nodded, Drew took a seat. "How many shots were fired from the gun that killed Peter Owen?"

"Two—one to the head and the other to the groin. Hell hath no fury like a woman scorned. He must have done something to really piss her off, but we never found out what."

"Was there gunshot residue on the mother's hands?"

"There was residue all over the place in that bedroom."

"Gloria West was naked," Drew read from the file, then looked up. "Was semen found?"

"Yes. That was in the report."

"The report also said nineteen-year-old George West found the body. Were his hands tested for gunshot residue too?"

"Yes, but he was clean."

"Do you remember if he looked like he had taken a shower or something?"

"I can't remember if his hair was wet. We just tested his hands, that's all."

"What about his brother Alex? I don't see anywhere that you interviewed him."

"What do you mean—his brother? Alex who?"

"George's twin brother, Alex West?"

Detective Wood frowned. "George West doesn't have a brother, Mr. Thompson. He was an only child."

Chapter Thirty

Shocked, Drew left the station. He had to warn Tara to stay away from Alex or George. One personality was a killer, maybe both. Driving in record time to Reagan National, he continued to call her number but kept getting her outgoing message. Finally, in frustration he left a voicemail. "Tara, it's Drew. I've got unbelievable news about Alex and George. Call me when you get this message. Whatever you do, stay away from Alex and George. Use any excuse you want but stay away from them. I know it's a strange request, but I'll explain when I see you."

Drew looked at his phone like something was wrong with it. Why was she not answering? What could she be doing that she doesn't have her phone on?

He called three more times as he moved through security. Running to gate twenty, he finally had a chance to look at the departure board and his flight to Milwaukee. Delayed twenty minutes. "Why now? I need to get back, and this happens."

He looked down three more gates and spotted a small bar and restaurant. He might as well have a drink while waiting, he thought.

Nothing's going to happen for a few hours until he got back and talked to Tara.

***

Alex pulled up in front of her apartment precisely at 9:30 in his black Jag convertible with the top down. He was excited waiting for her. He had the day's events planned out. He pressed her phone number and listened to it ring.

"Hi, it's me, I'm out-front waiting."

"On my way, just throwing stuff in my purse, including a new swimsuit. I think you'll like it."

"Great, but I'll like anything you wear."

A minute later, he watched Tara saunter out of the apartment building wearing a navy blue tee shirt, white shorts and white canvas topsiders with no laces. She had Ray Ban aviator sunglasses and a white visor.

"Wow. You look totally gorgeous today. And I see you brought your big purse. Are you packing heat?"

"Alex, you know very well I'm required to carry my gun, even when off duty. Rules are rules."

"Well, I don't think you're going to need it today. There haven't been any pirates on Lake Michigan for a very long time."

"Just relax. I promise I won't shoot you, OK?"

"That's fair, but please turn off your phone, will you? It's a special day, and don't want it ruined with you getting an emergency call about a killing or something that wrecks what I have planned."

"Fine. I can do that just for you." She grabbed her iPhone and switched it off. "There. Happy?"

"Yes, thank you."

***

Arriving at Milwaukee's General Mitchell Field, Drew phoned again. Jesus Christ, he thought in frustration, she's a cop. They always answer.

Getting into his car, an idea came to him, he'd call Pinkowski. He opened his wallet looking for the card Pinkowski had given him way back when he had first been questioned. He fumbled through all the credit cards, military ID, and money. "There it is," he said out loud. Drew had tucked it away behind the clear plastic pocket where he kept his Michigan driver's license. He dialed.

"Homicide. Pinkowski."

Motoring out of the harbor, Alex raised the sails and then turned *Passage Maker* north. Sailing half of mile out from the shore, Alex couldn't help but gaze upward at the large homes and mansions, perched atop the green bluffs, and then at the sandy shoreline, as he moved towards his favorite anchorage off Whitefish Bay. While not the typical harbor indentation most boaters looked for when anchoring, it was a good spot to swim and enjoy life.

He looked over at Tara. How beautiful she looked, especially today, he thought, but maybe she looked like that to him today because of the special reason for this trip.

"Would you like something to drink while we sail up to Whitefish Bay? I brought along a few bottles of champagne."

"Champagne? I can't remember us ever drinking champagne on the boat. Are you feeling all right Alex?"

Never better. I'm with the two females I love best in the world: my boat and you. That's why I'm so happy."

"You love me? That's the first time you've ever said that." She moved over to him, smiling, and sat on his lap. "The first mate has decided to get closer to the captain." She wrapped her arms around him and started kissing him. When they broke their embrace, Alex leaned over and flipped the autopilot on.

"Don't want to sail the boat into the shore because the captain can't steer a straight course. I think I need to give you twenty lashes with my tongue as punishment for getting the boat off course."

"Lash away, captain, your crew is ready for her punishment."

For the next twenty minutes, they enjoyed themselves feasting on touching and kissing.

"All right, we are here," he said, turning the boat toward shore and Klode Park's small indentation in the shoreline. Moving toward the bow as the boat drifted to the designated anchorage, he lowered the anchor and seventy-five feet of chain and line. Then he moved back to the cockpit and backed *Passage Maker* up until he felt the anchor grab hold of the sand bottom. Then he turned off the engine and moved back towards Tara.

"Now, where were we?" Alex took her in his arms once more.

After five minutes, Alex broke away, and went below to fetch the bottle of Dom Pérignon. "Let's freshen our glasses." He took her glass, dumped its contents overboard, then refilled her glass and his.

"There," he said with a smile.

A serious look appeared on his face, puzzling Tara.

"Did I do something wrong?"

"No, but I have something to ask you."

"I hope it's not that you've had too much to drink and want me to sail the boat back."

"No, that's not it, although I have had a little more to drink than you."

She watched as he moved closer to her and grabbed her left hand.

"Tara, my whole life I have only loved two people: my mother and you. I love you deeply and want to spend the rest of my life with you." She watched as he reached into his shorts pocket and pulled out a large diamond ring, slipping it onto her ring finger. "As you can tell by this, Tara Sullivan, will you marry me and be my wife?"

Tara let out a huge gasp that she was sure people on the beach could hear. Then she looked up into Alex eyes. "I can't believe this is happening. You want to marry me?"

"Yes, will you marry me?"

She started crying with joy, nodding her head yes. "Yes, Alex I'll marry you."

"I love you, Tara." And he grabbed her hand, pulling her up from the cockpit cushion and embraced her. Then he led her down below to the v-berth.

***

"Detective Pinkowski, this is Drew Thompson."

"Yes, Mr. Thompson. Do you have information for us, or is this a social call?"

"A little bit of both. I'm trying to get hold of Tara with important information, but I can't get hold of her. Do you know where she is?"

"No, I don't. I'll ask O'Malley." Drew hear Pinkowski's muffled voice, "Do you know where Tara is? This is Thompson. He's trying to get hold of her."

Drew heard O'Malley answer, "I thought she was going with that Alex guy, not Thompson."

"Yeah, I thought so too." Pinkowski said.

Drew heard O'Malley answer, "It's her day off. Maybe Sabina knows where she is. What's so important that he's calling us?"

Pinkowski answered, "Today is her off day. What's going on? Can't it wait until tomorrow?"

"Well if you want to know, I learned something this morning that might help her find her sister's killer. Besides that, she might be in danger. I really need to talk to her."

Pinkowski pounded his fist on his desk. "Thompson, we're the ones doing the murder investigation on Cate Sullivan, in case you forgot. Tara's not involved. You need to talk to us about anything concerning Cate Sullivan's case, not her."

"I understand that, but I'm worried about Tara."

"Where are you now? We need to talk to you right now about this."

"I'm pulling into McKinley Marina. Come down to my boat and we can talk about it but it's imperative I speak with Tara."

"OK. I'll call Sabina and see if she knows where Tara is. They usually talk every day. See you in ten minutes."

"Fine."

***

Pinkowski called Sabina Bennett's cell number after he and O'Malley got off the elevator to the parking garage. "Shit. No reception. I'll call her as we drive." Three minutes later, they were out of the garage. They turned onto Sixth Street and headed to McKinley Marina. Pinkowski dialed Sabina's number again.

"Yeah, what do you want, Pinkowski? You know it's my day off? Don't tell me you're calling to tell me to come in for another damn shooting. I've been waiting two weeks to get my nails and hair done. It's takes me all day for them to repair my chipped nails and braid my hair the way I like it."

"Relax, we aren't calling you in. We're looking for Tara. Drew Thompson called and is looking for her. He says he has information on her sister's murder and thinks Tara might be in danger. He wouldn't tell us much over the phone so we're headed to the marina so he'll fill us in."

"Tara in danger? I'm turning around and heading down there too. I want to hear what he's got to say. I'll meet you. I'm on Wisconsin Avenue near the river. I'll be at the marina in five minutes. Tara told me this morning she was going sailing with Alex West today."

"Yeah, I figured she didn't want to be interrupted, and had turned her phone off. We'll see you there. You might as well hear what Thompson has to say too so we're all on the same page." Pinkowski hit End.

His partner turned the police vehicle into the marina parking lot. "I still don't like Thompson," O'Malley said, "but if he's got something that could help solve Cate Sullivan's murder case, that's good."

***

Drew sat in the cockpit of *Courage*, drinking a bottle of water when he saw O'Malley, Pinkowski and Tara's partner Sabina hurrying down the dock. He got up to help them onboard after he noticed Pinkowski and O'Malley had on black leather-soled shoes. Sabina had boat friendly tennis shoes on. Smart lady, he thought.

"Now that we have a quorum, where is Tara?" Drew said. "Anyone want a bottle of ice water?"

Everyone shook their heads no.

"Fine. Where is Tara? I need to know. She might be in grave danger."

Sabina said. "Everything's fine. Tara went sailing with Alex today, around 9:30 this morning. She said they were going to do a picnic cruise someplace and anchor."

"Oh shit," said Drew, his tone arousing alarm among the others. "We have to find her."

***

"She could be anyplace out there," Drew said to Pinkowski.

O'Malley said. "I have an idea. Let's call the Coast Guard and have them fly their helicopter up and down the shore. We can also have two police boats check out the river although I doubt they'd picnic on the river."

"Good idea," said Sabina. "When they spot his boat, we can jump on one of the policeboats at McKinley and race to where they are."

Pinkowski said, "I still don't see why she is in danger. So Alex and George are the same guy—strange, but I don't see it as an apparent crime. Why are you so worried, Thompson?"

"I think George West is Cate Sullivan's killer. She was wearing a distinctive watch the night I saw her at Riptide. In Michigan, George took pictures of a friend of mine. When I looked at a few of the pictures he took, she had on the same type of watch and earrings Cate was wearing the night she died. When I asked George about it, he said the jewelry was his mother's, and he used it for dressing up his models."

"That doesn't make him a murderer," Sabina said. "There's such a thing as coincidence."

Drew shook his head. "Another coincidence: Stella Carpenter modeled for George and disappeared from here in Milwaukee. I think he had something to do with her death. Right now, I'm worried for Tara's safety. Who is she with: Dr. Jekyll or Mr. Hyde? Someone that cares about her or someone that might kill her?"

Pinkowski looked at the three others. "I suggest we wait here until we find her. West and her might be on their way back." He looked at his watch. "It's 2:30 now—long after lunch." He looked at the flags waving on the tall flagpole next to the boathouse. "It looks like a nice afternoon to be sailing. O'Malley, call the Coast Guard and see if they can find the boat. Thompson can give a description of the boat to the pilot."

"OK, we wait here," Drew said impatiently. Convinced Tara was in grave danger, he wanted to do something, anything, to save Tara.

"Any coffee?" O'Malley asked while Googling the Coast Guard headquarters.

"I'll make some."

***

"Do you want some more Champagne?

"Sure, but just one more glass. I'm lightheaded. It's been quite the afternoon." Tara leaned over and she kissed Alex. "Now can I turn my phone on, Mr. West?"

"Must you? I don't want to wreck this day. It's your day off. Come on, leave it off."

"Just let me turn it on and see if I got any messages or texts."

"Let's get the anchor up and start sailing back. I might need your help, First Mate," he said with emphasis. "Now that were a team."

"If you say so."

He got up and started the engine and then moved forward to raise the anchor with the power windlass. Once up, he rolled out the forward sail. "We'll just sail with the headsail so there's less fuss. Go ahead and turn your phone on for just a bit. I'm getting more Champagne."

She heard him pop the cork on the bottle as she powered up her cell.

* * *

Pinkowski walked over to A Dock and told the one remaining policeboat there to be ready to head out and intercept *Passage Maker* if it was located by the helicopters. Once they safely removed Tara from the boat, they'd ask Alex West to follow them back to the yacht club for questioning.

Pinkowski stepped back onboard *Courage*. "They're ready to go if we need them. The riverboats haven't spotted Tara and Alex."

"I can't believe Alex and George are one in the same," said Sabina. "How could he fool everyone?"

Drew shook his head. "Hell, I was with both of them for enough time and I didn't see it."

"We'll see if we have a killer when we question them, him, Alex or George . . . whoever," said O'Malley, turning to Drew. "I guess I owe you an apology. I really thought you were the killer. Now it looks like we might have a more viable suspect."

Pinkowski's phone rang. "Pinkowski . . . You've spotted *Passage Maker*? It's north of Atwater Beach, heading south towards the marina with just a front sail. Good, that will make it easier to identify from a distance. Roger, we're on our way. Thanks for your help. Yes, you can head back."

He hit End, then looked up at the others. "Let's head out on the policeboat."

* * *

Tara stared in disbelief at the number of phone calls she'd missed. "What the hell."

"What wrong?" she heard from below. Alex was opening and cooling another bottle of Champagne. "Is there another boat coming? We're far enough out we aren't going to hit land, even with the autopilot on, if that's what your worried about."

"No, it's not that, I just missed a lot of calls and texts." There was one phone call from the Milwaukee Humane Society, ten calls from Drew Thompson, three from Sabina and Pinkowski. "Shit, Sabina and Pinkowski called. There must be a homicide case I'm needed on. How long will it take to get in?"

"Just a little over an hour whether we sail or motor," he said. "Don't you think sailing is more romantic, future Mrs. West? Come on. We just got engaged. They can wait. It's a special day."

"Yeah, you're right. OK, let me just check this call I got from the Humane Society and from Drew. He called ten times. After I hear the voicemail messages, I'll turn off the phone, all right?"

"Thank you." Alex climbed up the steps from the cabin with the ice bucket and new bottle of champagne. "I think I'll get glasses instead of these red plastic cups," he said, heading back down into the cabin.

Tara scrolled through her voicemail messages. With the wind blowing, it was tough to hear so she turned on the speakerphone option, hitting first the call from the Humane Society. "Detective Sullivan, it's Sandy. I was moving boxes in a storage area and came across a shoebox of receipts and cards from the gala a few years ago. Much to my surprise, I found the receipt you were looking for. The person who bought the dog earring was George West. Here's his phone number. He paid cash." But Tara didn't need to know the number. "I hope this helps your investigation. Bye."

She stared at the phone. "My God, George is the killer." Then she hit the message from Drew.

"Tara, it's Drew. I've got unbelievable news about Alex and George. It's extremely important I talk to you right away. Whatever you do, stay away from Alex and George. Use any excuse you want, but stay away from them. I know it's a strange request, but I'll explain when I see you."

"From down below, she heard Alex say in a strained voice: "Why is the Humane Society calling you about a dog earring George bought? There's nothing wrong with a guy wearing an earring once in a while. I even wear one during Pirate Days at the Club. I even have a hole in my left ear just like George. It's no big deal." He emerged from below.

"Really!" said Tara. "I guess I never noticed your left earlobe." She leaned in closer to look at his left earlobe. "Why didn't I notice that before, not that it makes any difference?"

"And what's that shit Drew was saying about me and George? I know my brother can be difficult sometimes, but me? Hell, Drew was a suspect in more than one murder. And I thought he was my friend. Not anymore."

"I need to call Drew and find out what's happening. This is so strange."

"Why don't you wait?" Alex held up a finger and headed back down below. "I forgot something George gave me to give you for our engagement today. It was our mother's. He wanted you to have it today. I was going to wait but I think now is the right time to give to you."

"OK, I'll just call Drew quick, then turn off the phone." She didn't hear a response from below. Switching off the speaker on her phone, Tara returned his number on the screen.

***

Over the roar of the twin massive outboard engines on the policeboat racing north, Drew heard the phone ring. He looked at the name on the screen. "It's her."

"Tara, are you with Alex? Are you all right?"

"Yes, I'm better than all right, I'm engaged . . . to Alex, so why did you ask if I'm all right?"

"After I met with the detective who investigated Gloria West's death, I went to the County Records Department and looked up her children's birth certificates. There was only one. Tara, there's no Alex West. Alex and George are one and the same."

Tara gasped but tried to stay calm. How was this possible?

"We need to question George West. We're on our way in a policeboat. We should reach you in about ten minutes. So keep calm."

"Hurry up and get here. I'm afraid now."

"We're going as fast as we can. Just keep him unsuspecting about what is going on."

"I'll try. He's going to know something is different with me."

"Try to be relaxed, like you don't know anything."

"OK, hurry please." After hanging up, Tara looked up and saw Alex smiling. He had a watch in his hand and wore a gold earring.

"So what did Drew have to say besides stay away from me? A little late for that, don't you think, Tara?

"I don't know why he said that."

"Yes, you do. Very unsettling, Tara. But I have something for you. A sort of engagement present Alex was going to give you. But since you know about us, it's from me, George."

Tara's eyes got wide as she took the Piaget watch from George. She turned it over and saw the initials, MMS engraved on the back: Margaret Mary Sullivan. This watch had belonged to her mothers, then Cate. Tara was momentarily blinded by tears. "Why, George, why did you kill my sister?"

"I didn't plan on killing her, Tara, but she made fun of me, taunting me, calling me a bad boy, like my mother did. I loved and hated my mother. I had to kill her after Buddy died. All she loved was my fucking brother Alex. Alex the Great, she taunted me after he did something nice. When she was fucking someone, it didn't make any difference who, she'd tie me up with her scarves and gag me . . . until she was done. When I had a chance, I killed her and Peter Owen, her lover at the time. Too bad about the chauffeur; wrong place at the wrong time."

"George, we can help you."

"No, I don't think so. You might help Alex, but not me. I'm too damaged. You know, I liked you when we first met. You look like my mother too, and you were always kind to me. I craved that kindness, but then you fell for Alex and I was cast aside once again by Alex the Great—though I liked the fact that when you thought you were making love to Alex, you were really fucking me, black sheep George. I enjoyed playing that game with you."

Tara felt a chill. A revulsion run through her body.

"Poor Alex." George chuckled. "He was always weak. I was stronger, dominant. But Mother loved him, not me. And now, Tara, I have to kill you—like your sister, and Stella."

"You killed Stella. Why?"

"She was nice but called me nasty names. I hate getting rejected that way so I killed her on my boat and dumped her in the river like garbage." He shook his head, as if trying to forget. "Why don't you put on your sister's watch? I can't use it anymore after you found me out. I remember how Drew's eyes got wide when he saw the picture of the Piaget watch on lowly Roberta's wrist. Oh well, the time has come, Tara."

Tara looked in the corner of the cockpit and saw her purse. The Glock.

"Alex, Alex, are you there?" she asked George's menacing face while slowly sliding towards the purse. "I know you're in there. Save me, be strong. You love me. We got engaged today. We made love. Save me from George. We can help you and him, but you have to be strong and take over." Then she heard Alex's distinct voice. "I do love you, Tara, but George won't let me be stronger than him."

Tara lunged for her oversized purse, grabbing her gun, and pulling it out and pointing the weapon at Alex. "I'm sorry, Alex, I did love you for the kind, loving, person you are, but not George. He killed my sister and he has to pay for that.

But you both can get help. At least you can. I'm not sure of George."

Drew pointed as the policeboat cut through Lake Michigan's waves. "There they are. How far away are we?" he asked.

Piloting the craft, Officer Petropoulos answered. "We're about three minutes out."

"Good," said Pinkowski. "We should be able to board the boat, right?"

"Yes sir," the officer answered. "There is a light chop so we can come right alongside and board her."

Drew looked at Pinkowski and nodded. "If you want, I'll sail *Passage Maker* back, and you take West onboard the policeboat."

"Sounds like a plan," said Pinkowski. O'Malley nodded his head in approval.

Petropoulos turned on the boat's siren to let *Passage Maker* and other boats know they were in pursuit, if they couldn't see the flashing blue lights in the bright sunlight.

Tara stood. Her Glock leveled at Alex. She was aware of a large motorboat sound coming near their boat and behind her, and then seeing with her peripheral vision the big cruising yacht pass to the side of them about 300 yards off the left side. She could see the policeboat flashing lights in the distance and felt a sense of comfort that she might soon be safe. She was sad at the same time because she was in love with Alex. There was good inside this man, but also evil. George West needed to be stopped before he killed again.

Why was he smiling?

What he saw and she didn't realize was that the big cruising yacht that passed seconds before created a three-foot wave that was speeding toward *Passage Makers* broadside. He knew what was going to happen when the wave hit the side of their boat. In that instant, George West would have his chance to kill Tara.

***

"Oh my god," Sabina said, spotting Tara with her gun out, pointing at Alex. "Make this boat go faster."

Officer Petropoulos' hand went to the throttle levers, and pushed them forward, accelerating just beyond the redline of the tachometer. The boat hurled faster towards *Passage Maker* as all aboard grabbed for handholds.

***

Tara heard the hissing of the wave just before it hit the side of the boat. When it hit, the boat violently tilted. *Passage Maker's* long boom swung across and struck Tara's head, knocking her unconscious.

She dropped on the cockpit cushion. The Glock flew backwards from her hand, landing on the cushion behind her, just out of reach from where she was sprawled.

"Bitch," George spat as he leaped towards her, hands going for her long, delicate neck. "You're going to get just what Mother got, except I'm going to kill you with my bare hands, not those scarves." He didn't have much time to kill her before the policeboat arrived but didn't care. Tara had to die.

Drew saw the boom strike Tara in the head. He saw West leap at her.

"Tara's down! Can't we do something? Call on the speaker and distract him. He's crazy. He'll kill her."

Petropoulos grabbed the mic. "This is the Milwaukee Police, prepare to be boarded. Raise your hands or we'll shoot!"

Sabina and O'Malley moved out of the cabin and towards the bow of the boat. Guns came out as they got nearer.

Tara was unconscious for a few seconds. Coming to, Tara felt hands around her neck. George's knees straddled her. As her eyes flittered open, she looked into the eyes of a frenzied George, a gleeful smile on his face. She thrashed, trying to toss him off. Where was her gun? It had to be close by. She searched with her free hand but couldn't find it.

Please God, don't let me die, she thought.

Her right hand reached up and frantically searched for her gun. Toward the corner of the cockpit, she thought she felt the tip of its barrel. Tara needed to push herself closer, but how? Her foot hit one of *Passage Maker's* large winches and she pushed back hard as she twisted and moved a few inches.

"All I wanted was a little love, Tara, but once again Alex took everything. Now you're going to die, and your friends are going to be too late."

She felt his fingers tighten but as he leaned forward to pressure her neck tighter. He raised his body slightly. With waning energy, Tara moved them both an inch closer to the end of the cockpit. She felt herself fading. She couldn't breathe and things were getting hazy gray. She reached the gun's barrel. Rotating the weapon, she was able to grab the trigger guard and palm the pistol.

With one last ounce of strength, she raised the pistol. As her vision of the menacing face above blurred and faded, Tara squeezed the trigger.

***

"Was that a shot?" Sabina shouted.

Drew stood on the policeboat's bow. The craft pivoted to come alongside the moving *Passage Maker*.

"I don't see either of them," he said.

Sabina was panicked too. "Well it definitely sounded like a pistol."

As Petropoulos deftly moved the boat alongside *Passage Maker*, Drew leaped onto the moving boat. What he saw sent a chill up his spine.

The body of Alex lay flat atop the still body of Tara, blood covering both.

"Tara!"

Sabina jumped aboard. "Is she alive?"

They heard a moan. Drew grabbed the bloody attacker and rolled him off Tara and onto the cockpit deck. Next, he pressed his fingers to her neck, feeling for a pulse.

Tara's eyes fluttered open. "Drew, did I kill him? He was choking me. I had to shoot him."

Sabina reached over and pressed George West's neck. "He's alive, but barely."

She yelled over to O'Malley and Pinkowski. "We need to get George West to a hospital soon or he'll die."

Drew gently touched Tara's face, then reached over and turned off the Autopilot. He moved to loosen the headsail line, letting it flap in the breeze. *Passage Maker* slowed to a stop and started to rock. Drew grabbed the lines from the policeboat and tied the two together.

O'Malley called over to him. "I'll grab West's shoulders and you grab his feet and we'll move him over to our boat."

Drew nodded. One, two, three and they lifted him up and where Pinkowski and Petropoulos laid him down. The policeboat took off towards the marina.

Tara tried to pull herself up, "Drew, I had to do it. George was going to kill me."

"I know."

Sabina moved to her side, rubbing the small of her back. "It's over."

Tara looked at her, then Drew. "We got him, didn't we? We caught my sister's killer, and your friend's killer too."

"Yes, we did." Drew said. *And Stella's too.*

Epilogue

The Police boat raced toward McKinley marina and the waiting ambulance. The boat's captain had called ahead, standing by with paramedics familiar with gunshot wounds. The captain was pretty sure any of the paramedics covering Milwaukee were trained for that, because of the many shootings in Milwaukee. One of the other Police officers attending to George Alexander West had put a second gauze to his head wound and wrapped it up tight, trying to stem the flow of blood.

O'Malley looked at West. "The new gauze already looks red. He sure looks pale. Who do you think Tara thought she was shooting?"

Pinkowski shook his head. "Does it make any difference? The guy was trying to kill her. She had no choice."

"Yeah, you're right. It must have been the bad guy, not the good one."

"The way he looks right now, I'd be surprised if he lives. He might just bleed out right here in the boat." Pinkowski said.

O'Malley looked at the shoreline. "We're only a couple minutes away now. If they get him to the hospital, give him some blood in the ambulance, he just might make it to surgery. If he lives, we can convict him for murder. Then the State can send him to prison for the rest of his life. What a crazy system."

"We don't make the rules." Pinkowski said, "we just catch the bad boy and make him pay."

"Well, if he doesn't get there in time, he'll be dead. It will save the taxpayers a lot of money."

Five hours after surgery, they wheeled West into the intensive care area. Tara, Drew and Sabrina had arrived a couple of hours after surgery had started. Even though George's persona had tried to kill her, she was still in love with Alex—part of the dual person she had shot to save her life, a person who was loving and caring, but a person who was not as strong willed enough to fight off the dominant George.

Drew was his friend too. Sabrina was here to lend support to Tara. The three waited, not knowing what to expect until the doctor came out. When he did, they waited for the post-surgery prognosis.

"Hello. My name is Doctor Estes. We did all we could for him. He lost a lot of blood, and the bullet is still lodged against his skull. We didn't want to go in to remove it for fear in his weakened condition we might do more harm than good. We're pretty sure he's going to live but don't know what quality of life he'll have going forward. He's in a coma now and might be for a while."

"Can I see him? I'm his fiancé technically."

"Not yet. Maybe in a day or two. You're not going to like what you see right now. His head is all banged up, but at least then you can hold his hand. Just check with the nurse in a day or two and she'll let you know."

"Thank you for saving his life, Doctor."

"I'm amazed we saved his life with all the blood loss. He's one lucky guy so far. I've got to go now, but all we can do now is wait."

They watched him turn and go through the double doors into the surgery area.

***

The three sat down again. "Now what?" Sabrina asked.

Drew spoke first. "For me, I'm leaving for my cruise in a week. I feel better about life after finding Cate and Stella's killer. I also made peace and support with my best friend's wife, and his three kids. So now it's about me. I might have a friend I met in Sister Bay join me sometime along the trip. If you need to get away Tara, you can join me. I know you like sailing, but I'll leave that up to you."

Tara nodded. "Thanks Drew. I might take you up on the sailing, but right now I'm going to sit tight, do my job and try to get my life back on track. I need to somehow get over my love for Alex." She said as she looked at the ring on her finger.

Sabrina laughed. "I'm sorry about laughing. It's funny and sad Tara, that you still care about the guy you just shot. You can't make this stuff up. I'm here to help you get through this and be your friend if that's what you want. You're a good cop."

They all got up, hugged each other, and started walking out of the hospital.

"We'll all keep in touch. I care about you, Tara." Drew said, squeezing her hand.

"I will. I care about you too. You be good."

Acknowledgments

I would like to thank the following individuals for sharing their special knowledge with me.

Gust Petropoulos, retired Homicide Detective, City of Milwaukee, and Dana Isaacson, my editor.

Made in the USA
Monee, IL
19 April 2025

15835351R00218